HINSDALE PUBLIC LIBRARY

W9-AVL-738

© THE BAKER & TAYLOR CO.

THiS IS YouR LiFE

Also by Meg Wolitzer

Sleepwalking

Hidden Pictures

THiS /S YouR LiFE

MEG WOLiTzER

Crown Publishers, Inc.
New York

HINSDALE PUBLIC LIBRARY
HINSDALE, ILLINOIS

Publisher's Note: This is a work of fiction. The characters, incidents, and dialogues are products of the author's imagination and are not to be construed as real. Any resemblance to actual events or persons, living or dead, is entirely coincidental.

Copyright © 1988 by Meg Wolitzer

All rights reserved. No part of this book may be reproduced or transmitted in any form or by any means, electronic or mechanical, including photocopying, recording, or by any information storage and retrieval system, without permission in writing from the publisher.

Published by Crown Publishers, Inc., 225 Park Avenue South, New York, New York 10003 and represented in Canada by the Canadian MANDA Group

CROWN is a trademark of Crown Publishers, Inc.

Manufactured in the United States of America

Library of Congress Cataloging-in-Publication Data
Wolitzer, Meg
    This is your life: a novel/by Meg Wolitzer.
        p.   cm.
    I. Title.
PS3573.0564T47 1988
813'.54—dc19   88-11891

ISBN 0-517-56929-9

Design by Jake Victor Thomas

10   9   8   7   6   5   4   3   2   1

First Edition

For Richard Panek, with love

BT 11/88 17.95

PART
ONE

1

It was her sister who taught her how to hyperventilate. They sat facing each other on the bed, and they panted together like a husband and wife in a Lamaze workshop. When they could just about take no more, they felt that identifying swoon, the oxygen leaving their brains for good, the cells dying en masse. One day Erica put an end to it. She couldn't be bothered anymore, she said; she had other things to think about. Suddenly her walls were lined with posters; huge, disembodied heads of folksingers loomed down from above the bed and the dresser. Voices started coming from the stereo speakers: trembly underwater sopranos singing about medieval wood-nymphs and slain labor leaders. But the 1960s had already ended, and the records were strictly from the remainder bin. Buffy Sainte-Marie had a big orange 99¢ sticker slapped over her face.

Erica's room grew lush with things to touch, and fiddle with, and smell. Something was always burning in a dish. Once she bought a wand of incense from a man in a white robe on the subway and was later appalled by the literature he had sweetly handed her with her purchase:

> Thank-you for Buying "Lovely" Patchouli Incense.
> You're contributions will Go to help FIGHT the Rise
> of worldwide Judaism.

Still the incense burned, and now Opal stood and breathed in the bad air of her sister's room and thought longingly of how they used to hyperventilate together, and how all of that was finished.

In the past, sitting cross-legged on Erica's bed, the two sisters would allow their breathing to quicken. It was those first moments that Opal liked best. Erica had made a rule that they must keep their eyes closed, but sometimes Opal would crack open an eye and watch her sister heaving for breath, her shoulders moving up and down. It was embarrassing to see this, but somehow necessary. Erica was like a big sea creature that had washed up onto a rock, and Opal was the sea creature's diminutive sister. If someone had burst into the room then, it would have seemed crazy: two girls gasping for oxygen when there was certainly enough of it to go around. But no one *would* burst into the room; even the baby-sitters knew enough to keep their distance. Sometimes Opal could hear one of them practicing a routine in the den. She grew used to hearing the distant swoop and mutter of a voice, the rise and fall of words out of context. She rarely paid much attention, preferring the company of her sister. In Erica's bedroom it was just the two of them, breathing and falling.

One evening when they were hyperventilating, Opal actually thought she had died. She thought she had slipped into some narrow, dark province where she would be held forever. It was like all the hiding places she had ever found in the apartment: like the alley behind the refrigerator, where you wedged your body in and stood flush against the humming coils and wires until you were discovered. And you always were discovered; that was a given. But now Opal felt as though she might never get out, might never come to. She could not move, she could not open her eyes.

Goodbye, she thought, goodbye. She remembered Charlotte's babies at the end of *Charlotte's Web*, and the way they had parachuted off into new, separate spider-lives, calling goodbye to Wilbur even as a current carried them along. She had wept then, as she had wept pages earlier during Charlotte's death. It made sense to cry at someone else's departure, someone else's death. But this now, this was worse; Opal was mourning only herself. She would be found in her culottes and headband and knee socks. She saw herself being lifted gently, held in some anonymous adult arms and carried from the room.

That was when Erica reached out and shook her.

4

"Earth to Opal," Erica said, and Opal's eyes flew open like a doll's. "You should have seen yourself," Erica said, but her voice was kind.

No more was said about it. Together the two sisters caught their breath and went into the kitchen to hunt for supper. There was always a baby-sitter around to serve as a vague supervisor. Their mother had hired a string of young comedians to take care of Opal and Erica when she herself was away—men and women whom she had discovered at various comedy clubs around the city. She paid them decently and gave them a place to stay and a telephone to use and a pantry stocked with interesting food. The apartment was never empty; there was always the sound of one of the baby-sitters in the background, obsessively practicing a routine. The baby-sitters were like extremely lenient, youthful parents who let you do what you want and eat what you want.

Tonight Danny Bloom, who was doing a three-day baby-sitting stint, came out of the den and asked if they needed anything. He was a thin man in his late twenties, with a body like a piece of bent wire. His humor, said their mother, was very physical. He moved around a lot onstage at the Laff House, where she had discovered him.

"You two doing okay out there?" Danny asked them.

"Yes," Opal and Erica chorused. "We're fine."

"Well then, I think I'll keep practicing," he said. "I'll come out again in time for the show. She said she's doing all new material tonight."

When he had disappeared down the hall, Erica and Opal boiled water for wagon-wheel pasta and slathered Fluff on crackers. They ate in silence, and when they were through they flipped through their homework for a while, dreamily shuffling pages. Illustrations of colonial life drifted by; women in long dresses sat at butter churns, backs straight, hands busy. Erica and Opal looked up from their homework every few minutes, checking the clock. At eleven-twenty Erica carried in the television set, and Opal pulled the swivel chairs up close to the screen. Together in the kitchen with the heat from the stove and the soft, granular light of the television, they waited for their mother to appear.

5

Opal watched the long loop of commercials as though it were an opening act. It was strange; you barely had to focus on the commercials, and yet you still knew what they wanted you to buy. Opal loved television and watched as much of it as she could. You had to watch the shows closely, but during the commercials you could just let your thoughts fall around you while the music jumped and the coffee spilled and the bottle of detergent came to life and danced.

Opal swiveled her chair in time to the music and thought of all the things that crowded around her. She thought of the people she worshipped in the world: her mother, and her sister, and the new art teacher, Miss Hong. A few years before, she had worshipped Mickey Dolenz of the Monkees. She thought she had been shrewd about loving Mickey; everyone else loved Davy Jones, and the chances of ever getting *him* were slim, at best. More realistic to go for Mickey, she reasoned, with his elastic face and squinting eyes. No one else took Mickey seriously; they all went for the easy charms of Davy: the soft British accent, the tender skin. Opal remained patient, did not make a big issue out of her theory. She thought of Mickey constantly, wondered what time of day it was in California and whether he grew discouraged by all the letters Davy received. But as the months passed, and the flurry died down, Opal thought of him less, and somehow her love for him was unmoored. It had been her decision; she had not had to be forcibly restrained, like some older girls at school who tried to sneak into hotel rooms or backstage at the Westbury Music Fair. She had restrained *herself*, and suddenly she was way past the whole thing.

Everything kept changing as quickly as a film strip, frame after choppy frame. You loved someone and then you didn't, and then you loved someone else. You wept over a spider's death when you were eight, and a few years later you read that same death scene again with a cool, critical eye. You thought of ways in which E. B. White might have made the scene more true to life; you thought of writing to tell him.

There were very few things in the world that stayed hinged to you for too long. Each year there was a new teacher at the front of

6

the room, a new arrangement of chairs and desks, a new pale color slapped over the walls around you. Every class had a classroom pet: a guinea pig that drowsed in its window cage while you traced the outlines of the seven continents. You spent a whole year of your life caring for this animal, stroking its nervous fur and sliding in trays of pellets, and when the end of the year came, the animal was left back in the second grade while you kept moving up. You all knew that there would be another animal awaiting you in the third grade: a parallel rodent needing stroking and holding and water and food.

Now the commercials ended, and the theme music began, and suddenly Danny Bloom raced into the kitchen and perched on the countertop behind Opal. First there was the monologue, and a little joking around, and then Opal's mother was brought onstage. Sitting between Johnny and Ed, with the skyline tableau stretched out behind her, she gestured broadly and flooded the entire screen. In that moment the men disappeared, were swallowed up, and even the skyline was eclipsed. All that remained was an ocean of dotted fabric—her mother's fashion trademark—and the helpless laughter of the studio audience. They kept laughing and didn't show signs of ever stopping. This is what is meant by "convulsive laughter," Opal thought.

"I'm glad she's on first tonight," Erica said. "Not like last time when that woman from Sea World was on with her animals, and Mom got four minutes."

Things had changed since then, they acknowledged. Their mother was now allowed to come on first and ease into the still-cold chair by the desk. She was frantic tonight; she was huge and luminous. *My mother the moon*, Opal thought. *My mother the explosion.* Opal could not take her eyes off her mother. She was madly in love with her, as was half the country. Everyone wanted to meet her, talk to her, somehow nudge up against her.

"It's worse in California," Opal's mother had said. "Out there, everyone's lying in wait with their autograph books. They *expect* to see celebrities. They come right up and touch you; it's like a petting zoo." But Opal knew her mother wasn't significantly upset by this; it was clear that in some ways she took pleasure from the touch of strangers. Opal imagined her mother gliding down a street in Los Angeles under an archway of palm trees, while all around her, hands reached out to brush her cheek, her hair, the edge of a dotted sleeve.

Opal had not yet been to California. "I want you girls to stay in New York for now," her mother said, "and have as normal a life as possible. I don't want you to start missing a lot of school and falling behind. I know the situation isn't ideal, but the baby-sitters take good care of you, and I'm only a phone call away."

Opal begged to be allowed to go with her, but the answer was always the same. "Soon," she was told. "I promise you, soon."

But when, exactly, was "soon"? The word was used to represent any given period of time; it was fluid and could change shape freely.

"I will be back from L.A. soon," her mother would say as she stood before her closet, selecting dresses from the rack with the help of her assistant, Cynthia, who always leaned toward the loudest, most spangle-dipped items. Then a week or two might go by, during which Opal had her hair braided systematically each morning and her lunch packed by a live-in baby-sitter. *Soon, soon,* came the voice, this time over the telephone, but even long-distance it was as soothing and persuasive as a hypnotist's.

Finally her mother would return. It might be winter in New York City, with snow gathered in ragged drifts, but the limousine would pull up at the curb and the doorman would fly out to greet her, and she would emerge a dusty, mottled, coastal pink, her nose peeling, her suitcase swollen with citrus fruit. California seemed a remote, tropical island, having little to do with anything that went on here, in New York City, where the snow fell for days, and the world seemed locked permanently into winter. In California, Opal imagined, you were served crescents of papaya on a terrace overlooking the water, and speed-shutter cameras were always hissing at you like locusts. Opal would go there soon, she knew. But "soon" kept unraveling with no end in sight.

There were times, during that first year of fame, when her mother was home for weeks on end, either resting or playing a series of club dates in the city. "I really prefer it here," she would say as she got ready to go out for an evening in New York. "The audiences

8

are much more savvy. They laugh with discrimination. Out in L.A., you get the feeling that there's a laugh track going. Everyone's so desperate to have a good time; you could get up there and read a manual about oral hygiene and they would laugh. No, this is where I want you girls to live, not out there in Disneyland."

Sometimes she would sit down for a moment on the bed between her two daughters. "I hope I'm doing the right thing," she would say. "Who knows? Maybe if God had really wanted me to be a comedienne, He would have named me Shecky."

Opal and Erica looked at each other and laughed politely. They had reached a point at which they usually understood when their mother was making a joke and were able to respond fairly quickly. But sometimes Opal wasn't even sure whether her mother was really funny or not; she'd heard her jokes too many times. At home her mother practiced in the bedroom.

"You girls be my audience," she said. Opal and Erica sat solemnly on the edge of the bed and listened as she ran through her act. She usually opened with some rueful comments about her size. "I do have a weight problem," she said, looking down at herself and shaking her head. Then she looked up suddenly. "I just can't *wait* for dinner!"

Opal thought about this, and understood that her mother was making a little pun. She chuckled politely.

"Women's lib isn't so easy on large women," her mother went on. "I mean, I tried to burn my bra, and the neighbors called the fire department. It took hours to put it out. One of the firemen said to me, 'I don't know what kind of campfire you were making, lady, but those are the biggest marshmallows I've ever seen!' "

Opal and Erica laughed again, hesitantly. Their laughter had a familiar, rolling burble to it, like a water cooler. Opal was aware that there were probably some nuances she was missing, certain inflections that seemed to point to the approximate region of humor, although the particular meaning was lost on her. She recognized her own ignorance, her limits in the presence of this huge, wonderful mother. Opal was a knobby girl, especially small for her age. "My little ectomorph," her mother sometimes called her, touching the hair on the back of Opal's neck, making her arch and settle like a cat.

9

She preferred it when her mother did parodies of songs from musicals, which she had expressly rewritten for her act. Onstage she was accompanied by a piano, bass, and drums, but here in the bedroom, her voice had to survive on its own. She didn't have a brassy voice, as one might have imagined, but instead she sang in a girlish soprano, aiming tremulously for the top notes the way someone might reach for a delicate object on a high shelf.

"Okay, girls," she would say. "Now I'm going to do something from *West Side Story*. This one is to the tune of a song called 'Maria.' You have to know the song, I guess, but just bear with me." She paused, pulled at the throat of her turtleneck sweater, and began to sing:

"The most beautiful sound I ever heard/Pastrami/Pastrami, pastrami, pastrami/Say it loud and there's a carving knife carving/Say it soft, because I'm suddenly starving/Pastrami/I've just eaten a *pound* of pastrami . . ." She stopped singing and clutched at her stomach, rolling her eyes around. Opal was the first to laugh, and Erica followed.

"Oh good, you like that one," said her mother. "I'm glad. Here's another." She cleared her throat and sang. "There's *no* blintzes like *roe* blintzes, like *no* blintzes I know . . ."

After the songs she began to do characters, starting first with her most popular one, Mrs. Pummelman, then doing Baby Fifi, and finally Isadora Dumpster. She poked fun at her own weight problem, in the hopes, she often said, of having it cease to be a delicate subject. It was not this way with most overweight people. Opal thought of Debby Nadler at school, whose mother was a large, gentle ceramicist. Mrs. Nadler was constantly at work in her studio, standing over the wavy heat of a kiln, looking flushed and serious in a red smock. Her heaviness was just another part of her, along with her talent and her kindness and her breathy voice. It was a big package that you couldn't split up; it was all or nothing. And then there was Miss Coombs, the school nurse, whose wide, easy presence was welcome when you were throwing up or had strep throat and had to be sent home. Miss Coombs lay you down on a narrow cot and hovered above you, blocking out the stark glare of the room, and she placed a washcloth over your forehead, smoothing its edges with her heavy hands. Both Mrs. Nadler and Miss Coombs carried their weight around without referring to it all the time, and everyone understood that it would have been wrong to make fun of it, or even mention it. You couldn't make fun of someone's fat mother—the mother had to make fun of herself, like Opal's did—but on the other hand you *could* go up to another girl at school and calmly say, "You're ugly, no offense." The remark would blaze inside that girl forever.

Nobody ever said this kind of thing to Opal. She was popular already, good in gym, and quick at spelling. There was a small amount of cruelty in her, which surfaced at odd times and always surprised everyone, especially her. It sprang from nowhere, painlessly, like a nighttime nosebleed. She found herself occasionally joining in with a few others in the coat room at the end of the day and forming a tight ring around some unfortunate girl. Once they even stooped so low as to gang up on the new exchange student from Seoul, Korea, who couldn't even begin to imagine what they were saying to her in such mean voices.

Opal stood at the periphery, muttering a few vague insults that no one could hear. She barely had to do anything, and still she was liked. It had really all started the day that she brought her class to watch the taping of a television show her mother was on. It was a morning news show, and all the children sat bleary-eyed on the floor at sunrise among a tangle of wires and cables. They were so well-behaved that a cameraman came over and told them they were welcome back anytime. For the rest of the day Opal was treated with real awe. She found herself at the very heart of the lunch table, being offered sandwich halves and tangerines and an invitation to try Alison Prager's oboe, if she wanted.

After that, Opal had her mother make strategic guest appearances at school. On Carnival Day her mother dressed as a gypsy and sat in a booth, and everyone crowded around. All the other mothers felt snubbed. Mothers in clown suits milled around unhappily, smoking furtive cigarettes in corners. Peter Green's mother sat bone-dry on the plank of a homemade dunking machine, waiting for someone to plunge her into the water, but no one did.

It wasn't that the children particularly wanted Opal's mother to read their fortunes, as she had been prepared to do. Instead, they tore off tickets from a loop, and came up to her booth, shrilling, "Do Mrs. Pummelman!" or "Do Baby Fifi!" and Opal's mother would patiently oblige.

When they got back home at the end of Carnival Day, Opal stood in the doorway and watched her mother take off her gypsy costume. She watched her pull off her pantyhose, holding it bunched up on her hands for a second, as though about to make a cat's cradle of the nylon. Then she dropped it and reached around to unzip her gypsy dress. After that she unwound the turban from her head, and fished out the bobby pins from their hiding places in her hair. All she wore now was a pale yellow slip and two silver-dollar circles of rouge. She looked like a teenage girl sitting alone after a date that has gone poorly. That happened to girls sometimes, Opal knew; she had just begun reading books from the Young Adult section of the library. The books had titles like *Ready When You Are* or *New Girl at Adams High* or *Seventeen Means Trouble*. Sometimes in the book the boy stands the girl up at first, or else he says something terrible to her, like, "Oh, here come my friends. Let's pretend we're not together, okay?" Now Opal's mother looked so sad and exhausted that Opal had to look away. This was the only time she ever remembered wanting to look away from her.

Most of the time, like now, Opal could not get enough. As she sat in the kitchen watching the show, she laughed easily at all the familiar lines. Her mother torpedoed joke after joke, and everyone was satisfied. Opal could hear the beefsteak laugh of Ed McMahon, louder than anyone's.

When the audience finally quieted down, the camera closed in tight and her mother said, "I'd like to take this moment to send a special message to my daughters back in New York." No one moved. "If you're watching this, Opal and Erica," she said, "then you're in big trouble. You're supposed to be asleep now! It's a school night!"

It was like talking to her mother on a television phone, the kind that *My Weekly Reader* had insisted would be installed in every home by 1970. Opal had lived in fear. What if you were on the toilet and the phone rang? What then? But the threats had proven idle. *My Weekly Reader* also swore that America would go metric within the next few years. Opal had been terrified, knowing her own stupidity with ounces and inches, let alone kilos and meters. But this, too, was just a scare, designed to alarm, then be forgotten. Everything settled down, went on as usual. Her mother showed up on television, sent satellite love messages to the East Coast, and later that night, after the credits rolled and her mother stood as if at a cocktail party with Johnny and Ed and Rita Moreno, Opal drew back the blanket on her bed and slipped inside.

Lying alone in the dark, she could hear the baby-sitter practicing down the hall, and then the sound of Erica preparing for sleep in the next room. There was the usual banging around, drawers sliding open and shut, and once in a while Erica would open her door and a line of music would drift out: ". . . And when will all the killing stop?/We cry into the rain . . ." Then the door would close again and Opal couldn't hear anything more. Erica's music was so depressing lately, and yet this was the way she liked to fall asleep at night; this was her lullaby of choice.

Opal flipped over onto her side and lay close to the wall. She summoned up an image of her mother onscreen, a pulse of color and motion. She was excited for a while, thinking about the show, but then the excitement shifted into something else. Now in her mind she saw her mother joined by her father, her sister, and finally herself. The whole family was up there, all spread out like the little winking lights of the "Tonight Show" skyline. They blinked at each other from across a great distance.

No, she thought, amending it slightly. She, Erica, and her father were all little lights, but her mother was something else entirely. She was a zeppelin traveling across the sky, traveling from light to light, and everyone was pointing at her. Cars stopped on the road. "Look!" children cried. "Look! It's Dottie Engels!"

In the next room, her sister was already asleep, but now Opal was wide awake.

2

As a family, they bore the name of their weakest link. They carried it for years without wondering at the irony of this. They were the Engelses, taking the name from the father who had once appeared only at dinner tables and during arguments, and who then disappeared for good. Still they carried his name; it was like living with the child of someone who has left you and whom you now despise. The child begins to take on its father's features: the same impassive eyes, the thin mouth you cannot bear to feed.

Engels was a beautiful name; they had not been saddled with a clunker, as had many children at school, but even so, Erica decided it was time to change it. She announced this to Jordan Strang one day after school as they sat together on a bench by the river. The day was much too cold for them to be sitting outside, but still they sat coatless, trying to keep a pipe lit. It was a tiny pipe, packed full of green marijuana buds, and she and Jordan passed it quickly back and forth, as though taking part in a relay race. Jordan kept lighting matches, which stayed lit in the wind for barely a second.

"Come on, little guy," he kept addressing each match, and she watched him concentrate intensely, the way he did in Chemistry class, over a Bunsen burner. They had met in Chemistry, lab partners in an experiment involving calcium chips and Woolite. Soon they began to go down to the East River at the end of the day, where they would sit on a bench in Carl Schurz Park and try to smoke unlit green marijuana.

She and Jordan felt separate from everyone else at Headley— separate from the army of hard-working, wincing tenth-graders

14

who marched through the day with their heads full of S.A.T. words, lips moving as they formed "vernacular" or "sybarite." They were also separate from the group of mongrel tenth-graders who were always nodding out or laughing inappropriately in class or being excused to attend group sessions with Miss Klingman.

Erica and Jordan inhabited some limbo territory, one that was reserved for those who were homely and bright and liked to take drugs. If you fit into this category, then you wrote haiku in your locked bedroom at night, and you spent every afternoon in the park by the East River, fumbling to stuff little buds into the bowl of a ridiculous pipe, and you inhaled wildly in the wind, waiting for results.

She looked at Jordan's long face, the new wisps of hair growing above and below his lips. She watched him suck furiously at the pipe, then exhale what appeared to be smoke but was more likely vapor from the cold. The pipe was dead; Jordan let it drop into his lap.

"You're really going to change your name?" he asked.

"Yes," she said.

"What to?"

"I don't know," she said. "I'm not sure yet."

"Won't you miss having people know that you're Dottie Engels's daughter?" he asked. He paused. "Was that a stupid question? I just always wondered what it would be like to have famous parents. My parents are both endocrinologists. Now that's *really* exciting."

She was surprised to hear him speak with any measure of irony; Jordan usually had such a flat voice, and the things he said seemed to suit it. He talked about school, and the books he was reading, and where his family was going for vacation, and usually Erica would stop listening somewhere in the middle of a sentence. She would hook around a single word and run with it; *vacation*, he might say, we're going to New Mexico for *vacation*, and Erica would flash back to her own family vacations: Knott's Berry Farm, or Hershey, Pennsylvania. She saw herself at six, standing in wonder before a giant, gleaming vat of chocolate, and she suddenly had no more use for Jordan's droning voice.

"Do you *like* having a famous mother?" he persisted now.

She nodded and gave him a formulaic response about how it had its ups and downs. There were several children of famous people at the Headley School: offspring of politicians, actors, an occasional athlete. Erica sat next to the daughter of black torch singer Minx Janeway in French class. But somehow having Dottie Engels as your mother was different; it meant having a mother who was large and loud and overexposed, someone who appeared everywhere you looked, and who made you laugh until you felt sick. It was a strain to laugh like that; it was unnatural.

At sixteen, Erica knew she looked like Dottie, already running to fat, settling in to a life of being heavy. Erica had a round face with an absence of cheekbones; there was nothing planar about her at all. She wrapped herself in layers of Indian-print fabric: long skirts and scarves and shirts that looked like college dormitory bedspreads. Her hair was parted in the middle and fell straight to her shoulders. It always smelled edible from the apricot shampoo she used. Every day she looked and smelled exactly the same. She observed herself in the mirror each morning after a shower, and as the steam settled she was startled all over again by how terrible she appeared. In a minute, regaining composure, she forced herself to leave the mirror and head for school.

Occasionally, when her mother had been on television, someone would mention it the next day in class. "We saw your mom last night on the Bob Hope special," Meredith Gertz said, mincing up to Erica at the lockers, flanked by two friends.

"Oh, good," Erica said. She spun the combination lock, but suddenly all the numbers were lost. She spun and spun.

"Do you get to go to L.A. at all?" Meredith asked.

"Not really," said Erica.

Meredith shot her friends a meaningful look. "Ever meet Johnny Carson?" she asked.

"No," said Erica.

"Ever meet *anybody*?" Meredith asked.

"No," Erica said, and her voice had disappeared, sinking back into her big face, the recesses of her throat, the long, hollow

16

column that led down to her heart, her lungs, everything private and beating and desperate.

"Oh, forget it," said Meredith Gertz, and, as if on a drill team, she and her two friends wheeled around and walked off, heads close, already talking mean.

After that, Erica found herself left alone. No one was particularly interested in her, the way they were in Senator Peel's son, or the daughter of that astronaut. Still, the fact that Dottie Engels's daughters went to Headley was often mentioned in passing, and even referred to casually by the headmaster for recruitment purposes. Erica was Dottie's child, but she was also a lurking mammoth in the corner of the girls' locker room, doing an awkward little jig as she struggled into her size XL gym suit.

And now she was Jordan Strang's friend, his "girlfriend," probably, for that was the way everyone figured out the world. The beautiful held hands with the beautiful, the homely with the homely. Erica Engels and Jordan Strang sat together on a bench by the East River, coatless and frozen. It was as if neither of them had a sense of self, she thought—as though their bodies needed nothing—like those people who lived in the Himalayas and ate only air. But it seemed odd to think of herself this way; there was so *much* of her, so there ought to have been so much need.

"I have to leave," Erica said finally. "I'm supposed to spend more time with my sister."

"Whatever gets you through the night," Jordan said. His expressions often made no sense in context, and he spoke as though he were a foreigner clumsily trying to adopt a hip idiom. Perhaps he thought he was being clever in a cryptic way, like the characters in the novels he read. Jordan was obsessed with paperbacks from the Sixties; Hunter Thompson was his hero. He referred to him continually as "Hunter," as though they were in homeroom together. Jordan had given Erica a copy of *Fear and Loathing in Las Vegas*, and she had stared blankly at it for hours, missing the point. It was all about messy, crazed men driving fast and taking hallucinogens. This side of the counterculture, or what was left of it in the 1970s, seemed to have been designed specifically for *boys*—those boys who liked nothing better than to sit and talk

17

about Hunter Thompson or Carlos Castaneda until even their dreams swam with images of birds and clouds and the desert sun. Jordan had no one else to talk to, and so he talked to Erica, using her as a sounding board to ramble on and on about whatever book he was reading this week.

Erica kept her own obsessions to herself. Lying alone in her room at night she played the music of Reva and Jamie, a male-female duo who sang with exquisite harmonies. She especially loved their song "Cup of Tears," and always felt a chill at the part about the soldier's ghost coming back to haunt his lover. She would turn the volume up very high, but even so, she could still hear Opal calling her and banging on the locked door.

"What are you doing in there?" Opal called. "You want to hyperventilate?"

Erica paused. "I'm busy!"

"Doing what?"

"Homework!" Erica yelled. She turned over onto her back and lay staring up at the ceiling, listening to the harmonies spiral upward, then fall, thinking of nothing but herself, big and form-less, a jellyfish floating on a bed. She might as well give in to it now, she thought—give in to the future that was rolling toward her at an alarming speed. She might as well accept it, and spend the rest of her life out in the open. She would no longer have to squirrel away cartons of Pepperidge Farm Milanos, leaving the little fluted paper shells scattered around her room like doilies. No more sheepish pining away for food or conversation; all her needs would be worn up front like a badge of some dubious honor. She would be a big, pathetic thing, but everyone would *know* and would grow to accept her. There goes that poor fat girl, the neighbors would think, and maybe they would leave a plate of something outside her apartment door. She would have a place for herself, a specific role. Maybe that would be better than all this pretending that a little smudge of eyeshadow, or a special grapefruit diet, or having her ears pierced might help. The days were relentless, and she huddled behind her desk in school, keeping the desk top up as long as she could, searching for some imaginary pencil.

"Oh, sweetie," her mother sometimes said, "adolescence is *like*

18

this, but it will get better, I swear it will. Believe me, I know from experience."

Erica had certainly gathered enough stories about her mother's adolescence, but the picture she was left with was still vague, sepia-toned, involving V-J Day and D-Day, and the stoop of a row house on which a thirteen-year-old girl named Dottie Breitburg sat and ate Pez. In truth, Erica didn't want to think too much about that fat girl; she didn't really want to know her. Erica had heard many times about how her mother, as an unhappy teenager, had been sent off one summer on scholarship to Camp Hatikvah. This was during the height of the war, when Brooklyn was a newsreel of brownouts and victory gardens and grieving mothers. At the end of August, when Dottie returned from camp, she had changed profoundly. She, who had been miserable and sullen and unpopular, was actually *funny* now. A new personality had suddenly revealed itself from beneath the unpromising surface. Dottie now took it upon herself to entertain the mothers on the block in Flatbush, women whose coffee tables displayed bar mitzvah albums of the dead.

"I simply changed," Dottie explained now. "It didn't happen overnight; it was a slow process. I made some wrong turns here and there, some really big mistakes. But Erica," she would say, her voice slow and reflective, "you don't have to do that. You can have a good life; you don't have to settle. So you're not Twiggy, so you'll never shop in the Missy Petite department. But you'll get *through* all of this; I personally guarantee it."

Erica could not respond. Dottie had a formula; she told jokes and sang and made shameless googly-eyes at the camera, and everyone fell for it. But this was something that Erica would never do; she would rather die than get up onstage and show off. She had almost fainted once when she had to do an oral report on "The Fall of the House of Usher." There was no formula for her, no preordained way to live her life.

Why aren't you tired all the time? she wanted to ask her mother. Erica could barely make it through the afternoon sometimes. She walked from Chemistry to Study Hall to French, and she heard music in her head in time to her step: some deep

19

belching tuba-sounds that might have represented the entrance of a rhinoceros or an elephant in a deleted section of *Peter and the Wolf. Too many animals already*, the composer would think. *Let's stick to the quicker ones, the lighter ones.*

Things will get better, her mother repeated like a litany, and although she probably believed her own words, Erica could not take any comfort from them. She could no longer take comfort from anything her mother said or did, in fact. Her mother had recently betrayed her, and she could not forget it. The betrayal had happened the day after Erica announced during a telephone call that she was going to change her name.

"Oh?" Dottie had said over the phone. "And what are you going to change it to, may I ask?"

"I don't know," said Erica. "I haven't decided."

Her mother laughed gently. "I think we can wait until I get home to discuss it. In the meantime, don't do anything drastic."

The very next night, on "The Merv Griffin Show," there was a lull between jokes, and Dottie said, "You know, Merv, my older daughter announced last night that she's planning on changing her last name. She says 'Engels' is too ugly, too cumbersome. She wants something refined and graceful and ladylike."

Erica froze. "Oh, really?" Merv was saying. "Engels is a perfectly nice name. What is she thinking of changing it *to*?"

"Shmutznik," said Dottie, her expression a perfect deadpan.

The audience roared, and Joey diSalvo the baby-sitter roared, and even Opal, who was sitting about an inch from the set and eating Cheezettes by the handful, opened her mouth and let out a single bark of a laugh. Erica looked at her with disgust. Opal thought it was *funny*; she couldn't take her eyes off the screen. She just sat there watching, her hand lifting and lowering between mouth and bowl. She was like a member of some bizarre cult, her lips ringed in bright cheddar orange.

Erica slammed the heel of her hand against the television, and the picture went to a quick dissolve.

"What are you doing?" cried Opal. "I was *watching*, you know."

"Hey, hey, come on, you two," Joey diSalvo said. "What's going on here? You sound like little babies."

20

"I can't believe she would lie like that," Erica said.

"It's just a joke," said Opal. "Turn it on. She's going to do Mrs. Pummelman; she promised me."

"Let her tell true jokes," said Erica, "and not use me to lie about. As if I would really change my last name to something stupid like that. Oh, that's likely. If I change my name, I'm going to do it with no help from anybody else." She snapped the TV back on, and a commercial filled the screen.

"If you get married someday," Opal pointed out, still not looking up, "then you'll have to change your name."

"I'm not planning on getting married," said Erica. As soon as she said it she knew it was true; saying it made it so. She would not marry, ever. She suddenly understood this fact about herself, as deeply and simply as the way in which anyone understood the basic information they had about themselves—the way women said, "Yes, I have a small frame," or "Yes, I tend to be very emotional."

Instead of marrying she would go away somewhere. She had seen a series of commercials for the Peace Corps lately and had begun to fantasize about joining. Erica had written down the toll-free number which you could call any time of day or night to get more information, and she dialed it one night at three A.M. when she had insomnia. A woman answered, and her voice sounded very far away. It seemed odd that you could call twenty-four hours a day; maybe, Erica thought, the woman was speaking to her from another time zone, maybe even another continent. For one flickering instant she imagined a group of operators "standing by" in grass huts in Nigeria.

"I would like some information about joining the Peace Corps," Erica said from the kitchen phone, whispering so Opal wouldn't wake up.

There was a pause. "May I ask how old you are?" the woman asked.

"Sixteen," Erica said. It had not occurred to her to lie.

"Well, I'm afraid you have to be eighteen to apply," the woman said. "But you can call back in two years. We'll still be here."

21

"*I* may not be," Erica said, and she hung up the telephone before the woman could respond.

In the dark kitchen the automatic ice maker in the refrigerator made a few whirring and thumping sounds, as new ice cubes dropped. Erica was too young for the Peace Corps now, but if she waited two years, she could make her useless self useful. She pictured herself teaching village women how to read or tie a tourniquet. But even when she turned eighteen, there was a chance that they still wouldn't take her. *You're too large,* they might say during the interview, wrapping a tape measure around her middle. *You're too slow. You're too sad.* Maybe she would be left here in the city forever; maybe she would eventually be forced to marry.

Suddenly Erica was depressed again. There were very few options left, she realized; nobody offered you a smorgasbord of possibilities anymore. By the time you turned sixteen, all your abilities had been fully tested and charted, and it was clear as day what you could and could not do. Opal, only eleven, still had a range of choices left. She didn't have to start thinking about any of this for years. That was why Opal could sit happily in front of the television all day, eating Cheezettes and thinking the world was swell. She could watch the show with her head cocked slightly to the side, the way a squirrel sometimes looks at things; there was that same robotic curiosity to her movements.

Opal had found nothing wrong with their mother's jokes on "The Merv Griffin Show"; she had just laughed along with the audience. My mother is a charlatan, Erica thought; this was an S.A.T. word that seemed particularly applicable. She loved the word, and repeated it aloud sometimes when she was having trouble falling asleep. *Charlatan.* She imagined approaching her mother and saying, "Mom, I've come up with a new character I think you should do. It's this woman named Charlotte Ann, and she's a pathological liar." Dottie would look a little confused, not getting the secret joke, and she would thank Erica for trying to be helpful.

After the night of "The Merv Griffin Show," Erica did not watch her mother on television again for years, until college

22

began and it was unavoidable. Occasionally Dottie's face would sneak up on her during the flipping of channels, but Erica would never deliberately choose to watch. It was hard to avoid; Dottie Engels was ubiquitous, between the glut of talk shows and seasonal comedy specials. There was always a holiday coming up in the near future, and Dottie could usually be found onscreen dressed as Santa, or the Easter Bunny, or a turkey being chased around the stage by Bob Hope, who was dressed as a Pilgrim. Opal could not understand why Erica would not watch these shows, and this was the beginning of the split.

Erica no longer had the patience she used to have, the energy required to spend big blocks of time with her sister. She came home after school and went directly to her room, where she lay on her bed and tried to keep out all distractions, but something was always in her way: some light in her eyes or interference in the background. Opal occasionally hammered at the door, begging Erica to hyperventilate, saying she would even *pay* her. It was like the slow failing of a marriage, in which everything begins to rust piece by piece. Erica remembered her own parents' marriage, and how in the middle of the night she used to hear the two of them stalking different parts of the house: Dottie in the kitchen, opening and shutting cabinets, and Norm in the den, doing who knew what.

Maybe this was bound to happen if you lived with someone long enough; maybe there was no such thing as extended harmony. Certainly Erica had never witnessed it. Peaceful times seemed to be on loan; you experienced them only briefly, and then you spent the rest of your life remembering: the perfect summer, the perfect meal, the perfect night's sleep. Erica remembered a time when she and Opal had been close, the big and the little. They had roamed the apartment together, talked on walkie-talkies from different rooms, set up obstacle courses, built a spookhouse in the hallway.

Sometimes at night Erica used to hand Opal a piece of paper on which the words ADMIT ONE were written in Magic Marker. This meant that there would be a floor show soon. Opal would come sit in the darkness of Erica's room, her leg jiggling with anticipation.

"Good evening, audience," Erica would say. "I am Erica Engels." Then she flicked on her flashlight and made guttural crowd-sounds low in her throat. "Tonight," she said, "we are going to take a trip around . . . my . . . room!" She swung the flashlight beam across to the bureau, the desk, the depleted beanbag chair, and finally let it land on Opal.

Opal shrieked, blinded. "Erica, Erica, don't!" she cried, but she didn't move away. In that moment she was like an animal trapped in the high beams of a car. Erica switched off the light, and her sister's cries died away. Opal was not really trapped; Opal would do fine. She was a limber little girl who could walk a balance beam or do a bird's nest on the rings. She floured her hands with rosin and swung expertly from the uneven parallels. She was a monkey of a sister, resilient, not yet damaged. She hadn't been weighed down by a large box of a body, or by a steady ration of melancholy. Unlike Erica, Opal would not have to settle. There would be men for Opal, with angular features and expensive camping gear and vows of fidelity. The word "settle" was odd; Erica pictured Opal never settling, always circling above the ground like a plane that can't see its way clear to land.

These days Erica kept to herself. She had to admit that the situation was much better than when they all lived in the tiny house in Jericho, with constant arguments at dinner and a father who paced the hall like a warden, clearly uneasy in that house of females. He expected treachery from them, abandonment, and finally he got both. But that was history now; it had all been resolved legally, financially. Now they had a new life, a peaceful one.

But still, Erica thought, there was no way to truly be alone. Opal was always somewhere in the background, banging on doors, wanting company. And elsewhere in the apartment, a baby-sitter was usually practicing a comedy routine. *Something* was inevitably going on; even when Erica shut herself away in her room, with the wonderful music of Reva and Jamie playing, and the odor of patchouli rising up and fanning out, she was always aware of one or two stray thoughts. She didn't know what their purpose was; it was like finding an old key in a drawer and having no idea of what it might ever have opened. You hold the slip of metal between your fingers and try to recall the chain it once hung from, the door that flew open day after day. But nothing comes to you, because the key clearly belonged to someone else.

What you were left with, Erica thought, what did belong to you, were all the tangibles of daily life: the sweater folded over the chair, the warm Thermos snapped into its tin lunchbox, the bench by the side of the river after school. And always, finally, there would be Jordan Strang waiting for you on that bench, Jordan whom you knew you could never love, but might eventually have to.

3

I think we are in rats' alley, where the dead men lost their bones," the three girls chanted, practicing one more time before the mirror, while Mrs. Fabricant fastened their arms together with rubber bands.

"Okay, Hollow Men," the teacher said. "You're on soon."

They walked sideways like crabs down the hall to the stage door. Oh, the school at night! Opal thought. What a place it was; the floors shimmered in the dark, and you could hear the heating system breathing in the walls. The school at night was like a sleeping animal. Opal followed the others down the hallway, her wrists attached to theirs.

Someone opened the stage door for them, and they silently waited in the wings for their cue. Opal watched the actors onstage; the fifth-grader playing Madame Sosostris was talking to Sweeney. "Those were pearls that were his eyes," she was saying. And then that tiny redheaded boy, the one who had missed so many rehearsals, piped up from stage left in a surprisingly sure voice: "What are the roots that clutch, what branches grow out of this stony rubbish? Son of man, you cannot say, or guess . . ."

Everyone in the audience was quiet. This fragile boy, with hair like fire, spoke the words almost as if he understood them. All the children listened. Even Madame Sosostris, who usually played with her crystal ball and looked bored when someone else was speaking, turned to watch.

Then the three Hollow Men staggered out. Dressed in burlap, their faces blackened from the cork that Mrs. Fabricant had held over a match, they stood center stage, swaying against each other, as they had practiced for weeks, speaking in the carefully articulated voices of the old and tired.

"We are the Hollow Men," they said. "We are the stuffed men, leaning together. Headpiece filled with straw. Alas!" They paused, swaying more severely. "Our dried voices, when we whisper together, are quiet and meaningless as wind in dry grass, or *rats' feet* over broken glass in our dry cellar." Their voices grew hard on the phrase "rats' feet," snarling as they had been instructed.

There was a murmur in the audience. Opal looked out, squinting. Someone had left one of the auditorium doors partly open, letting in light. She could see members of the audience rustle and turn to each other. And somehow, in that moment, she managed to catch sight of her mother, sitting way in the back, on the aisle. Her mother was laughing. Holding herself and laughing as though she might split apart. Had something gone wrong? Opal worried. Had they messed up their lines? Was someone's headpiece on backwards?

There was no time to wonder, for their brief part was done, and they shuffled offstage together. That dull girl began her speech now, the girl who always spoke in such a dead voice. *She* should have been a Hollow Man, Opal thought. Let *me* be the Cruellest Month girl.

"And when we were children," the girl was saying, as though reciting the Pledge, "staying at the arch-duke's, my cousin, he took me out on a sled, and I was frightened. He said, Marie, Marie, hold on tight. And down we went."

The Hollow Men sat together on folding chairs. They were not allowed to untie themselves from each other because they still had to do curtain calls.

"Move in closer," Susan whispered to Opal. "You're hurting me."

So they sat there listening as the play wound down, and finally there was the line about the world ending in a whimper. On "whimper," the three Hollow Men shot up; this was their cue. Out front there was tremendous applause. Soon they were onstage again with the others, raising their bound arms up in salute.

27

Afterwards, riding home in a taxi, Opal asked, "Did we bomb in some way? Was that why everyone was laughing?"

"Oh, God no," said Dottie. "You were just so *dear*. That's what that was all about."

They were in a Checker cab, and Opal and Erica sat on the jump seats. Dottie and Ross Needler sat facing them. "You were wonderful, Opal," Ross said. "Maybe I should sign you on. Need a manager?"

"Har har," said Opal.

It had been an Evening of Eliot at the Headley Middle School. Each year the theater department attempted something ambitious.

"You *were* wonderful," said Dottie. "I mean it."

As a treat, they stopped off to celebrate at an ice cream parlor on the East Side. The parlor was bright and busy, and Opal noticed several people staring at her mother and poking each other as they walked in. As usual, Dottie seemed oblivious. She was saying something to Ross and laughing. Her earrings were huge silver disks that swung wildly when she turned her head even slightly. Everything was festive, and Opal kept thinking of herself onstage, swaying and chanting. ". . . where the dead men lost their bones," she thought, and it was a line that made absolutely no sense to her, and yet thrilled her all the same. Dead men losing bones— what did that mean? Could dead people lose bones the way regular people lost gloves? During rehearsals, they had never really talked about what the words meant; instead, they had spent time on what Mrs. Fabricant called "motivation."

"You're like scarecrows," Mrs. Fabricant had said. "You have no muscles or blood or anything. You're not human. You're just dried-out pieces of straw. Now what would that feel like?"

"Kind of bad and scary?" Susan Berwell said.

"Are you asking me or telling me?"

Susan paused. "Telling you," she decided.

"Good," said Mrs. Fabricant, smiling. "I *want* you to feel bad and scary. I want you to pretend your bodies are like old newspaper."

They stood up and walked in circles around the empty stage, pretending their arms and legs were crackling as they walked. Opal began to feel light, as though she might fly away. It was like

28

hyperventilating! she realized. Letting yourself disappear for a little while, because you knew you could come back later on. I have no bones, she thought; I have no skin or blood or muscle. She walked around and around, until Mrs. Fabricant put a strong hand on her shoulder and told her, "Enough."

But tonight, at the performance, the audience had laughed at the Hollow Men. They had been *dear*, dressed up as though it were Halloween. They might have come onstage clutching UNICEF cartons, they were that dear. But it was better, Opal knew, to be dear than embarrassing. Embarrassing was when you came onstage and forgot all your lines, and had to run off weeping, which had happened to Connie Delman the year before, in the sixth-grade production of *Summer and Smoke*.

Opal had the sense that no matter what she did in her life, she would probably never be embarrassing. She might fail at things, or annoy people, but probably no one would look away in shame. It relieved her to know this; it freed her up somehow. She swung just a little harder from the uneven parallels in gym class, and even the time she missed the upper bar entirely and fell with a *whump* to the mat, no one had made fun of her. Instead, the gym teacher had swiveled her gaze over to Alison Merkin and shouted, "*Alison, why aren't you spotting Opal?*"

Opal had stood up shakily and dusted herself off. No one was snickering. All the other girls stood against the wall in their gym suits, waiting their turn. Opal walked back to the end of the line, and there was a new spring to her step. "Too bad you fell," Karen Lewis whispered. "Are you all right?" Opal nodded. Alison Merkin, on the other hand, was walking toward the line with her head down.

This was the way it was; at the very beginning of school, everyone's role had been cast in stone, and they all spent the next several years living up to what was expected of them. Rude kids made obscene noises in front of substitute teachers, slow kids moved their lips when they read, and popular ones fell off the uneven parallel bars and walked back to rejoin the line with a certain cocky grace.

Opal ruled at school, with her tight cluster of friends and their elaborate projects and secrets. On her report card the year before, her teacher had written, "Opal is a joy to have around, always cheerful. It's been a pleasure to have her in my class!"

It was only when she went home each day that everything changed. At home, no one ruled. Opal and Erica shared the responsibilities, and none of the baby-sitters had much experience, or even interest, in asserting authority. When their mother was in town she tried to make their lives conventional. She insisted, for instance, in looking over their homework with them, and nothing made her happier than having the chance to sign a permission slip to go on a class trip. She also liked to cook breakfast for Opal and Erica, even if she had been out playing a late club date the night before. She would walk into the kitchen at seven A.M. and say, "How would you two like a big stack of flapjacks?"

Flapjacks; the word itself had a false hominess to it. They let her cook for them, watched her pour pale batter onto a griddle even if they had already finished eating. They didn't want to disappoint her; she seemed to take great pleasure from cooking them breakfast. Opal would gaze sleepily across the room at her mother. Even in a housecoat she looked beautiful, glamorous in quilted aqua.

When she was in town she often took them out at night for ice cream, like tonight. Every evening spent with her was special, and yet Opal always worried about something going wrong. Usually something did, and lately it was Erica who caused the problems.

Tonight, across the marble table, Erica was hunched over her sundae, eating quickly, as though afraid it might be taken away.

"Something wrong, honey?" Dottie asked.

"Nothing," said Erica. "Everything's great." Her voice was sour.

"Are you sure?"

Erica looked up, letting her spoon drop into the glass. "You really want to know?" she asked.

"Of course," said Dottie.

Opal rubbed her wrists nervously; they still bore indentations from where the rubber bands had been.

"Okay," said Erica. "Last year, when the Upper School did that Lorraine Hansberry Night, you didn't come. But you can conveniently make it to Opal's show."

Dottie looked stricken. "Honey," she said, "now let me think. Hold on. I must have been working; why else wouldn't I have come? There must have been something I couldn't get out of . . . oh, I know, it was the Sands! I was opening at the Sands! I wanted to see your play, Erica; we had a big talk about it."

"She wasn't even *in* the play," Opal cut in, the meanness piping into her from outer space. "She was in the lighting booth, remember?"

Erica stared for a minute, then burst into tears. The evening was ruined completely, and Opal began crying too. She wasn't sure exactly why, and yet she was unable to stop. Ross Needler looked around nervously. Two waitresses, who had begun to approach the table for an autograph, were now discreetly backing away.

"My girls," said Dottie, when they were finally calmer, "have I really hurt you so much? Don't you know that I only try to do what I can? That I can't be two places at once? I hate traveling so much, but what can I do? If I thought you'd be happier in L.A., then we'd move in a minute. But you'd hate it there; it's so awful, all swimming pools and valet parking. Oh, please bear with me, girls. Don't I always try to do something special for you? Aren't you happier now than when we were in the suburbs with your father? Isn't it a little better, a little more peaceful?"

And the two girls, ending their crying fit in phlegmy little sobs, nodded finally and admitted that they were happier now. Opal thought of her father; she dragged out the stock image she had of him: a bony man, the boniest father anyone ever had, coming through the door in the evening. He was the real Hollow Man, she thought; he would lose his bones someday.

It had always seemed wrong to her that he had a key to the house in Jericho, that he had *access* to their lives, when they were much happier without him. He would come into the front hallway, bringing with him the cold night air and his raincoat folded over his arm, and as soon as he walked in, everything changed. Opal and Erica, who were leaping around the house, stood frozen in their places as though playing Statues. The television, which had been yammering unnoticed in the den, was quickly shut off.

"Your father doesn't like television," Dottie had once whispered to them, and this fact had been astounding. Not like television? That warm flood of light, that endless stream of fun? Opal could not get over it. But there was a whole catalog of things her father did not like: chocolate, any kind of fish, carpeting, restaurants, among others.

"You girls help set the table," their mother whispered. "Hurry now."

After a long dinner of studious eating, there would often be a terrible fight. It would start from nothing, but fairly soon their mother and father would be at odds, spitting words back and forth. Opal and Erica would try not to listen. They would go into Erica's room and say their special code words again and again, placing a spell over the argument.

Fishka fishka foon, they said a dozen times, bobbing up and down like the old men in the synagogue. *Fishka fishka foon*. But it went on every night, and began to get worse, and finally Dottie took Opal and Erica away, first to Dottie's aunt Harriet's house in Queens, and eight months later to Manhattan, where they found an apartment, the three of them. When they moved to Aunt Harriet's, Dottie was nothing—not yet famous, not even a comedienne at all. In the past she had entered a few local talent contests and usually came in second, but it hadn't occurred to her that she could make a living from it. That would come later: the idea of actually putting herself out there, up on a stage alone. Dottie would learn quickly about the Open Mike nights at comedy clubs, the smoke that stayed in your hair and on your clothes forever, and how you had to sit for hours in dubious waiting rooms of buildings in the West 40s of Manhattan to find a manager. But for now, all she knew was that she had to leave her marriage.

"I want you girls to think back on your childhood when you're older," she said, "and not remember it as having been miserable. There's no reason for two little girls to have such a childhood."

What did they know? Opal was going into the second grade at the time, Erica the sixth. Their mother took them away one night without asking their opinion. She packed up the white Rambler station wagon with all their clothes and belongings and left before their father came home. It was July, and she rolled all the windows down. As they drove along the road, she shouted to them over the wind about their new life. "Think of it as an adventure, girls!" she said.

Opal looked out at the rush-hour traffic traveling in the opposite direction. Their father might have been in one of those cars on the other side of the divider, heading home, and he would pass the station wagon on the way. For one terrible instant, the two cars would be side by side and her eyes would meet his. Opal quickly looked away; she didn't want to see. She leaned forward against the front seat, her head resting near her mother's.

". . . *he took me out on a sled,*" the Cruellest Month girl had said in Opal's play, "*and I was frightened. He said, Marie, Marie, hold on tight. And down we went.*" Down they went, Opal and Erica and Dottie, driving off to Aunt Harriet's house and having no idea of what would happen to them. The car had been like a sled, swerving and speeding and finally landing them at the bottom. When they pulled up in front of the house in Flushing, Queens, it was eight o'clock at night. The porch light was blazing, and the poor old German shepherd was barking in the yard. Aunt Harriet peered out through the blinds at them, but for a little while nobody could bear to get out of the car.

Later that night, settled uneasily into the bedroom that had once belonged to Cousin Kenneth, Opal looked around her at the athletic trophies on the shelves, the map of the world on the wall. This was a real *boy's* room, dark and paneled and long ago abandoned. Cousin Kenneth hadn't lived here in many years.

Opal switched on her walkie-talkie to speak with Erica, who lay on the other side of the wall. Over the spray of static, Opal said, "Do you think we'll be okay?"

"Yes," said Erica. "She knows what to do."

"But it's weird here," said Opal.

"I know," said Erica. "You should go to sleep now, Opal. It's getting really late."

"All right," Opal said. She didn't want to let go of her sister's voice. The voice was so human, so real, contained in a plastic handset, held close against her ear; she could have listened to it forever. "Well, good night then," Opal said, signing off. "Over and over."

Erica laughed. "Over and what?" she said. "You've got it wrong. It's 'over and *out*.'"

"Oh," said Opal, embarrassed. "Well, over and out, then."

She clicked off her walkie-talkie and placed it on Cousin Kenneth's nightstand. *Over and out.* That was so definite. How much better was her own version, which meant: This will never end. Always we will listen to each other's voice, blanketed in static, before sleep. Always we will talk like this, across walls or states or continents. Even years from now, when we are both married and living far apart, I will say to you before we click off for the night: Over and over.

4

She had never gone through horses. She had skipped over that stage entirely, declining to be one of the many who sat in their rooms at night, making lists of potential horse names:

> **Velvet**
> **Prancer**
> **Windy**
> **Charcoal**
> **Silver**
> **Cinnamon**

She didn't take down an ancient copy of *Misty of Chincoteague* from her bookshelf each night and read for hours, then close her eyes to seal up the vision of this island where horses ran loose. She didn't pray for a foal for her birthday, fingers crossed into knots, making herself sick with want. She didn't *need* a horse; her longing was already there for her, laid out plainly. It wasn't attached to any animal or object; it hovered over her like a cartoon cloud. One day Erica woke up feeling it so deeply that she decided she had to do something. The following week, she and Jordan Strang began to change the nature of their relationship.

After school she and Jordan no longer went to the park. Instead they got right on the bus and headed crosstown to his family's apartment. First he would feed the schnauzer, then leaf through his parents' mail, then drop a dozen Nilla Wafers onto a plate and carry it into his bedroom. Erica followed silently behind like a Japanese wife.

Sometimes, in the bedroom, Jordan turned on his black light, and everything took on a purple hue and what seemed to be a dusting of lunar lint, and Erica and Jordan's teeth stood out like bright little game tiles. They examined their bodies in the light, holding out arms and legs for self-inspection, and then they examined each other. Soon it became something else, something that required the tenting of a blanket.

Jordan was as smooth as any boy in the tenth grade, his hips narrow, his muscles untried. He moved differently here, as though the air under the blanket contained all the properties of water. Slow, cautious, he pushed away at space as if it were a burden to him. Anyone could do this, popular or not; it was the great equalizer. Erica was amazed at the way her own want could be so easily poured into him, given shape. He could have been any boy in the tenth grade; it wouldn't have mattered. Not every boy in the tenth grade would have been willing, though. Most of them would have let out a sharp, incredulous little laugh at just the *idea* of touching such a fat girl. But somehow Jordan knew he had no real choice, and when he kissed her for the first time it was punctuated with resignation more than desire.

Jordan's long face peered down at her from a new angle; the whole perspective had shifted. They were not coatless in the park; no wind lifted their hair or snuffed out a tiny light between them. Jordan looked sidelong at her breasts, then looked away, then looked back once again. She felt a shiver watching him do this. Her breasts, suddenly, were no longer just the ledge she pressed her school books against as she walked the halls of Headley, nor were they a reason for turning away in the girls' locker room to make a quick, furtive scoop into the cups of a bra. Now they were something to be looked at, then turned away from, then looked at once again. Her whole body was meant for looking at now, and this was astonishing. She was so *big* compared with him; she was all broad expanses of skin and breast and hair. How could he want this?

It made her think, inevitably, of her parents in bed together. Years before, Erica had been aware of their lovemaking, because they made such a big show of it in their desire for privacy. Her father had installed a chain latch on the master bedroom door of

36

the house in Jericho, and his carpentry skills were poor. The latch had to be toyed with in order for the little knob to slide correctly into place. *Scritch, scritch, scritch,* Erica would hear, the scrape of metal much more audible than the lovemaking would ever be. Why did they feel the need to lock the door? she used to wonder. It was humiliating, as though they thought she or Opal might run into their room in the middle of the night, unbidden, seeking refuge from a dream. She and Opal knew better than that; they knew what went on in there. Opal occasionally did need to have things explained, however, for not all of her facts were right. She had assumed, for instance, that a man's penis looked just like that of the neighbor's dog Triscuit: crayon-bright and retractable into its casing. Erica showed Opal some color plates from the book *Treasures of the Renaissance,* which lay on the coffee table in the den, and set her straight.

But there were more complicated ideas about sex that Opal would not be able to grasp for years, and that Erica would not even try to explain. There wasn't much to say about the way in which two people, even in the throes of unhappiness, after days of screaming and days of not speaking, could suddenly approach each other with their warm mammal bodies and declare a truce until morning.

Erica knew very little about her parents' marriage, and even less about their divorce. Her father had been extricated permanently from their lives. Erica knew only that he had moved to Miami several years before.

"I don't like to talk about your father," Dottie would say when pressed. "He did enough damage to our family. It was a mistake for me to have married him, but what can I do? You girls are the only good things to have come from that marriage. I just don't want you to have to *deal* with him; there's no reason for him to be in your lives. Just forget about it."

So Erica and Opal stopped asking questions. In the beginning, after Dottie had moved them to Aunt Harriet's house, Norm had come to visit them a few times. The visits were awkward, though, and finally, after a particularly bad afternoon, he stopped visiting altogether. He called on the phone every few weeks in the beginning, keeping the girls on the line for ten excruciating minutes, trying to pull scraps of conversation from them, but it was no good; they were afraid of him, and what he might say or do. After a while Norm stopped calling, and they were deeply relieved. He sent Dottie child-support money each month, but there was no other communication. Erica imagined him down in Florida, with a new wife and new accounting job. She wondered if he thought about his first marriage and his daughters every time he turned on the television and saw Dottie's face shining out at him from behind the glass. He could never really forget; in this family, television kept everyone bound together for life.

Erica remembered how, the afternoon of his last visit, he had shown up at Aunt Harriet's door in a heavy overcoat. "I don't want to see him," Dottie had said, and she had stayed hidden in the upstairs bathroom until he took the girls out of the house. They walked around the neighborhood, which was nearly city, nearly suburb. In one direction there was a park, in another direction an expressway. You could sit on a park bench and listen to the sound of cars sweeping by in the distance.

"Are you girls doing okay?" he asked them.

They both nodded elaborately, like toy dogs in the back windows of cars, whose heads are forever bobbing.

"Look, your mother and I," he began, "we weren't made for each other. It wasn't a marriage made in heaven." At this point, Opal grew restless and started to walk around, plucking at bushes, snapping off low branches of trees. "Opal," her father said, "could you come here? Could you just listen a little longer?"

Opal wandered back, and he continued, telling them that he knew he had a problem with his temper, that he was trying to keep it under control, that he was sorry they were frightened of him. "I'm not so bad," he said. "Just look at me. There's nothing scary here." He pulled down his collar so his whole head was revealed: the skeletal face, the narrow eyes. Opal and Erica said nothing, just continued to stare.

"You know, you're both very cold," he said quietly. "You're both going to grow up to be frigid women."

The words meant nothing then, but Erica held tightly to the

phrase, the way one holds on to nonsense words from childhood until they can be deciphered at a later date. There had been a commercial on television for the Campfire Girls, she remembered, and it had depicted a group of beaming campers around a blazing fire. "Sing wo-he-lo," they sang. "Sing wo-he-lo . . ." Erica had loved the authentic American Indian sound to the syllables; she pictured two squaws meeting in a clearing, touching palms and saying "wo-he-lo" to each other in somber tones. But years later she had learned that "wo-he-lo" wasn't an Indian phrase at all, and that in fact it was shorthand for "work, health, love." Everything seemed to be in code; nothing in the world was simple.

"You're both going to grow up to be frigid women," her father had said, and Erica thought of this again now, as she lay in bed with Jordan Strang.

Her father had been wrong. She felt many things; she was alive with nerve bundles, alert to Jordan's careless touch. There was no fury between Erica and Jordan, as there must have been between Dottie and Norm. Instead, there was just the inevitability of going ahead with what they had begun. They no longer needed to say, "Meet you at the end of school." Instead, one of them was always waiting under the Exit sign at three o'clock. Finally the other one would show up, and together they would push through the double doors, not saying a word. They would walk through the school-yard, she struggling to keep up with him, and he loping along quickly, not even checking to see if she was by his side. Sometimes, in her hurry, Erica would drop a few papers or books in the snow, and have to call, "Jordan, wait!" He would stop on the path and sigh heavily, as if thinking: *This is what girls are like. All my life I will have to wait for them.* His own books and papers were always fastened into place by a thick rubber strap, whereas Erica clutched hers against her. Something inevitably got separated from her pile and flew away—some note to bring to her mother or a failed quiz—something she didn't really want, anyway.

They were both doing poorly in school. Erica had recently been called down to the guidance counselor's office and given a serious lecture.

"I'm going to do something I've never done before, Erica," Mrs.

Shub had said. She had her hand pressed down on a piece of paper, fingers splayed. "I'm going to show you your I.Q.," she said. "It's probably unethical of me, and maybe I'll lose my job, but I just want you to see how very bright you are." Then Mrs. Shub started to lift her hand off the page, all the while keeping her eyes fixed on Erica. It was like a magic act; Erica expected a flock of doves to thunder up from under Mrs. Shub's palm. "Look at that," said the guidance counselor, and Erica peered down to where the number "160" was typed. "That means genius," said Mrs. Shub. "Now maybe you can explain to me why you are failing Math and French and Gym."

Erica had only shrugged and muttered a promise to try harder, and finally she was let go. But she knew that she couldn't focus on school any longer; she was too far behind in everything to even think about catching up. She and Jordan began to try new drugs. He had an older brother at M.I.T. who spent a lot of extracurricular time in the laboratory, mixing together hallucinogens and amphetamines. Neil's latest discovery was a new drug called Bali. It had been christened Bali, he had explained, because it was a place everyone wanted to visit. Bali was a small translucent capsule filled with an amber liquid. There was a story going around M.I.T. about somebody's mother finding a capsule on her son's dresser and mistaking it for vitamin E. Supposedly she broke it open and spread the contents on the lines around her eyes and mouth. No one seemed to know what, if anything, had happened.

Now Jordan held two capsules in his hand and instructed Erica to take one. She plucked it up and swallowed it quickly, and then they both waited like expectant fathers. They sat on the floor of Jordan's room, looking through his vast record collection, and finally Erica felt something buzzing around the back of her head. She swatted at it absently before she realized it was the drug taking hold. Jordan was sprawled across the floor, and at just that moment he jerked his head up sharply. "Erica," he said, "I feel very strange."

This began, for her, what was to be five hours of taking care of Jordan Strang. Luckily, it was a Saturday afternoon and Erica didn't need to be home until the evening. Opal was off at somebody's birthday party on the East Side. Jordan stood up and began to walk

40

around unsteadily. He lifted small objects and put them back down.

"I'm not used to this," he said. "It's usually not so strong. Something must be wrong here. I think we've been poisoned."

"Could you sit down?" she said. "You're making me nervous." Jordan came and sat down on the edge of the bed, twisting his hands together in anxiety. Erica was aware of little waves of color rimming her vision, but she ignored them, put them on a back burner. She knew that she had to keep an eye on Jordan. This drug seemed to be a souped-up version of all the drugs people had done back in the Sixties, all the drugs that Jordan spent his days reading about.

"Hunter would approve," Jordan said finally, nodding his head and smiling. "I want to write him a letter. Please, Erica, let me dictate it to you, okay?"

Reluctantly she agreed, and they sat there like an executive and his private secretary. Erica wrote down what he was saying as fast as she could, although later, when she tried to read back what she had written, much of it was indecipherable. The words jerked across the page like the lines on an EKG:

Dear Hunter,
    I know you don't know me and I don't know you,
but I feel as though somehow we know each other anyway. Maybe we met during a trip somewhere, if you know
what I mean. I am sixteen and live in New York City
and have read all your books. Congratulations on being
such an amazing writer. I've been sitting here on the floor
of my bedroom and doing a drug called Bali, which I think
you would like, so I am enclosing one capsule for your
own personal use. There's more where that came from,
believe me. Doing this drug reminds me a lot of some
of the best scenes in *Fear and Loathing*. You'll know what
I mean when you take it yourself. Maybe I'm being pre-
sumptuous, and you don't trip anymore, it being the Sev-
enties and all, but I'm just assuming that you do. I know
that things were very different back in the Sixties, and that
you tripped practically every day. I was too young for
any of that, and I really regret it. I would appreciate any

anecdotes you might care to tell me, any stories about life back then, etc. Be well, Hunter, and keep up the good work. Hope to hear from you.

Your fan,
Jordan Strang

"How's that?" Jordan asked when he was finished.

"What are you going to do?" Erica asked. "Tape a capsule to the letter? It'll get crushed in the mail, or you might get arrested. You'd better not put a return address on it."

Jordan looked worried. "You're probably right," he said. "But then how could he write back? Suppose he thought this was a great letter? Suppose he was coming to New York and wanted to look me up, and I took this big precaution and didn't sign my name and address? I'd *die*." Jordan stood up and began to pace again.

"Oh, relax," Erica said. "Just take it easy."

"I want to hear some very loud music," he said. "That's what I want."

No, Erica thought, please make it acoustic. Make it soft and melancholy and sung by Reva and Jamie: "Oh bonny maiden, come walk a ways with me/We'll go down to the valley, where the wild fern grows free/Oh no, kind sir, I cannot go with thee/For there I'll find my brother, a'hanging from a tree/ . . ." Erica hummed to herself wistfully as Jordan busied himself at the stereo.

All of a sudden the room was pierced by shrieking music. The Phantom Limbs were singing their only hit, "Touch the Moon." Jordan played the song four times in a row, the bass turned way up high, and then decided that he had had enough.

"Let's go outside," he said. "I need some air."

They walked into the hall, with the schnauzer yipping at their heels, and rode downstairs in the elevator. Tony, the elevator man, eyed them suspiciously the whole way. Finally Jordan looked at Tony and said, "I see you are staring at my feet."

"What?" said Tony. "You're on drugs."

Jordan started to laugh, and Erica looked away in embarrassment.

"Did you get the reference?" Jordan asked her as they left the building. "Seymour Glass."

"Yes," said Erica. "I *got* it." The entire tenth grade was reading Salinger this month.

She ran alongside him on the street, struggling to keep up. They stopped at a "Don't Walk" sign, and in that moment Erica looked closely at Jordan, watched him do a little speed-induced softshoe next to her, and she wondered how she could bear to be with him much longer. He never looked at her, really, except when she had her blouse off, and even then he often bore the expression of an eager boy-scientist. She could picture the two Strang brothers, Jordan and Neil, as elementary-school kids doing experiments with the science kit they had been given for Chanukah. Two boys keeping busy with test tubes and iron filings, because there is nothing else in the world for them to do, nothing that will give them pleasure. Such boys don't expect pleasure, anyway, and this is why their bodies take on a permanent, retreative slouch. Jordan would never truly be interested in Erica; it would never occur to him to be. But be fair, she told herself; you aren't interested in him, either. Still, she felt relief that he existed, because she had to do *something* with all that need. Jordan was like a bucket you placed under a leaky roof.

Erica grabbed his hand as they walked, and he seemed so shocked that he pulled back as if he had touched something hot. They had never held hands before, never touched each other outside the confines of his room, or in any light other than black light. Nothing was purple now, or covered in space-lint. Erica and Jordan observed each other and sighed at the same time, acknowledging what they saw and somehow accepting it.

They hailed a taxi then and rode all the way down to the East Village. During the ride, Erica was finally able to sit back and close her eyes. Small paisley objects floated across a dark field, then vanished. It was an unobtrusive hallucination—not really a hallucination at all, she thought; more like a memory. Then she remembered what it was: the pattern on a jumper she had worn almost every day in fifth grade. She felt embarrassed that the only visions she had were *fabric* patterns; it seemed such a parody of what a girl would hallucinate while doing drugs. Jordan, on the other hand, was probably seeing pictograms drawn by ancient Yaqui tribesmen.

43

When they got out of the cab on St. Marks Place, two men were playing guitars and singing a medley of Bob Dylan songs.

"Let's listen," Jordan said, and they stopped for a few minutes on the sidewalk. Jordan took out a dollar and ostentatiously fluttered it down into the open guitar case. When the songs were over, and Jordan and Erica were walking farther east, he shook his head and said, "I wish I had been conscious of that music the first time around. I missed it all; it just kills me. My parents were sort of leftist back then; they liked Bobby Kennedy, and they had this group of endocrinologists that used to get together every month and have political meetings. But I was just a little kid; I didn't pay attention. I played Candyland in my room all day, and I didn't have a thought in my head." He paused, squinting. "Maybe that's what's wrong with us," he said. "We were born too late. Kind of like those men who think they were supposed to have been women. Maybe I was supposed to have been born a few years earlier, but something went wrong. Maybe my parents were supposed to have fucked one night a few years before, but my mother said, 'Not tonight, Jack, I have to look at a few more thyroid levels,' and that was that."

They walked for an hour, making a big circle around the East Village. Since it was so cold, most of the streets were empty except for a few stray people dozing on stoops, and a gathering of Hell's Angels and their girlfriends building a bonfire in a garbage can on East Fourth Street. On Second Avenue two old women wheeled luggage carts overspilling with laundry.

"That's what's on the street now," Jordan said. "All the hippie freaks went to business school and got married, or joined EST. There's no community at all. Just bag ladies and a few girls from New Jersey. Six years ago, this street was hopping. Music playing, dope in the air. *And I was too young for any of it.* Now look at it—it's like death."

Erica didn't know how to answer him, but it didn't matter; he didn't really want a response from her. He just wanted her to walk with him, to keep up with him as best she could. She was relieved when he finally wanted to sit down. They went into the Kiev on Second Avenue and sat at a table in the back, drinking coffee, which they both loaded up with sugar. Under the unnatural light she noticed how sickly Jordan looked, and it shocked her. I touch him, she thought. I kiss him and do other things. The thought repelled her for just a moment, then was gone, like one of her little paisley hallucinations. All thoughts, all visions, got absorbed right back into the atmosphere. She could take note that Jordan looked sickly now, but when she lay in his bed on Monday after school, under his *Hobbit* poster, she would forget that she had ever thought this. Somehow she would welcome his arms and legs, taking pleasure in the way they swung open and closed on their hinges. In his bed everything smelled sweet: a combination of Erica's apricot shampoo and the Nilla Wafers on their breath. It made sense that people wanted to spend their whole lives in bed, because if they did they would never have to face up to the truth: *My wife is a shrew*, a man might think over breakfast. *My husband is a bonehead*, the wife might think. In bed, these perceptions were of no consequence.

This was the big payoff of adulthood, the thing that no one told you. Just as your cynicism started to rise up, because of novels you were reading in your tenth-grade English elective, "Man's Search for Identity," it was quickly extinguished by the sweet goofiness that sex provided. You saw the light, and then *bam*, no more light. Just a calm, spreading glow.

"I'm completely down now," Jordan said. "It's totally worn off."

"Me too," said Erica, although for her the drug had never really grabbed hold. This was her role in life: to take dictation, to sit and watch as other people had visions, to tend and comfort. Maybe she ought to get a job as a volunteer at Odyssey House. She could talk teenage boys down from bad trips—all those boys, like Jordan, who had missed drugs the first time around. She could just *be* there, her large, welcoming self, telling them it was okay, everything was okay, and exactly how much did they take? But her desire to help wasn't innate, the way it seemed to be in some people. Erica could see it in the eyes of the Salvation Army bell-ringers at Christmas. Standing in front of Macy's, bundled up like refugees in the cold, clanging heavy bells until their elbows were stiff from the repetition of movement, those people actually

45

looked happy. They were in their element, their eyes dreamy as they stood over a kettle of money. They didn't mind the cold, or the fact that everyone around them was laden with wrapped packages and running off to homes and families. That would come later on, after a good day of work. They would go to their own homes, take off their coats, put up their feet, and think: *I have done something worthwhile with my day. I am a decent and noble human being.* And for them, it was enough.

It should be enough for me, too, Erica thought. I should not want all the things I do. It made her ashamed, how much she required, how much relief she took in the pleasures of her solitary life: sitting alone in her room and breaking the seal on a jar of Planters cashews, lying with her eyes closed in the heat of a bath, listening to the opening chords of almost any Reva and Jamie song. She gave nothing out; she was like a balloon, endlessly filling.

"I've got to go home," Erica said. "My sister."

"Me too," said Jordan. "My parents." He paused. "They want to meet you," he said. "But I told them no."

"Oh," said Erica. She could imagine Jordan keeping her from his parents, not wanting them to see her.

"You understand, right?" he asked.

"Oh, yeah," she said, and in fact she did understand; it didn't even bother her.

No more was said about it. They stood shivering in the street again, waiting for a cab, already anticipating their separate evenings at home. For him, there would be a chorus of parental voices as his key turned in the lock. The Drs. Strang would be sitting in the kitchen and chuckling over the latest copy of *Endocrinology Today.* Jordan would go in and say the requisite hellos, then he would palm a Milk Bone for the schnauzer, and make a quick exit into his bedroom for the night. *Sensitive,* his parents would think, shrugging helplessly at each other. *Troubled and bright.* This was acceptable in boys, but in girls it implied that something was really wrong.

"I wish you had more friends," Dottie often said. "I wish you had someone special in your life. I don't want you to be lonely;

you have so much to offer." There was always a kind of agony in her face when she spoke like this, and it was difficult to watch.

Erica had thought about telling Dottie about Jordan, but finally vetoed the idea. She didn't know what she would say when her mother asked specifics. Jordan wasn't someone she particularly liked, so how could she explain herself? It was better kept as an awful secret, something that existed only between Jordan and Erica, and which they both knew enough to keep under wraps.

Now the cab pulled up in front of Jordan's building. A doorman came and opened the door for him, and Jordan hopped out, not saying a word. They would see each other on Monday, and not before; this was understood.

Back in her own apartment, Erica walked down the hall and found an envelope, addressed to her, lying on the table outside the den. It was a thick letter with a return address in Indiana. She stood, woozy in the light, and opened it. "CONGRATULATIONS MISS ERICA ENGELS!" it read. "YOU HAVE BEEN SELECTED FOR INCLUSION IN THE HIGHLY PRESTIGIOUS 'WHO'S WHO OF AMERICAN HIGH SCHOOL STUDENTS'!" This was absurd; she was standing in the hallway with dilated pupils, winded, aimless, and someone wanted to put her name in a leather-bound book. Erica balled the letter up and stood with it in her fist.

From inside the den she suddenly became aware of someone talking. It was Joey diSalvo, practicing impressions. "My fellow Americans . . ." she heard him say. "Do you know who that is?" he was asking Opal. "No? That's our President. Did I do my Cagney for you? Let me run that by you . . ." And Opal was no doubt just sitting there, patiently listening.

"You dirty rats," Erica heard, then the voice grew harder, more insistent. "*You dirty rats,*" it wheezed.

Dozens of voices were known to come from that room, entire bewildering monologues about politics and sex and pushy women, and impressions of people about whom Opal and Erica knew absolutely nothing. All the voices had begun to meld together into one. Joey diSalvo was just another baby-sitter, just another comedian trying desperately to become famous.

"I know you're too old to need supervision," Dottie had explained to Erica, "but Opal isn't, and I didn't think you wanted the burden of being a full-time baby-sitter for her. So please bear with me, Erica."

Each of the sitters had his or her own particular style. Joey diSalvo cooked elaborate pasta dishes and did impressions and preened before the bathroom mirror; Mia Jablon smoked cigarettes and played board games; Danny Bloom complained about his dormant love life, offering details that were intensely personal; Lyman Huddle ignored Erica and Opal completely, and spent the evening listening to jazz with headphones on. He would sit in the butterfly chair in the living room and close his eyes and roll his head in slow circles. Hours would go by. Occasionally, as if prompted by some silent alarm, Lyman would surface, unclamping the headphones and blinking in the light. "You girls need anything?" he would ask softly, and when they said no, he would return to his cave of music.

Tonight Joey diSalvo talked on and on; who knew how long he would make Opal sit there? Erica continued down the hall and went into her bedroom. In darkness, the room was cool and blank but still familiar. Erica sat on her bed for a moment, letting her eyes adjust. She thought of her mother in a hotel room across the country, coming in alone after a late performance. Or perhaps Dottie wasn't alone; maybe there was a man with her. It sometimes seemed to Erica that her mother must have a secret life that involved men. Once in a while Erica could hear a man's voice in the background when Dottie called from California. "Oh, that's just a friend of mine," Dottie would explain. Erica wondered if her mother sometimes lay in a broad bed with one of these men and made love all night, Dottie's stage makeup sliding off onto the man's face and chest like war paint.

But there was probably nothing warlike about Dottie's love life. All the fire, all the bristle and scratch, had most likely left with the marriage. "I am leaving your father so I can have some peace," Dottie had said. "So we can all have a new life." But still Erica couldn't forget, still she tried to imagine what had gone on between her mother and father all those years they had stayed together.

There was no window into the intimacy of parents. And even if there was, would you really want to *look*? When Erica tried to imagine her parents making love, all she could summon up were two darkly angry faces, mouths open in criticism, yet the bodies were soldered together, as though her parents were two earthworms cut in half, and the halves had their separate needs and plans. The heads were furious, but the bodies, astoundingly, were liking it.

5

All vacation they told everyone their names were Betty and
Veronica. Nobody thought there was anything fishy about
this. "Good morning, Betty. Good morning, Veronica," the stew-
ards at the hotel would say when Opal and Erica came down to
breakfast. "How are you girls doing today?"

Fine, fine, they would answer, and Opal could barely contain
herself. She thought she would explode with laughter, but Erica
remained cool. They sat in the ornate dining room, drinking
thimbles of tomato juice, while all around them the air churned
with sluggish conversation. It was still very early, and most of the
guests at the hotel stayed up very late at night gambling and didn't
come out of their rooms until well into the day. There were plenty
of other children in the dining room, Opal noticed—children
who had been sent downstairs by mothers who lay in bed until
noon with eye-masks on. Opal's own mother was at this very
moment slumbering in the round bed of the Queen Victoria
Suite, where special guests of the hotel stayed.

It was winter break from school, and Dottie had decided to take
them with her to the Royale in Las Vegas, where she was opening
for Tony Bennett. "You girls need some sun," she had said the
last time she returned from the West Coast. "You're as white
as milk."

"Will we get to go swimming?" Opal asked.

"Every day," said her mother. "They have an indoor and an
outdoor pool. Rain or shine."

This practically sent Opal into convulsions; she ran in circles around the apartment, moving her arms as though she were doing the Crawl. Erica observed her coolly.

"I'm not going," Erica announced. She was sitting on Dottie's bed with a large book open in her lap.

"What do you mean, honey?" Dottie asked.

"I mean, I'm not going," said Erica. "Plain English. I have to study for the S.A.T.'s."

"You can do that anytime," said Dottie. "I want you to get out a little, have some fun. You're only a sophomore; the S.A.T.'s aren't for a long time. And since when are you such a conscientious student?"

And so they left for Las Vegas, Erica's suitcase loaded down with S.A.T. study guides. Opal packed lightly, choosing clothes she hadn't seen all year and which she had forgotten about. She loved delving into the summer closet, where her culottes and bathing suits were stored for the winter. Everything was densely smothered in camphor, but the smell was somehow pleasing. She held her one-piece bathing suit, with its starfish pattern and layer of ruffles, up to her face and inhaled deeply. It was as though certain articles of clothing had actual *lives*; in hibernation, a bathing suit smelled woody and medicinal, but in the sunlight it would once again smell jubilantly of coconut oil and chlorine: rich, affirmative summer smells.

On the airplane to Las Vegas, Opal and Erica sat together, while their mother took up two seats across the aisle; she had had written into all her contracts that the seat next to her on airplanes would always be free. "I'm a large woman," she had explained to Ross Needler. "I need to spread out."

A few of the stewardesses cooed discreetly over her before the airplane took off, and she was as gracious as ever. "May I ask what you're working on now, Miss Engels?" one stewardess asked. In her hand she held a demonstration oxygen mask.

"Well, I'm on my way to play at the Royale," said Dottie. "I'll be there for five nights, and then I'm coming to New York for a little break, and then it's back out to the West Coast again, for a CBS comedy special."

"We all just love you," said the stewardess. "I watch you

51

whenever I'm on the ground. I think you're the funniest lady in comedy today, and I'm not just saying that." She paused. "I've got to begin," she said, gesturing in annoyance, before bringing the oxygen mask up to her face.

The airplane lifted over New York, and Opal pressed her forehead against the tiny window. They hadn't gone anywhere as a family in a long time; vacations were more common in families that were still intact. Usually there had to be a mother and father who could split the driving, a mother and father who could close their motel door for a little privacy while the kids jackknifed into the pool only a few feet from the window. That was what it had been like when they were all together, or at least that was the way Opal remembered it. Her memories all centered around miles of early-morning road, and waking up crabby in an unnatural sleep position in the back of the station wagon, a strange, raised ridge-pattern worked into the left side of her face, from where she had been pressing it against the seat. In her memory, they were always going off *somewhere*, for that was what unhappy families did; they roped suitcases to the roofs of their cars and hit the road.

Opal never remembered the actual vacations themselves; she only remembered the ends of days, when she and Erica lay in their motel beds, the air conditioner mumbling across the room. Maybe that would be all she would remember of this trip to Las Vegas: the end of each day, when they were confined to their expensive suite at the Royale, while Dottie performed in the gigantic nightclub downstairs.

She did two shows a night, and between them she would pop upstairs to say hello, dressed in her blazing black and gold floor-length gown. "I can only stay a minute, you two," she would say, but even for that minute she would kick off her pumps and climb onto one of the twin beds. "Tell me what you're up to," she would say. "What have you girls been doing tonight?"

The answer was evident, for here they were, trapped in the suite, the television booming in the corner. Spread across one of the beds was an array of picked-at room-service food: jumbo shrimp in iced silver bowls, tall glasses of chocolate milk, wicker baskets of fried chicken.

"How did it go?" Opal asked.

"Not bad," said Dottie, "if I do say so myself. They really seemed to go for that new material. I was a little unsure of it, but they ate it up."

Opal had gone with her mother, the day they arrived, to inspect the sound system at the hotel. Opal sat in the last row of the huge, empty nightclub while Dottie stood on the dark stage, saying, "Testing, shmesting," into a microphone. "I'll just do a little of my routine," Dottie had said. "Is that okay?"

Opal settled herself in at the table. A barmaid appeared out of the darkness and silently handed her a drink. It was a Shirley Temple, Opal saw, and she brought the straw up to her lips in what seemed a polite and restrained fashion. The barmaid stood against the curving wall, and Opal realized, as her eyes adjusted to the dim light, that there were several other people in the night-club: four waiters, and three cleaning women, and a busboy. They had stopped what they were doing and were now lingering quietly, excited at the idea of getting a private performance. They leaned against walls, perched awkwardly at the crooked little tables, wait-ing. As Opal's eyes continued to become accustomed to the dark, she could make out all the separate figures standing and sitting, like spirits gathering after a long absence.

Dottie seemed aware of their presence. She was speaking now not just to Opal, but was looking around the room, making eye contact in all directions. "You know," she began, "I'm not ashamed to tell you that I married for money. My father said, "Here's fifty bucks, Dottie, now get out of my sight.' "

From the darkness came a long fluted column of laughter.

"You hear so much about girls giving themselves away on their honeymoon night," Dottie went on. "But I had to *pay* him before he'd even let me take off my dress." She paused, waiting for the response. "Finally," she said, "I get all undressed and lie down, and he's still standing by the door. I said, 'Norm, Norm, why don't you come over here and climb on top of me so we can make a little whoopee.' He said, 'Climb on *top* of you? Dottie, you know I'm afraid of heights!' " At this the barmaid and the waiters and the three elderly cleaning women really started laughing. The busboy in the left corner of the darkness began to applaud.

"The marriage was off to a bad start right away," Dottie said. "We went to Mexico on our honeymoon, had a lousy time. You know, Trotsky was liquidated in Mexico; I guess that's why you can't drink the water." There was puzzled, polite laughter.

"One night my husband told me he was into S and M. I thought he meant Stiller and Meara." Someone began to clap again. Dottie shaded her eyes and peered out into the room. "You're a great audience," she said. "I'm feeling kind of loose, kind of relaxed. I had three shrimp cocktails before the show; maybe I shouldn't drive home. Maybe I should *swim* home. But I'll tell you one thing," she went on. "On nights like this, I'm glad I'm not married anymore. My husband always hated it when I ate a huge meal before coming to bed. He said he had trouble falling asleep on a full stomach."

The audience laughed again, and Dottie smiled, waiting for them to grow quiet. "I remember when I was a young bride," she said. "I used to beg my husband for a floor-length fur coat. Finally he said to me, 'Dottie, you know we can't afford that. But I've got a solution—just don't shave your legs for a week!' "

At this the scattered audience joined together in applause. Opal chewed hard on her straw for a minute, and then she clapped her hands along with everyone else. But she felt disoriented; the jokes didn't make sense, and the ones about her father were so peculiar. They made her feel uneasy, as though she were eavesdropping on something extremely private.

She watched her mother from across the nightclub, and was startled by how small Dottie looked at this distance, how *wrong*, somehow. It seemed so much more natural to see Dottie Engels from up close, where she could fill an entire screen, rather than from far away, where she took on ordinary dimensions. On the stage of the nightclub at the Royale, she could have been any fat woman impersonating Dottie Engels, and no one would have known the difference. From her cocktail table at the back of the dank room, Opal felt a small stirring inside her, and the desire to leap up and run down the aisle to verify that this was indeed her mother onstage, and not an impersonator.

Now, between shows, her mother lay flat on her back in the hotel room, as if captured and landed. "Erica," she called out, her eyes closed, "what are you doing, honey?"

Erica was in the bathroom, sitting under the infra-red lamp, studying for the S.A.T.'s.

"I am trying to work," Erica called. "Is that permitted?"

"Of course," Dottie said. "Who am I to stop you? Although I've heard that there *are* child labor laws in this country."

"Did you talk to Tony Bennett?" Opal asked, propping herself up on her elbows on the other bed.

"Yes, he's a very nice man," said her mother. "Extremely gracious. The women are knocking down the stage door trying to get his autograph. It's different when men perform." She shook her head. "Well, enough of this," she said. "I've got to get downstairs again. For the late show, I'm going to spend ten minutes on that parody of *Oklahoma*, and it strains my throat to sing that much, so I'd better not tire it out." She walked over to where Opal lay, and bent down to kiss her. Opal inhaled what she thought of as her mother's nightclub smell: a mix of smoke and flowers, as though someone had set fire to a garden. The odor seemed dangerous, completely beyond Opal's frame of reference. After children went to sleep at night, the whole world changed.

"Don't go," Opal suddenly said, clutching onto the knot of pearls around her mother's neck.

"Why not?" asked Dottie. "What's the matter? Don't you feel well?"

"Yes," she said, but she was unable to explain the sudden urgency. She turned her head away, embarrassed. Dottie sat on the edge of the bed for a few minutes, stroking Opal's hair. And soon it was all right again, and Dottie slowly got up, straightening her gown, and started to leave. She stopped in the bathroom on the way out and said a few words to Erica. Opal perked up, listening to the conversation.

"Well yes, I know, Erica, but you could spend just a *little* time with her," Dottie was saying in a low voice. When she was gone,

Opal went and stood in the bathroom doorway. Erica was sitting on the bathmat, reading, the orange light beating down from above. It was the kind of light that was always shining on rotisserie chickens as they turned slowly in delicatessen windows.

"She wants me to play with you," said Erica, looking up briefly, "but I don't think you need to be entertained, do you, Opal? You can entertain yourself, can't you?"

"Yes," Opal muttered. "But it's boring here."

"We're on vacation," Erica said. "Remember? You were the one who wanted to come here." She turned back to her book.

"I like it during the day," said Opal, "when you can swim. It's just different at night. At night we have to stay in. And all we do is eat."

" 'Flower' is to 'artificial,' " Erica read aloud, "as 'death' is to blank."

"What?" said Opal. "What are you talking about?"

" 'Rain' is to 'torrential,' " Erica went on, "as 'hunger' is to blank."

"You're weird," said Opal. "I have a weird sister. I have a big, fat, weird sister."

Erica looked up. "Why don't you find something to do?" she said. "Why don't you go downstairs and maybe Mom will put you in her act. She could use you as a footstool or something."

"Oh, that's so funny I forgot to laugh," said Opal. This line was enjoying a current vogue among Opal's classmates, but it was usually reserved for desperate moments when you were looking to stall for time, and no other words would come.

This was another one of their standstill fights, a little circular argument that kept spinning and spinning like a hamster wheel. It could be called off at any time, simply by one person suddenly speaking civilly to the other. Whichever of them bored of it more quickly would just change her tone, and that would be that. Opal was unsure of how to proceed now. She paused in the doorway, looking down at the top of her sister's head, at the even part that divided a field of flyaway hair.

"I'm going out," Opal announced.

Erica paused. "Do you have your room key with you?" she asked.

56

"Yes," Opal said, reaching into the pocket of her Bermuda shorts and closing her fingers around the oval of plastic. She didn't want to go out, not at all; it was almost midnight and she had no idea of what she would find. But she had to, now that she had said it. There was suddenly no choice.

"Goodbye then," said Erica.

"Goodbye," Opal said, stepping into her thongs. "See you later." The door made a resonant suck and click as it closed behind her.

Outside, the hallway was hushed and glowed dimly, the only real light radiating from the distant beacon of the exit sign. Opal looked down at the carpeting, which she had never really noticed before. It was decorated with a very mod pattern: amoeboid shapes in green and blue, like the things that rolled and floated in Erica's lava lamp at home. She followed the pattern down the hall to the elevators, and rode downstairs with no destination in mind, no thought to her actions, only the need for constant motion.

Opal understood her own invisibility then, the fact that she could probably go anywhere in the world and no one would stop her. She was so small that she slipped between the cracks. She shuffled along in her flat rubber thongs at midnight, and found herself waking up, coming to life at a time of day when usually she would be drifting off. She could go *anywhere*; she pictured herself walking, in this same trance, out into the middle of a field in an electrical storm. She would be perfectly fine; the rubber thongs would ground her, keep her safe from lightning.

The hotel lobby at midnight felt like an indoor city, all lit up and fluid. It gave the illusion of movement, like one of those neon signs in which the pattern of light leads the eye forward, only to drag it back again in its tide. Opal walked through several low-ceilinged, sedate passageways, which reminded her of the ramps you walked down to board an airplane. The last hallway emptied into an enormous room. The lighting here was as uncompromising as it is at a supermarket, and people clustered around tables, everyone loud and willing. There was hooting and laughter and the constant rake of chips across felt, and over all that noise was another layer, a transparency of sound that could be lifted off from

57

the din: It was music, the calm, gentle vocals of the Carpenters singing "Close to You."

Opal felt a sudden swell of vertigo. She was so obviously under-age, so obviously *not* supposed to be here, and yet no one minded. This fact no longer excited her. Instead, it only depressed her, and she stood shivering, bare-armed, in the casino. As easily as she had entered, Opal shuffled out, her thongs slapping against the floor.

The casino was not the only room in the hotel that was alive at night. Opal followed a trail of music and walked unnoticed into the entrance of a disco that abutted the dining room. A sign on an easel outside the door read, "Teen Nite: Parents Keep Out!"

Over the stereo speakers, Ike and Tina Turner were beginning to sing "Proud Mary," and a dozen teenaged couples were dancing on the small, strobe-lit floor. Every girl had a blond flip and wore a short dress and tights; every boy wore a double-breasted blazer, and all the couples moved mechanically. Opal stood at the side of the room and watched. "First we're gonna take it nice . . . and easy," Tina Turner was saying, feral and persuasive. "And then we're gonna take it nice . . . and rough."

The music began to speed up, and everyone struggled to keep the rhythm. This was the world Opal could enter in a few years, if she chose. Erica never could; Erica was denied entry.

Opal moved farther into the room, staying close against the wall like a crab. "Left a good job in the city . . ." Tina was singing. "Working for the man every night and day . . ." Without realizing it, Opal was singing along in her raspy little voice.

"Sing it out," someone said, close to her ear.

Opal looked up, startled. She had been standing, she realized, inches from the deejay's booth. A teenaged boy was leaning over the ledge on his crossed arms, smiling at her. "You want to come up here?" he asked.

In the speckled light, Opal took a serious look at this boy. He seemed to be about seventeen, and he had vacant, pleasant eyes. He looked like somebody's older brother, or a lifeguard at a pool.

Opal climbed the two steps that led into the booth. She barely thought about it; she just accepted the invitation. Something about small spaces had always excited her. Anywhere you could slip your body in, find a surprising fit, make it work—that was the kind of place she wanted to be. She remembered how it had felt to be wedged into the space behind the refrigerator at home.

From the deejay's booth, Opal could see out across the dance floor. The room seemed bigger from this vantage point. And Opal herself felt bigger, nervier. "Can I pick a record?" she asked the boy.

"Well, okay," he said. "Within reason. *Not* the 'Hokey Pokey' or the 'Alley Cat,' please."

She knelt down on the patch of orange shag carpeting and began to flip through the miles of 45's. From beneath her knees the floor was quaking, as though straining under the great burden of soul music.

"What's your name?" the deejay asked.

"Veronica Lodge," she said, the lie coming to her with surprising simplicity. Erica would have been impressed.

Then he surprised her in return. "Yeah, and I'm Jughead Jones," he said.

Opal flinched. No one had caught on before; no one out here seemed to have *heard* of *Archie* comics. All anyone did out here was drink and gamble and order room service. The boy was laughing, and she saw in his eyes that he liked her. Not *that* way, certainly, for she was too young for that, but in some other way that was still not ordinary. It was almost as if he understood what she might turn into at some point, and was able to carry his imagination far enough ahead to picture her at sixteen, and be interested.

Opal had all the makings of a good-looking girl; she knew this about herself, could tell the way her looks were headed, the features sharp, the skin hairless and pale, the neck and wrists long. She would eventually grow into these looks, the way a puppy grows into its oversized paws. However she ended up, it would all be fine, and soon she would be loved by older brothers and lifeguards, and would sit on a blond boy's lap atop a high wooden chair, overlooking lanes of light blue water.

Opal found herself suddenly nervous with the deejay so close to her now, leaning over her shoulder and watching as she made her selection. Then, with no warning, she felt his hand cupping the nape of her neck. He was not really touching her skin at all; his fingers were barely grazing the fine baby hair that sprouted there. She could only feel *presence,* not pressure—similar to the way you somehow know when someone is standing over you while you sleep. The deejay's hand gave off a slight, gauzy heat. Opal took in a hard breath, and moved to look. But by the time she had turned her head, his arms were relaxed at his sides. Opal didn't know what to say, and he gave her no help.

"Pick a record," he said, his voice flat.

So she chose quickly and stupidly, fishing out a record she didn't particularly like. She chose "Jumpin' Jack Flash," a song that had probably been played hundreds of times in this room, but he took the record from her hands without a word and put it on the turntable, and soon one song faded and the next one bled in, and Opal stood with him inside this little cocoon of sound.

She did not want to leave; she just kept watching as he fiddled with the knobs, looking as attentive and serious as a navigator in a control tower. All around them the music surged and the lights blinked and the teenagers kept dancing, rolling their heads and arms in little epileptic thrusts, staying in a small, designated area of space on the dance floor, never venturing outside that proscribed circle. Opal saw that the deejay was what was called "well-built," with a strong line that bisected his back even through his shirt. She was so pleased with herself, so happy to be here with him alone, that she could think of nothing better. She would tell no one about this.

But then, looking across the room, Opal saw a figure in the doorway, hovering uncertainly. She knew at once that it was Erica, and her spirit suddenly dropped, as if through a trap door inside herself. Erica had come looking for her, come to bring her back; she must have been looking everywhere. At first, Opal thought to hide, to kneel back down behind the deejay, where she would never be found. She could even sleep here tonight, on this patch of orange carpeting, curled up like an old dog. But now there didn't seem to be a choice, and so Opal stepped down from the booth.

Walking back along the edge of the room, she raised a hand in salute to Erica, who stood in her poncho, waiting. There wasn't any anger on Erica's features. Her face bore a look of resignation, like a chaperone at a dance who senses how much fun everyone is having, and for whom there is no access to that fun.

It was in this manner that Erica retrieved her, and Opal went, pliant and wordless. She did not even say good night to her deejay, her boyfriend in a future life. She just left him with his hands sliding over the controls, palming records easily onto spinning surfaces.

6

The Junior Peace Corps was conducting interviews at the Stanhope Hotel one Saturday in February. Erica sat alone on a couch in the lobby, a brochure open in her lap. "Helping Friends Around the World," read the caption on the first page, and above it was an illustration of a white girl and a black boy shaking hands in what appeared to be a field of wheat. The illustration conjured up images of plantation life, more than anything else. It reminded Erica of the illustrations in the biographies she used to read in elementary school, books with names like *George Washington Carver and His Magic Legume.* Her school had certainly encouraged a real fascination for black history, even though there were only a handful of black students. George Washington Carver, Harriet Tubman, Frederick Douglass—Erica couldn't think of a single biography she had ever read of anybody white.

According to the brochure, the purpose of the Junior Peace Corps, or JPC, as it was informally called, was to "foster harmony and understanding between our world and the Third World." The JPC was a new organization, with no real affiliation to the Peace Corps proper. You were required to be between the ages of fifteen and twenty, and it cost a sizeable amount of money to join. If you were accepted, you were sent to one of a variety of Third World nations, where you lived with a family and labored at an assigned job for the summer. It seemed peculiar that there were no photographs in the brochure, only illustrations, as in the rendering of a courtroom trial.

"I don't like the sound of this," Dottie had said when Erica initially proposed the idea of joining. "If you're unhappy there, or sick, or need me, how can you reach me? You say there aren't any telephones where you'll be; I don't like the sound of it at all."

But it wasn't much easier reaching Dottie *now*, Erica thought. Whenever she and Opal had to call her, they had to leave a message with the clerk at the hotel, and it was usually hours before Dottie picked up the message and called back. She was always "running around" Los Angeles; that was the way she described her life there. She went from one engagement to the next, and wherever she went people stopped and smiled at her, or reached out to touch her. They loved the fact that she really did wear dotted clothing offstage. Children reached up at her; they loved her big, accessible face, and the way she clowned around. Dottie never grew tired of the affection of strangers. This was so peculiar, Erica thought—to actually want to be touched by someone you didn't know.

"Do you really like that?" she had once asked her mother after Dottie hugged a child who had come up to her at the Russian Tea Room. The child's parents stood smiling behind him, urging him forward.

"Honey, it's just another part of what I do," Dottie told Erica. "I put myself right out there, and I have to take what comes."

"But do you *like* it?" Erica persisted.

Dottie looked uncomfortable. "I don't mind the touching," she said. "Although I'd frankly rather it came from my own girls." This comment was directed at Erica alone; Opal was extremely physical. But Erica didn't want to make contact with her mother; Dottie's touch contained too many components, and they couldn't be sorted through quickly enough.

Now Dottie was in California, and Erica couldn't see the children her mother hugged in stores or on the street, or backstage after a show. Erica could only imagine what went on. And Dottie, for that matter, could only imagine what went on in Erica's life. She knew nothing about Jordan, about what he and Erica did together.

"I want to join the Junior Peace Corps," Erica had said long distance. "You don't know anything about it, only that they don't have telephones. Please let me at least be interviewed."

Dottie had finally agreed, but she was wary. "I want to hear all about it when I get home," she said. "In detail, miss."

So Erica went to the interview, and she was the only one there without a parent. She sat waiting on the deep couch, in a dress and pantyhose, which felt as though they were actively straining to contain her. She kept looking off into space and surreptitiously plucking at the crotch, where all the nylon gathered.

Erica had prepared her responses in advance. "Why do you want to join?" a soft-spoken young man or woman would ask, leaning in close, and Erica would look down at her hands and reply that she had always wanted to make herself useful. She wasn't afraid of roughing it; the elements didn't frighten her. In fact she wanted to put herself right *out* there, on the edge of a continent, out in that wheat field with that black boy, shaking hands under the African sun, which would surely bake her like a piece of pottery by the time the summer was through.

But no one asked her any such question, and the interview seemed almost a formality. When it was Erica's turn to go up-stairs, she was ushered into the elevator in a group of four, and she found herself in the middle of a dauntingly athletic crowd. The two boys were as thin and lanky as whippets, and the one other girl was tall and strapping, and looked as though she uprooted trees from the ground after school. Erica was the only heavy one here, and she knew it made her stand out from the group.

It had never occurred to her to wonder what kind of person, other than herself, might join the Junior Peace Corps. Up until now, she had only pictured herself alone in the world, and in everything she did. No matter how she envisioned herself, she could not take the leap of imagination that was required to further populate the image. Even the most dramatic of scenes—herself lying in bed with Jordan Strang, for instance—contained just Erica, her mouth twisted in striving, her legs fallen open. It was as though her boyfriend was *Topper* or something. But it wasn't just her boyfriend who was absent, if indeed that was the right word for Jordan. It was *everyone* in the universe; she could not see a soul. It

64

was as though there had been a nuclear holocaust, and everyone had been swallowed up into a big barbecue pit, and Erica was left wandering the earth's surface all by herself. Did this make her an egomaniac, the fact that she saw herself alone on the continent of Africa, hoeing rows under a sky wavy with extraordinary heat and light? She didn't even *like* what she saw, she didn't *like* that fat girl out there in the field, stripped down to khaki fatigues, pumping away with those thick arms and legs.

But all of a sudden her vision of Africa had become densely populated, colonized by other teenagers who attended private school in New York, members of the President's Fitness Team who joked and flirted with each other and would probably sneak off on a hot night in Upper Volta to smoke dope and listen to Fleetwood Mac tapes. Erica didn't want that at all; if she had wanted that, she would have stayed home.

I am here to make myself useful. I am here because I want to try something new. This is what she would tell them. But all they asked, when finally Erica and the three others were sitting in a suite on the ninth floor, was whether or not she had any allergies.

"No," she said, her voice small and disappointed.

"*I'm* allergic to cats," the tall girl offered.

"Well, there won't be too many cats where you're going," the interviewer said. He was a middle-aged man, not young at all, no beard and mustache, so small round glasses. He looked tired, like someone's father at the end of the day.

"Only *big* cats," said one of the athletic boys. "Lions."

Everyone laughed politely.

"I'm afraid that that's a romanticized view of Africa," the interviewer said. "At least the parts of Africa that we send our students to. You're more likely to stumble across a McDonald's than a lion this summer."

Everyone laughed again. All this artificial laughter, this nervous little exchange, and what he wanted to know was did they have any *allergies*. He explained a few details about the program, and asked them the kind of work they would be most interested in, but never once did he question why they were here. He passed around some forms, which listed the different work categories.

65

Field labor was the first choice. Erica quickly glanced around and saw that no one was jumping to blacken the box next to that category. *Food service.* Forget that one; she could just picture herself standing behind a steam table under a tent, her nostrils dilating as the steam rose into her face and she repeatedly dipped a ladle deep into a bottomless tureen. She would be able to think of little else but food all summer; the smell would stay with her at night as she lay under mosquito netting. It would fold around her in her sleep. She would eat like an animal and return home larger than ever. They would allow her one fewer piece of luggage on the airplane.

Hygiene. Now that was a possibility. Erica had always been very clean; this was something no one could argue. Her room, though dense with small objects, had an internal logic to it. She knew where everything was, and could locate things easily. She washed her hair every night, and spent a long time drying it, standing with the blow-dryer pointed at her head like a pistol. She could teach people how to be clean; she was certain of that. Being clean was the one thing you could take control of; dirt didn't overwhelm you, the way weight did. Your body was always ballooning, erupting, talking back at you, and you had no way to stop it. But at night, when the day was over, you could lock the bathroom door and fill the tub with Strawberry Blossom Bath Jewels. Then you could immerse your big self and slide on in, making that underwater bump and squeal as your body touched bottom.

Erica blackened the box next to Hygiene. After they had all handed back the forms, the interviewer asked them a few more superficial questions: What was their favorite subject in school? Had they thought long and hard about joining, and did they know that the summer would entail serious work? Were they ready for that challenge? Every head bobbed in synchrony.

"You're the kind of young people we like to see," the interviewer said. And they all congratulated themselves for nothing.

Who else but a group of "young people" would spend money to work in a field all summer? Who else would have enough energy to put in such long hours? There was a boy at school named Martin Wolf who had spent the summer at Outward

Bound. He had written an essay about it for class, and it was filled with details about being shaken awake at four A.M. every day and forced to scale a mountain, barehanded and whimpering. If you were afraid, the others humiliated you, jeering at you in the darkness. You didn't know who your friends were anymore, and you had to grab onto handfuls of crumbling mountain wall, thinking only of ways to make it to the top. Once on top, of course, everyone liked you again, and you all jumped around and hugged each other, and poured cold canteen water down each other's throats. There was nothing as exhilarating as that day, Martin Wolf had written.

But Erica was not Martin Wolf. She had no desire to make it to the top of anything at all, and she felt she had very little in common with other "young people." At Lincoln Center there were always Young People's Concerts, and her class had once gone to one on a Saturday field trip. She had been to concerts before, of course, but it had always been at night, and with her mother. This matinee had a very different feeling to it. The audience was composed almost entirely of children, as though they ruled the world. They were all dressed up, the girls holding little white purses ("clutches," her mother called them), the boys standing self-consciously on the balcony at intermission, leaning down over the burnished rail, hands shoved deep into pockets. It was a big joke, Erica had thought. And when the performance started (something blending Aaron Copland with Moog synthesizer) and the lights went down, Erica couldn't see anyone anymore, but she still felt the presence of the children all around her. It was wintertime, and the flu was swirling through the coatrooms of all the private schools of New York. In the darkness a child coughed from time to time, and another child coughed back in echoing response, like two dogs tied in separate yards, barking to each other to keep company throughout the night.

She was not a part of any whole. Not even with Jordan, she was reminded, as they lay together in bed after school. Winter was hanging on, and steam knocked through the pipes of the Strangs' old apartment, and snow fell outside the window by the bed.

67

Occasionally Erica sat up, looking out. She had established that in winter the streetlights in New York were illuminated at exactly five-thirty each day, and she liked to watch for that moment, when suddenly, before falling into shadow, the sky was sharply lit. It reminded her of television shows, when the light is shut off in the bedroom, but the ensuing "darkness" is just as bright as it was when the lights were on. It's a different kind of light, one meant to illumine the face of the character as he or she lies in bed, twisting and turning before sleep. Perhaps it's one of the Brady kids, troubled over a lie told during the day, or perhaps it's Lucy Ricardo closing her eyes and dropping off, the screen misting and whirling to let us know there's about to be a dream sequence.

Erica watched the lights pop on at once on Central Park West, and Jordan pulled her back from the window. "You don't have anything on, for God's sake," he said.

"Oh yes, I'm sure everyone's looking," said Erica. For certainly no one could see up to this darkened window on the eleventh floor, where she leaned forward, her breasts resting on the cold sill. After the lights came on, Erica knew it would soon be time for her to leave. In apartments all over the city, smells were rising up from kitchens. In Jordan's building, mothers on each floor were beginning to prepare the same exact dinner. This was the Year of the Wok, the year that everyone's mother had gone out and purchased one. The wok was treated as reverentially as a piece of art, rubbed each day with a cloth dipped in imported oil. Families ate with chopsticks every night, and the fragrance of ginger and scallions stayed in the air for hours after the dishes were washed. Only Jordan's apartment remained odorless. His mother was working late at the office tonight, and he would have to fend for himself.

Now here is something we have in common, Erica thought about telling him. Neither of our homes has any smell to it. It's as though we live in libraries, in office buildings. But he would only stare blandly at her, as he always did, drumming his fingers on the bed. He didn't care if she left or stayed, just as long as she was certain to leave before his parents arrived. This pattern would probably go on until the end of the school year, when they would separate for the summer. Jordan would go off to a computer camp in the Berkshires, and Erica would join the Junior Peace Corps and be stationed out on the veldt. But for now, here in this room, something held them fast.

She found herself wanting to go home soon, yet the thought of pulling her clothes back on right now was unbearable. She didn't want to step back into the clothes that lay formless on the floor. Her naked skin was warm from the dry heat that poured in through a vent above the door. Only her breasts were cold, from where she had pressed them against the windowsill. Erica crossed her hands over them, warming herself.

"Oh, you're suddenly shy?" Jordan said. "After what we've done? Isn't it kind of late for that?" He was smiling a little meanly.

"I wasn't hiding myself," she said. "I just got cold, is all."

He shrugged. "Whatever," he said. He lay on his back, arms folded beneath his head. His hair fanned out on the pillow like a woman's. He looked so gentle, his elbows jutting out like that, his features delicate, and yet he was loveless, a fact that repeatedly surprised her.

You only end up with what you feel you deserve, she had once heard someone say on a talk show. A psychologist was talking about women whose husbands beat them, and who still stay married. *He needs me*, they said, or *He's promised to change*. But Jordan didn't abuse Erica, certainly. He just showed her a kind of perverse, studied disregard. Erica was like a giant billboard, a big, screaming Day-Glo girl, the biggest girl in the tenth grade, and he seemed not to see her at all. Which was just fine, since she didn't see him, either. She never thought about him, never lay in bed at night, her mind fading to a dream sequence in which Jordan hovered above her, his body patiently working.

Suddenly there was the sound of a door opening in the distance. Someone upstairs, she thought, a family joining forces for the night. But then Jordan shot up in bed. "Fucking shit cock!" he said. Even his cursing was a little disjointed. "Someone's home!" he said, frantic, and he leaped off the bed and shimmied into his jeans. He had no hips; he slid right in. He threw Erica's clothes at her. "Here!" he said, and she grappled with her mohair sweater, forcing her head into one of the armholes three times before getting it right.

"Oh God, oh God," he was muttering, buttoning up his plaid flannel shirt. "Comb your hair or something," he said.

He handed her a broken comb from the dresser, and she pulled it dutifully through the top layer of her hair. She didn't feel nervous, oddly enough; there seemed to be very little at stake here for her. What was the worst that could happen?

Then the bedroom door swung wide. Dr. Strang stood there, her coat on, saying, "Honey?"

Jordan turned to her. He and Erica were both fully dressed now. Only the bed was twisted up and practically bore full-body imprints of where they had lain. "Hi, Mom," Jordan said, his voice revealing nothing. And then, with some bitterness, he said, "This is Erica."

He blamed her. For many things: for being here when his mother came home, for being herself, for being fat, for making him have to admit her existence in his life. The whole beauty of what they had was in never having to admit to any of it. It was all unspoken, just an act done in darkness, just something that satisfied them both in a peculiar, unhappy way.

"Nice to meet you, Erica," Jordan's mother said, smiling a little. There was a strong resemblance, except Dr. Strang's hair was red, the color that many mothers had gravitated toward over the years, a sort of dark, unflashy, acceptable red. "You kids want something to eat?" she asked. "I came home early, two cancellations back to back. Hope I'm not disturbing anything."

"No," Jordan said. "Erica was just leaving."

"Oh," said his mother. "Well, come talk to me a minute, will you?" she said. "I never see you, Jordan. You too, Erica. It's a rare treat to meet your friends. I feel honored."

They followed Dr. Strang down the hall to her study, an impressive room in which diplomas and Ben Shahn prints were

70

given equal wall space. Dr. Strang sat down behind her desk and took off her coat and shoes. "Oh, my aching dogs," she said. She paused. "Why do you suppose they call them dogs?" she asked. "Do either of you have any idea? No? That's the kind of thing Jordan always seems to know."

"I do not," he said.

Dr. Strang leaned back in her chair. She was quite pretty, Erica thought; the delicacy of Jordan's features was more appropriate in a woman. And yet, like Jordan, there was still something brittle there, something that had grown spoiled. She had gone to medical school late, Jordan had told Erica, had been a young mother at home with small children first. And perhaps she had waited too long, for there was no generosity in her voice, no warm expansiveness.

"I'd like to offer a bit of unsolicited advice, if I may," Dr. Strang said.

From behind her great desk she rummaged around for a while. Finally she found what she wanted and hoisted it up in both arms onto the desk top. "Oh, not this," Jordan said.

"Yes, this," said his mother.

The object was made of plaster, a large blank modern sculpture of some sort. Abruptly, Dr. Strang swiveled it around on its base, and Erica and Jordan were staring closely at a hideous rendering of a woman's reproductive organs. This side had been painted as carefully as a model ship.

"You know how strongly I feel about protection," Dr. Strang was saying. "Do you need me to run down the basics, perhaps remind you both of a few things?"

Erica closed her eyes. "I have to go home," she said faintly, but nobody seemed to have heard. When she opened her eyes again, Dr. Strang was pointing to the ovaries, two small orbs that had been painted a bright but inappropriate robin's egg blue. "And so it's very easy for a woman to become pregnant," she was saying, "the most natural thing in the world, unless you do something to prevent it. Do you get my drift?"

They both nodded, stunned and mortified. They sat and listened as she went through her lecture with as much confidence and general good nature as a museum tour guide in front of the Pietà.

71

The lecture somehow changed things between them. Erica and Jordan still spent afternoons together, still took off their clothes and fumbled with each other, and Erica continued to make Jordan cry out in a distinctive, strangled voice. But there was a difference now, one that she couldn't name. It struck her sometimes when they were lying quietly, still panting, staring up at the ceiling and not touching each other at all. Suddenly Erica would think back to Dr. Strang's lecture. She pictured that plaster model forever swiveling on its base, the pelvis moving back and forth in gentle, persuasive suggestion.

7

In the summer the baby-sitters were back in full force. Erica was off to Rwanda and Dottie was on a seven-city tour, and so Opal was home alone with a baby-sitter. Danny Bloom showed up on Tuesday and Thursday, while Wednesday brought Lyman Huddle, who was just a ghost of a presence in the apartment, with his headphones clamped on. On Friday Joey diSalvo the impressionist came, and the weekend was spent with Opal's favorite of them all, Mia Jablon.

"Poor girl," Dottie said about Mia. "She's so talented, but unless she finds some new material, she'll never get any work. She's too *angry*; I keep telling her to soften things up. I send her out on auditions, and she hears the same thing again and again: great delivery, but change the act. At this rate, she's going to spend her entire life baby-sitting."

Opal secretly wouldn't have minded that. She liked all of the baby-sitters, and waited by the door like a dog as they let themselves in with their duplicate keys, but Mia was by far the best. Once, in an unusual burst of emotion, Opal informed Mia that if anything were to happen to Dottie, she would want Mia to adopt her.

"I'm very flattered," Mia had answered. "But nothing's going to happen to your mama. She's indestructible."

This was a common view, and it had mostly to do with Dottie's size, as though a woman so large could never be downed. But the people who thought that never got to see Dottie after a night of shows, when she took off her clothes and sat smoking in her bedroom at dawn. They never got to see her sitting in a slip on the edge of the queen-sized bed, a cigarette hanging unattended from her mouth, her stockings bunched up on her fists like hand puppets.

Mia Jablon worshiped Dottie Engels, for it had been Dottie who had come up to Mia at Open Mike Night at the Laff House, after Mia had just bombed onstage with her jokes about the catcalls construction workers yell to women on the street, and had taken her aside and told her she had real promise. Dottie had shaken the hand of the younger comedienne and asked her if she wanted a few pointers. Over coffee the following week, Dottie had gone over Mia's routine line by line, helping her iron out the inconsistencies and gently suggesting where she might want to lighten the act up a bit. Mia had been wildly grateful. Dottie was her idol, a woman who had actually made it in this terrible business.

Dottie's story had become public knowledge; she was unusual, a woman with two kids, a divorced mother who had dragged her girls with her to every audition in the beginning, because she could not afford a baby-sitter and because she did not want to burden Aunt Harriet with them all the time. Opal vaguely remembered sitting with Erica in the waiting rooms of office buildings, reading *Highlights for Children*, while behind a frosted-glass door, her mother's silhouette loomed. Opal sat on a plastic chair, listening, bored to death by the same puzzling jokes, and then the same expression on her mother's face when finally she burst through the door. Dottie's color had always risen by that point; she was red and exhausted, and she called out to the agent, "Thanks for your time!" in a cheerful voice, and then she fetched Opal and Erica and walked swiftly out with them, hand in hand. There had been many offices like this, all of them equally depressing. Occasionally Opal would look up at the photographs on the walls of the waiting room; there were a few faces she recognized, but most of them were obscure: men and women with names like Frankie Vincent, The Hollis Twins, April Wells. And always Dottie would emerge from the inner office, trying to look triumphant even after she had been refused.

When Dottie was given her first job, serving as emcee at the Four Aces Club in East Brunswick, New Jersey, she took the girls with her on the bus. Opal remembered the ride—the Jersey Turnpike in the rain—and how she and Erica had stayed backstage in the dressing room. Their mother had instructed them not to move, not to go anywhere without her, because you never knew what kind of oddballs might be lurking in the wings of the Four Aces. From her post in the dressing room, Opal could hear Dottie's voice onstage; it resonated even from far away. Opal was comforted as she sat among the strange, feathered costumes, inhaling the smells of talc and oil-based makeup. Erica sat on a cracked plastic couch, her legs up, reading a book entitled *Susie Belvedere, High School Sleuth.*

Dottie started getting more work, and Opal and Erica traveled with her on weekends to New Jersey or up to Massachusetts. They stayed in cramped, bad motels, some with numbers for names. "Motel 12," she remembered, had plaid wallpaper and a waterless pool congested with leaves.

"Think of it as an adventure, girls!" Dottie continued to tell them. She never let them stay in the motel room alone when she wasn't there—not back then, when the motels were so seedy. She brought them with her to the clubs at night, and came backstage to visit between shows, making sure that dinner had been sent out to them from the kitchen, as she had requested.

One night at the Third Rail in Springfield, Massachusetts, Dottie met Ross Needler, a talent agent who was having a drink by himself. Ross was sitting in the bar, drinking Scotch and water, when Dottie Engels came onstage, a massive, brassy woman who somehow seemed maternal as well. He put down his drink and listened. When he learned that she had two young daughters sitting backstage, he was even more curious. Most of the female comics he saw were much younger, he explained later: dissipated Barnard girls in black turtlenecks doing beatnik jokes. But this woman was shamelessly overweight, and a delight to watch. He came back to the dressing room after the show, and Opal looked up from her connect-the-dots book just long enough to say hello, and then he sat there and talked to Dottie for an hour. They talked and talked, and soon Opal fell asleep against her mother's shoulder. The next morning, Ross Needler sped them all back to Queens in his big green Pontiac.

Ross booked Dottie into better places, clubs closer to the city, ever circling it, until finally he got her work right in Manhattan. She appeared at the Laff House, and from there he sent her to California, where she was booked onto a talk show as part of an undiscovered-talent segment.

"I don't know where she gets the courage," Aunt Harriet said to Opal and Erica as they sat up late in her living room waiting for the show. "She amazes me. First leaving your father, and now this." Aunt Harriet did not move from her easy chair. She sat, a thinner version of her niece Dottie, but definitely a Breitburg— lips pursed, hair arranged in a pile on top of her head—and waited. Opal and Erica sat on the floor at her feet.

Dottie was on during the final three-minute segment, which in the profession was nicknamed the Death Slot. When she came onscreen, Opal got so excited she started grabbing at the brown shag carpeting in her hands, almost pulling up clumps of it, like weeds. The excitement couldn't be contained in her great-aunt's tiny living room. Even the television set, an old black and white Zenith, couldn't possibly contain all of it. They had probably had to *stuff* Dottie in there, Opal remembered thinking, but Dottie fairly shrieked her way out, bursting through the glass. Opal lay on the tortured carpet in front of the set, gazing up, gasping with love.

After that night, it never stopped. Opal was forever gazing up, forever staying up half the night to watch. Her mother moved them into Manhattan, to a big apartment on the Upper West Side which she could barely afford, but whose huge mortgage she would pay off all at once in just a few months. In this apartment, the television was given its own shrine in the den. It was a large, oiled rosewood color set, with a built-in stereo and wet bar. The day after one of Dottie's late-night television performances, Opal and Erica were allowed to go to school late, equipped with bogus excuse notes that mentioned "a slight cold," notes that Dottie had pre-written and pre-signed before she left for California.

It was understandable that Mia Jablon would worship Dottie Engels. This worship brought Opal closer to Mia; there was a shared understanding at work between them. Now Mia Jablon baby-sat all the time, and she and Opal had developed a real rapport. Mia was small and tightly constructed, with wispy red hair that she wore pulled back in a short braid like Pippi Longstocking, and a mouth that was always twisting into exaggerated expressions. She was new to stand-up comedy, having gone to clown college first, which she had quit after a few months because the other students depressed her too much. There was so much false mirth in the classrooms of clown college; when you walked down the halls, she said, all you would hear was laughing and screeching, as though you were in a monkey house. If you had a bad day—a fight with your lover or menstrual cramps—then the whole thing seemed a mockery, and the laughter rang out at you as if in reproach.

Mia didn't seem to mind that she wasn't having any luck at comedy, and she actually seemed to enjoy sitting for Opal. She would get down on the floor with her and play Trouble or Candyland for hours. Occasionally she showed up with her friend Lynn, a graphics designer with whom she shared an apartment in Brooklyn. Lynn was older and somber and smoked even more than Mia, but she too seemed to enjoy playing Opal's board games. Once the three of them played Mystery Date, which Ross Needler had given Opal for her last birthday. The rules of the game were very simple; the board came equipped with a plastic door, and you turned the knob and flung the door open, finding yourself face-to-face with an illustration of your "date" for the evening. There were three different possibilities lurking behind the door, three men waiting on the porch. The one you were supposed to like best was "The Dream Date," a man in a white dinner jacket, holding a bouquet. His hair was slicked back and gleamed like wet paint. The second choice was "The Beachcomber," who was dressed casually, in shorts and a Hawaiian shirt, and who offered you a less ostentatious bouquet. The third choice, referred to on the lid of the game, in no uncertain terms, as "The Dud," wore a ratty T-shirt and bore no gift. Mia and Lynn were fascinated with the game.

"Oh my God, I've gotten 'The Dud' again," Mia shrieked, and she and Lynn poked each other and rolled around howling.

"I don't think it's so funny," Opal said. She took the game quite seriously; she felt sorry that Mia kept drawing "The Dud." It seemed ominous, as though this was Mia's fate spelled out in front of her on a Ouija board, and yet Mia refused to understand.

"*I*, on the other hand, am going out with 'The Dream Date,' " Lynn said.

"Make me jealous," said Mia. "Where's he taking you?"

"Oh, we thought we'd stay home," said Lynn. "You know, sort of cozy up around the fireplace, listening to old romantic love ballads by Jerry Vale or something. Then I'll woo him with a tempting dinner, and we'll spend the night doing the most beautiful thing a man and woman can do together."

"Their taxes?" asked Mia, and then she and Lynn broke out laughing again. "What a hoot this is!" Mia said. "Opal, I love this game! Can I borrow it some time? Some of our friends would love it."

Opal agreed, but she was uneasy. She could imagine Mia and Lynn and their friends, a group of wisecracking women crowded into a tiny Brooklyn kitchen, smoking pot and hunching around this poor, worn Milton Bradley game, turning the knob and making smart, snappy jokes that Opal would never understand. But still she said yes, because she loved Mia and didn't want to disappoint.

Sometimes at night she and Mia would go for long walks down Broadway. Summer was just settling in, and the crowds were out. Sidewalk vendors sold electric yo-yos and phosphorescent jewelry, and the night seemed lit with hundreds of fireflies. One night, Opal and Mia walked to Lincoln Center and sat on the lip of the fountain, feeling the water dust their hair.

"If I ever make any money," Mia said, "I'm going to live in Manhattan."

"Brooklyn's not Manhattan?" Opal asked. She could never quite keep this straight.

Mia explained to her about the different boroughs. "Brooklyn is for grandparents, and for starving uncompromised types like me," she said. "You're a lucky kid, growing up in the city. I grew up in Brooklyn, and I'll probably die there too; I'll be found dead on the N train. There but for the grace of your mother go I. She's a very generous woman, you know."

It was true; Dottie was tireless. She did her clown act at the Headley carnival each year, she helped young comics get a start in the business, gave them money and food and introduced them to talent agents, and she personally wrote back to as many of her fans as she could manage.

Erica would have been the only one to disagree. "She's a monster," Erica had taken to saying lately. "You don't see it, but it's true."

"You're so nasty," Opal had said. "What did she ever do to you that was so bad?"

"It's what she didn't do," said Erica. "But you're too young to understand that."

Erica liked to make Opal feel as though she was a little bit retarded—not enough so she had to attend a special school, but just dense enough to miss the critical point of most conversations. Erica wrote sheaves of poems, some of which had been published in *Insight*, the Headley literary magazine, and to Opal they made no sense. It was like trying to read the cryptogram in the newspaper; everything needed to be translated before you could proceed.

One of the poems was called "The Nadir"; Opal remembered that this had been among Erica's S.A.T. words:

THE NADIR

How can I reach the top
When I am ever slipping downward
Life is a big mountain
Whose bottom looms before us
Oh catch me please
Before I fall
Down the spiral
Into nothingness . . .

The poem was signed E. J. Engels, and it was printed on a page opposite a woodcut of a bag lady sleeping in a doorway. Many of the poems in the magazine were as meaningless as Erica's, and all of the illustrations were of old people or deserted beaches in winter. And now Erica was off in the farthest place she could find: Rwanda, which Opal had never even heard of, and about which Dottie had sung a little song before Erica left. "Help me, Rwanda," Dottie sang. "Help, help me, Rwanda . . ."

Now, sitting on the edge of the fountain outside Lincoln Center, a chill touched Opal's shoulders and lifted the edges of her hair. She wondered what her sister was doing then, wondered it with the same profound longing she used to have for Mickey Dolenz. This surprised her, for Erica had been so unfriendly to her. Erica didn't really deserve Opal's longing, and yet that didn't seem to matter. Longing was something you owned, like a birthmark; it was there, and you couldn't do anything about it except live with it. But she suddenly hoped Erica was all right. There had been no postcards from her yet.

Now it was just Opal and Mia. They were like two runaways sitting outside Lincoln Center, two lost girls waiting to be claimed by their parents when the concert was over. Mia Jablon looked like a kid in her Keds high-top sneakers, and she swung her feet as she sat on the fountain. What they had in common, Opal and Mia, was one important thing: They both loved Dottie Engels. They both needed her to watch over them, and Dottie always did. She was their guardian angel; she called them from wherever she was, and over the sputtering connection she asked how they were, and whether everything was going well.

We're fine! Opal screeched back, her voice tightening like a screw. We had pizza and watched "Get Smart"! As though these were the significant details, as though Dottie really needed to hear about "Get Smart" long distance. And yet somehow she did need to hear this; she always asked Opal about the small things: How was lunch? Did you finish Harriet the Spy yet? Dottie wanted to know the answers, for this was what their love consisted of.

Erica no longer wanted to take part in this ritual; Erica was beyond the reach of telephone lines now, in a place where you needed to be inoculated before you could enter, a place halfway around the spinning world. This staggered Opal. It had always been peculiar enough when her mother went to California and moved into a different time zone, but the other side of the world was unfathomable. When Opal fell asleep at night now, Erica would just be waking up.

In a week Dottie came home and Mia returned to Brooklyn, her knapsack on her back and Mystery Date tucked under her arm. Dottie was planning on staying home for much of July, and no baby-sitters would be necessary. The guest room was cleaned out, the bed stripped bare, and the adjoining bathroom no longer had a box of Tampax on the shelf, or a shaving kit on the windowsill. All of the baby-sitters' eight-by-ten head shots, which had been left scattered strategically around, were now relegated to a drawer in the den. The apartment, Opal realized, had grown completely silent.

For her entire first day back, Dottie stayed in bed. Opal walked gingerly through the rooms, trying desperately to entertain herself. Occasionally she peered in through the doorway. How could anybody sleep that much? she wondered as the morning dissolved into afternoon, and all the good television shows were replaced by bad ones. Game shows became soap operas, and Opal was bored. She missed Mia; she wanted to play a game, go for a walk, do a card trick, learn to do an impression of President Nixon, *anything*.

In a moment of boldness, Opal walked right into Dottie's room and stood over the bed, staring down. She picked up a pink feather which had fallen from a costume boa, and she dangled it over her mother's head, letting the point brush against her hair. Dottie swatted at the air in her sleep, and burrowed in deeper under the covers.

In desperation, Opal went to the thermostat in the hall and turned the central air conditioning way up. Then she waited, hoping to freeze her mother out, but that didn't work either, and so she went back into the bedroom and slipped into the bed beside her. Opal was so lightweight and unnoticeable that there was no movement to the mattress as she climbed in, no stir as she slipped under the comforter. She felt like a bug jumping onto the back of a dog. *Oh, please wake up*, Opal said silently, but there wasn't a sound except for Dottie's steady, peaceful breathing. Listening to that sound, Opal herself began to drift off.

When she woke up, or rather, when Dottie shook her awake hours later, Opal felt as though she were in a meat locker. The room was an alarming temperature.

"Why is it so cold in here?" Dottie was asking, standing over the bed. "Did you touch the AC?"

Opal could only nod, embarrassed. "Jesus," Dottie said. "We could have gotten frostbite!"

But she wasn't angry very long. She adjusted the controls and returned the apartment to a more reasonable climate. Then she came back to the bedroom. "I'm sorry I've been asleep so long," she said, "but that tour really knocked the wind out of me. Tell me what I've missed since I've been gone."

"Nothing," Opal said, shy at first, but as the evening wore on she gradually began to take objects from drawers and tabletops and present them to her mother: a diorama she had done, a spin-art painting, a beaded necklace she had strung. And she felt that pull of love once again, the real luxury of being alone with her mother. This would go on for all of July, she thought. Opal never wanted to go outside; who needed it? She would much rather stay in and listen to Dottie's new jokes, sit in the kitchen while her mother talked on the telephone, her head tipped to the side, cradling the receiver so that her hands could be free to sift through Opal's thick head of hair, making braids.

But on Dottie's third day back, the telephone rang while she was in the shower, and Opal answered it.

"Is your mother there?" a hesitant female voice asked.

"No, she can't come to the phone," Opal said. "Can I take a message?"

She grabbed a pen and pad and wrote down everything the woman said: that there had been a coup in Rwanda, and no one was hurt or in any danger whatsoever, but the Junior Peace Corps

82

program was terminated indefinitely. Opal understood very little of this at first, and yet after a few seconds what was important made itself known, coming into focus slowly, like a photograph gently shaken in a tray of chemicals.

In the background the shower churned, and she could hear her mother singing to herself under the spray. Opal hung up the phone and listened as the glass door slid open and Dottie stepped down. Now she would be drying off and coming out, and Opal would have to tell her the disappointing news: Erica was coming home.

8

She had been in Rwanda barely a day when the government was overthrown. Erica had just moved in with the Baptiste family, who lived in a small apartment house on the outskirts of Kigali. She was supposed to stay with them for three days, and would then be shipped out to the uplands to begin work. But as it turned out, she would see little of the country, except what could be viewed from the living room window that overlooked the crowded street below. Everyone's clothes looked slightly floured, as if caught in a dust storm. The heat was astonishing, and men and women held handkerchiefs up to their brows and walked dazed, as though suffering from concussions.

On the first night, the Baptiste family served dinner in their cramped kitchen, and there was painfully little to say. Finally the mother, a tired woman in a floral housecoat, turned on a transistor radio which hung from a hook above the sink, and an announcer spat out the evening news in French in a desperate voice. Everyone stopped eating and listened.

The father turned to Erica. There was political unrest in the country, he said in slow, careful English; surely she knew that. This was a difficult time for Rwanda; the government was on shaky footing. Hadn't the people from the Junior Peace Corps warned her? Erica shook her head, embarrassed. Everyone kept looking at her, their faces expressionless. No one else in the family spoke English. Even the daughter, Juvenale, who was exactly Erica's age, observed her with bland disinterest.

After dinner they all stayed poised around the radio, and Erica was startled to hear songs by Helen Reddy and Gladys Knight and the Pips. It was an American top-ten show, she realized. She looked around the room at this circle of black faces. Everyone was intently listening; no one said a word. A fan turned slowly in the window, and outside Erica could hear random, occasional noises. She was in Africa, exactly where she had wanted to be, and yet she could not give this scene any meaning. It felt more like an apartment in a housing project in Queens.

Late that night, looking into the mirror in the tiny bathroom down the hall, which the Baptistes shared with another family, Erica's own face looked different to her—flushed already from one day under the sun, and collapsed in on itself from travel. When she finally got to bed, climbing onto the cot that the father had set up for her in the doorway of Juvenale's room, Erica's eyes stung with fatigue. It was much too hot in the apartment, and her body felt peculiarly moist under the sheets. Across the room, she could hear turning and sighing. Juvenale was a thin girl with deeply black skin and hair that was twisted into dozens of braids the size of fingers.

In the dark, Juvenale asked, *"Z'êtes fatiguée?"*

Erica was so relieved to be spoken to, that she gave a long, rambling answer in painful high-school French about how, yes, she was extremely tired, due to the days of rigorous training at a campground in Maine, then the all-day plane trip, and then the bus ride. But then she abruptly stopped, realizing that she probably wasn't making much sense.

There was nowhere to go from there; the conversation had been hurled along to its finish already. The two girls lay in that dark room flat on their backs. This was only a way station; Erica would soon be living out near a chain of volcanoes, demonstrating dental care to villagers. She would be passing out spools of dental floss to women and men, and holding up giant placards that had illustrations of teeth painted in cheerful colors. But for now, resting in the home of this family who had for some reason agreed to take her in, Erica felt as though she had lost her sense of gravity. She gave in to it finally, letting herself drop. Juvenale seemed to be asleep already. Erica tried to follow her, pretending that this

85

warm, close air was the water of a bath, surrounding Erica, calming her. It almost worked. She was nearly asleep moments later, when three gunshots cracked in the street outside. Erica's eyes snapped open.

Suddenly voices called from down the hall. Juvenale's father appeared in the doorway; he bumped right into Erica's cot and stubbed his foot against its metal frame, shouting something in rapid French. Erica had no time to grab her Rousseau pocket dictionary from her luggage; she barely had time to pull a robe around her. Within seconds the father was ushering everyone out into the hallway of the building. The neighbors were gathered there, and they were all talking at once. Erica could not understand a word. A single bulb swung like a pendulum from a chain, and as the light moved across the line of faces, she felt as though she were at some strange new discotheque, or had taken some strange new drug. Her tongue was thick and wouldn't work. She could only remember the simplest things in French. *Un, deux, trois*, she whispered to herself. *Un, deux, trois*. Then she crouched against the wall between Juvenale and an ancient man who lived next door, and waited for instructions.

And so Erica found herself returning home, without ever seeing the volcanoes or the Kagera River, or anything else that sounded at all foreign to her. Her arm still ached from where she had been inoculated weeks earlier, but the inoculation had been for nothing. She hadn't drunk any water, hadn't gone near any native food. The Baptiste family had served her macaroni from a can, and then she had fallen asleep, and that was it. Now, still exhausted from the first plane trip, Erica was headed back to the States. She felt somehow personally responsible for the coup, as though her presence had thrown off the equilibrium of an entire African nation. The fat girl had arrived, and it was as if the other side of a seesaw had swung way up in the air. Bodies went flying; a government fell.

Dottie was waiting at the gate when she landed. Erica allowed herself to be hugged, and was then ushered into the limousine. Opal was there too, of course, leaping about in the backseat, watching television and pouring herself one Coke after another from the miniature bar, but Erica was so exhausted that she barely paid attention. She leaned back against the crushed velvet seat, and slept hard for the entire ride back to the city.

Her mother told her that she could go to summer camp if she wanted, that perhaps it wasn't too late to get her into a good one. She named a few—they were popular places that were always being advertised in the back of the *New York Times*, camps with euphonious names like Golden Lake and Iroquois Valley. And then, of course, there were programs for fat girls, which had names like Belle Rêve Camp for Overweight Teens. That was where Erica really belonged, not out on the veldt with strong, able teenagers, but in a tent with others like herself, shunted off to the farthest region and starved for six weeks. But Erica didn't want to go anywhere; she would stay home, she decided, and seal herself back up in her bedroom, which she never should have left in the first place.

Opal and Dottie were real pals these days; lately they had taken to sitting on the piano bench side by side and singing show songs. This was a truly disturbing development, and Erica couldn't bear to listen. She turned the volume of her stereo up as high as it would go, until the voices of Reva and Jamie were thoroughly distorted, but at least nothing else could be heard underneath, no jaunty chords leading into a reprise of "Happy Talk." Erica was swallowed up by sound, and even though it hurt her ears to listen, she lay on her bed and let the sound roll over her, the way that, when a subway train rushes past, you stand on the platform and tolerate the intolerable: the great wall of noise that seems to take you in as it sweeps by, only to drop you at the last minute. Once again there is silence in the station—the groan of turnstiles, and little else.

She didn't enjoy the music so loud, but enjoyment had very little to do with any of this. She didn't enjoy smoking dope with Jordan Strang, either; she never liked the way her hands and feet felt loose, as though they had been unscrewed halfway at the wrists and ankles, nor did she like the way her usual desire for food was magnified to a comical degree, so that she had visions of specific

87

dessert items floating in cartoon bubbles over her head. Twinkies appeared, and Yodels: anything that was soft and sealed in plastic—anything that had no resistance, no crust, nothing to come up against. The best food was as pliant as flesh.

The syllogism worked, too: The best flesh was as pliant as food. At least Jordan seemed to feel that way when his hands rambled along the edges of her body, stopping occasionally to feel something. Sex with Jordan, in which nothing was at stake, allowed you to swim through it to its resolution. Nobody asked you to enjoy it; nobody even asked if you *were* enjoying it. Erica was certain that Jordan felt as she did: that their lovemaking was both necessary and fulfilling, although neither of them would ever admit this aloud. Their needs were freakish, as though they had both discovered that their bodies were missing the same rare enzyme.

Erica lay alone in bed, with the music steamrolling over her, and she realized, to her astonishment, that she actually missed Jordan Strang. Not *him*, exactly, but sex with him. It was yet another act that she did not exactly enjoy, but that didn't matter at all. When you became lovers with somebody, you gave up all resistance. Erica felt as though she had let herself become exposed to a thousand new elements, some of them toxic, some not. She would need to be put in a plastic bubble for the rest of her life, like the boy in that TV movie. Only Jordan's touch was safe. How peculiar that she actually *required* the touch of this boy who did not love her: Jordan Strang, who loved no one but himself and, possibly, Hunter Thompson.

Jordan was off at computer camp in the Berkshires. She imagined him lying on his back in a bunk at night, falling asleep to the gentle, clicking chorus of computer terminal keyboards, more comforting to him than any insects would ever be. All around the camp, bunks glowed green or amber from the computer screens that lit the darkness like night-lights. And sometimes, around a campfire, the head counselor would tell stories about the ghost of the mysterious Computer Hacker, who returned to the camp every summer, wielding an axe.

Erica wanted Jordan's address. She wanted to write to him, to tell him she missed him. The letter would read like a deep confession, she knew, and yet she wanted to do it. But she couldn't remember the name of the camp, and in a fit of courage, Erica called Jordan's home telephone number; someone there would give her the address. The phone rang three times and then Jordan's mother answered. A nerve jumped in Erica's eyelid.

"Dr. Strang, this is Erica Engels," she said. "I'm Jordan's friend?" She said it like a question, giving his mother room to respond, "No, you're not."

But his mother seemed pleased. "Of course," she said. "How have you been, Erica? I thought Jordan told me you were off to Ghana for the summer."

"Rwanda," said Erica. "But I'm back. There was a coup and I was sent home."

Jordan's mother laughed once, sharply, then paused. "I'm sorry to hear that," she said. Her voice righted itself, became professional. "What can I do for you?"

Erica asked for Jordan's address, and Dr. Strang seemed delighted. "That's lovely of you, wanting to write him," she said. "I know he'll appreciate that." There was another pause. "You know," she said, "a thought just occurred to me. My husband and I are going to visit Jordan at Moccasin Hill on Saturday; it's Parents Weekend. Would you like to come with us? It's a three-and-a-half-hour drive and we're just going up for the day. I'm sure Jordan would love it."

Without thinking, Erica agreed.

On Saturday morning at seven, she showed up at the Strangs' apartment building. Dottie had been thrilled about the trip, so happy that Erica was actually doing something with a *boy*. Dottie was more excited about it than Erica, who was beginning to dread the whole thing. Erica sat in the back of the Strangs' brown Mercedes, flanked on either side by large, bulky items. Jordan's parents had packed a picnic hamper, and had also brought Jordan a few boxes of books he had requested. In addition, they had brought along some lawn furniture, and Erica couldn't see out of either window.

Jordan's father said almost nothing, a stance that Erica had

89

come to expect from fathers. Fathers were the ones who did the driving; that was how she thought of them. She remembered her own father at the wheel of the paneled station wagon, and the way she had observed the shape of his head as she sat behind him. In the summer he always drove with his left hand hanging out the window, and this was the only part of his pale body that ever tanned. The Engels' car wasn't air-conditioned, and on the hottest days, inching along the Long Island Expressway, Erica and Opal would make faces at people in other cars that did have air conditioning.

"Jesus," she remembered hearing her father say to her mother. "It's bumper-to-bumper traffic." For years, Erica thought that the phrase was "bumpita-bumpa traffic," because of the way the cars nudged up against each other. She could picture her father in the driver's seat better than anyplace else; when she thought of him now, which she rarely did, it was in a short-sleeved shirt in summer, his right hand palming the steering wheel, his left hand tapping the roof of the car, drumming out a tense little rhythm on hot metal.

It had been a long time since Erica had been around anybody's father for more than a few minutes. She had forgotten the dynamic, the way you were supposed to act, but soon it came back to her: shy deference, with underpinnings of respect and fear. But the father of a *boyfriend* was a new dynamic, one she had no grasp of. She wondered if this man, whose features she could not see now, this man whom she could identify only from the back of his head, which was shaped like a garden spade, knew that she was sleeping with his son. It seemed likely. Probably Jordan's father had come home one night in winter and found the plaster reproductive organs on his wife's desk, and had figured everything out. Would he approve of Jordan sleeping with a fat girl? Or would he be disgraced by it, taking his son aside and telling him he could do better? She wondered why it mattered what this man thought; he was just a cipher, after all, just a back of a head, and two hands grasping a steering wheel. He asked her no questions, seemed to possess no curiosity.

It was Jordan's mother who wanted to talk. She kept pivoting around at intervals during the trip. "Jordan tells me that your mother is Dottie Engels," she finally said. "I was so impressed; I've always enjoyed your mother's work. Humor is extremely important to everyone's well-being." Then she pivoted forward again, finished for the moment.

Erica turned back to the book she had brought along, *I Never Promised You a Rose Garden.* She had read it before, and it was one of her current favorites. She liked it up until the end, when the girl gets well and leaves the mental hospital, no longer needing to retreat to the secret land of Yr. Erica wished that the book had ended with the girl staying forever in her little universe, a place as magnificent and cordoned-off as the unicorn's garden in those tapestries at the Cloisters.

Jordan's mother interrupted her reading again. "Erica," she said. "I just had an idea. This may be way out of line, but do you think your mother might be available to speak at a medical convention sometime? I know she's a star, but we'd love to have someone like her, and I know that it pays handsomely."

"I don't know," said Erica. "She's very busy. You could call her manager. He handles all of that." She instinctively felt protective of her mother, which surprised her. Why *shouldn't* Dottie Engels address a group of physicians? Why was she above all that? Let her stand up there and make her usual fat jokes, and get all those physicians to laugh until they choked. But Erica knew that her mother would never accept an engagement like that; Ross Needler was very particular about where he allowed her to work. Every fall, Dottie was approached by a variety of companies that wanted her to perform at their annual industrial shows. The fees were impressive, but she still said no. When performers started doing the Tekwell Breakfast Show at the Dorset Hotel, then you knew that something was wrong, that some erosion had already begun, and the career was usually unsalvageable from that point on.

Dr. Strang faced forward again, and the rest of the ride was spent in silence. When they reached Moccasin Hill in Lenox, Massachusetts, Erica straightened her hopelessly creased clothing and strained to see out the front window. They drove through a log archway, following a line of other cars. At the side of the dirt road, a counselor dressed in white was waving everybody on. Erica felt a sudden anxiety at the thought of seeing Jordan. As the car reached the parking field, she squinted to see if she could pick Jordan out of the group of campers who milled around with hands in pockets, waiting to be claimed. Finally she saw him. He was not alone, a fact that surprised her. He was in the center of a group of boys, slouching against a parked car in the sun. His hair was very long; it now fell nearly to his shoulders.

When he recognized his parents' car, Jordan lifted a hand up in hesitant salute. He walked toward them, and the Strangs opened their car doors simultaneously, leaving Erica in the backseat. She watched as Jordan allowed himself to be loosely embraced by first his mother and then his father. Erica would be trapped here until someone unloaded a few lawn chairs or the giant picnic hamper. Finally they remembered her; through the glass, Erica watched his mother turn and point to where Erica sat. Jordan tilted his head and peered inside. He looked shocked to see her there. Surely they had told him she was coming; why did he seem so surprised?

But it turned out that they *hadn't* told him; they had left it as a surprise, which Erica knew was a misguided gesture. Jordan did not think of Erica as someone to look forward to, to be delighted by. He stared at her through the glass, and made no move to open the door and release her. Finally his mother said something which Erica couldn't hear, and Jordan reached out and opened the door. Silently he lifted a few lawn chairs from the seat, allowing her to pass. Erica slid across the leather seat and stood up, facing him.

"What are you doing here?" was all he asked.

"Your mother invited me," Erica said. "I thought she'd told you."

"No," Jordan said. "Nobody told me. I only got two tickets to the computer demonstration this afternoon. I guess I'll have to try to get another."

He looked different to her, somehow. It wasn't just that his hair was longer and his skin patched with light freckles. He held himself differently—straighter, she thought, as though he had been given posture lessons at Moccasin Hill.

92

"Well, come on," he said, and he turned around and led them to where they were supposed to go. Erica and the Strangs followed behind meekly, carting furniture and food.

They spent lunchtime on a blanket in a clearing in the woods. All around them, boys sat on blankets with parents. A few of the boys were talking with animation, but most of them were hugging their knees and looking off at some point in the distance, or studiously picking at scabs. Mothers unloaded Thermoses and plastic drums of food. Erica seemed to be the only "girlfriend" among the crowd; here and there were other girls, but they definitely seemed to be the boys' sisters. It was easy to recognize sisters: They showed just as little interest as their uninterested brothers, staring off at their own imaginary oases, or leafing through *Seventeen*. Only Erica sat close to Jordan, trying to make him talk to her.

"So why did you leave Rwanda?" he finally asked.

She told him the story of her trip, and he asked one or two questions. Everyone began to relax; Jordan's mother passed around a platter of barbecued chicken, and they all ate.

It was much later in the afternoon that Erica went alone with Jordan to his bunk. His parents had insisted that Erica and Jordan have some time to themselves, even though Jordan didn't particularly seem to want it. So while the Drs. Strang watched a skit in the field house about the Age of Computers, Erica followed Jordan up a narrow path to a wooden box on stilts in which he lived with seven other boys. No one else was there now; the room was dark and neat and smelled of calamine.

"This is it," he said, gesturing around him. On a shelf by the bed, Erica noticed several small trophies. She picked one up and examined it. "First Place in Freestyle Swim Meet," it read. Erica stared at him.

"Is this yours?" she asked, and Jordan nodded. All of the trophies on the shelf were his; he had won competitions in swimming, archery, and tennis. Jordan, one of the least athletically inclined boys at Headley, had somehow changed during the course of the summer. She could not get over it.

The screen door swung open then, and two boys walked in. They resembled Jordan, Erica saw, although they were smaller than he

93

was, and their hair was not nearly as long. One of them kept scratching at a dotted line of mosquito bites along his bare arm.

"How are you doing, man?" Jordan asked.

"Pretty good, Jordo," the other boy said. "You get any good shit from your folks?"

Jordan shrugged. "I doubt it," he said. "The usual."

"Whatever," said the first boy.

Erica stood by the shelf, still grasping Jordan's archery trophy in her hand. She felt as though she had been caught in some illicit act, as though her hand were curled around his penis. She put the trophy back down on the shelf with the others.

"We've got to go," the first boy said. Jordan still hadn't introduced Erica to them, but neither boy seemed particularly curious; perhaps she was wearing a cloak of invisibility. The two boys dropped a couple of care packages from home onto their own beds, and turned around and left, the thin door shuddering shut behind them.

Jordo; they had called him Jordo. Most likely Jordan had been hoping for a nickname like this his entire life. He had found his niche in the world: a computer camp, of all places, where everyone who was an untouchable during the school year could gather and try out the vocabulary of the cool. Stammering, paper-thin boys could slap each other five and call each other "my man," without having the whole thing be viewed as hilarious. In this safe, pine-shrouded place, for eight measly weeks, these boys could rise up and join forces. And somehow Jordan, perhaps because he was the tallest, or because he was the one who had brought drugs from home, or perhaps simply because they had drawn straws, was their leader. Jordan was in charge here; Erica could sense it. She had held one of his trophies in her hand, she had seen him lean against a car like James Dean. And when it had come time for him to introduce Erica to his henchmen, he had been ashamed. He had pretended she didn't exist, that she was a sister, a cousin, an apparition who had somehow blown into Jordan's territory, and the boys had gone along with it.

She looked at him and knew that whatever she said now would be infused with desperation. "Can we lie down?" she asked.

94

Jordan glanced around the room. "I don't know," he said. "Someone might come in." He stood there considering.

"No one will come in," Erica said, and finally he climbed with her into the bottom of his bunk bed, but his eyes were still surveying the room. His body had become stronger, she realized when he took off his T-shirt. His chest seemed mapped off into separate sections, and the divided muscle was hard under her palms.

After five minutes Jordan steadied his hands on her shoulders and pushed himself up. "Erica," he said, "you shouldn't have come."

"I know," she said.

Jordan looked beyond her, out the screenless window. "I've got to get back," he said. "I want to catch the end of the skit." He sat up swiftly. She watched as he pulled his T-shirt on, forcing his head through the hole, eyes squinted with effort like a baby being born. Erica sat up too, and her head slammed against the upper bunk.

They walked in silence back down the hill toward the field house. As usual, he walked a few feet ahead of her. She could have sat down on the path, and he probably would have kept walking, not realizing she wasn't right behind him until he was miles beyond her. Jordan had changed. He was more distant than ever: he, who had always been a *given*, the one constant in her life. This whole summer had been unbearable; first the disappointment of the Junior Peace Corps, and now this.

It was in that moment, stumbling down the incline, that Erica decided she would attempt suicide. She came about this decision dispassionately; the idea seemed right, a snug fit.

"I have to go to the bathroom!" she called down to Jordan, who was almost at the bottom of the trail. "I'm going back to your bunk for a minute!"

He stood with his hands on his hips. "All *right!*" he said. "If you really have to. Can you find your way back alone?" He probably thought it was some menstrual thing that he did not fully understand.

"Yes!" Erica called, and Jordan disappeared into the woods at the bottom. Erica returned to the empty bunk, and this time she began looking around with purpose. Each bed was neatly made; these outcast boys couldn't throw off every uncool habit in one summer. Disarray would come with time, until one day their rooms at home would look as though someone had broken in. Only the record collections would remain perfectly neat. If someone's mother happened to put an album out of alphabetical order during cleaning, the son would scream at her until she wept.

Erica knew nothing about the lives of boys, except what she had learned from Jordan. But there was no way for her to have known much, really; even when her father had been living with the family, he had been more of a shadow puppet than anything else. His *maleness* was always well-protected from both her and Opal. Neither of them had ever seen him without his shirt on. Erica remembered that when Opal was very young, she did not know that men had nipples. She had assumed that their chests were flat, unbroken planes, like tabletops.

Now everything that came into Erica's field of vision was exclusively male. She felt like a divining rod as she walked about the room. She picked up the yellow cannister of Desenex on the windowsill. "For Relief of Jock Itch," it read. *Jock Itch*; this term embarrassed her, although she did not really understand it. It was genital, she knew, and male, and cryptic. On the shelf next to the upper bunk was a selection of what she perceived as *male* reading material: two science-fiction novels by Robert Heinlein, a computer manual, and a stack of *Mad* magazines. Thrown across the back of a chair in the corner was a pair of red bathing trunks, hung inside-out, exposing a little wet twist of elastic sewn inside.

Erica sat down on Jordan's bed. She noticed a shoe box on the floor beneath the shelf, and she picked it up and opened it. It was filled with various items: Band-Aids, shaving supplies, an asthma inhaler, and a bottle of St. Joseph's baby aspirin. This man, this *Jordo*, who tried new, untested drugs manufactured by college freshmen, still took baby aspirin when he had a headache. Erica picked up the bottle. This was the best she could find, but it would have to do. She opened the lid, which took her several minutes and made her resort to using her teeth, because it was child-proof, and then she extracted the ball of cotton and shook out a generous handful of tablets into her hand. She would take them, she decided, when she got back into the Strangs' car, and she would travel down to New York City, and by the time they got home she would have died. Erica dropped the aspirin into the pocket of her shirt, replaced the bottle in the shoe box, and went to join Jordan and his family. She felt oddly excited as she walked back down the path.

Later that night, sitting in the backseat of the car, once again flanked by lawn furniture and the picnic hamper, Erica waited until Jordan's mother was done speaking to her, done talking about Moccasin Hill and how well Jordan seemed to be doing, and then she discreetly took the handful of aspirin from her pocket and put them into her mouth all at once. The taste was surprisingly familiar and resonant; it burned her throat, crumbling like chalk dust. It made her think of things she hadn't thought of in years: Sweetarts, Chocks vitamins, tossing feverishly in her bed; it almost made her choke. This was the right thing to do, and a gentle way to do it. If, by some chance, she were to live, she would wake up in a psychiatric hospital like the one in *I Never Promised You a Rose Garden*. That wouldn't be so bad, she thought. The Strangs' car swung onto the highway heading south, and Erica settled in for the duration.

Three hours later they were shaking her awake.

"You slept the whole way," Jordan's mother was saying. The overhead light was on inside the car, and Erica was now fully conscious. She didn't even feel woozy in any way. She automatically gathered up her book and her purse, and the night doorman came to the car and helped move the lawn chairs so she could get out.

"Well, thanks a lot," she said.

"Our pleasure," said Jordan's mother. "You're a wonderful traveling companion," she added. "We hope to see more of you, Erica." Her husband nodded and gave a small wave.

After the car pulled away, Erica stayed at the curb for a few seconds. The doorman stood looking at her quizzically, his hands behind his back, but he didn't say a word. She would go upstairs now, where her mother and sister were probably singing duets, or painting each other's toenails pebble pink. Opal would be sitting with her foot in Dottie's lap, and Erica would breeze right past them. She had to *live* with them; she had to be there because there was nowhere else for her—not Rwanda, not Jordan Strang's bedroom, not death. The taste of baby aspirin was still thick in her throat, the sweet sting of it, and probably would be for years.

PART
TWO

HINSDALE PUBLIC LIBRARY,
HINSDALE, ILLINOIS

9

Suddenly, no one would laugh at a fat woman. When Dottie stood up and told those jokes now, she was met with a wall of silence that was wider and denser than her own body. Actually, the decline wasn't sudden, or even dramatic, although Dottie liked to tell it this way. She liked to say that her audience had fled one day like lemmings, when in fact they had been diminishing slowly over a period of years.

"Everyone has their season," Dottie said. "What am I supposed to do, move to the Fanny Brice Retirement Home?" She was keeping it in perspective, she said, and trying not to grow too depressed. Opal was the one who was depressed. From a safe distance, she watched as her mother was offered fewer television spots, fewer club dates. Often Dottie was forced to share billing with an illusionist or a hypnotist. There were cages of doves backstage now, and young, leggy women smoking and waiting to be sawed in two.

"Ross and I are going to brainstorm," Dottie said over the phone. "We're going to put our heads together and come up with a master plan, a way to get me back on my feet. He's not worried, so I'm not, either."

But she seemed vague when she telephoned, Opal noticed. Sometimes in the background, Opal could hear the slap of cards as her mother laid down a hand of solitaire. Lately the conversations lasted only a few minutes. "Listen, honey, I've got to go," Dottie would suddenly say. "There are a million things I have to take care of." Opal could imagine her mother hanging up and restlessly scavenging the apartment for food, cigarettes, distractions of any kind.

Soon, Opal knew, something would have to give; either Dottie would find decent work, or else she would lose herself. Opal imagined her mother simply collapsing in a great heap in a restaurant or on the street, mourning the death of what had been, and no longer was.

"If it was me, I would die," Opal told her friend Tamara Best over dinner one night in the dining hall. "I mean, I wouldn't be able to go on."

"Well, that's you," said Tamara. "That's not her. I think performers have a different outlook." Tamara was a Theater major; she had just been given the lead in *St. Joan,* and had cut her shoulder-length spray of hair for the occasion. "I don't know your mother," Tamara said, "but she sounds like she's doing something right. Like she's surviving." She paused. "Why are you so involved?" Tamara asked. "I'm concerned about my parents' lives too, but only up to a *point.*"

Opal didn't know how to answer. They sat in a corner of the large room, and all around them she could hear the hiss of the steam table and the mumble of adolescent voices. Opal tried to picture what her mother was doing for dinner tonight. Chances were, Dottie was standing in front of the refrigerator right this minute, poised in its light. Opal could see her holding a bloody packet of steak in one hand and a frozen pizza in the other, weighing the possibilities. For a moment Opal imagined inviting Dottie to come live with her at Yale; they could be roommates, she thought, and enroll in all the same classes. Dottie would crack jokes during seminars, would shout and whoop in the middle of lectures.

Finally it wasn't just a question of aimlessness, or pride; Dottie needed to find work because she was going through her money at an alarming rate. One afternoon she called Opal in New Haven and made an announcement.

"I found a job," she said.

"That's terrific," said Opal. "Out in L.A.?"

"No," said her mother. "Right here." She paused. "This is a

little different." And then she began to explain that she had agreed to lend her name and image to a line of clothing. "It's going to be called the Dottie Engels Collection for Large Women," she said. "That's what it will say on all the labels. And there will be three little dots sewn on to every garment, either on a pocket or sleeve. Kind of a trademark."

Opal held her breath for a moment, wondering how to respond. "Is this definite?" she finally asked.

"Why? Do you think it's a mistake?" Dottie asked.

"I don't know," Opal said. "I don't know what to tell you." She paused. "What does Ross say?"

"Oh, what can he say?" Dottie said. "He says he wants what's in my best interest. He knows I need money; he knows things are getting tight, what with your tuition and my extravagant ways. He didn't push me into this; we both talked about it for a long time. I don't know, honey, I think I'm just going to have to *do* it. There really isn't anything else."

Opal remembered her mother drifting across a stage to kiss the host of a talk show. Back then, her gowns came all the way down to the floor so you couldn't see her feet, which gave the illusion of one swift movement, as though Dottie were on wheels.

"You've agreed to do it?" Opal asked, and her mother softly said yes, she had, and all Opal could do was congratulate her. But as she did, she could feel something within herself shift position and drop. She wanted to tell her mother not to do it, to stop now before it was too late. Don't look back, Eurydice, she thought, and she imagined Dottie disobeying and turning to look, finding only this new image of herself: someone huge and overripe and desperate, with three dots marking her sleeve.

The commercials were released during October of Opal's junior year at Yale. She closed the door of her single room in Silliman, turned on her television set, and kept a private vigil for hours. She watched several new sitcoms and a few old standards, until finally the first commercial appeared.

Her mother swung into camera range, while on the soundtrack a heavy disco beat kept time as clearly as a metronome. "Sizes fourteen to forty-six!" Dottie was saying, her voice agitated but

103

buoyant. The camera crawled across a wall of dresses behind her. The clothes themselves were not terrible, Opal thought, just big and formless and light, like maternity clothes for angels.

She kept an eye on her mother as though Dottie were a child performing in a school play—a child who was somehow managing to strike out in a small, miserable role: a forest animal during Fire Prevention Week, or one of the lesser von Trapp girls in the fall musical. It was painful for Opal to watch her mother onscreen, but Dottie held herself with dignity. She never flinched or gave one of those clenched, ironic little smiles that try to let the home viewer in on a secret.

Dottie had claimed that she didn't entirely see this venture as a sign of failure. "Of course, I'd rather be opening at Caesar's," she said, "but in the scheme of things, it's somewhere between death and a few of the clubs I used to play." She paused. "I have to make my peace with it," she said. "I thought to myself: It's a decent project. It's moral. Why should large women have to look like Sicilian widows? If I got anything from those years on tour, it was the confidence to dress bright. Other women should be encouraged to show themselves off, too; they shouldn't have to wear dark colors and vertical stripes their whole lives. They shouldn't have to be ashamed."

But Opal told no one about the commercials. Eventually, everyone at school would find out on their own, she knew, but for now she didn't want to talk about it. She sat in bed and watched her mother drift by in first a peach dress, then a sky-blue blazer, and finally a long, pale green chiffon number with little fluted ruffles that looked like leaves of Bibb lettuce. Then Opal lit a cigarette and closed her eyes as the commercial faded to its conclusion.

She would have to call Dottie that night and tell her she had seen it. "So what's the verdict?" Dottie would ask, her voice bright but nervous, and Opal would tell her the commercial was impressive, that the clothes looked good, and the music was catchy. Her instinct now was to protect Dottie in a way that she had never done before. But there had simply never been a need before; Dottie had always been a kind of *Brunhilde* figure, armored and huge and fearless.

104

Opal glanced at the clock; one-fifteen, and Dottie would probably still be waiting up. She decided not to call. Tomorrow she would call; tonight Opal just wanted to be left alone. From outside in the hall, she could hear various noises: two anorexic roommates were studying aloud for a Latin exam, tossing declensions back and forth. Someone else was taking a shower, and Opal could hear the water smacking tile. Finally Opal heard Andrea, her next-door neighbor, coming home with her boyfriend. First there was a thud of books dropping, and then a lighter thud of bodies dropping. Then there was whispering, and low, knowing laughter, and finally the unmistakable sound of two people making love. None of it really interested her, she realized. After a while it was just noise, and barely human.

Opal could not get over the idea that her mother had fallen. "You mean you never thought about this before?" Tamara had said. "It seems so inevitable."

But Opal just shook her head. There was no way to explain the fact that Dottie had always been a fixture, a *given*. Opal thought of the way she used to sit in front of the television's gentle light, and how every once in a while she would look up, smiling and blinking, as her mother's voice called to her as if from above water. Dottie Engels was always somewhere nearby. Finding her— and you usually could, if you looked hard enough, whether on television or in a newspaper or in the pages of a magazine—was like finding the North Star in an unfamiliar sky. A new location disoriented you, but you had to be patient, and look and look until finally the star made its presence known behind a stand of trees, or over a darkened lake.

Now, whenever Opal looked for Dottie, she felt as though she were searching for her mother among footage of the war dead— intently looking for something she just as intently hoped she wouldn't find. But still Dottie turned up, a bright, swirling, unmistakable tornado of readywear fabric.

Opal began staying up late at night looking for her mother's commercials, and sleeping through most of her morning classes. She had recently declared herself an Art History major, and there were sheaves of prints she needed to examine in the slide room, and hours worth of reading to be done each day, but suddenly it all ceased to hold interest; suddenly she could think of little else but her mother's decline. Opal remembered how, the year before, she had loved standing before a painting at the Yale Art Museum, notebook open to a clean page, watching as the image went from static to fluid. She had felt *held* there, much the way she used to feel as a child, centered in front of the big TV.

Now Opal spent most of her time in front of the television once again. She scouted the airwaves for her mother, cringing her way through each ad, praying that it would fly by swiftly and silently. Before midterms, when the library was packed and everyone on campus stayed up all night, drinking gallons of potent coffee and living in terror of failure, when everyone suspected they weren't as smart as they had been told all their lives, and now the moment of judgment had finally arrived, Opal stayed alone in her room, a bar of blue light shining steadily beneath her door as she watched television in the dark.

In November, Opal received two notices of academic warning, and her advisor urged her to come see him, but Opal didn't know what in the world she would say. Thoughts of Yale became more remote; she felt a surprisingly small amount of guilt about how little time she was spending on her work. Tamara had agreed to tape the nine A.M. lecture each day, but the recordings were poor, and the professor's thin voice was usually swallowed up by the coughs and rustling of one hundred students who were waking up for the day.

"Do you know what you're doing?" Tamara asked. "I've seen people fall apart here. Remember that girl, Julie Litman, who got the lead in *The Belle of Amherst* last year, and got so wrapped up in it that she stopped going to all her classes?"

Opal nodded. She remembered Julie well, with her long Emily Dickinson dresses and bun and fishy glances. "This is nothing like that," Opal said.

"Well, be careful," said Tamara. "Really, I'm worried about you. And it's not just me. Peter told me that he walked past your door at four in the morning the other day—who knows what *he* was doing, prowling around—and he said you were up watching TV. He heard 'The Love Boat' theme song coming from your room."

106

"It's for a project I'm doing," Opal said. "Sort of a deconstruction of popular culture. I'm comparing and contrasting the aesthetics of Aaron Spelling and Quinn Martin."

Tamara laughed and shook her head. "Just watch yourself," she said. "This isn't like you."

Opal had always been a good, if obsessive, student—never a genius, but consistently neat. Somewhere along the way it became clear that neatness really *did* count, or at least the adult version of neatness, which seemed to be scrupulousness. She wasn't innately gifted; nothing slid by with oiled ease, as it seemed to do for so many people around her. When she walked past the practice rooms of the music building at school, down that narrow corridor of vacuum-sealed glass cells, she was overwhelmed by the explosion of chords. And in the microbiology lab one afternoon, waiting for her friend Peter to finish for the afternoon, Opal had stared in awe at the line of students, all of them with heads tipped down, squinting into microscopes for hidden colonies of life. There was nothing in the world that Opal could do with any particular brilliance. She had been Dottie Engels's daughter; that was what she had done best of all.

On the Wednesday evening before Thanksgiving break, Opal traveled down to the city in Shelley Carper's dented Pontiac packed with students. The ride quickly turned into a party on wheels; someone lit a joint, which immediately stank up the enclosed space, and Shelley popped in a tape of some new band that sang like androids. Up front, Debbie Flynn opened a bag of trail mix and everyone held out their hands.

"Are we there yet?" Peter Lipman asked when they had been traveling for ten minutes.

Everyone was jokey and easy and able to unwind; only Opal stayed slightly apart. She rolled the window down an inch and leaned upward toward the small jet of air.

"As soon as I get home," said Peter, "I'm going to open good old Panofsky. He's the only art critic in the world who says, 'As you can see from the following quote in Latin . . .' and then doesn't bother to translate. Shit, I'm not even going to have time to eat the turkey."

107

Everyone clucked and murmured in agreement. When they reached the city, Opal was let out first, right in front of her mother's building. She thanked Shelley, and waved as the car pulled out into the quiet, wide street. Opal stepped onto the curb, clutching her knapsack, and she realized, as she hefted its light weight, that she had entirely forgotten to bring any of her notebooks or texts home with her. She would not be able to work at all during break. It astonished her that she had lost hold of herself in this way, and that she felt no grief at all.

The next day, as she and Dottie stood in the kitchen preparing dinner, Opal suddenly said, "I'm failing." She spoke without drama. She was at the sink, running warm water over the frozen dome of turkey.

"What's that?" Dottie asked, and Opal turned off the faucet.

"I'm *failing*. I got two probation notices," said Opal.

Dottie didn't say anything at first. She shook her head slowly, and sat down at the island in the middle of the room, lighting a cigarette. "Well, honey, is something wrong?" she finally asked. Opal shrugged. "Is it personal?" Dottie tried. "Something love-related, if I may ask?"

Opal shook her head. "No," she said. "It's definitely not that."

"Animal, vegetable, or mineral?" asked Dottie. "Come on, Opal, I hope you know that you can talk to me. It would take a lot to shock me."

"I know," said Opal. She found a towel and wiped her hands dry. "I've just sort of lost interest," she said.

Dottie observed her fully, head tilted. "Honey," she said, "maybe it's too hard for you. Could that be it? I mean, maybe you're pushing yourself. I'm hardly an expert, not having gone to college—having received my degree from the school of hard knocks—but maybe this is too much. I've looked at some of your textbooks, and God knows they're way over *my* head."

"It's not that it's too hard," Opal started, but she had no idea of where she might possibly go from here. "I think about other things," she said, "and I start worrying." She paused. "Like about you," she said.

Dottie looked puzzled. "What's all this?" she asked. "Why

should you worry about me? You're a twenty-year-old girl; you've got your whole life up there in college. You've got better things to think about than me. Really, Opal, I don't know what you're saying." But Dottie seemed thrown suddenly, unnerved.

Opal came to the counter and slipped a cigarette from her mother's pack. "I hate that you smoke," Dottie muttered.

Opal ignored this. They sat with the oven preheating and the smoke lifting, and outside the sky looked dark, even though it was daytime. The sky often looked dark from the kitchen window, which granted a narrow view between buildings. Opal could just make out the skull of the planetarium across the way.

"Look," said Dottie, "I appreciate your concern. It's not as though I haven't stayed awake at night obsessing about this myself, worrying whether or not it's career suicide." She poked her cigarette out in a saucer. "But you know," she went on, "my career is already as good as dead. In a way, I have nothing to lose." She shook her head. "Comedy isn't where it used to be," she said. "Turn on the television; have you seen that man, the one who calls himself the Unidentified Flying Comic? You know, the one who comes onstage with that cape and that accent? *That's* what people pay money to hear. Gone are the days when I was getting famous—the nightclubs, and the real excitement in the air."

"Well, doesn't that depress you?" asked Opal.

"Sure it does," Dottie said. "Sometimes, if I really start to dwell on it, I get blue. When I first started out, everyone said it was so wonderful how far I'd come, what a good role model I was for other women, and now they're saying that my humor is *insulting* to women. So comedy has changed, so I'm making a living with a line of women's clothing. Is that so bad?" She looked at Opal as though she really wanted an answer. "It's a good cause," Dottie went on. "These women need to wear something other than potato sacks." Suddenly Dottie stood. "Come on," she said. "Enough of this depressing talk. We've got to get this show on the road, if we want to eat dinner tonight."

But a real gravity had already set in, and nothing could change it. Later, Dottie pulled the turkey pan from the oven and extracted the meat thermometer from the shining flesh of the bird. When

109

she stood up, her face was pink with heat and worried, and Opal felt miserable for having brought anything up.

She compared this with the year before, when Dottie had been in L.A. for the holiday, taping a sixty-second spot for something called "Kaleidoscope of Stars," and Opal had been invited to Tamara's house in Vermont. There were three good-natured, attractive brothers present, all of whom had nouns for names: Clay, Hull, and something else bucolic that Opal didn't quite remember, either Forest or Park. Both of Tamara's parents were hale and angular and cheerful. There was no *subtext* to the weekend, no hidden rage or regret. They had all sat around a large parsons table and drunk a lot of wine, and after dinner they went for a night ski through the trails out back.

She could not imagine what Tamara's childhood had been like, living there, singing madrigals with her family at night, having three brothers to jostle and goad at the dinner table. Every year Tamara invited friends home for various vacations, even the unimportant vacations, like Columbus Day, so that no one should have to stay alone at school in an echoing dormitory. She seemed to take for granted the pleasant agitation that thrummed through her house all weekend. Everyone in her family slept late, and staggered from bed in the morning at their leisure. The three brothers drank long slugs of milk right from the container, and came to the table in only their pajama bottoms. Their chests were broad and hairless and beautiful, Opal thought, looking away.

But now, a full year later, Opal and her mother sat alone in a darkening kitchen, slicing meat into parchment with an electric knife, and Opal found herself grateful for the hum of the blade. "You know," Dottie said, "before you start feeling *too* sorry for me, I'd like you to see some things for yourself. I'd like you to see a little more of what this is all about."

"What do you mean?" Opal asked.

"Well, I'd like to take you to the factory where they make the clothes for my line," Dottie said. "I just want you to *see*."

So the following Monday, two hours before the caravan of students was due to take her back to New Haven, Opal went with her mother to the Amwoolco factory on Chrystie Street in lower

Manhattan. The limousine cruised through the unfamiliar streets, and Opal realized that in all her years in New York, she had never once been to this neighborhood; she didn't even know what it was called. Dottie had the driver stop in front of a factory. Opal looked up and could see yellow light shining behind some of the large, smeary windows on the third floor. Higher up in the building, most of the windows had been punched out, and all that was left was a map of glass, with no light behind it. Opal was seized with a crazy fear of this place. There was nothing familiar about it, nothing she could grasp on to, except the bizarre fact that this was her *mother's* factory, her *mother's* line of clothing.

A guard let them in, and they traveled upstairs together in an ancient elevator. When they arrived at the third floor, Dottie pulled back the grate and opened the door of a large room that was chattering with machinery. On the far wall was a banner that read: DOTTIE ENGELS FASHIONS FOR LARGE WOMEN . . . SAY IT LOUD, I'M BIG AND PROUD!

Opal sucked in a hard breath. Was this shame she felt, in its purest form, or did it have something else stirred in? She couldn't be sure.

Then the noise slowed and lessened, as word went around that Dottie was here. Machines were abandoned and several operators, mostly women, gathered around. Opal realized that her mother was the only island of color among this crowd of people. Everyone else was wearing dark gray aprons, and their hair was pulled back in netting, away from their faces and the machinery. Dottie was clothed in an orange dress from her line. The dress hadn't actually been released yet; this was only a prototype.

"Miss Engels, we're so glad to see you," an old woman said, coming up to Dottie and embracing her with chicken-bone arms. Opal turned away; she felt as though she were witnessing a scene from Dickens. But her mother was calling Opal back, wanting to introduce her.

"This is my daughter Opal," Dottie announced.

"You have two girls, is that right?" the woman asked.

"Yes, that's right," Dottie said, and then her face closed up and went peculiar for just a moment, the way it always did when someone mentioned Erica.

"She's so streamlined," said a young woman, herself overweight and wearing a Dottie Engels dress under her apron.

At twenty, Opal did not feel streamlined. Instead, she felt that she looked strange, with her round face jutting off a tall, lanky body with breasts. It was an odd hybrid: the presence of both child and adult when the two halves were supposed to meld. It reminded her of the way Shirley Temple had looked as an adolescent, at the end of her career.

Now Opal followed her mother around the factory, peering down at the tops of women's netted heads that were nodding over small machines. When the tour had ended and they were back downstairs, Dottie said, "See?" but Opal wasn't at all sure of what she was supposed to have seen.

"See what?" Opal asked.

"See that this is something real, something worthwhile," said Dottie.

"Real isn't the same as worthwhile," Opal said, and she immediately regretted it. This sounded like some stupid comment uttered in a freshman logic tutorial.

"Forget it, then," said Dottie. "Just forget it."

She pulled open the elevator grate and walked out ahead of Opal, nodding to the guard but not stopping. Opal trailed behind, struggling to keep up as she had done as a little girl. They walked across the street, where the limousine was double-parked, and Dottie got in first. "Look, I'm sorry," Opal said as she ducked into the car. "Please, I'm just not sure of what I was supposed to *see*."

Dottie didn't answer. She unzipped her purse and fished around inside for a pack of cigarettes. Because no one would laugh at a fat woman anymore, the silence had spiraled all the way downward to a factory at the bottom of Manhattan. Opal watched her mother smoke, saw the way Dottie inhaled as though she were hungry. It was just the two of them now, traveling together in this car that Dottie could no longer afford and would soon be selling. Opal remembered how she and her mother used to sing duets together, and how Erica would storm past, her hands over her ears, not wanting to listen. They had sung "Happy Talk" and "Dites-Moi." The music traveled back to her now, unbidden, and it brought with it a trail of other things. Opal thought of the way her mother used to look in a full-length gown, and the way the baby-sitters used to sound as they practiced all night. There had been so much going on back then; now it all seemed whittled-down and disappointing. This was the result of those years of excess, she thought, leaning back as the car bumped lightly across a few potholes. Then, for some reason which she did not entirely understand, Opal thought of her father.

In thinking of him, she suddenly wanted to see him.

The desire struck with an astonishing simplicity, but there it was: Opal wanted to talk to him, to write to him, to ask him questions. Years before, after the divorce was official, Dottie had often said, "Your father doesn't know how to show love, and I see no reason for him to have *your* love, girls. I'm afraid he'd only hurt you. Better to let the whole thing drop."

So they had dropped it, dropped him, and it had been a painless release, with very few echoes. Opal thought about him occasionally over the years, but always with a kind of distracted curiosity that had a short half-life. Once in a while she would be reminded that she had a father living in Florida, and for a moment she would close her eyes and summon up an image of a tall, reedy man in a business suit, loosening a striped tie under the Miami sun. That image would satisfy her, and she would not pursue it. Back when she and Erica were both still living at home, they would occasionally discuss him, but it always felt *wrong*, as though they were holding underground meetings of a subversive political organization and might be discovered at any time. Soon their voices would grow frail and hesitant and the discussion would end.

But now Opal felt herself swell with longing; it seemed as real to her as matter, as real as muscle and bone and lipid. It might have filled her clothes and ballooned her up to size 46. In her head, she began to compose a letter.

10

Erica lay back on the table while the girl attached two electrodes to her temples. They seemed to spring from her head like branches, she thought, peering at herself in the mirror on the wall. She had thought she would look like a vivisection victim, wired and stunned on a slab, but instead there was something mythological about this whole thing: a tree growing from a woman. Erica vaguely remembered reading a story like that in the Bullfinch book, years before.

"I'm going to sit on the other side of the glass, where you can't see me," the girl was saying, "and I'm going to ask you a few questions. The machine will monitor your brain waves as you respond. So just relax, okay? Think of something peaceful; think of your favorite place."

The girl disappeared into the next room. Erica shifted slightly on the papered table, as the first of the questions began. "In your mind," came the girl's voice, "do you use food as a replacement for love?" She was young, about Erica's age, and had not sloughed off certain childhood cadences. She spoke as though reciting a nursery rhyme.

"No," Erica answered. Jordan had suggested she tell lies during the test; it would be interesting to throw off a whole study, he said, to screw up whatever theory was being proposed.

They had been making a living from this sort of thing for months now. It had originally been Jordan's idea; he kept seeing advertisements in the back of the *Village Voice*—graduate students wanting guinea pigs for psychological studies—and he and Erica began making the rounds. It was like selling blood, Erica thought: a slightly sleazy thing to do, and yet she actually enjoyed herself. The graduate students always treated you very well, and you were paid as soon as the tests were done. Sometimes they were looking for overweight people, like today, and Erica was always accepted into the study right away. During one such test, she had to eat a bag of cookies while a young blond man told her jokes. He wanted to see what sort of correlation there was between humor and the enjoyment of food. But the cookies were dry and uninteresting— Stella D'Oro—and the jokes strictly knock-knock. Erica never doubted the worth of the studies; she obediently answered the questions and left with her money. Today, when she left, her temples were still damp with conducting grease.

She walked out into Washington Square in the late afternoon, clutching the twenty-five dollars she had earned, and decided to go visit Jordan. He had left for NYU Hospital the night before, where he was participating in a two-week study of young, healthy males with a family history of heart disease. He wouldn't be able to falsify any information there, Erica thought, because all they wanted of him were blood and urine and his recorded heart rate. She pictured him lounging on a high bed in a warm, pastel room, and she envied him. Back in the apartment they shared, the heat was erratic and the street below was alive with drug deals throughout the night. Erica was often kept awake by the sound of arguments—somebody being cheated, or cheating someone else.

It was an early winter; December had barely begun, and already the wind was fierce. Erica walked through Washington Square, passing the usual assortment of dealers and homeless people and a bevy of well-bundled NYU film students shooting a scene. Over the years, Erica had watched dozens of such movies being shot in Washington Square Park. Sometimes film students advertised in the *Village Voice* for actors, but since there was no money involved, neither she nor Jordan ever responded. Today a woman in black was sitting on a bench with a parrot on her shoulder; the camera stayed trained on her for minutes.

115

She walked on. A young man at the fountain said, "Hey, baby, I like them fat. More to hold on to," but Erica didn't even flinch, the way she would have a few years before. A few years before, that sort of remark would have been enough to send her to bed for the day. But now she just kept walking, not even stopping to give him the evil eye.

Erica was the kind of woman who was never sprayed with perfume in department stores. She would step off the escalator and watch as the grimly smiling models turned from her and aimed their atomizers elsewhere. All around her were clouds of fragrance, but she walked right between those clouds, untouched. She had become nearly invisible at twenty-four, which was interesting, since there was even *more* of her now than ever. In the past few years Erica had made a conscious decision to "let herself go." Her body had swelled outward in all directions, the ankles thickening, the neck disappearing into her shoulders. She had to dig like an archaeologist to even locate the outline of her bones beneath the skin. The clavicle was several inches under; her fingers found it like a prize.

Jordan didn't care that she had gotten so enormous; in some way, she thought, he liked it, because now the two of them were even more of a perverse couple than they had been, more of a contrast, he with his skinny hips and long, deadpan face, she with all that excess baggage.

"I find the two of you very, very sad," Jordan's mother had said on the telephone. "Something went wrong somewhere." Now Jordan refused to talk to his mother. Occasionally she left messages on the answering machine, but Jordan never returned them. He just listened, unmoved, to his mother's recorded voice, and then he fast-forwarded the message until her voice was distorted into a high-pitched animal squeal, like a Chipmunk Christmas record, urgent and meaningless.

Soon Erica stopped talking to her own mother. It started the first day that Dottie came to visit. "My God," Dottie had said, picking her way across the cluttered living room. "How can you two live like this?" She had brought with her a little potted fern, and she held it tightly between both hands, suddenly unwilling to relinquish it to this new environment.

116

Was there anything sadder, Erica thought, than grown children being descended upon by their parents? *This is it*, you said to each other. *This is what I've become.* Dottie sat on the ratty futon couch in a bright blue dress, and when she got up to leave twenty minutes later, her entire back was coated with white cat hair. They had no cat; the couch had belonged to Jordan's brother, who kept a houseful of pets. When Dottie stood to put on her coat, Erica and Jordan stared at her back, not saying a word. It was a private moment, a mean joke shared between them. Dottie would go to lunch at the Four Seasons covered in cat hair. No one there would say a word either, not even the maitre d'.

"Please, Erica," Dottie said again at the door. "Think about what I said. And it wouldn't hurt if you spruced yourself up, too. If it's money . . ." she said, and her voice trailed off as she opened the clasp of her purse.

"It's not money," Erica said, but she accepted fifty dollars anyway, and then felt regretful about it all night. She lay in bed with Jordan, thinking about the strained afternoon and how her mother's critical eye had roamed the apartment, looking for a good place to land.

"I can't see her anymore," Erica announced.

"Why not?" said Jordan. "At least she gives you money; that's better than my parents. Mine just want to *talk*, no cash involved."

But whenever Dottie called now and asked Erica to come visit, to at least come talk things over, Erica said no. "If I've offended you in some way," Dottie said, "then I apologize. But you do live in squalor, Erica, and I couldn't help but say so. You know I always speak my mind."

Erica wanted to be disowned; she wanted to be cut loose, legitimately disenfranchised. "Please," Dottie said. "I know we haven't been close. I know I haven't been the best mother, but I feel as though you're punishing me, Erica."

"I'm not punishing you," Erica said, and she knew she had to get off the telephone quickly, for she was afraid she might say things she hadn't prepared. Sometimes words tumbled out against your will, but you were responsible for them anyway. "I need to be alone with Jordan," Erica said. "For now, it's what I need."

117

"All right, if you insist," said Dottie, her voice cold. After that day, Dottie began sending Erica letters. In each one, she asked Erica to reconsider, to at least call and talk. "If you want," Dottie wrote, "we can go into mother-daughter therapy. I'm sure such a thing exists; everything *else* does these days." Erica didn't answer any of the letters, and after a while they just stopped coming. Slowly, Dottie began to fade from view.

Sometimes at night, Erica looked out the window and thought about her mother, imagined her sitting in the window of the apartment on Central Park West. "I'm home, kids!" Dottie would say, flinging open the door, but it was a few years too late. One daughter was off at Yale, of all places, and the other one was living "in squalor," in Alphabet City.

Nobody had thought that Erica and Jordan would stay together so long. Erica herself had thought they were through after she had gone to visit him that summer, many years before, at computer camp. But Jordan had returned to Headley in the fall and found that he was powerless again. He had had a brief summer of popularity among other outcasts, but at the end of August all the outcasts were sent back to their cringing lives. Jordan approached Erica at the water fountain one day in September of their junior year at Headley and asked if she wanted to come home with him again. He did not plead; he spoke simply, and she nodded in response.

That afternoon, lying once again in his bed, she knew that they would stay together for the long run. Perhaps it was by default, but she didn't dwell on this point. Jordan was back, his body still hard and brown from summer, but soon he would soften again, and the color would drain from him, and the equation would once again make sense.

Even when high school ended and they separated for college, Erica was not worried. She somehow knew that neither of them would do too well on their own, and that they would return to each other when the four years were done. She had discouraged Jordan from applying to schools where he might once again wield some offbeat, microchip-generated power.

"Why go to MIT and live under your brother's shadow?" she said, and he finally agreed. The MIT application lay untouched

118

beneath his bed for months. Jordan ended up at Michigan, which was such a vast metropolis of a university that no one ruled, no one was in power. Erica ended up at Bennington, mostly because they agreed to take her. Her high-school grades were bad and her S.A.T. scores disappointing, but she had written her admissions essay from the point of view of herself at ninety looking back on her entire life, and Bennington went for that sort of thing.

What Erica remembered most from college was the relentless snow that fell all winter, and the string of parties held in the Carriage Barn: big, noisy mixers with tropical themes, and blue drinks sloshing in coconut shells. All around her, great quantities of dope were smoked, and the air in dorm rooms never really had a chance to clear. Tentatively, girls slept with boys, or with each other, mixing and matching all the time, so you could never be sure *what* would walk out of someone's room in a towel in the early morning. Erica had no interest in any of this. It wasn't that her body didn't cry out for attention; it certainly did, sometimes with a fierceness that she was positive could be heard across the room at night by her slumbering roommate, Nilda Guy. But still Nilda slept, undisturbed. She was a Hispanic scholarship student from the Bronx. Erica was grateful for the lack of attention Nilda paid her; it allowed her to be left alone, and not have to lie in bed at night unburdening herself from across the room. It had occurred to Erica that what people consisted of, really—or at least what she herself consisted of—was a big, rolling mixture of solid and liquid. Perhaps, she thought, it was in her best interest to *expand* rather than unburden. She would hold on to everything— all of herself, and all of Jordan—gathering it to her the way a mother gathers her children to her in the shopping mall, so no one gets lost. Nothing would slip away now, Erica thought. None of her strength would dwindle. Not a single calorie would burn.

Over Christmas vacation freshman year, Erica returned to the city and went right from the Port Authority to the Strangs' apartment. She and Jordan retreated to his bedroom, which looked the same except for the absence of posters. All that was left behind on the walls were tiny tack marks.

"So what are you taking?" Jordan asked.

119

Erica was confused. What drugs was she taking? No, he meant what courses. She dutifully recited, "Anthro, Macro, Death and the Twentieth-Century Novel, Japanese."

Jordan nodded and reeled off his own list, which consisted of science and math courses. Then he sighed and lay down on the bed. He looked too big for this room, too lanky and sprawling, too old.

"Are you going to stay in Ann Arbor?" Erica asked.

Jordan shrugged. "It sucks," he said, "but I'll probably stay. I can't think of anything else to do. You?"

She nodded. "Me too," she said.

"Same difference," said Jordan, and Erica remembered that this was the way he spoke, sometimes making little sense, and it moved her, the familiarity of it, the comforting rhythm. She straddled Jordan, leaning down over him so her hair was in his face. She still smelled of Greyhound—smoke and disinfectant—but she didn't care. You had to rope men in like steer, Erica knew. You had to find little ways to trick them into loving you, because it might not occur to them otherwise. When Jordan was with her, he remembered what he had forgotten he needed. Now her hands worked the planes of his chest, and he sighed and let his mouth go slack.

They had somehow gotten from there to here, so that now, at twenty-four, she found it difficult to be without him. She visited him in the hospital every day that December, although he always seemed slightly annoyed when she showed up. He was usually sitting up in bed watching television or playing cards with his roommate, a bus driver with emphysema. In the evening the hospital was as lulling as a department store, with its resounding chimes that might have summoned doctors to surgery, or saleswomen to lingerie. Erica arrived just as the dinner trays were being stacked and carted out.

Tonight Jordan was watching a game show and eating canned peaches. His roommate, Ray, was asleep, his breathing a long, slow rasp. Erica whispered at first, but Jordan waved his hand impatiently. "Old Ray here can sleep through everything," he

120

said. "His breathing drowns out all other sounds. He's like a white noise machine."

Jordan looked happier than Erica remembered ever seeing him. His life was pacific here; he floated through the day in his open-backed gown, hair streaming, paper shoes on his shuffling feet. She watched him eat the last of his peaches, and when he was done he lifted the little fluted cup to his lips to swallow a drizzle of syrup.

"They treating you okay?" she asked.

"Just great," he said. "This drug they're giving us, it has interesting side effects. Makes you feel kind of dreamy. We have to describe the way it feels, and I swear, they write down everything you say. If I said to the nurse, 'It makes me feel like my heart is an elevator whooshing through the shaft of life,' she would write it down and it would appear word for word in *The Physician's Desk Reference* in a year."

"When are you coming home?" Erica asked. She hadn't meant to say this, because she knew fully well when he would be back, but somehow it got out. As she expected, Jordan was annoyed.

"We've been through it," he said. "Two weeks minimum, or else I don't get paid; you know that. You can be alone in the apartment for two weeks, can't you, Erica?"

She nodded and looked down. Of course she could be alone; she always had been, and it hadn't ever bothered her before. Erica had never thought there was really a choice. You *were* alone, and that was that; without knowing it, she had adopted a rudimentary existentialist attitude sometime around puberty, and it had stuck.

"You're very dependent on me," Jordan said, and although he pretended to dislike this, his voice sounded boastful.

"We're dependent on each other," Erica tried, and Jordan almost flinched.

"That's your interpretation," he said, turning the television back on. "Think what you want."

What was it, she wondered when visiting hours were over and she was walking back through the dim and gleaming halls, that had made him like this? And what was it, also, that had made her accept it, even need it? Maybe it was because she knew nothing else,

121

and could only guess at what was involved in the love between men and women. She could mimic it pretty well, and sometimes the mimicry cracked open, revealing a tender center. During those times she would forget herself, and say something to Jordan in a hushed, surprising tone, and he would look at her as if she were mad. "What are you *doing?*" he would say, disengaging, and she would find that her arms had been wrapped around him like ivy.

When Erica got back to the apartment, she stood in the darkened doorway for a moment. This went beyond loneliness; she was actually frightened without Jordan there. "Hello?" Erica called out, just to make sure, as if a burglar or murderer would actually answer when called to. But she couldn't stop. "Anybody here?" she went on, in a voice thready and high. They had lived together in three different apartments in the East Village since college. This one was the most inhabitable of the three, but still she was frightened.

Now Erica snapped on the overhead light and watched the roaches zip into the seams where the walls joined the floor. Then she climbed the ladder up into the loft bed. Almost everyone she knew slept up at the ceiling in a loft bed, and the ones who didn't slept close to the floor, on futons. The real sign of adulthood, she thought, would be having a bed of normal height. But everyone's apartment was too small, and a bed was a thing to be hidden from view during daytime hours, away from eye-level. A bed was something you needed to climb up to, or kneel down onto. Erica peered down at the apartment. From this angle, the room looked out of whack; if she stared long enough, it seemed to tilt and list like van Gogh's room at Arles.

There was a shelf up in the loft where she and Jordan stored cookies and a bent tube of spermicide and a television. This last item was a small black and white set that Jordan had purchased on the street. Surprisingly, it worked fine, as long as you didn't want to watch CBS. Erica almost never watched television; it was Jordan who did, and he favored strange shows: relics of the Sixties like "Hawaii Five-O" and "The Mod Squad."

"Oh, oh, look at this!" he would call out. "Peggy Lipton's in a Nehru jacket tonight!" But Erica always ignored him.

Now, alone, she listened to the agonized street-opera outside, and when she had had enough of all the shouting, she turned on the television to drown the sounds out. Erica lay back against the pillows and began to eat from the bag of cookies on the shelf. Mallomars were perfect, as round and smooth as doorknobs. She wolfed them down happily and watched a talk show on which all the guests appeared to be losers. Maybe she could rush over to the studio in a cab and be allowed on the air to tell her own story.

The first guests tonight were the most terrifying couple Erica had ever seen. It seemed that twenty years before, when they were dating, the woman had decided to break up with the man. In a rage, he bought some lye, poured it in a Dixie cup, and threw it in the woman's face. If he couldn't have her, he reasoned, then no one could. The woman was blinded and disfigured, and the man, in his intense guilt and continuing passion, took care of her and soon they were in love again, and eventually they got married. Now they had written a book explaining their story. "We have been virtual pariahs," the woman was saying. She wore dark glasses and had a high head of jet-black hair. "No one will be friends with us," she said. "As soon as they hear our story, they don't want anything to do with us. But they just don't understand."

Her husband squeezed her hand and moved closer. "That's right," he said. "I love this lady very much. She means the world to me, and always has."

Erica could not turn away from the set. She imagined them at night, getting ready to make love, Mr. Lye gingerly removing Mrs. Lye's dark glasses, revealing a set of eyes as empty as a statue's. He had rendered her blind, and now they would be together always— she with her neediness and he with his overwhelming burden of guilt. That was enough, it seemed, to keep people bonded for life.

The television show dissolved to a commercial. Erica couldn't move; she was groggy from sugar, dazed by the testimony of Mr. and Mrs. Lye. And then something happened: An old dog whistle went off, silent to the world but audible to her. Erica leaned closer

123

to the screen. She had heard a voice, a familiar summons. *"Are you a large woman?"* the voice asked, and Erica dutifully answered, "Yes," as though she were being administered a psychological exam by a graduate student. *"Do you hide inside unfashionable fashions, embarrassed to show your body?"* the voice went on.

"Yes," Erica said again, "oh, yes," and then the screen was filled with Dottie Engels.

11

Her father lived at Sixteen Coconut Court. All day Opal conjured up images of that street: its small, pastel houses shaded by exotic foliage, its automatic sprinklers turning on in the morning and off at night. Finally, she saw her father walking out onto the porch of number sixteen, reaching his hand into the mailbox, his fingers curling around the edges of what would soon prove to be her letter.

She wished she had never written him. It wasn't that her letter revealed anything personal; in fact, it was brief and unremarkable:

> Dear Norm Engels,
>   I am not sure why I am writing you, but you have been on my mind lately, which I suppose is normal, considering. To make a long story short, I was wondering if you have any interest in corresponding with me. It wouldn't have to be on a regular basis or anything; I'm just curious to know some details about your life, and maybe tell you some details about mine. I'll leave it at that for now. Please write, if you're so inclined.
>
>   Opal

Opal remembered the kinds of letters Dottie used to send back to her fans, how they were trimmed with extravagant punctuation. "Dear Susan," Dottie would write. "Thanks very much for your kind words!!! I'm *so* glad I make you laugh. That's my job!!! Love & polka dots, Dottie Engels."

Opal had gotten her father's address from a Miami telephone directory in the reference room of the library. He was the only Norman Engels listed, and as she sat with her finger poised beneath his name, it struck her as peculiar that she had never looked him up before, that she had never really been curious. But Dottie had eclipsed that curiosity, had stood directly in its light.

Opal wondered what her father's reply would be like. Certainly he would be surprised to hear from her, but not too surprised. In all probability, Norm still thought about her, about *all* of them, fairly often. He couldn't simply have erased an ex-wife and two daughters. Or maybe he could have. It was impossible for her to guess what Norm Engels would think when he went out onto his porch and opened his mailbox. He might stare quizzically at the letter for a while, letting the facts settle. *Once I had another family,* he would remember. But then his new wife would call to him from inside the house, where a ceiling fan spun slowly above her as she lay in bed. "Norm, any mail?" she would ask in a sleepy voice, and he would have to call back no, there was nothing important, just a circular, just a throwaway.

You could never predict anyone else's response, Opal knew. Most people had hidden itineraries, and the surface never matched what rolled around beneath. Weeks passed and her father did not write back. She checked her mailbox at Yale Station each morning, but all she ever received were notices of academic warning, each one more threatening than the last.

When the dean finally telephoned and insisted she come talk to him immediately, Opal felt a surprising wave of relief. "Come in, come in," he called when she arrived, and Opal walked past his secretary and into the bright office. Dean Marsden was springing up and down in his chair like a baby in a bouncer.

"It's one of these Scandinavian kneeling chairs," he explained. "Ever seen them? Very good for the back." He kept springing as he talked. He asked Opal if she was happy at Yale, and she admitted that lately she was not, that she couldn't focus on her work. She had "personal problems," she said, knowing that this was the kind of vague term that kept you immune to further probing. Opal sat in Dean Marsden's office for twenty minutes, and by the end of

126

the meeting she had agreed to his suggestion that she take next semester off. This was not a punishment, the dean said; it was important to him that she understood as much. It was merely a helpful measure designed to give her some time to "rethink" her commitment to undergraduate life. She could definitely come back to school in September; there would be a room waiting for her on campus. He spoke in a decent, careful voice, and Opal felt like Julie Andrews being sent away from the convent in *The Sound of Music.*

Then she remembered something. "What about my mail?" she asked.

"Your mail?" The dean stopped bouncing.

"Will it be forwarded to me, or can I have someone pick it up from my mailbox?" Opal asked. Her father would be writing to her soon; it was important that his letter did not get sent to the apartment, where Dottie would find it.

"Well," said the dean, "I'm sure you could have a friend pick up your mail for you. You'll still retain your mailbox. We think of this as a *leave*; it's not permanent. Look," he said, "would you like me to approach your parents? It might make it easier." But Opal said she would do it herself.

When she got back to her room she called her mother, who listened as Opal stuttered out the news. When Opal was done, Dottie told her it wasn't terrible, it wasn't the end of the world. "I don't want you to crack up under all that pressure," Dottie said. "I've read about kids who freak out at these pressure-cooker schools."

"You're not angry?" Opal said. "Or disappointed?"

"No," said Dottie. "So it's not the best time in the world for you. So we're both having a little trouble. Look, Opal, you'll come home and we'll spend time together. We won't starve; we won't have to do a mother-daughter act on skid row." She was quiet for a minute. "I think I should tell you something, though," she said, her voice strange. Opal tensed. "I've met someone," Dottie said.

For a moment Opal didn't know what her mother was talking about. The phrase, coming from Dottie, made no sense. Opal thought for a moment. "Like a man?" she asked.

127

Dottie laughed. "Yes, '*like* a man.' To my knowledge he *is* a man, in fact."

Opal felt her whole body flex, then stiffen. Over the years she had assumed that her mother had taken occasional lovers. There had sometimes been men in Dottie's hotel suites when she was on tour, and as a child Opal had heard sounds in the background over the telephone: the flushing of a toilet, or laughter that was frankly male. "Just a minute, Opal," her mother would say, then she would cover the phone so all Opal could hear was something that sounded like the captive roar inside a seashell. Dottie had never come out and actually spoken of these men, and Opal had assumed they were just accessories and didn't really count. Dottie had always seemed self-contained: a huge, autonomous machine that ate and joked and generated its own heat and light.

But now Dottie was talking about this man, Sy Middleman, and saying that she wasn't sure she was falling in love, but that she felt comfortable with Sy. "It's just the thing I need," Dottie said. "It makes me forget about my problems for a little while. I thought I should tell you now, before you come home, so you're not too shocked. Sy's been spending a lot of time around the apartment."

Opal listened as her mother told her the story of how she had met him. Sy was a garment manufacturer who had been called in as a consultant for the Dottie Engels Collection, and he was the only man who would listen to Dottie's ideas, the only one who paid any attention when she got up the nerve to speak during merchandising meetings.

"When you get home, I'll tell you everything," Dottie said to Opal. "We'll stay up all night talking."

"All right," said Opal, but her voice faltered.

"Will you be okay until then?" Dottie asked. "You know, taking a semester off isn't the end of the world. If you need it, then you shouldn't be ashamed. And advertising a line of clothes isn't the worst thing either. We've got to keep these things in perspective, both of us."

That night Opal sat on her bed and looked around her small dormitory room, trying to memorize its dimensions, the molding

128

around the doors and windows, the slope of the floor. In a week she would start to dismantle this room, taking down the print of the *Arnolfini Wedding Portrait* from the wall and the books from the shelves. Her friends, when they heard the news, would come to visit one by one. As a joke, Peter would cover the mirror and Tamara would wear black.

I am being *suspended*, Opal would explain, and the word implied that she was still somehow fastened in place. But that wasn't what she felt at all; what she felt was that she, too, was slipping. It was a part of her lineage: a family act that performed without a net.

She should have been buoyed up by the fact that her mother had fallen in love, but somehow she was dubious. What kind of man could Dottie love? she wondered, and what kind of man could love Dottie? Opal tried to imagine someone substantial enough, someone tough and generous and a little raucous. The only person who fit this description was Dottie Engels herself. Dottie was hopelessly reflexive, Opal thought; she would have to have herself cloned if she wanted true companionship.

"Your mother is an original," the baby-sitters used to say, watching Dottie perform on late-night television. It didn't seem likely that Dottie had really found her match; what seemed likelier was that she was desperate, and in her desperation she had begun to flail. She would take *anything*: an ad campaign for fat women's clothing, and a man who listened to her when everyone else no longer would. The thought of Sy Middleman depressed Opal in advance.

"So?" Tamara would say, if Opal told her about Sy. "So what's the big deal? Your mother's a grown woman, she hasn't been married to your father for ages. I think it's nice that she's finally found someone. It isn't *your* life, you know. Leave her alone already."

But Opal dreamed about her mother, saw her laughing and talking with poise on a talk-show stage. She saw the familiar sweep of dotted material, and the head of hair blown up like a skillet of Jiffy-Pop. Opal clung to this image, even though it no longer

129

existed. But that was all that anybody was left with, really: a series of stills that could be brought out and sifted through occasionally, as though visiting the permanent collection of a small museum. That was the only way Opal could maintain contact with her family, the only way she could get them all together.

The desire to keep a family together seemed primitive. Opal remembered watching *The Parent Trap*, in which Hayley Mills, playing identical twins, schemed to reunite her mother and father. There had been something frighteningly determined about the awkward split-screen image of those twins manipulating their parents' lives, forcing them into an awkward meeting and finally an embrace.

But all Opal wanted was to see everyone in the same room. It was a simple, visceral desire. She wanted to line her family up, the way she used to line up her stuffed animals on a windowsill. No one kept *still* in this family; everyone kept springing free and disappearing for extended periods of time. She thought again of her father, and wondered if he would write her this week. Then she began to think of Erica.

The last time Opal had telephoned Erica, it had been at Dottie's request. "Please," Dottie had said, "call your sister up and make sure she's all right. I'm so worried about her, down there in the East Village, living God knows what sort of a life, and she doesn't want to talk to me. Do it for me, Opal, and *don't* tell her I told you to call."

So Opal dialed her sister's number, and was relieved that it was Erica who answered and not her terrible boyfriend. "I just called to say hi," Opal said. She glanced up at Dottie, who had busied herself at the other end of the room and was actively pretending not to listen.

Erica's voice was level. "Is Mom there?" she asked.

"No, of course not," said Opal.

"Put her on," Erica said, and Opal went silent. Then she shrugged and held out the telephone to her mother. Erica was not stupid; she knew she had been set up, and Opal didn't blame her for being angry. There wasn't exactly an antagonism between the sisters; that was too forceful a word. It was just easier, Opal knew,

130

for Erica not to have to *think* about this failure of a family. And yet there were times when Opal longed to talk to her. She wished they still had their walkie-talkies from childhood, and could signal each other when they were feeling bored or melancholy. She remembered the way Erica's voice would split right through the layers of static.

Opal wanted to come out and say: *Our mother has fallen in love.* She could imagine Erica's sharp intake of air, then the slow release. No shit, Erica would say. Tell me all about it. And Opal would launch into everything she knew, filling in the blanks. Maybe she would even tell Erica that she had written to their father. She didn't even *like* Erica anymore; she was embarrassed at how Erica had turned out, so big and formless, so freaky, and yet Erica had *been* there over the years; she was the only other witness.

Opal's suspension began on a Sunday. She packed her dorm room up in boxes and had them shipped to New York, and then she took the train down by herself in the early evening. When she arrived at the apartment, she rang the buzzer three times but there was no reply, so Opal let herself in. The apartment was odorless and quiet, but the living room was softly lit. Dottie was probably home.

"Hello!" Opal called, putting her knapsack and keys down on the hall table.

"In here!" her mother called back, and Opal headed in the direction of the voice. She found her mother in her bedroom, sitting in front of the vanity in a kimono. Dottie stood and embraced her, and Opal let herself be wrapped for a moment in fabric and perfume, while her mother asked about the trip, about her mood, about whether or not she was hungry.

"You're getting all dressed up," Opal said when they had disengaged and Dottie was sitting back at the vanity, fiddling with the back of a pearl earring. "Are you going somewhere?" Opal asked, and Dottie told her that she was going out for the evening with Sy.

"I hate to be away your first night home," Dottie said, "but Sy got these tickets ages ago. Bobby Short. I figured you could amuse yourself for tonight."

131

Sy arrived half an hour later, before Dottie had finished dressing, and Opal let him in. He was short and soft around the edges, with a damp, downturned mustache. Sy appeared loud and coarse and amiable all at the same time, and he possessed one surprising feature: his clothes. As a garment manufacturer, he had access to elegant, beautiful clothes: unstructured linen suits in pale wheat tones, ties with intricate, delicate patterns etched in the weave, Italian shoes that were as glossy and tapered as race cars.

"I think I'll wander around until your old mother is ready," Sy said after he and Opal had shaken hands and exchanged a few awkward words in the doorway.

It was clear that Sy had spent a lot of time in the apartment, and Opal watched as he walked casually through the living room. He picked a few browning leaves off a coleus, and then he plucked a handful of pistachios from a silver bowl on the table. Finally he sat down on the couch and unfolded the daily crossword puzzle from his breast pocket. "Care to join me?" he asked, but Opal shook her head. "I'm a fanatic about puzzles," he said, and he uncapped his pen and gazed off into space for the answer to the first clue.

Finally Dottie was ready. She entered the room quietly, her perfume slightly preceding her, and Opal saw that she was wearing one of the dresses from her line of clothes. Her hair was swept up off her neck, and her head seemed smaller than usual. Or was it just that her body was *larger* than usual? Since she had fallen in love with Sy, Dottie seemed to have been eating more than she used to. Sy believed in excess, Dottie said, and he often took her to twelve-course banquets at a dumpling house on Mott Street. He referred to her flesh as "love handles," and he grabbed her by the waist and swung her around like a Tilt-a-Whirl.

Opal watched her mother and Sy together, saw the way they touched frequently, using small, understated gestures. Dottie lightly fingered his collar, and he rested a hand on her hip as they stood at the door.

"We'll be home very late," Dottie said. "You know where everything is; just help yourself." Then they were off. Opal stood and stretched, listening for a moment to the uncompromising quiet of the apartment. There was no chorus of stereos up and down the hallway, no whiffs of dope and hot-plate cuisine, no one accidentally setting off a fire alarm with a Frisbee. All she could hear was the intermittent hum and whir of the refrigerator making ice, and the sound was lulling, deadening. She knew she would have to do something while she lived here, or else the semester would just keep unrolling, with Dottie and Sy breezing in and out of the apartment and Opal stationed once again before the TV.

Two days later, Opal sat in a chair in Ross Needler's office while the lights on his telephone blinked and a secretary kept coming in to silently hand him pink memos. Opal glanced above his head at the assortment of photographs on the wall. Somewhere up there, in that collage of faces, loomed her mother. Opal tried to peer at the wall surreptitiously.

"Top row," Ross said, "all the way on the left."

Opal was embarrassed. "Sorry," she said.

"Why be sorry?" Ross asked. "If my mother was on somebody's wall, I'd want to look too."

"Not if it was the post office," Opal said.

"Very quick," said Ross. "Just like your mother." He sighed and leaned back in his chair. "Look, I don't know of any real jobs," he said. "Nothing that pays, anyway. You have no experience whatsoever, and you're young. I could maybe find you an internship, but it would be scut work. Nothing challenging, but you might have fun. In fact," he said, "I do know someone who owes me a small favor. If you'll bear with me, I'll see what I can do."

She watched as he spun a fat Rolodex file. Years before, Ross used to squeeze the flesh of her face and call her "kiddo," and he would bring an armload of presents when he came to the apartment. He and Dottie would sit in the den all night, and Ross would have a big notebook open on the coffee table, or sometimes an adding machine. Together, they figured out salaries, schemes, dates for performances. The room always seemed rosy and swollen with smoke.

Ross hadn't changed dramatically since then, Opal thought. He had always looked old to her, his face long and lined. Now Ross made a few brief phone calls, and finally he located an assistant

133

director friend who said he would probably be able to give Opal an internship at the television show "Rush Hour." It was strictly gofer work, Ross warned her when he hung up. "The staff is young and smart," he said, "and the ratings are good, as you know, so there's a decent morale around the set. They've already been renewed for next season."

"Rush Hour" had been enormously popular at Yale. There always seemed to be a group of people clustered around someone's television set every Friday night at ten to watch it. The show had a frenetic, young cast: souped-up, razzing men and women who sang and danced and improvised their way through the hour. The format was modeled after the old "Mickey Mouse Club," with cast members lining up and calling out their names at the beginning of each show. One of the men would always announce himself as "Annette."

Before Opal could thank him, Ross said, "I wonder what your mother will say."

Opal shrugged. "She'll be pleased, I hope," she said. "She thought it was great that I was coming to see you."

"Well," said Ross, "I once mentioned 'Rush Hour' to her, just in passing. I was talking about how there was a new wave of young talent out there, and your mother argued that there hasn't been a decent comedy show on TV for years. It's hard for her, I guess; you really can't blame her." Opal agreed. "You know," he said, "she's had a long, solid career. Over ten years. Compare that with most other performers, and it's incredible. Dancers are lucky if they last until twenty-five—their knees go and they get arthritis— and singers' voices are shot way before they're old. Some of the folksingers from the Sixties—those girls with their long hair and sweet voices—they sound like crap now, they really do. You can hear them on all the telethons. Dottie isn't necessarily *done* yet, you know."

"Do you think she could really make a comeback?" Opal asked.

"Oh, who knows?" said Ross. "A career gets sleepy for a while, so you put it on hold. I've seen people snap back like you wouldn't believe. They appear somewhere for the first time in years, and then they get letters from people saying, 'Oh, we thought you were

134

dead.' There's a chance of reincarnation for your mother; she's just got to be patient." He shook his head. "I just want to make sure that she's doing all right, you know, emotionally. I thought maybe you could tell me that."

"My mother's fine," Opal said. "Really." Ross kept watching her, waiting for her to elaborate. "She's fallen in love," Opal added in a small voice, and she realized, as soon as she said it, how much she had wanted to tell someone. She looked for his response.

"Oh?" Ross said. "That's news. I'm glad to hear it. Anyone I know?" Opal told him about Sy. "Your mother deserves to be in love," Ross went on. "It's been a long time."

He fingered a few of the pink sheets of paper on his desk, and Opal stood awkwardly to leave, thanking him for his help. She had told him about Dottie, and now it was done. It didn't matter that she had told *him*, particularly; what mattered was the simple act of telling.

Opal thought back to the monologues she had listened to as a child, the rush of words that had poured out at her over the years. "Just listen to this," Dottie had said. "Just listen to this," the baby-sitters had said, and Opal had sat very still in her chair, patiently listening, until all the words ran out.

12

When Jordan left the hospital, he refused to take his identification bracelet off. Erica was reminded of those girls in her high school who had worn POW and MIA bracelets even when it became apparent that no one was ever coming home. There had been something dramatic about it, the way the girls had compared wrists in study hall, reciting unfamiliar names as though they were the names of lovers. Now Jordan lay in the loft, his long arm dangling over the edge as he slept. Erica walked by and saw the strip of plastic, his own name typed in faint purple ink. He had been wearing the bracelet for weeks now.

Jordan hadn't been able to find any more work through the back of the *Village Voice,* and so he began to spend the days at home. Erica had no trouble finding surveys of overweight women; these seemed boundless. Between the two of them, though, they had very little money, and Jordan was down to cashing the last of his bar mitzvah savings bonds. He decided, at the end of December, that he would try to sell drugs—nothing serious or scary, he said, just a small-fry operation—and so he got several names from his brother, a chemist who used to supply everyone at MIT.

Erica objected at first; she stood over him in the kitchen as he sat at the table, sifting and separating. "It's dangerous," she said. "You could get arrested. I could get arrested." Jordan didn't respond; he just kept working. Finally she gave in and watched; there was something gradually mesmerizing about the quick movements of his hands. He folded pages out of magazines into little origami packages that held half-grams of cocaine. Erica watched as he measured out the powder and poured it onto a color photograph of Miss Clairol, and she understood then how a pioneer wife must have felt watching her husband clean and load a gun.

Jordan's first customers would be coming over in half an hour. Erica found herself walking about the apartment before they arrived, taking little swipes at the furniture with a cloth; this was the closest thing to *company* they had ever had. When the downstairs buzzer rang, she flew down to open the outside door. Two teenage girls stood on the stoop bundled up in bright ski parkas. "We're looking for Jordan," one said.

Erica stared, then let them in. She flattened herself against the wall and let them go up ahead of her. The girls were about sixteen, she guessed. They smelled of snow and shampoo, and they took the stairs two at a time. "Cute apartment," one said when they were inside. They opened their jackets and shook their long dark hair free.

Jordan came out of the kitchen then, holding a large mirror as though it were a tray of hors d'oeuvres. "You're Mandy and Parker?" he said, and they nodded. "Want to try some of the sniff before you go?"

Erica cringed. As usual, Jordan had his terminology wrong, but the girls didn't know. They sat on the ratty couch while Jordan opened the little packet and sliced up a few thin lines on the mirror he had taken down from over the dresser. Erica had had to use guesswork to make a part in her hair that morning. Now she stood in the doorway and watched as two shining heads bobbed down over the round mirror. The girls inhaled loudly, like truffle pigs.

They stayed for hours, doing lines and talking happily. Both of them, it turned out, were seniors at Headley. Jordan seemed thrilled to have them here, and Erica realized, with true surprise, that he was actually flirting with them. He was sitting up straighter than usual, his voice lively, and he was in no great hurry to have them leave.

"Is Mr. Catapano still teaching math?" Jordan asked.

Parker rolled her eyes. "What an old ass," she said.

"Exactly!" said Jordan, his voice rising. "He'd be drawing a

137

rhombus at the blackboard and he'd nod off." Jordan sliced out another set of lines, more vigorously than before; his hand shook, and the lines came out streaky and thick as skywriting. "Is that awful mural still up?" he asked. "The one with Susan B. Anthony and Helen Keller and everybody?"

From the way he was speaking, Erica thought, you would think he had been president of the student body. Jordan was suddenly infused with nostalgia for a place he had despised, a place that had despised him. And now he was chumming around with two girls who thought he was something because he could get them what they wanted.

Erica felt like an old fishwife standing in the background. She walked through the small rooms aimlessly. Next time, she thought, she ought to wear a housecoat and pink scuffs on her feet; that would complete the picture. As it was, the two girls weren't paying her any attention. They were doing imitations for Jordan of one of the English teachers. Mandy was standing up and saying, "People. Pee-*pull*! Remember, it's *your* time you're wasting, not just mine."

When the sky darkened and they were finally about to leave, Jordan was bouncing up and down a little on his heels. "Any time," he said. "Call any time, day or night." Then he carried the mirror back into the bedroom.

The two girls pulled on their coats, and Erica was suddenly seized with need. She opened the door to let them out, then spoke quickly. "Look," she whispered in the hallway, "he was very unpopular in high school. We both were. You would have hated him, really. You would have made fun of him."

The two girls stared at each other, their faces suddenly emptied of expression, a trick they must have taught themselves to keep from cracking up at moments like this. Without saying a word, they were gone. Within seconds, Erica could hear them howling in the stairwell.

After that day, Jordan put all his energy into the business. Erica would walk into the apartment and find the stereo blasting, and Jordan sitting in the kitchen, bent over what looked like a small city of anthills. Erica didn't really like cocaine, and didn't understand what all the excitement was about, all those articles she had

138

read about white mice mangling each other to get at a dropper of spiked water. Sometimes at night Jordan would bring the mirror up into the loft and slice out a few careful lines. What startled Erica most was seeing her own reflection, big and wavy and florid in the glass. It was too close, too much; how were you supposed to relax when you were practically touching foreheads with yourself? And the sensation itself was nothing more than a kind of thready anxiety followed by a viscous, bitter drip down the back of the throat. For some reason, everyone in the world wanted to be anxious, wanted to be hopped up. Erica was the exception, the mouse that stayed curled in the corner, ignoring the shadow of the dropper overhead.

She wondered if Jordan was really interested in cocaine, either; what he liked best, she thought, was the company. People suddenly came to him—called on the phone and showed up night after night. Mandy and Parker returned, and they sent some of their friends as well. Jordan began playing host to every twelfth-grader in New York. The apartment had a steady hum to it, the buzzer going, the stereo playing. "Put on an album; whatever you like," Jordan would say magnanimously to sixteen-year-old boys, because he knew it was their idea of heaven.

Boys with transparent mustaches would crouch down over the records, or stand at the bookshelf going through Jordan's science-fiction collection. "Oh, God!" they would say, slapping their heads. "You have a first edition of *Alpha State Centurions!*"

Erica was the housemother of them all; she brewed sun tea on the kitchen window and stocked the cabinets with extra Pepperidge Farm cookies, even though the bugs got to them within hours. There were bugs everywhere in the apartment, and they didn't care if you watched them or not, that was how nervy they were. In the morning they staggered off Erica's toothbrush, drunk on fluoride.

She had to get out; everything was too close, too much. One morning she went over to NYU to take part in another study. The graduate student running it was obese himself, which surprised her. His name was Mitchell Block, and he had a large, intelligent face smothered in a beard. Everything about him was drawn on a much larger scale than ordinary; he looked like one of those plaster lumberjack statues that stand outside pancake houses off interstate highways.

Scale was always a source of fascination; Erica still remembered looking at a Diane Arbus photograph in high school called "Jewish Giant at Home with his Parents," and how she had cried out softly when she first saw it. The young giant had towered above his bewildered, shrunken parents, ducking so as not to go through their ceiling. When you were big, whether it was tall or wide, you worried that no place could contain you, that you were taking up too much space in the universe, swallowing too much air.

"Erica," Mitchell Block said, his voice soft. "Erica, listen closely."

When he spoke her name, she felt a chill ripple across her forearms; it was as though he somehow *knew* things about her. But her name was typed plainly on the index card he held between his fingers. He had probably sat there all morning, saying, "Susan, Susan, listen closely; Michelle, Michelle, listen closely." And those overweight women, peering out from inside their caves, had suddenly become alert, because no one had called them by name in years, and no one's voice had ever carried so far inside the cave.

Mitchell said they were going to play word association, and Erica wanted very much to do well; perhaps, she thought, she could respond in a way that would make him think he was really onto something significant here. He would say "food," and without skipping a beat she would return with "love." He would say "body," and she would answer "hate." His eyes would widen, and the list of words would come quicker; the two of them would volley for minutes.

But the words he gave her had no logical connection to one another. There was not a single food reference, unless you counted "table," but that was stretching it. When Mitchell had gone down the entire list, he put his pencil down and smiled.

"Thank you, that was fine," he said. "Now comes the time for me to confess something. I wasn't really paying attention to your responses at all. I was just looking at your eye movements; that's what the study is all about. I'm curious to see if very overweight people really feel connected to the world, or whether, even when they're engaged in conversation, they're somewhere else entirely. Hiding in their own world."

"And what did you find?" Erica asked.

Mitchell Block smiled again. "I'm not supposed to go into it," he said. "But let's just say I think you're still living in the real world."

"Oh, I try to drop in whenever I can," said Erica.

He laughed, and she felt herself flush. "Well," he said, pushing back his chair and standing up. "I've got to get on with more of these. But thank you, Erica; I've enjoyed talking to you." He held out his hand, and she felt as though she were grasping a big catcher's mitt, one that was humanly warm.

That night Jordan was jumpy—itchy with the static of winter, and wanting to move around. He stuffed a little lump of cocaine into his nose and let it melt there; he didn't have the patience to go through the whole chopping ceremony. "Let's go out," he said. "Anywhere."

They walked through the lightly falling snow to a bar in the West Village that Jordan said he knew well. He had an embarrassing habit of trying to engage old bartenders in conversation at the end of the night. He would hang around while a bartender ran a rag across the wood. Jordan would sit and swivel on his stool, gnawing a swizzle stick, talking compulsively about anything, nothing. It excited him to be in the company of old men, men whom he thought of as having *lived*. In the spring it was worse; Jordan liked to sit in Washington Square Park, talking to the old chess players who sat concentrating at stone tables. Erica sometimes had to pull him away so the men could finish their game. He was a joke, she thought, although none of the old men ever laughed at him. They just seemed to tolerate him, looking up at him with slow, surprised eyes every time Jordan said something that made no sense.

When Erica and Jordan walked into the bar, it was apparent that it had changed management since Jordan had been there last. Several men stood milling around, a few of them in leather, and others sat by themselves at tables, chairs tilted back against the wall, beers in hand, eyes closing sleepily. On the wall, a television

141

with a screen the size of a picture window showed Joan Collins in close-up, but the sound was turned off. It was a slow night at a gay bar, Erica realized.

Jordan looked perplexed. "It used to be called Paddy's," he whispered. "I'm sure of it. Just a little neighborhood place with a pool table." He walked back outside to peer at the sign over the door. "The Grist Mill," he said. He plucked at the knees of his corduroys. "We can go if you want; you might feel uncomfortable here, being a woman."

"*You* might feel uncomfortable here, being a man," she said.

At that moment the overhead lights clicked out, and a spotlight was pointed on the small platform in the back. Erica quickly sat down to duck the light, and Jordan followed. It was a drag show; the opening number was a decent lip-synch version of "New York, New York." A man was dressed as Liza Minelli, with a black wig plastered to his head, and false eyelashes as big as starfish. "This one's for Mama!" he was saying.

"Do you want to go?" Jordan whispered. "We could sneak out when he's done."

But something made Erica want to stay. Maybe she saw it coming, maybe in some way she knew. She settled in, ordered a Scotch, and watched the show. The man onstage was now doing a medley of Barbra Streisand numbers, crossing his eyes on every other line, saying, "Oh, Mr. Arnstein," straining for laughs. The Wednesday-night audience was small and scattered but polite. They clapped when each song was over, and no one left the bar.

It was right after the requisite Diana Ross number that the man came back onstage in a huge, billowing dress with a polka-dot pattern. The imitation was dead-on: the big spheres of rouge, the fleshy orange lips, the hair piled up like hay. And all the movements were right, too; the man traveled the stage the way Dottie used to—arms flailing, describing circles in the air. "Look, look, is it what I think?" Jordan said. "Is it? Is it?"

She didn't even answer him. She just kept watching as the man launched into one of Dottie's oldest routines. "I went to the circus recently," he was saying, "and I offered to buy the tent. They said fine, and asked if I wanted it wrapped. I said no, I'd *wear* it home!"

142

Erica's heart was thudding furiously. She swallowed what was left of her drink, and kept the ice in her mouth, biting down hard; it felt as though she were breaking rocks in a quarry inside her head. Most people were able to shake themselves free of their parents; most people could just get on a bus one day and disappear. But it was as though her mother was writing in the sky, sending Erica messages that she would see every time she tipped her face up to the sun. First there had been that awful commercial for women's clothing, and now this. Her mother had ceased being actively famous, and Erica had thought it was all over, but apparently Dottie Engels had a half-life—she stayed in the blood forever, you could not get her out. She was always there, with that wide, familiar face, and all those jokes that made you hate yourself because you were big too, made you feel that if you were fat you had better be funny.

"Honey, you're so *serious*," Dottie used to say to Erica. "Lighten up a little, okay?" But Erica would shrug her mother off. At Bennington there had been a group of very heavy, purposeful women who spent all their time hunched around a table in a corner of the dining hall. They were deeply involved in the Women's Task Force and the Rape Crisis Hotline; they were what Dottie would have called "humorless." Once, one of them approached Erica at the salad bar and thrust a petition at her. Erica scrawled her name quickly and slid her tray along the slats. She didn't want to be identified with them, not at all, and she hated herself for it. But just because she looked like them they thought she *was* like them: moon-faced and wounded and well-intentioned.

"Do you want to go?" Jordan whispered now, and they slipped from the bar just as the man onstage was pulling off his Dottie Engels wig and taking a bow.

The next day, something woke Erica up, lifted her from sleep. She was up before Jordan was awake, and before the first of his customers started arriving. She peered at him as she climbed from the loft; Jordan was a mouth breather, and when he slept he often looked as though he were pausing in the middle of a sentence.

Erica zipped up her old green ski jacket and walked downstairs.

143

The morning was exceptionally cold, but she didn't mind. The wind rearranged her hair, blew some of it across her eyes. She marched across town to NYU and headed right for the psychology building. It had become as familiar to her as her own apartment building. She liked the sulphur smell here and the perceptible overlay of animal smell. Erica walked along the hall, peering into the small square windows. In one window a fist of light blossomed from a slide projector, then closed in on itself as the frame changed. Students sat in the dark, heads tilted upward at a screen which Erica could not see.

Several windows down she found Mitchell Block. He was sitting in a small room, and his broad back was to the door. Erica could see the young woman who faced him; she was definitely over-weight, too, and sat with her hands in her lap. Her eyes, Erica noticed, never once raised up to meet his.

13

It stinks," said the voice.

"What?"

"It stinks. No offense to you, of course, but it's just not funny."

Opal had come home late one night, after a taping of "Rush Hour," and found that her mother was waiting up for her. In the dark living room, all Opal could see was the orange point of a cigarette, but Dottie's voice was clear and surprising.

Opal slid her palm along the wall to turn on a light. Her mother was sitting on the couch in a kimono that Sy had given her, with a full ashtray before her on the coffee table. "I just find it a little sophomoric," Dottie went on. "I may not be up on today's trends, granted, but I still know when something doesn't work. Did any of those writers ever see 'Your Show of Shows'? Did any of them ever hear of Sid Caesar?" She paused. "Did any of them ever hear of me?"

Something stirred in Opal then, made her feel an uncoiling of despair. The show was good; there was no question about that. The humor was uneven, and sometimes a joke was run into the ground, but most of the time there was a rhythm that kept the audience excited. The first sketch tonight had been about a support group for men with inadequacy problems, and the patients consisted of actors playing Sonny Bono, Ike Turner, and Tom Hayden. Later in the show there was a mini-musical called "Long Day's Journey into a Hard Day's Night," in which the entire Tyrone family wore mop-head wigs and spoke O'Neill's lines in Liverpool accents. Sitting in the wings with Walt Green, the other

145

college intern, Opal had realized how different this was from watching her mother perform. There wasn't so much at *stake* now; Opal wanted the show to do well, but her whole life wasn't standing onstage, and she didn't need to hold her breath when the houselights lowered.

Now she looked at her mother sitting on the couch, wrapped in a green kimono, her eyes small with exhaustion, and she wanted to lead her to bed like a drowsy child.

"Why don't you sit down awhile?" Dottie said, and Opal reluctantly agreed.

"Is it just me?" Dottie asked.

"Is what you?"

Dottie gestured. "Oh, this whole humor thing," she said. "Not *getting* it. I feel as though I'm from another country—no, another planet—and I'm learning about the local customs. Opal, I just don't *see*. What happened to the old kind of comedy, where you stand on a stage and you talk to the audience conversationally? None of these pyrotechnics. Just a simple routine, maybe a little music to go along with it, a couple of impressions. Now the simplicity is lost."

"I guess," Opal said, "there are other things now. A variety." But her voice was soft and not very believable. Dottie wasn't looking for consolation, she realized; tonight, Dottie just wanted to talk. Opal watched as her mother lit another cigarette and then held out the pack to Opal, which she had never done before. Usually Dottie complained terribly about the fact that Opal smoked. "Just because I have a disgusting habit doesn't mean that *you* should," Dottie sometimes said. But now she was actually striking a match for Opal and holding it out to her, as if to say, *Oh, well; we're all going down.* Opal hesitated, then took a cigarette and leaned forward to meet the light.

"The first time I was on Carson," Dottie began, "I was so nervous, the way everyone is their first time."

Opal nodded, remembering how her mother had called from California the day of the show, and had run through her monologue long-distance while both girls listened on separate extensions.

"The hairstylist backstage was telling me little anecdotes about other people who had been on," Dottie said, "except she kept calling them 'antidotes.' When you finally get onstage, the lights are so hot that you sweat like a pig, but you're supposed to pretend that you're at this wonderful cocktail party. If that was really a party, I would have left in five minutes and hosed myself down. But I just had to sit there, and after a while I got used to it, and they liked me, as you know. I was funny," she said. "Not to blow my own horn, but I really think I was pretty funny."

There was a sound from across the room. Opal looked up to find Sy standing in the doorway in his matching kimono. "I thought you were funny," said Sy. "You certainly made *me* laugh back then." He yawned, struggling to wake up.

"Where's that record?" Dottie suddenly asked. "You know, the one we were listening to just the other day." She stood up slowly, steadying herself, and walked across the room to the shelf of record albums. She flipped through them for a minute until she found what she wanted; it was the first record Dottie had ever made, a live concert album entitled *Everything's Coming Up Dottie*. She slipped the record from its sleeve. The record was deeply scarred from use, but it was unmistakably Dottie's voice that blazed through the rooms.

"Dot, the neighbors will call the police," Sy said, but he sat down to listen.

Opal watched her mother's face, saw the pleasure Dottie was taking from this, her lips moving silently to accompany each spoken word.

"You know," Dottie was saying on the record, "I've been asked to be on 'Hollywood Squares.' I only hope they don't put me on the top row, because the whole thing would collapse!" There was a wave of laughter. When it ended, Dottie went on. "The bags under my eyes are so heavy," she said, "I even had the delivery boy carry them home for me the other day!" Another wave, and then some applause. "You like that?" the younger Dottie said. "I'm glad, because there's plenty more where that came from."

When the record ended, Dottie's eyes were shining. "Well, ladies, I guess we should turn in," Sy quickly said. "I've enjoyed this trip down memory lane, but I, for one, need my beauty sleep."

147

Opal watched as Sy held out his hand to Dottie. After they had gone, Opal stayed up for a while. She picked up *Everything's Coming Up Dottie*. The cover art depicted a field of huge sunflowers, but in the center of each flower was a photograph of her mother's face. Opal wondered what it would be like to go from being everywhere—from populating an entire field—to occupying one small space. Her mother was physically larger than ever, but there were no longer multiple images of her wherever Opal looked. Right now Dottie and Sy were getting ready for sleep—taking off their kimonos and climbing into bed. Opal imagined them sleeping together—sleeping, not making love—their bodies shifting to accommodate each other, changing shape throughout the night like sand dunes.

Next to Opal on the couch was the crossword puzzle Sy had been working on that day; she picked it up and saw that all the squares had been filled in. When she looked more closely, though, she realized that several answers made no sense. Sy had filled in words just to have the satisfaction of completing the grid. She glanced up at the clues. *Author Anaïs*, read 24 Across, and Sy had filled in *Pin. Anaïs Pin*; it almost made Opal cry out. Sy was a decent man, and right now he was lying next to Dottie. "You make do with what you're given in this life," Dottie used to say. "I'm no Twiggy, so I use my weight; I throw it around a little. Is that so bad?"

It was better, wasn't it, than what most people had? Back when they all lived in Jericho, Opal and Erica had had a code phrase for the times their mother cried. "Pink eyeshadow alert," Erica would whisper, poking her head into the doorway of Opal's room. With Sy, there would be very little crying. Instead, there would only be peaceful sleeping, and Chinese meals that went on and on in a parade of silver dishes. Maybe it was sheer companionship that Dottie wanted; maybe after a certain point in life, that was enough.

Opal took for granted the fact that she would always have a knot of people around her. At Yale, she woke up to the sound of voices in the morning, and fell asleep to those same voices at night. But now, back in the apartment, the pitch had lowered,

148

the voices were fewer; you had to fend for yourself here, make your own noise.

She realized that every day at work she inordinately looked forward to spending time with Walt Green. He had become her companion, her sidekick, the only person there she really spoke to. Opal spent much of her time at work at the Xerox machine or picking up props from a manufacturer downtown. She was treated well by Joel Macklin, the assistant director who had hired her, and largely ignored by most everyone else. A couple of the writers occasionally asked her how she was getting along, but there was a nervous, dislocated atmosphere in the studio that made extended interaction unlikely. The cast members kept away from everyone else and remained in quarantine down the hallway where their dressing rooms were. Sometimes Opal would see them slip back and forth between each other's rooms, like characters in a bedroom farce.

On Friday nights Opal sat in the wings with Walt, while all around them men and women in headphones cued each other for sound and lights. Once Opal watched one of the cast members, a wiseguy named Stevie Confino, preparing to go onstage. He stood only a foot away from her, and she watched as he exhaled a few hard, short breaths and faked a small feint to the left, like a boxer about to duck through the ropes and into the ring. Opal thought of her mother, pictured her standing backstage, blotting her lipstick and waiting anxiously for a cue.

At lunch hour, she and Walt went off by themselves to a coffee shop on Seventh Avenue. Walt was a junior at Columbia who had taken a year off from school to work at the show. He spoke freely about the job in a way that impressed Opal, made her relax. He also asked her questions about herself, seemed to want her to talk. When he told a joke, she laughed without the self-consciousness she usually felt when she was being set up.

"What do you get," Walt asked, "when you cross a Mafioso with a semiotics expert?"

"What?" said Opal.

Walt smiled. "An offer you can't understand."

Opal laughed and lit a cigarette. "That's great," she said.

149

"Too arcane for the show, though," said Walt. "I tried it out on the writers. No go." He shook his head. "So, have you figured out the way things are around the set?" he asked. "I'll steer you in the direction of the people who are worth knowing, and keep you away from the ones who will make your life a living hell."

Opal smiled. "Thanks," she said. "You like it here, though, right?" she asked.

"Well, yes," said Walt. "Depends who's asking. You and I are strictly *serf* material, of course, but you really get to see a lot of things. It's kind of an education."

"What kinds of things?" Opal asked.

"Well, for one thing," said Walt, "have you noticed the way some of the cast take five-minute breaks about every *fifteen* minutes? Guess what's going on in the bathroom? But they make a lot of money; they can afford it. Unlike some of us, they have salaries." He paused. "Not that I would spend my salary on cocaine. I don't know," he went on. "My parents think I'm crazy to want to work in comedy. They think it's a really depressing world. It's gotten so I don't tell them things. It's like that Billie Holiday song goes: 'Don't explain.' But I've always wanted to work in comedy."

"What do you mean, always?" Opal asked.

"Ever since 'The Dick Van Dyke Show,' " Walt said. "I used to fantasize about sitting around that office all day, goofing around and coming up with ideas. Having lunch every day with Morey Amsterdam and Rose Marie."

"Poor Rose Marie," Opal said. "Unable to find a man. Forever single!" she said.

Walt smile. He was attractive; there was something persistent and fierce about him. He was like a little muscle, Opal thought.

"What about you?" he asked. "Do you actually want to do something in this 'depressing line of work,' as my father would say?"

"I don't know what I want to do," Opal said. "I've grown up around all this; my mother's a comedian."

"Oh?" said Walt. "Anyone I'd know?"

She told him, and realized that as she spoke, her face was quickly heating up, as though she had confessed something intensely private.

Walt squinted. "*Really*," he said. "That's amazing. But you're so . . . petite. I didn't make the connection."

"We don't look alike," Opal said quickly.

"Do you look like your father?" he asked.

Opal shrugged. "I'm not sure," she said, and her voice dropped away.

"I'm sorry," said Walt. "I didn't mean to pry."

"You didn't," said Opal. "I'm just weird about certain things."

"Everybody is," said Walt. "Everybody has a *theme*. You talk to somebody awhile, and you realize they have one particular thing that rules them. The best you can do is a variation on the theme, but that's about it." He shook his head. There was a protracted silence, and Opal became tense, wondering what he would say next.

But all he did was lift his wrist to look at the time. "We'd better go," he said. "They may not pay us anything, but they want us back in time." They walked back to Rockefeller Center, where flags were flicking and slapping in a strong wind, and Walt took her arm. For a moment Opal felt as though she and Walt had important jobs, as though they were U.N. delegates returning from lunch. She thought of her father and wondered if her face had given too much away when Walt asked her about him. Was her father her "theme"? She really couldn't be sure. It seemed impossible to extricate Norm Engels from this whirling family. She thought about turning to Walt and trying to explain further, but suddenly they were pushing through the heavy glass of the revolving door, and the time had passed.

"Let me *look* at you," Mia Jablon said. She spoke with the inflections of a mother who has been separated from her child for a long time. If the child knows what is good for her, she will stand back, arms at her sides, and let herself be appraised. A wrist will be lifted and dropped, strands of hair swept from left to right. A shirt

151

will be tucked in hard, hands digging down the way only a mother would dare. But Mia simply wanted to look, and Opal didn't mind. Mia had been her baby-sitter, after all: someone who had cooked for her, and put her to bed, and sat drowsing all night in a tiny white rocking chair during croup season. Opal stood still now while Mia observed her for a long moment, and then they embraced.

"You're a beauty," Mia whispered. "I knew that would happen; I could see it even then."

Opal had been working at "Rush Hour" for three weeks, and Mia Jablon had just been brought in, mid-season, as the newest cast member. Mia had been discovered by one of the show's producers at a small club in Tribeca, where she was performing with Synchronous Menses, the women's musical comedy troupe she had founded. She did characters: Her best one was an old black blues singer who had worked as a dishwasher her whole life, named Soapy Waters. Mia's humor had a deliberate edge; she stood onstage and said, "Sure, I'd like to have children one day. I think *one day* would be long enough."

It had been nine years since she and Opal had seen each other, they calculated that first night over dinner at Mia and Lynn's loft. In those nine years Mia Jablon had barely changed at all, except to take on a kind of definition around the edges, as though she had been outlined in magic marker. Her body had stayed tight and small, her red hair only slightly threaded with something darker and less felicitous than it had been. The braid, Opal was pleased to see, was still intact.

"Television, *finally*," said Mia, leaning over the table to gather plates. "I was always told I didn't have the face for it. Too scrunched up, they said; it won't hold up under the camera, it'll collapse like a soufflé. Now your mother, she's got a face. The camera used to eat her up."

"If she didn't eat the camera first," Opal said, and was immediately ashamed.

No one dared laugh. "How's Dottie doing?" Lynn quickly asked. She and Mia had recently moved from their old apartment in Brooklyn to this large loft in a warehouse on Franklin Street. They had very little furniture, and Opal wasn't sure if this was because

152

they had moved in so recently, or whether it was the desired aesthetic. Either way, she liked the feel of this big, spare gymnasium of a room. Mia and Lynn moved about the space like two cats, Opal thought, watching them as they cleared the table. There was a balletic, married rhythm to their actions, and Opal realized, for the first time, that Mia and Lynn were lovers. It had probably always been common knowledge, and Opal was suddenly embarrassed about her ignorant child-self, that skipping, yammering *other* that she had been. Adulthood put a new spin on things, gave them a certain clarity. Mia scraped crumbs from the tablecloth with the side of a knife; Lynn snuffed out the fat candles in the center of the table. Everything was familiar, and tacitly coordinated.

"My mother's fine," Opal said. "She's got a boyfriend. His name is Sy, and they seem happy together. They're together all the time." Nobody said anything in response; they all observed an extended silence, as though speaking of the dead.

Mia plucked at a cluster of green grapes from her plate until she had pulled them all off, and the knobbed stems looked like a pile of jacks. "I've thought about your mother a lot," she finally said. "I've followed her career pretty closely." She shifted in her chair, settling in. "In the beginning, before I'd ever met her, it was so amazing to me that a woman had made it like that in comedy. And she was original, too; in those early shows, if you watch them now, you can see that she's really got her own voice. It's not so much that she was hilarious; she was just so outrageous, so nervy. Sometimes I didn't even think she was funny, but I never minded."

Opal nodded. "When Erica and I were little, we never really got it," she said.

"Well, I *got* it, I think," Mia said. "She was very much her own performer, and warm too, unlike some of the women who came later and made a big thing out of being bitter. You know, that kind of whiney humor that became popular. I remember watching her on Mike Douglas. It was exciting to see—like the beginning of something important, where there's still all this anticipation, but you're not sure what's going to happen. She was this huge, wacky *mother* figure let loose onstage. And then later on you can see that

153

she's really in charge there, doing those weird songs and all those characters, and everybody is crazy about her. And then, finally, everything just *stops*. I couldn't understand why your mother wasn't on any of those comedy specials anymore. Lynn and I used to spend hours looking for her name in *TV Guide*. But then I realized that it had less to do with *her* than with what else was going on at the time. I mean, look at how the women's movement changed everything. Suddenly everybody got a little embarrassed if women made jokes about their bodies, but Dottie wouldn't stop; she was like a machine. God, all those jokes about breasts."

"Boobs," Lynn interrupted. "I believe the word here is 'boobs.' If you're going into television, you'd better get your terms straight."

Mia laughed. "Right," she said. "I'll remember that. Range wasn't her big thing," she went on. "It was consistency. If you wanted a certain kind of comedy, you could get it from Dottie. She satisfied your expectations."

"And now she's doing fat women's clothing," Opal said. Her voice surprised her, resounding in the room as though she had suddenly started shouting in a museum.

"That upsets you?" Lynn asked.

Opal looked at her. "No," she qualified, "it embarrasses me."

"But she's hanging on," Mia said. She leaned across the table, arms folded. "I've been hanging on forever. In these nine years since you've seen me, I've been a waitress at four different restaurants—in one of them I had to wear a bonnet and carry a basket of warm popovers—and I've word-processed at three in the morning for a law firm, and sold moisturizer at the Clinique counter at Bloomingdale's, and I used to come home on the subway to Brooklyn every night, so exhausted I felt sick, and I'd have to get my energy up so I could turn around and go back into the city three hours later to play at a club where maybe ten people would see me." She paused. "And now I'm going to be on TV, and I'm supposed to pretend that I'm still fresh-scrubbed and excited about it, that I'm not already exhausted by life. I wouldn't be so quick to criticize that mother of yours. She's a wonderful woman; I guess because of her you don't have to worry about money. You're not going to be living in a trailer park eating olive

154

loaf. You go to Yale, and that's terrific, but you should be a little more grateful, Opal; I mean, *look* at your life. Look around you."

When she had finished, Mia seemed self-conscious. "I'm sorry to go on like this, but I feel so strongly about it," she said. "I feel bad too when I see Dottie up there on TV with that rack of balloon-dresses, but what are you going to do? I think *anybody's* life, if you put it on display, would look like a commercial for fat women's clothing. It's your mother at her most extreme, the worst that can be made of the fact that she's big. So maybe someday I'll be on TV with Lynn and we'll be doing a commercial for *gay* women's clothing." Mia patted out a little beat on the table. "Gals!" she began. "We've got the biggest collection of designer overalls and work boots! Wear them home for Christmas and make your parents *miserable!*"

Opal leaned back in her chair and laughed easily. She could have stayed here for hours, she knew; she could have sat and listened to Mia Jablon talk about almost anything. Mia would be a success on the show; Opal was sure of it. Her appeal would be very different from Dottie's; Mia wouldn't fill up the whole screen. She would occupy one small part of it, ignite it like a match, so your eye was forced toward the point of light. You *wanted* to look at Mia; her face was intelligent and asymmetrical. Opal glanced across the table for a second at Lynn, who was watching Mia also. Lynn's smile was broad and full and Opal was suddenly envious of their love, of any married love that could sustain itself like this. She herself had never had it, had never known it was possible.

At the end of dinner, Opal was reluctant to go. She took time to pull on her jacket, slowly drawing the zipper closed. Lynn was stacking dishes in the kitchen, and Opal and Mia stood in the doorway together.

"You know, I'd like to see Dottie," Mia said. "Do you think she'd be interested in hearing from me? We sort of fell out of touch when you got too old to need baby-sitting. She had so many people in her life."

"I'm sure she would," Opal said, and this was true; her mother always expressed pleasure at seeing people she had not seen in a long time, or even at meeting people who claimed to be big fans.

"I wish I could help her," Mia went on. "Maybe we could get her an appearance on the show. Not that I have any power there. I've only just *arrived*, but maybe when I settle in more—if they still like me—I could suggest it."

"She hates the show," Opal said. "She doesn't think it's funny at all."

Mia shook her head. "Don't be so sure," she said. "Dottie hates being left out, I think. I've seen that happen. When I found out that I had gotten this job, everyone in Synchronous Menses acted really weird toward me, sort of nasty. They told me I wouldn't be able to do the kind of humor I was used to, that I was selling out as a feminist, blah blah. I mean, I'd heard all that a dozen years ago, when I shaved my legs for my cousin Judy's wedding. But I know that most of them would have taken this job in a *second* if it was offered to them. They're all living on food stamps, and they want to be seen, they want to be out there. Everybody feels left behind; you have to take that into account. Dottie feels like the whole world has changed, and maybe it has, but that's not necessarily a bad thing. It's just hard, when you've made a living out of certain kinds of attitudes. Lucky for me, I never had any success before, so I'm perfectly happy to ring in the new, to leave things behind."

"Just don't leave *me* behind," Lynn called from the kitchen.

"Never," Mia called back.

Opal rode the freight elevator down to the street. The world had coupled up, it seemed, overnight. But the coupling wasn't all that new, she realized; what *was* new was the fact that she had noticed it, and that it now troubled her. Mia and Lynn, she thought, Erica and Jordan, Dottie and Sy. She wondered again if her father was coupled, too. Maybe he lived alone on Coconut Court, and was one of those people who said he was "married" to his work. Opal had written to him a second time, had asked if he had received her first letter, but he still did not respond. Tamara, who checked Opal's mailbox at Yale Station every few days, said that nothing of importance had arrived. Opal would have to start thinking of other things.

But it was hard to think of other things on a night like this,

156

heading alone out of the warm light of someone else's home into the street. Lower Manhattan was perfectly still, and the streets were lined with shallow craters that shone with rain. Opal glanced up at Mia and Lynn's window, and could see a shadow elongate, then compress, behind the paper shade. Everyone had made their choices, had settled in for the long run. This was it, she thought, and yet she knew that she herself was still in suspension. All around her, women chose to be with men, wanting the complement of bodies, or, like Mia, they chose to be with women, wanting something else that Opal didn't even attempt to imagine. It was too much of a cliché to say that a woman wanted the sameness that another woman offered. Mia and Lynn were nothing alike: Mia so spritely, and Lynn with her lupine face and deliberate, ironic stance. In truth, Opal knew nothing about coupling of any sort. All she knew was that humans were supposed to gravitate toward one another, the ways plants bend into the light.

At college, freshman year, Opal had gone to bed with Tom Kennerly, a slightly undernourished, handsome boy she had met one morning in the dining hall. In the beginning, she told him scraps of information about herself, but he already knew who her mother was. She went about the relationship with a kind of clinical enthusiasm; it felt good to be one of the sexually active women in the dormitory who sat around at night with a copy of *Our Bodies, Ourselves* open on a table, like members of a Bible study group.

"Cystitis," a knowledgeable senior would say, diagnosing an underclasswoman who sat doubled over in pain. "*Definitely* cystitis." And someone would be sent on a run to the Stop and Shop for a jug of cranberry juice and some plain yogurt. It was a secret club, and somehow the clubbiness of it was the aspect of having a lover that Opal liked best. She actually began to read the question and answer columns in women's magazines; she took the quizzes they offered, and tallied up her score to learn her "intimacy quotient" or her likelihood for divorce. She did well on these quizzes, and somehow this gave her an embarrassing amount of pleasure.

Opal felt far less comfortable actually being with Tom. As she lay in his bed, she looked blankly at her reflection in the high

157

mirror over his dresser, where the arms of sweaters hung out of drawers, like the arms of people waving from a train. She clutched on to Tom's narrow torso late at night when everyone else was out at a double feature of *Harold and Maude* and *King of Hearts*—and he slid himself into her and then out again like a piece of light machinery. It works! she had thought with some pleasure, but her pleasure was that of a former disbeliever, not a lover. She had been convinced; her body was desirable and operated properly, and even if at times she felt herself hovering somewhere above the scene, looking down on the small room and the crooked mirror and the pink flesh of this young man from Lyme, Connecticut, it had still worked properly, and he had labored until she finally came, with a long, sibilant release of sound that surprised them both.

But there had been no continuity, for neither of them, they confessed guiltily over dinner at Naples Pizza two weeks later, was in love with the other. They had burst out laughing in relief at the confession; they even toasted it, clicking glasses to the absence of emotion. Then exams came, and they saw less of each other, although sometimes Opal watched Tom play Frisbee on the common, his arm flinging out to execute a throw, his feet lifting him off the ground. She would watch him from across the green and wonder where this need to be "in love" had come from, and why she somehow thought of it as a birthright. Maybe it was pure instinct, she thought. You strove dumbly toward this element that you didn't understand, and which certainly you hadn't learned from your parents.

"Your father doesn't know how to be loving," Dottie had said. "It's difficult for him to show emotion." But it seemed to have been a generation of bad fathers, Opal thought. Back in the Fifties, a husband was presented with a warm, sweet, and sour bundle that kicked. He held it awkwardly, slightly away from his body, like a teenaged boy holding an armload of flowers on a big date. Fathers had changed since then; now the world was crawling with a new breed: bearded young men who doubled over with labor pains, men who leafed through the Old Testament to find a good name for the baby. These men were foreign to Opal, another species entirely.

It was too easy to think of her own father as terrible. It was easy and mindless and she had done it for so long that she didn't remember any other way to think. But now she wondered; now she had her doubts. It had been a month since she had first written him, a month since she had been waiting. This was her private grief, one which she could not talk about with Dottie or Erica. As far as secrets went, it was a weak one. How much more extraordinary to have had a private correspondence with him, as she had hoped: an intimate, revealing exchange of letters, a body of information that would move and change and trouble her. They would secretly write for years, until finally there was nothing left to say, and then they would agree to let the correspondence die gracefully.

But he refused to write. Once a week, Opal called Tamara up at Yale, who said there still wasn't any mail of significance in Opal's box. "Are you definitely coming back in the fall?" Tamara asked, and her voice sounded suspicious, as if she imagined that Opal was in danger of staying like this, as if "suspension" was actually a permanent condition.

Sometimes, alone in the apartment at night, Opal wanted to look at her father's face, even though the photographs didn't tell her much. She stood in front of the hall closet and took down the old coat box from B. Altman's, which contained snapshots from that other life. Most of the photographs had been taken during family vacations, and in each one her father looked nearly the same: bone-white and untouched by the sun, even in the height of summer.

Opal remembered how Walt Green had asked if she looked like her father. She thought of this again one night, when Walt came home with her for supper after work. They sat eating in the kitchen, under the yellow table light, which gave Walt's eyes a certain unusual density every time he tilted his head up. Walt had brought a bottle of red wine with him, and they continued drinking even after the food was done and the dishes had been deposited in the sink. "God, you actually spent your childhood here," he said. "This room is huge."

"Do you want to see the rest of it?" Opal asked, and he nodded. They took their glasses with them for the tour of the apartment.

"It's great," Walt said as they stood in the living room. "You should see where I live, up by Columbia. There are three of us in this tiny rathole on 112th Street. I sleep on a fold-out couch like Mary Tyler Moore. But this is a whole *house* right in the middle of the city. I'm impressed."

When they had gone through all the rooms and were heading back to the kitchen, Opal stopped for a second in front of the hall closet. "I'll show you some other things, if you want," she said quickly. Walt shrugged and agreed, and Opal opened the closet door. She reached up with both arms and brought down the B. Altman's box, and then she carried the box into the den. Opal sifted through the contents until she found the photo album, and she opened it across both their laps, like a sleigh blanket. At the front of the album were several pages of Erica as a baby, then two pages of Opal.

"That's what always happens," Walt said. "They're less excited the second time around. There's much less documentation. Same with my sister and me." Finally, after all the baby pictures stopped, the family vacation pictures began. "Oh look, the World's Fair," Walt said. "My family went there, too."

"I think everyone did," said Opal. "Do you remember the Italian Pavilion?"

He nodded, smiling. "Of course," he said. "It was terrific. And I remember another pavilion where you sat in a chair that lifted you up through a shaft, and showed you the inner workings of the human brain. God, it was great." He paused. "What I remember most," he said, "is how hot it was. I always had to go to the bathroom."

Opal turned the page. There at the top, among the World's Fair series, was a picture she distinctly recalled posing for. She remembered the day well, and how she had traveled for hours through a series of dark chutes and tunnels, and how at the end of the afternoon, finally out in the wide reaches of sunlight, she could no longer see. She could barely hear, either. The same song was weaving through her: a chorus of cricket-children singing, "It's a small world, after all," and then singing it in other languages, each version less identifiable than the last, until finally the

160

children seemed to be chattering, "Gluka brznik faxmilgriv." What language *was* this? she wondered. Russian? Greek? She didn't know, but she couldn't focus on it any longer because her father was making her pose for a picture. She stood, impatient for him to finish, while all around her, other children posed similarly before domes and arches. Fathers adjusted the lenses on their bulky new cameras, and children sighed and swung their arms out, ruining the shot. Opal could not bear the protracted moment between the focus and the click, but her father had a bad temper, so she didn't dare complain. Instead she stood in the invisible frame he had squared off around her, jerking and rolling her eyes.

After the shot her father faithfully rubbed the print with a sponge soaked in some chemical that smelled like toxic salad dressing, and later, after the afternoon was over, he sat in the family room in Jericho and pressed it into an album, sealing the image of his younger daughter behind plastic.

Now Opal sat with that same album open before her, staring down at the photograph. "Look at that," she said.

Walt looked at the picture for a long moment. Suddenly he inhaled sharply, frightening her.

"What?" she said.

"I don't believe it," said Walt.

Opal looked again at the picture, looked where he was looking. "I don't understand," she said, and she glanced back at him, missing the point entirely.

"That's *me*," Walt said.

She looked again. There, behind six-year-old Opal, a small boy was wandering by, sullen-faced and tired. His hair was shaved into a colorless crewcut. His eyes were looking off somewhere into the hot, open distance. He and Opal did not see each other at all; each of them was a prisoner of a separate family. Over the sounds of people talking and laughing, of babies crying and music percolating from different pavilions, a harried mother was calling out, "Walt! Walt Green! You come over here right now! Walt! Walt!" And the boy kept walking.

It was him. She was almost sure of it. Looking back and forth between the photograph and his grown face, she saw that he had the same bones now as then, the same small, sharp eyes and full mouth. Only the hair was wild now, as if he were still punishing his parents for the skinhead they had foisted on him so many summers ago.

Opal and Walt threw their arms around each other and laughed giddily. "To think," they kept saying. "It's *amazing*. To think."

Walt poured more wine and they both started talking more freely, overlapping sentences, cutting in. He talked about his family, his voice changing tone a little. His older sister, Nissa, he said, had had a nervous breakdown three years before.

"It was terrible," Walt said. "We were all really thrown, although when I look back on the summer, the clues are right there. She just stopped eating. My parents went to visit her apartment, and Nissa had cleaned out the entire kitchen, and was keeping *makeup* in the cabinets. So they sent her to this place called Sojourn House, kind of a farm in Vermont for people with eating disorders. You have to do chores there every morning, milk the cows and so on. She lived there for six months and supposedly got better, and now she's back in her own apartment. It's just that she's *changed*. I mean, she has friends and goes to work, but she's sort of unresponsive to everyone. I don't think she's had a boyfriend since her breakdown. She's become the kind of woman," he said, "who is always taking her friends to have abortions."

"What does that mean?" Opal asked.

"The kind of woman who is never having an abortion herself," he said. "Who's never *involved* with anyone. My parents sometimes call her up and ask if she wants to have dinner, and she says, 'Oh, I can't. I'm taking Julie or Andrea to have an abortion.' My parents say that Nissa is their greatest sorrow." Walt shook his head. "Every family has their own secret," he said. "And whether you want to or not, you're supposed to *keep* it." His voice was thick now, and wistful. "No one ever asks for it," he said, "and yet there it is. It's like being born into the KGB."

"I know," said Opal, and she noticed the way he was holding his wineglass, the fingers curling into a fist around the stem. There was something bluntly made about Walt; he was like a kid, a

162

boy—the boy in the photograph. They were both quiet for a while. Opal picked up the album from the table and looked at the photo again, wanting to see that younger version of him. Walt had *been* there back then, she thought, and he is here now. Beside her, he leaned closer to get a better look at the photograph, and she could feel the sleeve of his sweater for a second against her wrist, and his breath on her hair.

"Let me see that," Walt said, and as he squinted at the picture he began to reconsider. "You know," he said, holding the album up to the light, "I'm not entirely sure now. I mean, it *looks* like me, but I think I was heavier. I mean, I was a chunky kid; I wore double-husky clothes for a while. You know, I'm beginning to think it isn't me."

"Are you sure?" Opal asked, and her voice had gone tinny with disappointment.

Walt shook his head and said no, he wasn't sure, but he didn't sound very convincing. It wasn't him, she thought now; it wasn't. He placed the album back across Opal's lap, and it felt suddenly heavy to her. She had drunk too much, she realized; she thought she might start to cry. Walt looked perplexed, even embarrassed, and after a while he stood to leave. She wanted him to go, and felt slightly unmoored, uncertain.

What *was* certain, she thought after he was gone, what could never be argued, was that the girl in the picture was indeed Opal. If she were to come across herself in the background of someone else's photograph, there would be no doubt. Opal looked again at that squinty girl in orange culottes, and was astonished to see that when it came right down to it, she had barely changed at all.

Winter wore on, and her father still hadn't written. "Nothing in your mailbox but advertisements," Tamara told her. "An offer to go to Fort Lauderdale over Spring Break on one of those student trips from hell. An invitation to join the Black Students Alliance. That kind of thing. What is it you're *waiting* for?" Tamara asked, but Opal insisted she wasn't waiting for anything in particular. As soon as she said this she knew it was true. If he hadn't written by now,

163

he never would. Opal had sent three letters to him, each one more needy than the last. Three letters from his own daughter, and he wouldn't budge.

Late at night sometimes, Opal would be awakened by sounds drifting out from the kitchen: the blender, the carving knife, the dishwasher. She could not believe how much Dottie and Sy ate; she didn't *want* to know, really, about their excesses. Opal began keeping to herself more, both at home and at work. Walt and Mia called to her from across the studio, but she sometimes pretended she hadn't heard.

One afternoon, Opal was sent to buy cocaine for Stevie Confino. He approached her discreetly, when she was on her way to lunch, and said, "Can I count on you for a favor? I have to be in makeup in five minutes, and you're the only one I would ask. I'll be indebted to you for life, Opal; I'll perform sexual services, I'll give you my first-born son."

Up until this moment, he had almost never said a word to her. She looked at his hopeful face, the hair matted down with water, the towel around his neck, and he seemed young and ridiculous, and so Opal agreed, just to be *done* with it. Stevie gave her four fifty-dollar bills and cab fare and sent her off downtown.

Opal got out of the cab on East Seventh Street and double-checked the address that she held in her glove. Then she rang the bell of a cruddy building on the south side of the street, and waited, shivering, on the stoop.

When the door opened, and the two sisters stood facing each other, Opal felt only a dumb thud of surprise, a big drop of it, painless and silent, like snow sliding off a roof. "Jesus," she said.

Erica was staring at her. She was wearing an ancient yellow T-shirt that Opal remembered from years ago. It read: REVA AND JAMIE: FIRST NORTH AMERICAN TOUR. Erica just stood there, leaning against the doorframe, not saying a word. It was early afternoon; the street was freezing. "You want to come up?" Erica finally asked.

Opal nodded. They walked up a narrow, dark stairwell. On the third floor, Erica opened her apartment door and the hallway was flooded with sound. Heavy-metal music groaned through the apartment like a buzz saw. Jordan Strang, whom Opal had not seen in

164

years, was sitting on the couch in the small, filthy living room. Jordan looked up from whatever he was doing, his eyes slowly focusing as he recognized her. Then he looked imploringly at Erica.

"It's okay," Erica said. "You remember Opal."

Jordan nodded and shrugged. "Easy come, easy go," he said. He got up finally, like an old dog, and ambled into the bedroom. Opal could hear the creak of a ladder.

"Did someone die?" Erica asked.

"What?" Opal said.

"Did someone *die*," Erica repeated, and this time she phrased it like a statement. It meant: I assume you are here for a good reason; I assume you have not just dropped in to pay a social call. Opal shook her head. "Look," said Erica, "we have some people coming over. Business. Maybe we could talk later."

"*Erica,*" said Opal, and she knew her sister still did not understand. Opal reached deep into the pocket of her pants and yanked out the four fifties, which she had folded up tightly. "I'm the one," she tried. "*Business.* I'm here to pick it up."

Erica finally understood. She let out a long breath and blinked several times.

"Should I go, Erica?" Opal asked. "Do you want me to go?"

But Erica shook her head. They sat down on the couch, which was covered with a fall of cat hair. "Can I smoke?" Opal asked, just to be polite, for she would have been shocked if smoke wasn't permitted here. Smoke would barely be *noticed* here, she thought. It would just blend in with all the other interference: the music, and the cat hair, and the dampness in the air.

"Sure," said Erica.

Opal lit a cigarette. "This is too weird," she said. "Too, too weird."

"I know," said Erica. "But I'm used to this. Not with you, with Mom. Everywhere I look, she's there. It's like those Venn diagrams in elementary school. Everyone overlaps in this stupid family."

"But it's not as bad as it used to be," Opal said. "She's almost never on TV anymore. Just those commercials."

"Yeah, those commercials," said Erica.

They were silent, thinking. Each of them, Opal knew, had an image in her head of a fat woman endlessly dancing. The woman spun and spun, her dress magically changing colors, dissolving slowly from red to green, like litmus paper.

"She's making a living," Opal said. "It was hard for me to take at first."

"Opal," Erica suddenly said. "I can't do this."

"Do what?"

"Talk to you. I just can't," Erica said. She stood up awkwardly, abruptly. "I can't think about any of this right now. I have enough on my mind."

Opal slowly stood. She hadn't said anything yet; she had just *gotten* here. She hadn't told Erica about Dottie being in love, or about all the letters she had written to her father. *Their* father. "Things weren't so bad back then," Opal tried, her voice high. "We had some fun together, Erica. You used to cook for me, and we'd watch television. We used to hyperventilate. Do you remember? Am I making this up?"

But Erica was looking away. "I'll go talk to Jordan," she said. "I'll get the coke for you."

She disappeared into the bedroom, and returned a moment later with two small paper packets. Paper in exchange for paper, Opal thought, as she handed over the money. It was all so flyaway, so flimsy. She felt a deep sadness as she stuffed the packets into the zippered pocket of her down coat, and then opened the door to let herself out. She walked slowly down the stairs, hoping that Erica would come to the landing and call her back. She could picture her sister's head leaning over the rail. *"Opal, come back,"* Erica would say, and the request would be plaintive and heart-stopping.

But Erica didn't want that. Erica wanted to be left alone, in that sad little apartment with Jordan Strang. It would be a good story, Opal thought, nearly elevated to the level of Greek drama: one sister selling, the other buying. And yet, she knew, there was no one she could tell. Opal pushed open the front door, and a slant of snow rushed in.

14

"And then my *sister* was standing on the front steps," Erica said. "I couldn't believe it. You'd think, in this huge city, you could have a little privacy, but apparently that's impossible."

"Me, I'm tired of privacy," Mitchell Block said. "My family lives in Wisconsin; I never see them. I've been trying to get my parents to New York for years, but they're too scared. I think they saw on 'Sixty Minutes' that you can't even walk down the street anymore without carrying a revolver, and that did it."

They were sitting in the snack bar of the Loeb Student Center at NYU. She and Mitchell both ate large quantities of food during the meal, and neither of them felt the need to be apologetic about it as they heaped mountains of potato salad onto their plates, or went back to the counter for seconds. They sat in the snack bar for most of the afternoon. The cleaning woman mopped all the other tables until finally theirs was the only dry surface left in the place. When the woman approached with her dripping sponge, they knew it was finally time to leave.

"Come on," Mitchell said, ushering Erica out, and they went to his office in the basement of the psychology building. The tiny room was ablaze with fluorescent light, but Mitchell had tacked up some *New Yorker* cartoons on the walls, and a huge calendar, in an attempt to create an atmosphere of some warmth. On his desk was a big magnet which had a cluster of paper clips clinging to it. Erica sifted the clips between her fingers, unwilling to leave just yet.

Mitchell finally looked at his wristwatch. "I hate to break this up," he said, "but I have to get back out there in five minutes.

167

You don't want to be responsible for halting the progress of science, do you?"

Erica smiled and stood up. They hadn't known each other very long. There had been two lunches, at which she had talked expansively, and Mitchell had somehow seemed to listen in an equally expansive way. He was thirty-one years old, she knew, and was halfway done with his doctoral thesis. He had been working on it for years, and it changed every semester or so—became slightly more bizarre, according to his professors. They advised him to take some time off, or else to just *finish* it, get it over with, get on with the rest of his life.

Erica had pushed her way into Mitchell Block's field of vision. That first morning, when she stood waiting for him outside the classroom, he had been cordial to her in a perfunctory way. She had quickly told him that his study interested her, that she had been thinking about it since they had met. It wasn't a lie; she *had* thought about that day very often. She had remembered the way Mitchell's voice had sounded, reciting word after word, and how he had held a pink index card between thick-jointed fingers. Like Erica, Mitchell had a weariness about him. At first she had thought he knew something about her, but then she realized, the more she dwelled on it, that he merely knew the same *things* that she did, that his perceptions were similar to her own. She had inferred all this just from a little list of words, a defeated light in his eyes, and a body that occupied as much space as her own.

Over lunch that first day he had told her some basics about himself, and she had responded in kind. Without thinking, she told him that her mother was Dottie Engels; it surprised her even as she said it, for she told almost no one anymore. It wasn't a fact that she was particularly proud of, but somehow she wanted him to know.

"Come on," he said at first. "You're pulling my leg."

But she shook her head.

"That's very interesting," he said. "I can't even imagine what that would be like."

They were both eating Soft-Serv ice cream from the dispenser in the snack bar. They had each filled a plastic dish with a tall turban of ice cream, and Erica felt as if she were on a "date," a word she could not think of without considerable irony. She suddenly felt very much a part of the boy/girl equation; she thought of the symmetry of Archie and Veronica on either side of a booth in Pop Tate's Chocklit Shoppe, sipping coyly at matching ice cream sodas. Erica suddenly felt exposed in an odd, sexual way. She deflected this by a sudden burst of candor; she spoke simply and clearly about her mother, and what it had been like growing up around someone famous. She had never even said as much to Jordan, who used to press her for details.

"Are you and your mother very close?" Mitchell asked, and Erica shook her head quickly.

"We don't speak," she said. The phrase sounded weighty and official.

"Why not?" he asked. This was the dreaded question, the one that she could not answer.

Erica hesitated. Finally, all she could say was, "I'm really not sure."

Walking home, she dismantled and reassembled the conversation several times. That last part, about not speaking to her mother, still troubled her. Mitchell would think she was filled with a dark sadness, just the sort of thing he expected of heavy women, according to the findings of his study. Erica no longer wanted to please him in that way, to satisfy his clinical expectations. Now she wanted to stand out from the survey in *bas-relief*, to be the girl with the brightest eyes, the one who had been wounded least. Erica desperately wanted him to know her, and yet she could not bear what there was for him to know.

All day long Mitchell sat with fat women, many of them deeply unhappy, and they spread their lives out before him like a smorgasbord, and he listened quietly, nodding and smiling encouragement. She would not be one of those women; she would be something entirely different, someone who did not fit into his study, someone who screwed up the beautiful, sloping curves of all his graphs.

The twelfth-grade girls were back. They were sprawled on the living room rug like courtesans, Erica thought, picking her way

169

over them to get to the bedroom. Jordan was standing in the middle of the room, arms outstretched, balancing a coke spoon on his nose for entertainment. Erica climbed back up into the loft. She lay down, feeling dreamily sated as she always did after a big meal. She was still aware of the milky vanilla taste of the ice cream she had eaten; it made her think of Mitchell, of sex, of things sweet and cold. She idly wondered how he would look undressed; she imagined his massive body shining beneath his winter clothes, as though he rubbed it with oil, like a weight lifter. But there were probably none of those discrete islands of muscle on Mitchell's body; instead, he was most likely rounded and soft and yet somehow still powerful, like a kettle drum.

When Jordan came back into the bedroom later and climbed up into the bed, Erica hoped he wouldn't touch her. She looked over and saw his long arms busy on the surface of the mirror. His hospital bracelet hung loosely on his poor thin wrist. Jordan's business was going well, she supposed. Customers would come over for the afternoon and Jordan would sit with them, cutting up and sampling what they had already paid for. Somehow, nobody seemed to mind. The apartment was becoming a salon of sorts, and Jordan was the good, benevolent host. He talked about the 1960s with his high-schoolers; this was a hoot, Erica thought. Suddenly Jordan was an expert on something he himself had been too young to take part in. He was only a secondary source, but it was apparently close enough. Just the other day she had heard him conducting a small seminar in the living room on the life and work of Hunter Thompson. Three boys sat transfixed.

She looked over at Jordan in profile, his head bent above the mirror, a straw perpetually in one nostril like a life-support system. She thought about the last time they had had sex together; it had been just over three weeks before. It was, she realized, right before she had met Mitchell. Mitchell's presence made a difference, she realized; suddenly there were other possibilities. It didn't *have* to be Jordan; it didn't have to be him at all. This was a thrilling revelation.

"What's funny?" Jordan asked, and she realized that she had been smiling.

"Oh, nothing," she said, but she could not get rid of her private

170

little smile. If only he knew, she thought, he would not sit there so calmly, with a Flexi-Straw up his nose, staring at himself like Narcissus leaning into the water.

That night, she dreamed of Opal's visit. She dreamed of her sister climbing the stairs, walking into the apartment, the door flying open at her touch.

Erica woke up in the stark middle of the night, the moment when night hesitates into morning, and when outside, garbage trucks and derricks lift and lower, ruling the earth like dinosaurs. Jordan was asleep beside her with his face pushed into the pillow. Erica sat up in bed, careful not to slam her head against the ceiling.

Why had she sent Opal away like that? What had been the purpose? I am a cold person, Erica thought, and was ashamed. Opal was the person she had spent the most amount of time with, after all, years and years of it. It was all irretrievable now, something to be relegated to photo albums and drunken, nostalgic evenings.

And what, she wondered, was Opal doing buying *drugs* for someone? This made no sense at all. Opal had always been so straight, so clean, so *legal*. How wrong to think of little monkey-girl Opal, buying cocaine in the dead of winter. Erica leaned back down and rolled over, pushing her own face into the pillow.

Mitchell Block said he loved his family, but it was much easier for him, Erica thought, because he never *saw* them. They never showed up on television in the middle of the night, or onstage at a gay bar, or on the front step. All of Mitchell's communications with his family took place over the telephone and in letters. When Mitchell thought of his parents, he felt nothing but a slightly melancholic love, the sort of twinge that was expected after a certain age. Being an adult child was an awkward, inevitable position. You went about your business in the world: tooling around, giving orders, being taken seriously, but there were still these two people lurking somewhere who in a split second could reduce you to *nothing*. In their presence, you were a big-headed baby again, crawling instead of walking. At Bennington, Erica had always been able to tell when someone in her dormitory was

171

talking to her parents on the telephone; the girl's voice would suddenly go flat and uninflected. You could hear it all the way down the hall.

"Don't your parents *criticize* you?" she had asked Mitchell. "Don't they make you self-conscious? I never heard of parents who didn't."

After giving this a little thought, he shook his head. "Not really," he said. "No, not that I can think of."

"But what about for being *fat?*" Erica said, and this was the first time she had used the word in his presence. She suddenly was terrified that he would be offended.

"I was hoping you hadn't noticed," Mitchell said, his voice light and amused. Erica waited for him to go on. "It's strange," he said, "but I never thought of myself as fat when I was growing up. My parents stressed the fact that I was *healthy*. I weighed in at ten pounds when I was born, and this was something they were really proud of—as if I was a prize heifer in a 4-H show. There was never even a hint of criticism about my weight, I don't think. Maybe there should have been," he said. "It might have been a good idea for me to have been put on a diet. But my parents were true innocents. They still are. They believe that it's healthy to eat clotted cream and big wedges of cheese and a *lot* of red meat. Just raise the cholesterol right up; create massive gridlock in the arteries. That's their credo."

"I always thought that being fat was terrible, but sort of inevitable," Erica said. "I just sat around waiting until the day I could wear my mother's hand-me-downs: Capri pants with Spandex waistbands, blouses with *darts*. My sister Opal is *thin*. She's like our father; he was *painfully* thin, I think. I can't even imagine what that would be like. It's like trying to imagine being the opposite sex."

"You really can't imagine that—being male?" Mitchell asked.

Erica shrugged. "Well, I can think to myself: Oh, this is what it would feel like to have hair all over my chest and this *organ* dangling between my legs, but beyond that—no, I can't imagine it." She looked at him. "Why?" she said. "Can you?"

172

Mitchell thought for a moment. "All those interviews I do," he said. "They really put you in another person's life for a little while. I've been hearing women's stories for months now; after a while something catches. Like the day *you* came in."

"What about it?" she asked, embarrassed but curious.

"Well, I thought you were interesting, of course," Mitchell said, "but not just as a specimen. I tried to imagine what your life was like. How you lived. What it was like being you."

"And?" she asked.

"And," Mitchell said slowly, "I wasn't sure." He became quiet now. "I'm still not," he said. "I think you must have had some extraordinary experiences growing up. Not just with your mother being famous, although I'm sure that's a part of it." He paused. "I'm curious to know what that was like," he said.

She thought of how Jordan used to ask her questions like that, back in high school, and how she had never wanted to tell him anything. But now Erica didn't mind Mitchell's questions; in fact, it pleased her that he wanted to know more. She tried to arrange her words before speaking. What was there to say? she wondered. She could tell him about the walks she used to take with her mother down Central Park West, and the way people would point to Dottie every couple of blocks. She could tell him about the way you get used to sharing your mother with the world, because you have no choice. Mitchell would nod and listen carefully, but finally, she knew, he would not *get* it. People couldn't just be opened up, window by window, like an Advent calendar. Suddenly, she didn't know what to tell him.

There ought to have been a club, Erica thought, for children of the famous. They could call themselves SOFA—the Society for the Offspring of Famous Adults—and they could all meet once a week in someone's apartment and have long, cathartic rebirthing sessions. She imagined herself part of a circle, swaying back and forth, her arms around the two Kennedy children.

Yes, let it all out, Caroline, everyone says. We know it's been hard, we know it's been rough. All those photographers around you like flies, and all those terrible collectible plates and calendars and beer steins with your father's face on them. Let it out,

173

Caroline, go back to your earliest memories, back to that green-velvet lawn with the fence all around, and your pony—Macaroni, wasn't it?—and the way you ran in a little tulle dress across the lawn toward those great bending knees, those powerful waiting arms.

Erica's own problems would seem insignificant compared with these. When it is Erica's turn to be rebirthed, Caroline and her brother stand up and stretch a bit, wander in boredom over to the bowl of nacho chips on the table, check the time, whisper in the hallway. But Erica perseveres; the others hold her, cradle her in their arms, and take her back as far as she can go.

Imagine you are very small, Harry Belafonte's daughter says, her voice low and soothing.

Erica pictures herself at twelve, watching her mother on television. Dottie is telling a joke about raiding the refrigerator in the middle of the night. Everyone in the audience is laughing so loud, it seems as though they may never stop. Now Erica starts to thrash, but they hold her down.

Go with it, Erica, says one of the Truffaut brood.

So she goes back even further, and now she is seven. Her mother isn't famous yet, only fat; she is stepping daintily into a swimming pool, dipping one toe in first. How is it that she manages to be so big and still look *dainty* when she chooses? Dottie tucks her hair into a bathing cap: one of those caps exclusive to mothers, with huge, floppy rubber flowers clinging to it like lichen. Then she plunges into the water, parting it evenly with her big body. She swims with her head above the surface, like a sea elephant. As she moves, pool water flies out everywhere, and now Erica recoils.

Keep going! shouts Margaret Mead's daughter, her voice excited. Go back as far as you can!

Finally Erica is back inside her mother's great body, floating somewhere in the birth canal, pushing herself against the walls, her own body vibrating in time to the heartbeat. Now Erica starts to flail around more violently, and everyone moves in closer to help her. Even Caroline and John grow a little interested, and amble back over to the circle. I'm coming out! Erica cries, and then, as though she's on a water slide at an amusement park, out she comes.

15

"So it's the Eighties and everybody's getting into shape," Dottie began. "All you hear about are these Jane Fonda Workout videos. Well, I've decided to make my own video, and I'm calling it the Dottie Engels *Pigout* video." She paused, looking around her. "There will be three different levels of difficulty," she continued. "Piglet, Porker, and Porker Plus. The video will show you my very own technique for mastering the fine art of gluttony. All you need is a comfortable leotard, a floor mat, and an invitation to a bar mitzvah where there's guaranteed to be smorgasbord and a Viennese table."

She went on for ten minutes more, and when the routine was finished, Dottie stood still for a moment in the middle of the large office. "Well, that's it," she said, twisting her hands together. "Just a few things I've been putting together."

Opal glanced to the side without turning her head. No one was moving or whispering or even scribbling notes on a pad. Everyone was just sitting still. Finally Joel Macklin stood up slowly, his swivel chair creaking. "All right then," he said, and the effort in his voice was perceptible. "Thank you, Dottie. It's a treat to hear you again. Ross, we'll talk in a few days. Things are crazy around here. We've got the whole season lined up, and we're swamped. But I'll call you this week."

In the elevator going down, no one said a word. Opal felt terrible for having encouraged Dottie to audition for "Rush Hour" in the first place. Mia had made the preliminary overtures to the director, and then Ross had put in a few calls. Dottie had been extremely skeptical from the start. "Oh, what would they want with me?" she asked. "That show is for young people; they wouldn't be interested."

"Don't you want to perform again?" Opal said. "Don't you want to work before a live audience?" And finally Dottie had agreed, and had put together an entirely new routine. As soon as Dottie stood up there and started talking, Opal knew it would not work. She had been allowed into the audition, but within minutes she wished she had been banned from the room, and would not have to witness the living enactment of her mother's failure.

Now the elevator opened at the white lobby, and they all stepped out. "Look," Ross tried, "let's all go get some coffee and talk about this." He leaned against the wall beside the bank of elevators. "I'm sure they would be willing to audition you again, Dottie. We can think about ways to make the routine crisper."

"A crisper is for lettuce," Dottie said. "Please don't patronize me." She shook her head slowly. "It was one of life's embarrassing moments," she went on. "I wish you'd never encouraged me. God knows what they're up there saying right now. I can just hear it: 'She's too campy. Too *shticky*. She's better-known for those late-night TV commercials; we might as well have on the guy who sells the Ginsu Knife, or that other guy from Wall Unit World.' "

"Oh, fuck them," Ross said quietly, and Opal and Dottie looked at him in mild surprise. "What I mean," he said quickly, "is that I *will* get you something, Dottie. So they weren't particularly impressed; so what? They don't have a monopoly on comedy. I'll make sure you get work somewhere; it's been too long, and I want to see you back on TV. I promise you, I will find you something."

One of the elevator doors opened then and a new crowd flooded out and dispersed. "I should go," Dottie said. "It's going to be murder getting a cab. I forgot what it's like, not having a car."

"No coffee?" Ross said, and Dottie shook her head. She leaned in and kissed him lightly. "I'll find you something, Dottie," he said again. "You'll be in the city for a while?"

She nodded. "Sy is going to Hong Kong tomorrow on business," she said. "I'll be home all the time. A war widow. Where else would I go? Dinner at the Rockefellers'? No, you know where to find me."

Back in the apartment, Dottie went immediately into her bedroom and sat down at the vanity. "I've got to get this garbage off my face," she said. "I wasted all this Lancôme makeup on those rude people." She saturated a cotton ball in witch hazel and ran it along her cheeks. The cotton came away a startling bright orange. "This is really hell on my skin," she muttered.

Opal looked at the makeup table. It was covered with a variety of bright bottles and jars and powders, but everything was lying in disarray, as though someone had broken in, and searched frantically for a certain rare shade of lip gloss.

Dottie suddenly turned to her. "You never wear makeup, do you?" she asked.

Opal shook her head.

"You'd look nice," Dottie said. She opened a paintbox of colors. "Do you want to try some on?" she asked.

Opal had no interest in this, but somehow her mother seemed so depressed, that Opal agreed. She sat down on the bench beside her.

"Here," Dottie said, and she tipped Opal's face up toward her, as though they were about to kiss. "I'll just use a light foundation, nothing heavy." She seemed to be talking to herself. "Your skin is young; it doesn't need to be steamrolled over, like mine does."

"Your skin is nice," Opal murmured.

"Yeah, yeah, as nice as the smoke of a thousand nightclubs," said Dottie. She turned Opal's head to the side. "That's what being on the road does to you. And the lights; I wouldn't be surprised if they cause sterility. I've read about that with fluorescent lights, anyway. Lucky for me I already had you girls before I went into the business."

"Oh, so lucky," said Opal.

"Don't you think I'm happy I had you?" Dottie asked.

"I guess," said Opal. "Happier with me than Erica, anyway."

"I love your sister just as much," Dottie said quickly. "It's just that things are more problematic with her. She hasn't been easy;

177

she never was. Even as a baby, she was so colicky she kept us up all night."

"Was I an easy baby?" Opal asked, but she knew the answer and was just fishing.

Dottie's voice became soft and reflective and pleased. "Oh, yes," she said. "The best."

The pads of her fingers pressed down gently onto Opal's closed eyes as she applied smoke-gray eyeshadow. Dottie moved in close, and her breath came in soft releases against Opal's neck. "I'm just going to even this out, nice and smooth," Dottie was saying to herself.

When she finished, Opal opened her eyes and stared into the big mirror, which was ringed with lights like a marquee. She saw herself and her mother at once, took them both in at the same moment, and for the first time in her life, she thought they looked alike. Makeup could steer you in any direction; Dottie had steered Opal right into her own arms, practically into her own image. Opal's face had filled out; rose blusher brought her cheeks into rounded relief, and a light orange lipstick made her mouth look somehow alive and sort of frightening, like those puppets you make by curling your fist and painting lips on the side of your hand. Not quite human, but still somehow of the flesh. And she held herself like Dottie, she saw. They were both peering into the mirror anxiously now, heads leaning forward like two turtles waking up and looking around.

"Do you like it?" Dottie asked.

Opal thought of the first time she had seen *Persona*, in a Friday-night crowd at Yale, and how excited she had been by the big scene in which Liv Ullmann and Bibi Andersen's faces merge onscreen. "Yes," she finally answered, but her voice sounded different; was it her mother's voice now? Did she hear a laugh track somewhere in the back of her head, an audience prepared to laugh faithfully no matter what?

"You know, men like makeup," Dottie said.

"What?" Opal pictured a public rest room full of businessmen, each of them dressed in a suit and leaning over a mirror at the sink, painstakingly applying eye shadow.

"Yes," Dottie went on. "It can look very sexy on a woman. I think you look terrific with a little color in your face." She paused. "Do you ever think about dating?" she asked. "Is this an appropriate question for me to ask? We never talk about this; I just wondered. You don't have to answer."

Opal and Dottie were still looking in the mirror, addressing each other's reflection. It was hard to stop, to look away from the mirror at the real thing. Opal strained closer to gaze at her own face. The makeup base had been applied so thickly that she couldn't see her pores; she seemed to have been cast in some kind of durable plastic. She ran a hand across her face and felt an involuntary shiver. What kind of man would want to touch such a surface? she wondered. What kind of man wanted to feel polyethylene instead of skin? She thought of her mother's lovers over the years, men who waited for her in hotel rooms after a performance. Did Dottie take off all her makeup before she went to them? Did she come up to the room smelling freshly of cold cream and witch hazel, her face raw and clean and open? Or did she leave it on, because the men who liked Dottie liked the image of her they knew from television: the clown makeup, the bouffant sprayed stiff as doll hair? Opal had an unpleasant vision of her mother lying in a big hotel bed with one of these nameless men; the man was lapping at her face as though it were a plate of milk. Makeup tasted good, Opal realized. Her own lips, she thought, pressing them together, gave off a warm hint of fruit gum.

"I've told you about Walt, the other intern," Opal tried, her voice breaking a little in the middle. "He's very nice, but I just don't know. I can't decide if he likes me or not."

"What's not to like?" Dottie asked. "You're a beautiful girl, Opal, and you've got brains, too. Maybe he's threatened by you; that could be it. Sometimes men are threatened by accomplished women; believe me, I know."

Opal paused. "You mean Dad?" she tried.

Dottie turned to her. "No," she said, "I wasn't thinking of your father in particular, but he certainly fits the bill."

Opal remembered the way her father used to act—how whenever Dottie entered a local talent contest at a school gym, Norm would wait in the car. It was too much for him; he couldn't take it. And it wasn't just Dottie, either; it was Opal and Erica as well. She thought of the last day they had seen him, and how he had taken them to a nearby park for the afternoon. He hadn't known what to *do* with them that day. Both girls were restless, and finally Norm had gotten angry, and said something about how they were both going to grow up to be fidgety.

Now Dottie was looking at her. "I don't *think* anyone is threatened by me," Opal said. "You should *see* the people I go to school with: women with double-800's on their S.A.T.'s, women who have already been flown to Sweden for *physics* festivals or something. There's this one woman I know—Jeanette Kovelman—who just had her first novel accepted. Actually, it's a trilogy; they're going to publish it in a boxed set. She's supposed to write like Virginia Woolf or something. And she's nineteen, and beautiful, too. Believe me," Opal said, "no one is threatened by *me*."

"Well," said Dottie, "you know more about it than I do. But really, Opal, if any romance should happen to crop up, I'd love to be informed." She paused. "I try not to be nosy," she said, "but you never tell me anything about your life. I want to know things about you."

"All right," said Opal. "But you know, we never knew about *your* life, either."

"What is it you wanted to know?" Dottie asked.

Opal didn't answer right away. "About the men," she finally said. "We always wondered."

Dottie smiled. "Ah yes, my mystery love life," she said. "It was a mystery to me as well." She was quiet a minute. "I always liked having men around," she said. "Back when I was on the road all the time, I would grow very lonely late at night. If there wasn't a man around, I would call down for room service and eat an entire three-course meal in the middle of the night. A nice man or a nice piece of veal—the satisfaction was the same. Anything so I wouldn't be bored." She paused. "But I never was with anyone I was serious about. I would have told you girls. At the hotels in

Vegas, the men were gamblers, mostly. No gangster types, just businessmen who claimed to be big fans, and occasionally men who were at the hotel for a convention. There was an anaesthesiologist once, I remember. They were sweet to me, brought flowers to the room. It was certainly more romantic than anything I'd known. We had fun together; it was a very giddy time. But I never had a real *relationship*. I was running around too much; it wasn't possible. I only hope you can have more than what I had," she said. "Now I've got Sy, and I suppose it's enough for me." Her voice was strained. "He wants to get married," she said.

"Really?" Opal asked. "What did you say?"

"What do I need with another marriage, at my age?" Dottie said. "He's always talking about 'settling down,' but I said, 'And do what, Sy, have a *family*?' Like Sarah in the Bible?" She broke off abruptly, switching gears. "Enough," Dottie said, "enough of my life. It's not very interesting, not even to me. Tell me something about you now. What is it with this Walt person? How can we give him a little kick-start in the romance department? How can we get him to ask you out on a date?"

Opal shrugged. "Nobody calls it a 'date' anymore," she said. "You just spend time together, go out to dinner or something. But you don't call it a date."

"Maybe that's my problem," said Dottie. "I'm not up on the current lingo. I guess the whole world is different from the way I thought," she said. "You can say things now that you never used to be able to, and you *can't* say things that you once *could*. Like about my weight," she said. "Those casting people today looked at me as though I was making jokes about handicapped children. I guess what they're looking for is this new kind of comedy. Like that Unidentified Flying Comic."

"Oh, you always bring him up!" Opal said. "He's just one person, just one stupid comedian. There are a lot of different kinds of humor out there."

"But no room for my kind," said Dottie. She turned from the mirror and looked directly at Opal. "I used to like what I did," she said lightly. "I used to look forward to being on the road, to opening at a new club, or appearing on a television show. I liked

181

the perks that came with it: the basket of fruit in the dressing room, the hotel suites. In Vegas, you'd drive down this long strip until you got to the hotel, and your name would be up on one of those giant signs. It always thrilled me, even after I'd done it a thousand times. I used to be funny!" she said, her voice elevating, as though she was surprised by her own words.

Suddenly Dottie Engels couldn't think of a single funny thing. Some gate had been left open, and all the jokes had fled: the horde of fat women with their enormous breasts, their shopping carts, their tortured husbands, their squawling children, their steaming plates of food, their overflowing washing machines, their telephone bills, their entire lives split open and bursting at the seams.

"I still think you're funny," Opal tried.

Dottie smiled weakly. "Thanks, honey," she said. "I appreciate that. I only wish you were a casting agent for a network show." She sighed. "I'm glad for Mia anyway," she said. "She's a nice girl, the two of them are very nice, Mia and Lynn."

"Did you always know about them?" Opal asked.

Dottie nodded. "*About* them? Of course," she said. "It wasn't so hard. One of your other baby-sitters—Danny Bloom, I think it was—asked me if I knew what Mia and Lynn's relationship was. I told him I'd draw him a diagram." She laughed. "I'm not dumb," she said. "It was always hard for those girls. I admired them, even back then. And now," she said, "look at Mia. She's getting written up all over town, she's getting famous, and I can't find work. It's just like *All About Eve*. I never thought Mia would get anywhere. I thought she was too hard-edged for the world; I told her to tone it down, but she didn't listen. And I guess she was right. But back then you couldn't have gotten away with humor like that; it seemed so angry, so man-hating. Today it's considered 'in.' "

"Something will come up," Opal said.

"Oh, maybe, maybe not," said Dottie. "I'll wait and see if Ross really comes through with something. In the meantime, the clothes are actually selling, and that will keep me in pastrami." Dottie fumbled around on the cluttered table to find her cigarettes. She lit one too quickly, and the flame shot up like a small blowtorch.

"Something will come up," Opal repeated, as if on automatic.
Dottie looked very tired, Opal thought, as though she had not slept for days or, rather, as though she *had* been sleeping for days—years, even. Dottie Engels had just woken up from a deep, enchanted sleep and found that the world was an unfamiliar place. Cars were compact now, lean runners lined the Central Park reservoir, a lesbian could be a star. And up in the air, high above everybody, the Unidentified Flying Comic was circling the sky.

16

Erica kept a close watch on Mitchell Block, almost as if he were part of a study she was doing, and not the other way around. She knew when he arrived at his office in the morning, and what time he left at the end of the day. She knew these things because he told her. He mentioned them casually, in conversation over lunch. He might say, "And then when I took off the other day, oh around four-thirty or so . . ." and the fact would become embedded in Erica's mind. She imagined Mitchell pulling together his books and papers and emerging from the basement of the psychology building into the light of a late afternoon.

She knew where he studied in the library, knew it not because he had told her, but because she had seen him there. She had been out walking and had seen Mitchell enter the Bobst Library on Washington Square; he went through the revolving doors in his red down jacket, a knapsack slung over his arm. Erica stopped abruptly. She resisted the impulse to run to him, to cry out his name. Their relationship was being forged bit by bit; she didn't want to force it, although she had to stop herself from doing so. A moment later, Erica was whirling through the revolving doors.

"Do you have an I.D.?" the guard at the desk asked. Erica patted around dumbly inside her jacket, and the guard waved her through.

Mitchell was nowhere to be found. Erica stood in the stark lobby and looked straight up. The ceiling seemed miles above her. Everything was done in dizzying black and white squares; it was like being inside an Escher print. Erica took the elevator up to the top floor and worked her way down. On every level, she walked through the rows of carrels, peered down at the heads bent over books. From a distance she saw a set of wide shoulders, a dark head, and stopped. The man turned around; his face was fair and hairless and not Mitchell.

Finally she found him. He was sitting in a modern armchair by a window on the third floor, his feet up on the sill. She approached him cautiously. "Erica," he said, looking up. He did not appear startled; it was as though, somehow, he had been waiting for her.

This, at least, was what she liked to tell herself: that he knew she would come, that he had summoned her there. He did not ask how she had found him; he accepted it as a given. "Can you take a break?" she whispered.

They went for a short walk around the block, but it was so cold that they stopped on the corner, and Mitchell said, "Do you want to go to my apartment and have some tea?"

Erica nodded. He lived on MacDougal Street, she knew, although he had never invited her there before. She wondered what the invitation meant, and felt suddenly unsteady. As they walked, she put her hand inside her coat, trying to remind herself of what she was wearing. Oh good, she thought, the black sweater. It looked all right, a little bit linty, but not too awful.

Mitchell put the key into the lock of a door on the second floor of an apartment above an Italian café. She heard the bolt slide and release, and then they were inside. The apartment was very small, and she remembered again how big they both were. The front room was narrow and overheated; steam spurted in uneven gasps from an old radiator. Erica and Mitchell took off their coats and threw them over chairs. Clots of snow fell to the floor, but he didn't seem to mind. They sat facing each other at a small round table, drinking Earl Grey tea and eating eclairs that he produced from a white bakery box in the refrigerator. Almost, she thought again, as if he had expected her. The eclair was cold and densely sweet. It had no resistance when she bit into it; it was all give, a crumbly shell surrounding custard. It was so good that she shivered. The steam from the tea rose up at her like a facial, and she

185

poured in honey from a plastic bear bottle with a dented stomach. Everything was intensely sweet; this was the way she wanted it.

When they were done, and the box was empty and the teacups drained, Erica put her hands on the table, fingers splayed, and peered down at them. "I don't know what to do," she said. "I'm very attracted to you." She said it as though admitting a weakness, a deficiency. Mitchell Block's face was red and kind, she saw, and his beard needed a clipping.

"Come," was all he said. Then they stood together, as if agreeing to the next dance, and went into the bedroom. His bed was big and neatly made, the covers pulled tight. Mitchell reached down and in one great sweep pulled everything back.

"Let me," he said when the bed was cleared. He was breathing with difficulty. He came around to her side and took the bottom of her sweater between his fingers, and lifted the whole thing up, inside-out, over her head. She was stuck in the tunnel for a moment, and then came out again into the light. Her hair was now standing straight out from the sweater's static; she flattened it down with her hands. Beneath the sweater Erica wore a white brassiere. It had, for some reason, always embarrassed her: the dazzling *whiteness* of it, and the hidden skeleton of underwire. Mitchell unhooked it, and then his hands caught her breasts at once, as though afraid they would fall to the floor like the snow.

"Oh, look at that," he whispered in this same hushed, thick voice.

And then he was unbuttoning his own shirt, and she felt she ought to help him, make herself useful. She unbuttoned one of his sleeves. Beneath the shirt, his skin was winter-white and covered with a bramble of fair hair. When he pulled off his pants, Erica quickly looked away. She thought of Jordan at home, thought of the first time she had seen Jordan naked, as an adolescent, and how she had looked right at him, unflinching.

But with Mitchell, Erica felt a kind of shyness that she hadn't been known to possess. "It's okay," Mitchell said, and he sat down on the edge of the bed. He circled her with his arms and drew her to him. She felt how much volume they took up; there was no room left in the apartment anymore, or in the bed. She didn't

186

worry, as she sometimes did with Jordan, that she might crush him. Mitchell was not crushable, she thought, running her hands along his sides. She moved against him and he sighed deeply. "That's right," she heard him say. "That's right."

In a while he asked, "Do you want me inside you?" and the image was startling: the huge Mitchell Block actually *inside* the huge Erica Engels. She thought of those rounded Russian dolls that fit into each other. Now Erica nodded yes, and Mitchell reached across her into the night table, his elbow grazing the point of her breast. She watched as he pulled a packet out of the drawer and tore it open. The tearing sound stayed in her head; it was as though Mitchell was swathing his way through a field. Then he was moving against her, and she was aware of the sheer *largeness* of her own body, for the first time in her life, without loathing.

Erica had once seen an episode of "Donahue" that featured slim, handsome men and their hugely overweight wives. "I love big women," one man admitted. "When I saw Connie in the typing pool, I knew instantly I wanted to marry her." Erica had been appalled, looking at the couples sitting blithely onstage, holding hands. They were as bad as Mr. and Mrs. Lye. To worship the flesh like that, to glorify it from a distance, was as bad as reviling it. But here she was with Mitchell, and it seemed that they were approaching something close to worship. She felt the contrast of warm skin and cold sheet, but soon it blended; the sheets heated up, and then they were kicked off altogether.

When they were done making love, Erica lay in the hollow beneath Mitchell's arm; it was the only concavity about him, she thought. Everything else, all the other surfaces she had touched, were wonderfully convex.

"I was just out for a walk," Erica said. "Look what happened."

"I was reading about glandular-generated depression," Mitchell said, "and look what happened."

"I had to leave my apartment," said Erica. "Jordan was about to read aloud selections from *Narcissus and Goldmund*."

"Do you feel guilty for being here?" Mitchell asked.

187

"No," said Erica. "Not at all. I feel good about it, I do."
Mitchell was oddly silent, and she realized that his question was
not entirely simple. "Do *you* feel guilty?" it occurred to her to ask.

He waited a moment, then put his hand over his eyes. "Yes,"
he said. "Extremely." He paused. "There's a woman," he began.
"She's a graduate student in Comp. Lit. We've been seeing each
other for about six months. We've never said we were going to be
expressly monogamous, but I guess it was understood. And now
this, I don't know."

Erica remained under the crook of Mitchell's arm. If she bolted
away, made any sudden gesture, it would have been too dramatic,
so she stayed there, lying close, but she felt a small panic rising
up. Her own heart, she could feel, was beating double-time; it felt
as rapid and fragile as a hamster heart.

"I didn't tell you," Mitchell said, "because I knew that you lived
with your boyfriend. I knew you liked me, but I didn't know it was
going to be like this. And then today, I didn't *think*, really. It just
happened."

"And it was okay," Erica said, "wasn't it? I didn't feel weird
about it with you, as though I had to hide myself or anything.
Because you're used to this, you knew what I would look like."
She stopped. "Do you even know what I'm talking about?" she asked.

"Of course," Mitchell said quietly. "But I don't know what good
that does me, Erica. If I went to Karen, I don't think she would be
particularly moved by your description."

Erica was silent. Finally she asked, "Is Karen fat?" But she knew
the answer, saw it clearly, saw the whole thing: the woman here in
bed with Mitchell on a Sunday morning, the sun flooding in, both
of them eating croissants and papering the bed with the *Times*.
Karen was curled like a cat against Mitchell's side. He protected
her, that was what she got from him. Big, bodyguard protection.
Her other boyfriends had been such little shits. Handsome, wiry,
slender, and nasty. Mitchell Block was different; he would never
quite understand Karen, but would feel a kind of dazed pleasure
that she loved him, or at any rate required his presence. They
could go on like that forever: the quivering delicate woman and
the big, bewildered man.

188

"Is Karen fat?" Erica asked again, her voice sharp.

Mitchell shook his head. "No," he said mournfully. "She wears a size-six dress. She's like a thimble."

"I get it," said Erica. She moved from the hollow of his arm.

"Erica, don't," said Mitchell. "Don't do this. I do feel guilty; I'd be lying to you if I said I didn't, but I don't feel *terrible*. I mean, I feel *guilty* that I feel so good, actually. This was very exciting to me, you know. When you touched me I thought I would *die*."

Erica was propped up on her elbows, several inches away from him. She slowly lowered herself and moved back against him, sighing heavily. It would be painful for her for a while, Erica knew; she would think of little else. She would think of how Mitchell had lifted the curtain of her sweater, and how she had felt no embarrassment with him, none of the distaste that was just another part of making love with Jordan. She had never known it didn't *have* to be there; it had always seemed a prerequisite, like foreplay.

"I ought to go," Erica said, her throat constricting. She sat up on the edge of the bed and began to dress. Bending down to find her socks, she felt Mitchell's large hand curving on her spine.

"Will you come back?" he asked.

She craned her head around to see him. Mitchell, leaning against the headboard, had a convalescent look about him. His eyes were plaintive, his hair and beard matted. She could see his shoulders and arms, which were a pale, milky color, barely a color at all. "I don't know," Erica said. "I don't think it would be such a good idea." She turned back and finished dressing. When she was done, she towered above him, fully dressed.

"Please come see me," he said.

Outside, the street air felt fine; it ruffled her hair and clothes, shook the life back into her. Erica thought of the heat of Mitchell's room, and the saline quality to his skin. In another life, she might have eventually *lived* with him, she thought. Together they would have taken up all the space in that mouse-house of an apartment.

Erica walked quickly along Washington Square South. She had stepped out for a walk hours before, and Jordan would wonder what had happened to her. Or maybe, she thought, he wouldn't. It depended on whether or not his customers were still in the apartment. Erica couldn't bear the idea of returning to that place now. How would she stay there and continue to live with him? How, in fact, had she lasted so long in the first place? It was so much easier to remain inert, to not have to take any action at all. The world was full of people who lay in bed with one person and dreamed of another. It didn't even have to be a particular person you were dreaming about; it could be just an *idea* of a person, someone whom you had to invent and assemble.

Erica realized that she felt suddenly hungry. She had been exerting herself much more than usual: all that walking, and then all that tossing in the bed. When Mitchell lay on top of her, giving her his full weight, she had felt the air pushed out of her for a second. It gave sex some absolute, tangible meaning: the heaviness of two bodies, each of them giving the other a full bulk of weight, saying, *Take this, it's yours,* passing it back and forth like a baton in a relay race. Soon a rhythm is established, and you can take more and more. You show off, like a weight lifter at a gym, piling iron bricks on the Nautilus machine. You go red in the face, you start to sweat, you are actually *laboring.* Sex isn't necessarily an ethereal pastime for two dewy teenagers in a field. When you were big, like Mitchell and Erica, sex was about *matter,* and the shifting and arranging of that matter. It was like sculpting in some thick wet clay and then casting it in bronze.

And now she was starving, longing for something sweet again. Erica was standing on West Fourth Street, and she saw that she was directly in front of a bakery, as though she had landed there divinely. She blinked a few times, then peered in the window. It was filled with tiers of pastry: petits fours iced in pink and white, with little silver balls peppering the top, and a round chocolate birthday cake, the frosting so thick and scalloped that it seemed to have been applied with a putty knife.

She opened the bakery door and a little bell trembled overhead. Inside, the fragrance was surprisingly strong. Erica knew exactly what she wanted. She hesitated before the slanted glass counter for just a second, and then ordered a single eclair.

190

17

Dottie was in the isolation booth. She had headphones on and was blithely listening to Pachelbel's "Canon in D," while outside the booth the double bonus answer was being revealed. "It's a hard one," confided the host of the show, a slender, giggling man named Jack Waring. "But if I know Dottie Engels, she'll be able to figure it out." He paused. "Especially if we tell her there's a free meal in it for her!" He put his hand to his chest and bent over at his own joke, and the laugh light blinked. The audience dutifully complied, although their laughter came in an unstable wave. It could be filled in later, Opal knew; it could be sweetened until everyone seemed to be roaring.

Ross Needler had found work for Dottie. It was a game show, and originally she had been depressed by the prospect and had said no, but after a while she changed her mind and called him back. Something was better than nothing, she had rationalized. It was work; there would be an audience, and a live set, and she would be back on the air.

"Think of the exposure," Ross had said.

"You can *die* of exposure," Dottie answered, but still she agreed.

"Run for the Money" was one of those game shows that relied on physical exertion as much as what Jack Waring termed "brain power." It was a fairly complicated show, Opal thought; if you answered a series of questions right, you made it into the isolation booth for the double bonus question, and if you answered that correctly as well, then you went on a chase for a large sum of money, which was strategically hidden along an extravagant obsta-

191

cle course. Dottie wouldn't be allowed to keep any of the money, of course. It would all go to her teammate, a law student from Fordham named Darren Helper.

Dottie had to pretend that she didn't need the money at all. This was the great irony, and everyone involved with the show's production understood it well. It wasn't just Dottie; most of the celebrities who appeared on "Run for the Money" were experiencing hard times. Alcoholic actors or desperate ex-child stars with faces puffed up and ruined by adolescence—all of them flocked to the show. This week, the other guest was Melanie Sweet, a young dark-haired British actress who had portrayed a villain on a nighttime soap opera before it was canceled. Neither Dottie nor Melanie was appearing anywhere else, but the host treated them as though their careers were blooming madly, and at the beginning of the show he thanked them both for taking time out of their busy schedules. "Of course," he said to Melanie, "viewers remember you best as Tempest Blaine on 'Sutter's Cove,' but I understand you're working on some new projects."

"Oh, yes," Melanie answered in her clipped, distinctive voice, and she went on to explain that she was reading screenplays and searching for the right part. She was afraid, she said, of being typecast as a villainess.

"You know," Dottie offered, "I have similar fears; I'm afraid of being typecast as an overweight woman!"

Again the host doubled over, his laughter exploding like thunder into his little clip-on microphone.

Opal sat in the third row. She had been given the morning off from work. Now she glanced up at the ceiling, which was speckled with recessed lights like a planetarium, as though the universe could be contained within the confines of a theater. Maybe it couldn't be contained, Opal thought, but it could be approximated. The full set of "Run for the Money" was as elaborate and distracting as much of life: all those bright colors, loud noises, and either elation or despair waiting at the end.

When people won big on game shows, their families piled onstage, hugging them and hugging the host. But when they lost, their families stayed safely in their seats, unwilling to be identified.

Nine-year-old kids looked away from fathers who had just mistakenly answered the pivotal question. Images of what *might* have been flashed through the kids' eyes: a Winnebago, a trip to Disneyland, a gleaming Jaguar. All of it wasted, tossed easily into the lap of the opponent. In the car on the way home from the taping, the kids sit sullen in the backseat of the old station wagon, trying to decide whether or not ever to speak to their father again.

At least it's something, Dottie had said all week, as the day of the taping grew closer. Just last night Opal had set up an obstacle course in the living room, at Dottie's request. Opal had held a stopwatch, and Dottie had made her way over the mine field of cushions and upturned chairs. Opal watched as her mother struggled through the clutter. It *was* "something," true, and "something" was given full credit merely because it existed, because it got Dottie out of the house. You had to look for gratification, Dottie often said; it wasn't going to miraculously appear before you. She found gratification in small ways: when her face appeared somewhere, or her name. It made her feel connected to the rest of the world.

Opal had read *Howards End* in her English class the year before, and for weeks afterward everyone had gone around campus murmuring, "Only connect," as though this were the only thing worth remembering from the novel. And what, even, did it *mean?* It had such an easy surface to it; of *course,* you thought to yourself, Forster is saying that we should all connect with each other! And you sat up in bed in the middle of the night, flicking on the lamp and waking your roommate to tell her how important it was that you two "connected." Your roommate lay there squinting at you in her Lanz nightgown, begging you to turn off the light.

So Dottie Engels only wanted to connect; what was wrong with that? You couldn't tell your mother *how* to connect; she had to decide that for herself. No one had told Dottie to be a comedian in the first place; that had been her own decision. It was, people had said in articles early on, her "gift."

During a break, Opal peered down at her mother and waved, but Dottie didn't see her; she was having her hair fluffed by a woman in a smock, and her eyes were closed, as though she were momentarily dozing. The hairstylist gently shook her, and Dottie's eyes opened. The woman disappeared offstage, the light went on again, and everyone was silent. The important round was about to begin, the part of the show that some viewers tuned in for exclusively.

Dottie was going to run the obstacle course. Melanie Sweet hadn't been able to hit the buzzer quickly enough, and she just kept shaking her glossy head of black-Labrador hair. Melanie Sweet's partner, a computer programmer named Suzanne, was given various sad parting gifts, and then her chair and desk began to move on their track, until she had floated offstage, waving forlornly, as though set adrift on an iceberg.

Now the obstacle course was ready. There would be small tasks for Dottie to carry out: "Nothing herculean," the producers had assured her. This was the part that Opal didn't want to watch. She thought about going out into the lobby for a cigarette. She could come back in when it was all over, when Darren Helper had won enough money to pay back his student loans, or else had gone back to the Bronx empty-handed. Her mother's failure shimmered back at Opal like a reflection: herself in the mirror, wearing full makeup. Dottie had started off so big and wide and powerful, and now she was going to run along a snaking track in her red-dotted dress while the audience watched and roared. But it wasn't just Dottie; it was Opal, too, who had started off so small and wiry and clever, and had ended up at this uncertain place. How did we get like this? Opal wondered. She gazed back up at the pinpoint lights on the ceiling. She thought of Erica, standing in the doorway of that lousy building, staring out at her.

Dottie stood at the entry of the obstacle course. Then a loud bell rang and she was off. First to the archery range, where she had to shoot at a target whose colors represented different dollar amounts. Dottie tried two arrows, and both missed the target completely. The third arrow hit the second-lowest amount, $250. The audience loved it. They screamed at her, urging her along. Dottie smiled up at the camera, her face a little crazed with triumph. Next Dottie went on to the pile of Buried Treasure. Somewhere underneath a big mound of dirt was a gold coin with a cash amount written on it. There were also a few dud coins in there, which had nothing written on them at all. Whichever coin Dottie found first was the one Darren would keep. Dottie paused, panting, holding the shovel in one hand. The clock overhead was ticking away, and the audience was quiet once again.

Then she started digging. She went at it with a vengeance, and dirt flew around the stage. Opal watched her mother lift and lower rhythmically; she was like a dog digging up a bone in a yard. Now she was slowing down. The shovel came up, stayed in the air, came down. The camera did a close-up; Dottie's face was a high color, shining with sweat and radiant, as though a light had been left on somewhere underneath the surface. Dottie reached slowly down. Her hand curled around something, but the camera hadn't left her face. Suddenly her expression changed; in close-up it was terrible.

"Oh, help me," Dottie said. She fell to the stage, and the shovel dropped too, with a resilient metallic clang. Opal sprang up, a small cry caged in her throat. The audience turned and murmured. Dottie Engels was flat on her back, a gold coin blazing in her hand.

PART
THREE

18

When the call came, all her clothes seemed to fly into her hands. Suddenly Erica found herself holding a blouse by the collar, a crushed pair of jeans, two socks. The telephone had shaken her from one of those strong afternoon naps, and now she was quickly dressing, stepping into her jeans and jerking the zipper closed.

On the phone, Opal's voice had been flat but frightened. She wasn't calling to buy coke, Erica knew at once. "It's about Mom," Opal had said. "She's had a heart attack."

Erica felt her own chest suddenly compress. She didn't know what in the world to say; finally she found a voice, but it sounded strangely hollow, as if she were speaking on an overseas call. "Where is she?" Erica asked.

"Roosevelt Hospital," said Opal.

What next? Something responsible, supportive. Erica picked at a ragged fingernail. She was breathing faster now, through her nose, like a bull gathering steam. "Well," Erica said, "I'll come there."

There really wasn't a choice, she knew, as she pulled the blanket back and swung her legs over the side of the loft. Crisis did not leave *room* for choice. All your conflicted feelings were supposed to fly out the window, making way for action. But even as you geared up for it, you weren't thinking: *Oh, I'm so humane; I'm such a decent human being.* You weren't thinking at all, you were just responding dumbly, from the porous human marrow inside you. Erica dressed quickly, then hurried into the kitchen for her

199

coat. Jordan was at the table with a box of Arm and Hammer baking soda and a box of safety matches in front of him. He was trying to figure out how to freebase.

"My mother's had a heart attack," Erica said.

Jordan looked up slowly, distracted. "You going there?" he asked, but he did not ask where "there" was. It might have been anywhere; New York was certainly filled with hospitals. Jordan himself had been a patient at several of them. Erica nodded and slipped on her coat, and then she was outside.

During the subway ride uptown, the enclosed space as damp and hot as a Swedish sauna, Erica felt her body rock with the movement of the train, and she wondered if her mother would die, and if she did, what that would mean. She could not even begin to imagine. The train stopped at 14th Street, and the doors slid open. A couple of people hobbled on, and the doors slid shut. At every stop, the train admitted more and more human tragedy, or maybe this was just the way she viewed the world today. Everyone looked specially beaten down by the ferocious cold weather, and the subway's warmth seemed to make it worse, almost highlighting the misery. The lights blinked and went out for a few moments, and they all traveled in merciful darkness.

Erica thought: If my mother dies, I will be lost.

She wasn't sure why this should be so, and yet it felt absolutely true. In some way she took comfort from the fact that Dottie was *out* there. She felt like a child lying in bed while her parents' dinner party rages in the other room. The child does not have to take part, but is somehow soothed by the fact that all night, as she sleeps, the voices will continue, the low murmur of jazz, the gathering of plates.

When Erica arrived at the hospital, she had to follow a labyrinth of colored tape to find the Intensive Care Unit. All she could think of, as she followed the yellow lines at her feet, was the Freedom Trail in Boston, which her family had gone on years and years before. They had followed the brightly colored footprints all over the city, past Faneuil Hall, and the Commons, and Boston Harbor where the tea had been dumped. Now Erica was passing terrible sights: stick figures strapped to stretchers so they wouldn't

200

blow off, nervous families clustered in anticipation around a doctor, an old man trying to wheel himself to the water fountain. She kept going until the yellow tape abruptly ended.

A nurse placed a cool hand on Erica's shoulder. "Do you have a pass?" she asked, her voice wafting straight from the Islands.

Erica shook her head. She tried to explain who she was, and her words came in a rush. The nurse led her into a crowded waiting room. It took her only a second to locate Opal. After an awkward moment of silence, Opal began to talk, giving a short, stuttering summary of how Dottie had collapsed onstage.

"It was really terrible," she said. "There were all these people everywhere, and one of the stagehands said he knew CPR, but it turned out he really didn't. I could barely get into the ambulance with her. And then when I did, I couldn't believe it; this paramedic took out this big pair of shears, like *garden* shears, and cut her dress right off her."

"So what did they say?" Erica asked.

"Nothing," said Opal. "Heart attack, that's all I know. They said to wait here, and somebody would come out and talk to us when they knew something." She gestured toward a pair of windowless doors. "She's in there," she said. "They don't let visitors in. We just have to wait." Opal glanced up. "There are two reporters here," she said. "I told them I didn't want to talk to them. If I *did* talk to them, I'd probably ask them where they've been for the past few years, when Mom needed the publicity. Now they're here when she doesn't need it."

Erica glanced up and saw two young men walking restlessly around the room, picking up old magazines and putting them down. They stood out from the crowd; everyone else was sitting with their families in anxious huddles. On the floor a young boy played with a set of plastic "A-Team" dolls. He sat at his mother and father's feet and talked to himself quietly, while his mother absently stroked his head.

If you brought a blind man in here, Erica thought giddily, he might think he was in a room full of people making love. All these *quiet* sounds, the hushed, agonized noises these desperate families made. It was just like the subway. Why wasn't anyone talking to

201

each other? Erica wondered. If there ever was a time to commiserate, this was it. She could imagine everyone turning from their separate family constellations and beginning to speak as a group. It would all happen at once, like a pivotal step in a folk dance, in which all the couples acknowledge each other and everyone steps back in a giant ring and links hands.

The mother of the little boy would look up and say, "Our daughter swallowed Comet."

Comet, the *cleanser*, Erica would realize, and she would picture the scene: a child clutching the shiny green cylinder, tilting her head back to receive the full flow of powder. Erica shivered. Right now, she thought, Jordan was at the kitchen table with a yellow box of baking soda in front of him. She felt an inexplicable rage toward him—the way he continued to wear his hospital bracelet when nothing in the world was wrong with him, the way he had lounged in his hospital bed for two full weeks, following the soaps and eating canned peaches.

In that moment, Erica made an easy leap onto her mother's side of the fence. Maybe it hadn't entirely happened in that moment; maybe, if she thought about it hard, she might have seen it coming. After all, she had not been able to look at Jordan very much lately. The change had started the day Erica went to bed with Mitchell Block. She had come home and found Jordan sitting up in bed, his hair hanging in strings, his restless hands dancing on a mirror like figure skaters. It was as though she had gone directly from the Bed of Heaven to the Bed of Hell. But she climbed in with him anyway, because she didn't know what else to do, hadn't yet worked out a plan.

In the waiting room, Erica fantasized everyone would have a chance to talk about their particular tragedies. The middle-aged man in the corner might suddenly say, "My wife had a stroke," and as he spoke he would claw at his tie, struggling to loosen the knot.

After each statement, everyone would murmur in sympathy. It was like being at a group therapy meeting, at which everyone was revealing their problem, their addiction, their own personal pattern of self-destruction.

"Our mother had a heart attack," Opal would say, and Erica

202

would be touched and startled by the use of "our." She suddenly remembered the two of them back in childhood, eating macaroni and watching television.

But Opal said nothing; no one did. The waiting room possessed the logic of dreams: You find yourself in a strange place and you're not sure why, and yet you do not question it. You simply move among the other people with grim purpose. Erica kept watching the sad eyes of the young couple and their son. Erica envied the boy. Imagine: to be absolutely lost in the world of the A-Team, to be thinking of nothing but victory and defeat, of good and bad. Imagine: to be sitting on the floor with your mother's hand warm on your head.

When they had been there for what might have been hours, Erica went out into the hall, fishing for change in her pockets. Neither she nor Opal was wearing a wristwatch, and she couldn't even guess what time it was. There were no windows in the waiting room outside the ICU; it might have been any hour of day or night. The only thing Erica had to mark time by was the fact that suddenly she was *hungry*. The method may have been more primitive than a sundial, but it was also flawed. Erica's hunger pains could occur at any time, whether or not she had recently eaten. Sometimes she felt her stomach scoop itself hollow just from fear, or boredom, or because she had seen an ad for McDonald's in the newspaper. Occasionally she woke up in the middle of the night and found herself flinging open the kitchen cabinets without knowing why.

Now the row of vending machines was overwhelming, and Erica pressed buttons randomly. She started with black coffee, and followed it with a Danish that had dropped from the machine for fifty cents. There were other, more bizarre items offered for sale here—old-lady rainhats, vials of cologne, Scottie-dog magnets—but all Erica wanted now was food. She wanted to eat, sitting under the waiting room lights, on the green vinyl couch, with the other exhausted people all around her. She carried an armload of food back down the hall, but when she returned to the waiting room, Opal was gone.

Erica panicked. A small hiss escaped her throat, like air from a tire.

"You looking for your sister?" the young mother asked, and then she pointed.

Across the room, behind the glass of the nurses' station, Erica could see Opal engaged in a pantomime conversation with a young doctor. Both of their hands were fluttering rapidly as they talked. Erica hurried across the room, and several packets of sugar went flying out of her grasp. She knocked on the glass, and a nurse buzzed her in.

Dr. Hammer was talking in a clipped tone. He was young and red-haired and unblinking, and he explained that Dottie's heart hadn't been able to sustain her massive weight, and that she had suffered a massive myocardial infarction.

"Wasn't she under the care of a physician?" he asked. Opal and Erica looked at each other blankly; neither of them had the vaguest idea. "I find it just *astonishing* that no one has ever put your mother on a diet," he said. "Really, it's unconscionable. How has she gone on so long like this?" he asked.

"Because she made her living from it," Opal said simply.

"Well, it may well kill her," he said. "We'll do everything we can on our end, of course, but I just want to prepare you. If your mother pulls through, she's going to be a very sick woman. She will need a lot of care, but we'll talk about that later. For now, we're just trying to stabilize her. I'm afraid that all I can tell you now is to hang around and wait."

Erica glanced at Dr. Hammer's wristwatch, but it was one of those stingy digital jobs that gave nothing away. The square face of the watch was darkly blank, like a television set at rest.

"I'll be checking on your mother periodically," Hammer said. "If there is any change, someone will let you know."

Erica and Opal went back to their post in the waiting room. Opal tapped a cigarette from a pack and lit it, sucking deeply. Erica watched her, observing the long, delicate arms and the round face, all of it at once familiar and *not*. Everything was like that today. Erica wasn't sure what was required of her; she had returned in the middle of a crisis, but there were no parents present, no instructions. They were two grown women with a dying mother, and that was all it was. The disenfranchised, the

204

alienated, the lost: No matter what you were, you returned home at times like these, because if you didn't, your mother's face would loom like a dark angel above your bed forever.

Opal smoked for a while, and they both sat in silence, with everyone whispering and rustling all around them. Every once in a while, one of the reporters drifted over to the couch, but Erica and Opal had nothing to say. Erica closed her eyes. When she opened them again, she realized that she must have fallen asleep. One of the reporters was gone; the other one was reading a magazine in the corner. The young couple and their son were gone too, had been spirited away while Erica slept. There were a few new replacement faces in the room. One of them, a woman in a waitress uniform, sat on the other end of the couch with her head in her hands.

"Opal," said Erica. "Do you know what time it is?"

"I have no idea," Opal said.

"Do you want to talk or something?" Erica asked.

"I don't know what there is to talk about," Opal said.

"Well," said Erica, "I want you to know that I'm not going to disappear again." Her voice, she heard, was coming out louder than she had expected. The waitress lifted her head to listen. "That's all," said Erica. "I just want you to know this."

"It doesn't matter," Opal said. She shifted away from Erica on the couch and closed her eyes, trying to look convincingly asleep. So Opal didn't want to talk; that was her choice, and there was nothing Erica could do about it. In her mind, she unscrolled the day that had just passed: the subway ride uptown, and the long wait, and the face of the redheaded doctor. Erica thought about the fact that Dottie might die, but then she could not give that thought any real meaning. She didn't know what to do with it; she couldn't reconcile herself to it, or in any way start to grapple with it. Instead, the thought slapped up against her and then simply *dropped*, like a baseball lobbed by a father to a dazed and hopeless child.

19

The doorman had lit a votive candle for Dottie Engels. "We're all thinking about your mother," he announced as Opal walked across the lobby, and all she could do was nod and thank him and hurry out into the street to flag a cab. She could not talk about Dottie yet; it was too soon, too much. Walt Green had left three messages on the answering machine, asking Opal to please contact him, but she hadn't returned his calls. She hadn't returned *any* of the calls on the machine yet, although the tape was thick with frantic messages.

Opal didn't know what she would tell anyone. Her mother was out of Intensive Care, momentarily out of "the woods," a nurse had said, but she still lay doped-up and sick, tethered to a monitor and an oxygen tank and I.V. drip. A private nurse named Mrs. Ramsay sat beside the bed and knitted an afghan with bundles of bright, unraveling wool.

At first Dottie didn't talk very much, and her voice, when she used it, was rusted and slow. "You girls still here?" she asked, and Opal and Erica piped up from the windowsill that they were indeed right here. "Did anyone call Sy?" Dottie asked. "Did anyone take in the mail?" Opal assured her that everything had been seen to, that Sy was on his way home, and that all Dottie had to do was lie still. "I don't feel anything," Dottie said. "No pain. Just a little nausea. Nothing." After a while she sank back into a chemical sleep.

Opal thought of Sal the doorman in his brown uniform with

gold braid, kneeling down to place a votive candle on the altar of a church somewhere in Brooklyn. The trappings of serious illness were so bewildering: rows of candles and tanks of oxygen and all those *flowers*. Dottie's room was choked with huge arrangements of peonies and gardenias that friends had sent, and a vine that spidered wildly across the windowsill and trailed like a comet to the floor.

In the evening, Sy returned from Hong Kong. He swept into Dottie's room directly from the airport, and Opal and Erica watched as he leaned over her bed to kiss her hello. "I got on a plane immediately," Opal heard him say.

"Sy, I had a heart attack," Dottie said, her voice tiny.

"No kidding," said Sy. "I thought it was an ingrown toenail."

"Please," said Dottie. "Don't."

Before Sy had even had a chance to take off his coat, Dr. Hammer swung into the room. "I'm going to examine her," he said, "but you people should stick around outside, because I'll want to talk to you afterward."

They walked out into the hall as the doctor was whisking a curtain around Dottie's bed. Opal quickly introduced Sy to Erica, who looked confused. Sy leaned against the wall and shut his eyes. She noticed that he hadn't shaved, and that his tweed suit was lined with creases. "You must be exhausted," Opal said.

"Ah," he said, "who knows. I'm still on Hong Kong time. It'll catch up with me later. For now, I'm not thinking about it. I have other things to worry about." The three of them stood stiffly together in the dim hallway, while in the background bells lightly rang and elevator doors slid open and closed. After a few minutes Dr. Hammer beckoned them back inside.

"I want everybody to hear this," he said. "It's very important." He adjusted his collar and positioned himself beside the head of Dottie's bed, looking pointedly at Opal and Erica. "As you know, your mother is very sick," he said. "But she has a choice. She can change her life and get well, or she can remain the way she is and soon die." He spoke with a kind of hushed intensity, and Opal imagined that he might have been a member of some cult religion

207

before turning to medicine. "And when I say change, I mean seriously," he said. "I'm not talking about some piddling, half-assed diet." He turned to Dottie. "Your blood pressure is sky-high," he said, "and your heart is the size of a ham. It's actually amazing that you've survived this long; it says something about your strength. But in your present state, you are a walking time bomb."

Opal looked over at Erica, who stood clawing at a fingernail, and at Sy, who was nervously smoothing down the creases on his suit. Finally she looked at Dottie, who was lying perfectly still.

"What do you mean, 'change'?" Dottie said.

"For one thing," said Hammer, "you have to stop smoking. Cold turkey. And you must lose weight. Not just some small amount, but over a hundred pounds. Exercise. This isn't a joke. You've got to change."

"I thought you said I had a choice," Dottie said.

"Maybe you didn't understand," said Hammer. "I'll say it again: If you don't lose weight, you will certainly die. Another heart attack very soon, I would guess. More severe, and probably fatal. Your heart is *huge*."

"Yes, I've heard," said Dottie. "Like a ham."

When he was gone, no one moved. Everyone stood where they were, until finally Sy said, "So, what do you think, Dot?"

"I think it's lousy," she said, her voice trembling. "*Change* myself. Nobody can really change."

"They're not asking you to change your inner self," Opal said. "Just your weight."

"Maybe that is my inner self," said Dottie. "You don't know what it's like being fat." She turned to Erica suddenly. "Erica," she said, "you know what I'm talking about, don't you? You know what it's like. Tell them."

But Erica wouldn't answer. She just shrugged and looked away.

"All right then," said Dottie. "I see I'm on my own here."

"Dottie, you're not on your own," said Sy. "You have all our

208

support. Whatever you need to do, you'll *do*. And we'll all help you."

"Forget it," said Dottie, and she began to cry. "I'm not up to it," she said. "I just don't have it in me." Erica reached over to the night table and pulled up a fistful of tissues for her. Everyone kept standing there while Dottie cried noisily. At one point, Mrs. Ramsay looked up from her knitting and suddenly said, "It's the drugs, you know. They make you depressed. I had one heart patient, a priest, who cried like a baby."

"I feel terrible," said Dottie, when she could speak again. "I don't want to be here in the first place, and now they come in and tell me I have to *change*. I've spent a lifetime a certain way; I'm not about to suddenly become someone else. The public knows me this way; it's who I am." She gestured loosely. "This is *it*," she said. "What you see is what you get."

"Maybe not," Opal tried. "Maybe there's more."

Dottie shook her head, twisting the tissues between her hands. "No," she said. "I don't want to live if it means becoming something I'm not."

"What is this?" said Sy. "You sound like that license plate, 'Live Free or Die.' "

"That's how I feel," said Dottie. "I appreciate all your concern, but it's my choice. Hammer said so himself. And I choose *not* to change my life. I'd rather just let go, just not fight it."

"What do you mean?" Opal said. "You're talking like a real nut case."

"No, I'm making perfect sense," said Dottie. "It's my life, and you've got to trust me. Anyway, you girls will do fine by yourselves; you always have. Please," she said. "Don't argue with me; I'm not up to it. I feel sick. I need to sleep."

And with that, Dottie pressed a button and her motorized bed slowly changed position, buckling like a wave.

Late that night, back in the apartment, Opal padded into the kitchen and opened the refrigerator. Faced with the solid wall of food, she was overwhelmed and could not choose. This was the way Dottie Engels ate; this was why she was so huge. Opal remembered one of Dottie's oldest jokes: "I do have a weight problem; I just can't *wait* for dinner!" She found herself smiling, thinking about it now, but then suddenly the humor was lost, and she leaned into the bright cold light of the refrigerator and began to cry.

She didn't know what she was supposed to do; she hadn't in any way prepared herself for this. To be orphaned at twenty had never seemed a possibility. And Erica would be no help at all; Erica kept herself at an arm's length from civilization, so she was untouched by disaster. What was to come? Opal wondered. What frightened her most was that she couldn't even begin to imagine.

Maybe she would become one of those nervous, lost women you sometimes saw in the city, prowling Columbus Avenue after work. The kind of woman who will probably spend the night watching cable TV at home, stabbing a finger up and down the row of channel buttons. Dozens of choices haunted the nighttime airwaves: phone-in psychics, nude talk shows, ancient black-and-white sitcoms that evoke a world of meddlesome neighbors and separate beds. It doesn't matter what is watched, finally, because *all* of it is interchangeable. What matters are the voices that expand to fill the room.

Opal thought of how Walt had walked around the apartment and marveled at the space, seeing it in a way that Opal no longer could. The ceilings seemed too high to her now, the walls too far apart. How strange that the temper of rooms could shift like the seasons. Years before, the apartment had been a perfect size; the rooms had spilled into each other endlessly, and it didn't seem impossible that a new wing or passageway might be discovered behind a closed door, like an apartment in a dream. Nothing had seemed impossible then. You could feel the presence of real life in those rooms, with the baby-sitters practicing and Erica's incense infusing the air with its sweet stink. Dottie had barely been home then, but it almost hadn't mattered. Whenever her mother was away, Opal prepared for her return. She waited under the awning

210

with the doorman, and when the limousine pulled up at the curb she skidded out onto the sidewalk, pressing her face to the square of smoked glass.

Now Opal went into her mother's bedroom and sat down on the large bed. She lit a cigarette, and the snap of the lighter, the friction of her thumb against the little wheel, was peculiarly satisfying. If Dottie listened to Dr. Hammer, she would never be able to smoke again. Imagine, Opal thought, never letting a cigarette take its time to burn between two fingers, never pulling in smoke and feeling it roll like water down your throat. This would be difficult for Dottie, she knew. But what would be much worse, of course, would be the food. Dottie would have to give up the important items: anything with a crust, or filling, anything glutinous or dense or set afloat in butter. No salt, either. When Dottie salted food, Opal remembered, her hand moved as rapidly as someone shaking a maraca.

But it wasn't just the food. It was something else that Opal couldn't really imagine: this notion of *losing* yourself for good, giving up the reflection in the full-length mirror. Giving up the known, the given, the thing that you had never really liked, but which you knew would always be there. If *you* couldn't recognize yourself anymore, how could you expect anyone else to? Even the idea of you would disappear. In a way, it was worse than a death.

Opal sat smoking in the bedroom, and she realized that she was actually talking herself into agreeing with her mother's decision, giving Dottie permission to let go. But this was all wrong; Opal needed to calm down a little, get her bearings. She reached across the bed to where the remote control lay, and she hit the power.

Immediately a medical drama sprang to the screen. "Is Rick going to be all right, Doctor?" a young woman was asking. She was dressed in elephant bell bottoms and a headband; this was clearly a Sixties rerun.

The doctor opened the door and let Katrina into the hospital room, where her boyfriend lay on a bed, his arms and legs

211

restrained by leather cuffs. He had apparently wigged out on LSD, and was now talking like a madman, or a mystic.

Even in the midst of everything, television still went on. What had Opal expected, that all the channels would have a day of silence out of respect for Dottie Engels? That they would all broadcast the static pattern that came onscreen at the end of a programming day, and all you would be able to hear was the flat, steady hum that told you there was nothing on, that the world was asleep, and that you ought to be, too?

This was what death did to you, or the possibility of death: It made you long for some stasis, for maybe just a measly fifteen minutes' worth, in which the whole world might slow to a wobbly standstill like a child's top.

Opal opened the drawer of her mother's night table. She found random, unconnected items inside: emery boards, a checkbook, a spool of dental floss. The smallest, most benign items were the worst to look at now; they hammered home the reminder that this person's life was made up entirely of daily acts: a life strung together on *dental floss* as much as anything else. Opal climbed off the bed and went to her mother's closet. She flung open the door and snapped on the overhead light, then she began rooting around as though she were looking for one particular item, when in fact she was looking for nothing at all. She let herself forage through Dottie's clothing, and all of it smelled shockingly familiar, as though Dottie herself were still inside each dress, her body warming and filling it.

Opal buried her head in the rack. Down below, she saw, were the shoes, lined up in a homely row. Her mother had extremely wide feet, EEE width; her shoes looked as though they were straining at the sides, gaping open like the mouths of baby birds. Dottie had tottered around onstage on wide women's pumps with narrow spiked heels, all her weight resting on two skinny pivots. Dr. Hammer had not gotten over how much Dottie weighed, and how no one had done anything about it.

Suddenly Opal was ashamed. But what *should* she have done? Put one of those horrible gag tape recorders in the refrigerator, so when Dottie pulled open the door, the refrigerator would seem to be speaking to her, saying: *You eat too much, fatso! Close me, I'm freezing!* Or maybe she could have sat her mother down in the den and said, "We're all worried about you, Mom. You simply must lose weight." This would have been reasonable, and yet it had never once occurred to Opal. Her mother was simply what she was, the sum of all those pounds, and always had been. Opal remembered the way Dottie used to hold her, years ago, taking her up on her wide lap, and how Opal had felt a flood of pleasure every time.

Once, a long time ago, when Opal was ten or eleven, she had sat on her mother's lap on network television, in front of millions of viewers. It was a Christmas special, and at the very end of the show, Opal, dressed in a white dress with crackling crinoline beneath, had been instructed to walk across the stage, into the hard gloss of the television lights.

Dottie was dressed as Santa Claus, and Opal walked right toward her, moving stiffly. She was aware of each careful, mea-sured step—straight-legged as a palace guard, making sure that she would not skid in her buffed patent leathers. All the way across the stage Dottie waited, dressed in a red flannel Santa outfit and authentic-looking beard. Opal went to her and climbed onto her lap, as they had rehearsed twice that afternoon. Even from under the thick flannel she could smell her mother's perfume.

Opal had one line of dialogue to say; the director had instructed her to wait until all the applause died down, until even the stray wintertime coughers were quiet. "Just take your time," the director had said. "We have all the time in the world."

So when everyone was silent, Opal gathered a breath, looked into Dottie's eyes, and said her one line: "Mom, when are you going to help me with my homework?"

At this, the audience broke into tremendous laughter. "Well," Dottie called out, "as you can see, I'm needed at home, but I hope you've had as much fun tonight as I have! Thank you, everybody, for making this a holiday to remember. Merry Christ-mas to all, and to all a good night!"

213

Then the orchestra began to play, and a bevy of Santa's Helpers did cartwheels across the stage, and Opal gripped the edges of her mother's flowing white beard, holding on for dear life.

20

The first thing Erica noticed was his eyebrows. "What have you done?" she asked when she walked in. "You look like Cat Woman." Jordan's eyebrows had for some reason been tweezed down to scraggly, arching lines. It was early evening, the night of Dottie's heart attack, and Erica had just gotten home from the hospital. All she wanted now was dinner—a plate of something steaming and aromatic, which hadn't come out of a machine—but she was startled when she saw Jordan. He was sitting on the living room couch, rolling a joint, and he looked a bit like a transvestite. Erica took off her coat, still staring at him.

Jordan shrugged. "I had a little accident," he said, and he looked embarrassed. "You know yesterday I was freebasing for the first time, and I cooked the baking soda with the cocaine, like you're supposed to—I mean, I had a detailed recipe—and then when it was all dried and ready, I lit a pipe of it, and it sort of exploded in my face. It's a miracle I wasn't hurt; the flame just jumped up and burned my eyebrows, but the skin was barely touched. I mean it hurt a *little*, but not really bad. So today I tried to even them out with a tweezer, and they came out like this."

Erica stood looking at him, shaking her head slowly. "What are we going to do?" she asked.

"A little witch hazel feels good," Jordan said. "Maybe you could pick some more up when you go out."

"I don't mean that," Erica said, but she was too tired to elaborate. She went into the kitchen and opened a package of pasta, and she set a pot of water to boil. She was looking for simple tasks to

215

occupy her, so she would not have to think. The hands could move and the mind could rest.

From the living room, Jordan called, "So what's with your mother?"

The question pierced her. She didn't want to answer; she didn't even know that she could. If Erica suddenly started to cry, Jordan would be shocked. He had never seen her cry, and he would not get it. "You never see her, as it is," he would say, in an attempt at solace. But Erica didn't cry, and instead she just sat listening to the hiss of the gas jets. Finally she called back to Jordan, "She's alive, my mother's alive, but she's still very sick." Then Erica dropped a fistful of spaghetti into the pot, and she waited until the sticks bent in the heat of the water. She wanted to eat her dinner alone, to find a quiet place in the apartment where she could sit and eat and not think about Jordan and their life together. She didn't want to look at his arched, Tallulah Bankhead eyebrows, or hear him recite selections from Brautigan or Vonnegut.

Erica carried her bowl of spaghetti up into the loft, and sat there with the lights off. The air was close up there, and smelled slightly medicinal. If she was a normal person, she knew, then there would be someone she could call to talk to about Dottie. She could even let her voice go all weak and then split with emotion down the middle. The friend would listen and respond appropriately, and then say, "Look, Erica, I'm getting into a cab and coming over to see you now. We'll go out for coffee; we'll do *something*. Don't argue."

She realized that she had never had any real women friends. Maybe there was a book in this: *Women Who Hate Women*, it could be called, and Erica could go on television talk shows to publicize it. Of course, she would have to change her image, sort of tone it up a bit. Very few of those women who wrote self-help best-sellers were actually glamorous; instead, they were sometimes plain, homely, or overweight women who had been treated badly their entire lives, and who finally gathered enough courage to write about it with a vengeance. And then they went on a diet, got an expensive Egyptian-style haircut, bought big hoop earrings and

216

an electric-blue dress with a big bow at the throat, and went on national television.

I could do that, Erica thought, twirling her fork in her dish. *Women*, she would say to the audience, *I grew up in a household of women, and I lacked a father figure, so when it came time for me to choose a mate, I selected one who treated me badly, who didn't appreciate my womanhood.*

But that was nonsense. She didn't think that Jordan treated her badly because she was a woman; he didn't treat *anyone* well; he didn't know how to talk to adults, or listen to them, and he couldn't look anyone straight in the eye. It was as though Jordan possessed a little boy's filthy, snickering secret, but had long ago forgotten what the secret was, and only the mannerisms remained. He was happiest when he was around his teenage customers; only then did he seem to come awake.

Every day now Erica and Opal went to the hospital and took turns sitting in their mother's room, watching her shift and sigh in the bed. On the third day, after Dr. Hammer told Dottie that she would die unless she lost a drastic amount of weight, Erica went home and wanted nothing more than to be left alone. She hoped that Jordan would be occupied with his chopping and cutting all night, so that she wouldn't have to talk to him. But at seven o'clock the buzzer rang and the teenagers returned. They made a few mocking comments about his eyebrows, but when they realized he was truly upset, they let up. Erica heard all of this from the loft, where she lay drowsing. She didn't even need to see the scene to know what was going on. It was Mandy and Parker and a friend of theirs named Frodo, who had recently been kicked out of Headley when Quaaludes were found in his paintbox in art class.

"They're sending me off to New Hampshire to a school where there are 'other people like me,' " she heard Frodo say. "Little do they know there are 'other people like me' right here at Headley."

"Here's to Headley," Jordan said, and Erica imagined that they must be lifting up cut pieces of Flexi-Straws to make a toast. Then they broke into the Headley School song, which Erica hadn't heard in years. Jordan's voice was the strongest, and he led the chorus of voices:

217

"As *the years go by and our life marches on*
There is one place that we'll remember
As *we gaze ahead to our future bright and bold,*
We think back to each September . . ."

Erica listened as they all hurried through the phrase "future bright and bold," which never quite fit into the line. She could actually hear emotion in Jordan's voice; there seemed to be a slight tremolo as he sang. She saw him transforming, before everybody's eyes, into a *chanteuse*; he already had the eyebrows, he just needed the dress, something off the shoulder. Jordan and his customers were sitting in the living room around the coffee table, where the old, scratched mirror was having a razor drawn along its surface. They would be there for hours, she knew, endlessly talking. What did they even talk *about?* she wondered, for she hadn't been able to talk to Jordan for months. The last good conversation she had had, she realized, was with Mitchell Block, whom she missed terribly.

Erica rolled over in the bed, drew herself up with her legs tucked into her chest, a position she used to assume during bomb drills at school. If she could see Mitchell now, she would tell him many things: She would describe the day and night at the hospital, down to all the smallest details—how the hallway had smelled of death and ammonia and something that was supposed to be chicken *française*. She would talk about how it had been, seeing Opal, and finally how Dottie had looked in that room full of flowers. She would tell him how her mother wanted to die.

Mitchell, who had been reading all day in the library, would nod slowly, his intelligent eyes taking everything in. He would hold her and rock her, and tell her there was hope still, that it was possible to think this through. Then he would tell her hopeful stories about his family in Wisconsin. Every fall, he would tell her, they went to a big Cheesefest, and during the ride back, the trunk packed with cheddars in varying degrees of sharpness, they would all sing songs and lean against each other and renew their familial love. Love could regenerate, he would say; it could grow like the arm of a starfish.

218

But she couldn't call him, she knew. It would only start things up again, and that was the last thing she needed. Erica felt a clean whistle of pain inside her. She had always imagined herself to be greedy, a constant consumer who took up too much space in the universe, but now it seemed possible that all along she had been denied so much: Could *both* versions be true? It was like stuffing yourself with carbohydrates; some urges were satisfied, but even when you could eat no more, you still felt hollow in some basic way. She thought of those Ethiopian babies who die even after they're rescued and given nutrients, because their bellies can't take it, it's too late, it's all wrong. They swell up and burst; they spontaneously combust.

My mother has spontaneously combusted, Erica thought. Dottie had been filled with so much, but most of it was garbage: all those acres of layered desserts, those pots of oleaginous eye makeup and lip gloss, those garish hotel rooms with their sunken tubs and round beds and room service, and, finally, all those hours of terrible, self-hating jokes. Night after night in the dark Dottie had stood under a spotlight and reeled off a catalog of grotesqueries, and the audience had egged her on.

"If you're fat and you're a woman," Dottie had often said, "then you'd better be funny." But Erica hadn't been funny; instead she'd been one of those moony, serious, do-gooder girls, although she secretly knew she possessed a cold heart. Erica had read somewhere that Florence Nightingale was supposed to have been a terrible person, a really compassionless nurse who went about her work efficiently, but who instilled fear in the hearts of her charges. It wasn't that Erica lacked the capacity to love; she loved Mitchell, she realized, in some deep, unyielding way, but it did her no good.

From the next room came the sound of voices again, rising up in an unsteady medley of Sixties hits. Jordan and Mandy were singing that song about the carpenter and the lady. His voice seemed to get lost under Mandy's wispy, delicate soprano. Suddenly the song ended because they had run out of words. There was some discussion, and then they broke into a version of "Both Sides Now." Suddenly the others joined in, and they were tone-

219

lessly singing the one song that all of them knew, slogging their way through the lyrics, as though it were a college fight song.

The singing would go on all night, if she let it. She could just lie up here in the loft, utterly forgotten, and wait until the others finally went home and Jordan reluctantly climbed the ladder. Erica sat up in bed, her head slightly grazing the ceiling. She peered out into the living room, and could see the tops of everybody's heads. They were all sitting on the floor, and Jordan, she saw, had his arm looped around one of the girls, and she was leaning against him companionably. It was Parker, Erica saw, leaning forward to get a better look, and she knew that they must have sat like this before. It seemed probable that they had a sexual relationship, although she couldn't imagine Jordan working himself up anymore into a real state of passion. Over the past winter, his attention span had been considerably shortened, snapped off sharply at the end.

Watching them, Erica felt a dull wave of surprise, but it transformed quickly into something resembling relief. She thought of Dottie, alone in her hospital room, sleeping uneasily in that strange place. Then she thought of Opal, alone in the apartment they had once shared. Erica was tired, but she climbed down from the bed and got dressed in the darkness, leaning against the ladder as she laced up her shoes. She had to stand self-consciously in the living room for a few seconds before anyone noticed her. When they did, they all looked up impassively.

Jordan let his arm drop casually from Parker's shoulder. "What's up?" he asked.

"Can I talk to you?" Erica said.

Jordan rose slowly, like an old man, and followed her into the kitchen. "It's not what you think," he said.

"You don't know what I think," Erica said. "I'm leaving. And don't flatter yourself why. It has nothing to do with that girl in there."

"Then what?" he demanded. "Are you upset about your mother? Is that it?"

Erica paused; she wanted to laugh. How could he miss everything that went on? How could he not know a thing about the world? "Yes, I'm upset about my mother," she said, "but that's not it." She felt herself growing giddy. "It's because of your *eyebrows*," she said. "That's it. I'm afraid you're prettier than I am now."

"Oh, very funny," Jordan said. He looked beyond her into the living room, where someone must have been signaling to him. "Do what you want, Erica," was all he said, and it was enough of a send-off; it was all she needed to leave.

When she had slammed out the door, she stood in the hall for a second, listening. She should have made a clean exit, she knew, and just kept going down to the bottom and out the front door, but she was much too curious. She stood for a moment with her ear against the apartment door. First there were mumbled voices, nothing she could make out, and then silence. And then apparently the discussion about her had ended, for Jordan burst forth with the opening lines of "Teach Your Children," and everyone joined in.

Sal the doorman didn't recognize her at first. She had to pull off her parka hood and stand right in front of him, before he said, "Erica! Hey, where have you been? We missed you." He stopped himself. "We're all really sorry about your mother," he said.

She thanked him and walked slowly through the lobby. It had been ages since she had been here, and yet she felt a remarkable tinge of nostalgia. The floor was as highly polished as a ballroom, and the same armless statues stood in niches in the wall. There, across the lobby, was the bank of elevators, which she had ridden in unhappy silence for so many years, standing between her mother and sister. It hadn't always been like that; when they first moved in, Erica had loved the apartment. She used to wander around while the painters were working, inhaling the heady latex fumes and fingering the drop cloths thrown over all the furniture.

Erica still had keys to the apartment, but she thought it was better to have Opal let her in. She pressed the bell and first heard footsteps, then her sister's nervous voice. "Who is it?" Opal asked.

"Erica," she answered.

There was silence for a moment, and then Erica could hear the locks sliding, one by one. The door opened, and Opal stood there wearing a bathrobe and clutching the *TV Guide*. She looked quizzically at Erica.

"I left Jordan," Erica said. Opal just stared. "I thought I should be here," she continued. "We have to talk about this."

Opal nodded and didn't say anything, and Erica took it as an invitation in, at least the best invitation she was going to get. The apartment was quiet, and perfectly neat. Erica walked down the hall to her old room, and was surprised to find it exactly as she had left it. There was still an ancient Reva and Jamie poster on the wall, and the same coffee can of Magic Markers still stood on her desk. She thought of how she used to sit there and write bad poetry, then illustrate it with rainbows and those cartoon dog heads that every thirteen-year-old girl knew how to draw. Erica uncapped a magenta Magic Marker and tested it on the desk blotter, but the tip was dry as a candlewick.

21

Erica had been home less than an hour, when she came to Opal's doorway and said, "Come into my room."

My room. How easy the territory was to reclaim. You didn't have to do a thing; the linens on the bed were clean, the drawers of the bureau waited to receive your clothes. Everything had been left intact, and all you had to do was show up and it was yours again. Even though Erica probably hated this place, she was already inhabiting it fully, walking barefoot in the lawn of beige carpeting.

So Opal followed her into the bedroom, remembering how thrilling such an invitation had once been. Now she felt only uneasy as Erica pushed open the door. As they settled themselves back on the bed, taking their places at the head and foot, Opal thought of how they had only one fact in common now: Their mother was dying.

She leaned back, resting her shoulders against the familiar curve of wood. They would discuss specifics, Opal thought; they would say how upsetting it all was, how unexpected, and Opal might even start to cry. Erica would look embarrassed, and would try to comfort her, moving closer and patting a big bear-paw on Opal's back.

But what Erica said was, "We should do something."

Opal looked blandly at her. "Such as?" she asked.

"You know," Erica said. "Give her *reasons.*"

Beneath the wild wreath of hair, Erica's eyes were narrowed with intent. Opal wasn't used to the idea of Erica taking charge; it hadn't happened in years and years, not since Erica had swung a flashlight around the room and Opal had sat in wonder, watching.

"But I don't know any," Opal finally said. "You never think about whether you want to be alive; you just wake up every day and you *are*. I can't imagine what it would be like if it were a decision."

"I can," said Erica.

Opal watched Erica across the bed, saw the way she sat with her arms crossed awkwardly over her breasts. "Is it so bad?" Opal finally asked. "Have you really been that miserable?"

Erica nodded. "I used to be," she said, and then she paused. "But I'm not now," she added. "You have this view of me, that I'm right out of *Panic in Needle Park* or something. That I live like an animal."

Opal started to object, but her voice died out quickly. It was really an accident, she thought, how each of them had ended up; it was only a question of where the hammer had struck. It was that way in most families, she knew: There was always someone who nobody spoke about. The older sibling at a special school upstate, or the one who stayed in his room during family dinners, or who had only a post office box somewhere in the Midwest for an address. It was easy to lose people along the way.

"I'm sorry," Opal said, suddenly embarrassed.

"Oh," Erica said lightly, "I didn't mean to start anything. We've got enough to deal with." She paused. "You've got to tell me things," she said. "I've been gone so long, I don't know anything."

"Things?" Opal said. "Like what?"

"Well, tell me about Sy, for a start," Erica said.

Opal nodded. "He and Mom have been involved for a while," she said. "He's sort of like her. They go out to eat all the time, they drink a lot." She shook her head. "He's very upset about all of this too, but I don't think he'll be able to do anything. I don't think anyone will." Opal thought of Dottie lying flat on her back, like a whale that has been speared and landed. Then she felt something stirring in her, and she placed one hand across her eyes.

"Opal," said Erica. "Hey."

224

Opal looked up; for a moment, staring into the wide plate-face of her sister, it might almost have been Dottie sitting there. Dottie at a simpler time, Dottie Breitburg as a girl in Brooklyn, making her relatives laugh. "We always had people around when I was a girl," she used to tell Opal and Erica. "It made up for my being an only child. I always loved the way our house was filled with visitors."

Visitors. Opal wondered if it would help her mother to have a few other people come see her in the hospital. Dr. Hammer had said that she would probably be up to it in about a week, although Dottie insisted she didn't want to see anyone. Opal imagined an endless stream of guests filing into her mother's room. She could picture Dottie slowly looking up from the bed and coming back to life. The influx of people would remind her of her populated childhood, and of all the years when her dressing room was always packed with friends and fans after a show.

"I wonder," Opal slowly said, "about bringing some people in to see her. What would you think of that?"

"It depends on what you mean," Erica said.

"Friends," Opal said. "People she's worked with. Something to buoy her up. She always had a lot of people around her, and I know she misses it."

"Well," Erica said after a moment, "it's a start. It's something. Sure, we could try that if you want."

They were both silent. "Can I ask you something?" Opal finally said, and Erica nodded. "Please don't take this wrong," she went on. "I just want to know why you've suddenly become so involved. Why you want to help like this. I mean, I appreciate it and everything, but it comes out of the blue."

Erica looked surprised, but she responded quickly. "Sometimes you just do things," she said. "I mean, she's *dying*. For that matter," she went on, "why did *you* call me in the first place?"

Opal thought about how she had stood at the telephone outside the emergency room and found Erica's number in the frayed Manhattan White Pages hanging from a piece of wire. At first she had made the call only because she thought Erica had every right to know. At first it had nothing to do with need. And yet, when

225

Erica stood in the door of the waiting room twenty minutes later, Opal had felt a rush of *relief*—for here, she thought, was someone who might split this wealth of grief down the middle. But grief didn't work like that. When it had to, she saw, it doubled in size so there was enough to go around, and only then did it split itself in two like a cell undergoing mitosis.

"I'm not sure why I called," she said. "I just did."

"*Exactly*," said Erica.

They might have been children then, Opal thought; they might have been sitting together in the wonderful peace of an early evening, with the TV babbling safely down the hall, and a baby-sitter hovering somewhere nearby.

"They said she has a heart like a ham," Opal suddenly said. "What a funny way to put it. Isn't that a song?" She began to sing. "Some say the heart is just like a ham . . ."

Erica cleared the hair from her face, and Opal saw that she was smiling. She also saw, once again, how little they resembled each other. There was nothing to mark them as sisters. Only the joint history that kept rearing up once in a while: a shared father and mother, the protoplasm in which everything floated. They had a father living on Coconut Court, and a mother whose every heartbeat moved in dramatic peaks and valleys across a screen, like a drawing done on an Etch-a-Sketch. All sharp points, no sloping curves. There weren't any subtleties here; just the rhythm of life, which was in itself unsubtle. You were either alive or dead; there wasn't a third choice. You couldn't stay suspended forever. Eventually, you had to land.

The next day at the hospital, Sy was busy unwrapping the gifts for Dottie he had brought back from Hong Kong. "Here's something I thought you'd like," he said, holding up a scarlet silk kimono with black calligraphy sewn across the back. "I thought it would look nice with your coloring, Dot. After I bought it, I asked a fellow I know to translate the writing on the back, and he told me it means 'Eat the American Capitalists.' Go figure."

"Sy," said Dottie. "I'm not in a very good mood. I ache all over. I just want some quiet in here."

226

He put down the kimono. "All right," he said. "Quiet you'll get. I'm going to go downstairs and get some ptomaine on rye." He left the room quickly, leaving the gifts scattered across Dottie's bed.

When he was gone, Dottie said, "What's with him?"

Opal stared at her. "We're all upset with you," she said. "It isn't just Sy."

"I'm sorry to hear that," Dottie said. "I don't mean to interfere with your lives. I want you to go back to work, Opal. You don't have to spend every day here with me; it can't be too interesting. You have better things to do."

"It's all right here," said Opal. "I'm going to stay until you're feeling better. Less depressed. Until you talk about getting well."

Dottie smiled grimly. "Don't hold your breath," she said. "Hammer sent a social worker up here, and she told me about some weight-loss clinic in California. The Lexington Clinic. You live there and lose weight, she said. She really was pushing me to go, but of course I told her I was *not* interested."

"Why not?" Opal asked.

"I'm just not interested," said Dottie. "*Please.*" She closed her eyes and shifted in the bed. "Oh, when is Mrs. Ramsay coming back?" she asked. "She went out to some store called Yarn 'n' Things, and I haven't seen her since. She told me she would be back in time to wash me. I feel like I've been sleeping in sand."

"Do you want me to wash you?" Opal said, and even as she spoke she was afraid her mother would say yes.

"That would be very nice," Dottie said, her voice suddenly soft and grateful. "I would like that very much."

So Opal found herself dipping a washcloth into a plastic basin of soapy water, and running it along her mother's face and arms and neck. The skin flowered as it was touched by heat. Everything white spread to pink.

"Oh, this is lovely," Dottie said, closing her eyes. "Lovely."

Opal was careful not to go near the tubes and wires that were taped to Dottie's chest. She lifted the gown carefully, realizing that she did not remember the last time she had seen her mother's body. Opal had nearly forgotten there was something underneath

227

the clothes. But now she drew the thin fabric up above Dottie's thighs, and her breath caught for a second. She had to stay in motion, had to keep dipping and wringing the cloth until she was done. Her hand moved along the thick band of flesh. Imagine owning this body, she thought, picturing herself suddenly encased in this unlikely shell of fat.

Dottie purred as the warm cloth traveled the width of her stomach, and Opal felt ashamed at her own disgust. She was making her mother happy for a moment; she was giving her pleasure. This, she realized with shock, had always been her goal.

"Thank you, honey," Dottie said when she was finished. Opal moved back to the windowsill and watched for a while as her mother eased back into sleep. It was a peaceful scene, but still troubling. Dottie was letting herself fall, Opal thought. Even now, fast asleep, Dottie was probably dreaming of tumbling down a rabbit hole, dropping slowly through a dark well, impatient to get to the bottom. In a way, Opal was grateful lately when Dottie slept. Sometimes, when she was awake, Opal couldn't stand to be in the room. She would excuse herself and walk down to the fire doors at the end of the hall, and there she would light a cigarette, smoking fiercely and guiltily, inhaling so hard it charred her throat.

It went on like this for days. Every afternoon, Opal and Erica took turns visiting. Sy came in the evenings after work, and each night he seemed more and more beaten down.

"She just *insults* me," he told Opal. "Tells me I'd better start looking for a new girlfriend, that I'd better face the facts." He fingered his beautiful plum tie. "I don't know," he said. "I'm very worried. She seems worse every day. But she's very difficult to deal with. It *gets* to you."

It had gotten to all of them. No one wanted to stay very long in Dottie's room, and they couldn't wait for the moment when the next shift started. Opal, looking up to see Erica in the doorway, would quickly put on her coat. "Good luck," Opal would whisper as she hurried from the room.

Downstairs, pushing through the revolving door, Opal was always surprised at the sensation of being outside. When you spent the entire day inside a hospital, the outside seemed a dream from an earlier life. There was an abundance of natural light, and air that actually moved against your face and hair: How different this was from the overheated, linoleum glow of the hospital.

At home, Opal began making calls. She and Erica had put together a list of several people they thought Dottie might want to see, and now Opal was inviting them to come visit Wednesday night. Dottie claimed she still didn't want to see anyone, said she still wasn't up to it, but Dr. Hammer had told her that visitors might be helpful. No one quite knew what to *do* with Dottie. She could not stay in the hospital forever. Soon she would be well enough to leave, but then, Dr. Hammer had assured her, she would just be returning home to die.

"That's fine with me," Dottie answered. "Better there than here." At that, the doctor scratched something on her chart and made a quick departure.

Now Opal called Aunt Harriet, and had a brief, emotional talk with her frail great-aunt, explaining the situation. Aunt Harriet said that she barely got out of the house, but would make an exception to see Dottie, whom she loved. Everyone talked carelessly of love on these conversations. "I *love* your mom," Ross Needler said. "I *love* Dottie," Mia Jablon said. Their voices were earnest and grave, and Opal didn't think she could take much more of this. As usual, she realized, her mother had eclipsed all else. College seemed a long time ago. Opal vaguely remembered her room in Silliman, its narrow bed and metal shelves, its walls that had been punctured with thumbtacks for years and years— punctured and painted over—as generations of students left and new ones arrived. Opal had once been in that tide of students, but now she had slipped away. Now her life was spent in a hospital room, with a dying woman who would not listen to anyone.

At least there was Erica. It was astonishing that she thought this, but there it was; Erica's presence was the best thing that had happened all winter. At night, the two sisters convened in the kitchen and cooked for themselves. They would never have to go food shopping again, Opal thought, for Dottie kept the kitchen as well-stocked as a bomb shelter. They settled in at the large table

229

and ate dinner. Sometimes they wheeled the TV up close and watched the news or an old sitcom, and sometimes they just talked, their conversation clumsy at first, easing up after a while.

Erica talked about Jordan, and why she had finally left him. "There's someone else," Erica said shyly, poking at her dinner as she spoke.

"Who?" Opal asked. This amazed her: Ungainly Erica had *two* lovers, *two* men. She existed in the world of sex in a way that Opal did not. Was there some secret to being so large? Was this why Dottie did not want to give it up? Maybe if you were heavy you experienced touch differently; maybe it really moved you when a man placed a burning hand on your breast.

Erica told her about this man Mitchell, and the quality of her voice changed a little, lowered to nearly a whisper. "I'm trying to figure out what to do," Erica said. "I'm not done with him."

Opal understood well the idea of unfinished business, of walking around knowing that there was something else that had to be done. Sometimes you weren't sure what it was, and it plagued you until you figured it out.

Thoughts left you without warning, and suddenly, much later, came tumbling back in pieces, like Skylab. Opal thought of all the people who would be showing up at Dottie's hospital room Wednesday night, and she wondered if there was anyone she had forgotten. Sitting at the kitchen table, she looked across at Erica, who seemed deep in thought. Erica was holding her fork lightly, balancing it on one tine.

It was getting late already, Dr. Hammer had said. The hospital could do only so much for a recovering heart patient. Just that morning Hammer had shown up with a flock of medical students. The students peered anxiously over the doctor's shoulder, hands poised on their beepers. They were just a little older than Opal, the men with new beards and wire-rimmed glasses, the women with worried, intelligent expressions and hair pulled back in barrettes. All of them were dressed in tablecloth white, and when they examined Dottie a couple of them made clicking sounds with their tongues and shook their heads.

There was not much to do; there was only Opal and Erica and

230

Sy, and this planned bombardment of visitors. Opal pictured the Wednesday procession into Dottie's room, as grand as "The March of the Siamese Children" in *The King and I*. In the center was Dottie, washed and powdered on her bed, waiting to be convinced, waiting to be startled back to life. Then Opal had an idea. It was certainly a bad idea, she thought as she let it form slowly, a terrible idea, but still she seized it, because she didn't know what else to do.

"I'll be back," Opal said, standing up from the table and pushing in her chair.

"Okay," said Erica, looking up in half-surprise.

Opal walked down the hall to her mother's bedroom and sat down on the bed. She picked up the receiver of the telephone and dialed Miami information. The number was delivered to her by a robot.

He wasn't home, of course; that would have been too much. What she got was a recording of a woman's neutral voice, saying that Norm and Ellen were out right now, but a message might be left after the tone. When the tone came, it was loud and prolonged, and Opal had a moment to wonder if she really wanted to do this. The tone seemed to go on and on.

"Yes," she said, when the line went quiet, "this is a message for Norm Engels. This is Opal Engels calling." Her voice had only a slight quaver to it at first. "It's about Dottie," Opal continued. "She's in the hospital and she's very sick. I guess you've read about it. I don't even know why I'm telling you this." Opal paused and laughed a slightly hysterical, mortifying laugh. "God, I'm sorry," she said, "I'm a little nervous right now. Well, anyway," she went on, "I just wanted to say that we're going to be at the hospital on Wednesday night. A bunch of people. Roosevelt Hospital, that is, in New York City. Look," she said, "you can just ignore this call if you want. I'm sorry; I've been really upset. I just wanted to tell you. Maybe you could do something; I don't know. Oh, just ignore this message."

And then there was another tone and Opal's time was up, and she was left to sit there and realize what it was she had done.

231

22

"Party" was Dottie's word for it, and she said it over and over, even after they told her it wasn't a party at all. "This 'party' you girls have arranged," she said, "will it be black tie or casual?"

"Oh, stop it," Opal said. "Aren't you tired of this?"

"I am only going through with the party," Dottie said, "because you're my daughters and I love you. But I hope no one expects me to be a thousand laughs tonight."

"Don't worry," Erica said. "No one's coming for the atmosphere."

But that evening, when visiting hours began, Erica found herself taking notice of the atmosphere. She saw the way visitors of the dying clutched flowers and wandered the halls like jilted suitors. From a radio behind the nurses' station, Erica could hear an all-night talk show murmuring like water. Everything here felt as though it had been slowed down, lowered a pitch.

She walked back to Dottie's room and found Sy sitting in the corner, hunched over a puzzle, and Opal on the windowsill, swinging her legs like a kid, her heels banging against the radiator.

"Where's the dip?" Dottie asked from the bed. "Has anyone made the dip yet?" No one even answered. Dottie took a lipstick out of her night table drawer and streaked its blunt tip across her pale lips. When Erica approached, she could see the new blur of orange on her mother's face, and even she—who understood nothing about fashion—knew that it looked all wrong. Tonight Dottie resembled several of the other women who lay in rooms along the hall. Each day Erica peered into the open doorways, noting the similar look to these women, the way many of them lay open and broken but still somehow *adorned*: ribbon threading through thin hair, a slash of lipstick across the mouth, like patients in a doll hospital.

"You look nice," Erica said flatly, then she turned away and settled herself in a chair by the door. Down the wide, quiet hall, an orderly bumped a gurney through a set of double doors, and somewhere in the distance the elevators lightly chimed. The first to arrive were Mia and Lynn. They poked their heads into the room and Mia said, "Someone call for a baby-sitter?"

Dottie smiled and waved them in. "Just don't *look* at me," Dottie said. "That's all I ask. Keep your eyes closed. I look like garbage."

"You've been *ill*," said Mia. "What do you expect?"

"Well, you two look great," Dottie said. "Both of you, so stylish. I bet you have to keep the men away with sticks."

Everyone hugged and kissed hello, and Erica stood for a moment while Mia exclaimed over her. The past was brought out and examined; Mia told baby-sitting stories, anecdotes from years before. "There was one time you were on Merv," Mia said, "and I was sitting for the girls. I made a tape of your monologue and listened to it over and over, trying to see what you were *doing*. And how I could maybe do it."

"I remember that," Opal said. "You borrowed my tape recorder."

"So you figured it out," said Dottie. "How I did it."

Mia shrugged. "Took me long enough," she said.

"But it's wonderful, what's happened to you," Dottie said. "I want to hear about it, about both of you. The show, the new apartment. What it's like having this whole new career."

Dottie began to ask questions, and her interest seemed genuine. She didn't sound bitter at all, Erica realized, and the evening actually seemed to be working. Dottie was warm and inquisitive and generous tonight. There was no envy here, or even wistfulness. When Ross Needler and his wife showed up a little while later, Dottie told them to pull up chairs. "And, Erica," Dottie said, "keep on the lookout for that mean night nurse. She may try to break this up."

Erica gave her chair to Anne Needler, a small, nervous woman who seemed far removed from anything to do with television, and she stood in the doorway, leaning against the frame. From here Erica could view the whole room, could watch the way everyone circled Dottie, as if trying to levitate her. Dottie was suddenly so cheerful, that probably no one here would even believe the dire stories that Opal had told them on the phone. *Oh, you're exaggerating,* Ross would say tomorrow. *Dottie seemed terrific, better than she's been in a long time.* And Dottie did seem that way, certainly; even the muscles of her face looked relaxed.

Maybe, Erica kept thinking, the worst is over, the storm has passed. But this sudden shift didn't feel quite right; it was too quick and artfully done. Erica kept watching from the doorway, and after a while she began to understand. Dottie was relaxed, Erica knew, in the way of someone who has accepted the inevitable. Dottie had already removed herself from the race; she wasn't a part of the scene at all. She should have been the one standing out in the doorway, watching all the fuss inside. No, she should have been farther away: outside the window, up in the sky, looking down at the whole skyline from a great, benevolent distance.

Erica's mouth suddenly seemed to suck itself dry; she ran her tongue over her lips, watching the scene around the bed. She couldn't speak; she couldn't plunge in and accuse her mother of anything. For once, the atmosphere in this room was tranquil. More people arrived: ancient Aunt Harriet, and a cameraman named Lou whom Dottie had always liked. Everyone looked relieved when Dottie made an effort to sit up and embrace them.

How strange, Erica thought, to lie in bed and watch your life just flood into the room. Maybe dying would be like this. Erica had seen interviews with people who spoke of such experiences— women who swore that while in a coma they saw high-school gym teachers, pieces of birthday cake eaten in 1943, episodes of "My Little Margie." What if this visit expanded, and *everybody* from Dottie's life suddenly showed up at the hospital?

"Dottie Engels, *this is your life!*" an offstage voice would say in a thrill of bass and vibrato. And Dottie, lying in her high, railed bed, would watch as one after another her visitors appeared in the spotlit doorway.

"Dottie," an ancient voice begins. "Dottie, do you know who I am?"

Dottie pauses in the bed, blinking. "No," she answers. "I'm not sure . . . It sounds familiar."

"I was the first person in the family to ever think you were funny," the voice continues. "Think hard now."

Dottie inclines her head very slightly toward the voice, remembering. She thinks of the summer, over forty years before, which she had spent at Camp Hatikvah, and how, when she had returned, everyone thought there must have been something in the water, for Dottie Breitburg had become *funny*. She had won first prize at Talent Night, doing impressions of Hitler and Mussolini and Carole Lombard, and then, buoyed up by her improbable good luck, she who had been first in *nothing* returned to Brooklyn somehow changed.

At first they thought it was only that she was louder; it seemed as though Dottie shouted when a normal speaking voice would have been sufficient. They had her hearing tested; she sat in a small room hooked up to a box while a technician fiddled with dials and instructed Dottie to raise a hand each time she heard a tone. Sounds came at her from both sides: calliope-swoops in first her left ear, then her right. Her hearing was declared perfectly fine. After a few weeks it became clear that not only was Dottie loud, she was also amusing. Even Aunt Pigeon, still in mourning since the telegram about her son, looked up from her station at the window where she sat gazing sadly at traffic all day, and laughed.

At the seder that year, Dottie made little puns about the *affikomen*. "What a clown," Aunt Pigeon said, and as if this were a cue, all the uncles unloaded their pockets of change. Suddenly Dottie was being *paid* for telling jokes; it was astonishing.

At night, even after she was sent off to sleep, she stayed awake in her room and listened to everyone talk about her. She liked nothing better to hear her name, no matter what was said. The women carried in the crystal, washing it gently in the sink, and over the hiss of water Dottie's name occasionally rose and rose like a creature of purpose, finding its way to the top.

But "This Is Your Life" has only begun. Next a voice in the hospital room booms, "Dottie, I always thought you were swell." It is a voice that everyone recognizes from night after night of television. Ed's voice is more familiar than his face, actually, for usually he is off-camera. When Ed looks into the monitor sometimes, all he can see of himself is one ankle, crossed over his left leg and poking out into the frame that houses Johnny and the guest of the moment. Ed has become just an ankle and an infectious laugh; nothing more. Sometimes he lets himself laugh on and on, knowing the mikes will pick it up, because he wants to be sure he *exists*, to have something better than a mere Cartesian proof of it.

But the night Dottie Engels was on the show, Ed hadn't had to force himself to laugh congenially. Everything she said was just so damn funny, he couldn't help himself. He was having a good time for once, really loosening up, until Johnny shot him a sidelong glance, meaning *Enough, Ed,* and he was forced to end his laughter with a forlorn little cough, his fist to his mouth.

Now the guests come faster, one after the next: men Dottie dated when she was on the road, waitresses from the clubs she played, next-door neighbors from Jericho. Everyone is swarming her, pushing their way through the flowers to touch her and sing her praises. Her whole life is here; how can she turn it down? How, Erica thinks, can she possibly say *no?*

"Yes," Dottie was saying, "oh, yes. But then I took one look at the dressing room and said, 'It's one thing to fit into that costume, but how do you expect me to fit through this *door?*' "

Everyone was laughing, even Aunt Harriet. "Dottie, you should do a whole routine like this," Ross was saying. "Something about the old days, about being on the road. I think it could be very funny."

"Oh, I doubt it," Dottie said, but she seemed pleased.

When the telephone call came, Dottie was telling a story about the day she auditioned for Ed Sullivan. The phone rang three times before she seemed to notice it. "Could you hand that to me, Sy?" Dottie asked, and Sy picked up the phone and said into the receiver. "Miss Engels's dressing room, hold the wire," and, then stretched the cord across the bed to hand it to her. Everyone kept talking during the call and Erica couldn't hear what was being said, but from across the room she could see her mother's face rapidly change, as though something terrible had been revealed. Someone had died, Erica thought. But who? Everyone was here; there was no one left who would upset Dottie so much. Now Dottie's voice was lifting above the laughter.

"Well, I really don't know what to say," she said. "Yes, that's all well and good, but *really*." Her voice was shrill and a little wild; it reminded Erica of the Mrs. Pummelman voice, which she had not heard in years. The room became quiet. Erica looked over at Opal, who was back on the windowsill now. Opal was staring fixedly at Dottie, and her mouth was slightly open, in wonder or fear. Opal seemed to understand what Erica did not.

"*Goodbye*," Dottie said. The telephone was handed back to Sy and replaced on its cradle. Dottie raked her fingers through her hair and said, "Look, everybody, I'm feeling a little worn out now. I hate to cut this short, but I think I should. Please, no offense. Promise me you'll come back another time." Her lips were tight, and she was staring hard first at Erica, then at Opal, with something that bore a close resemblance to rage. Erica's heart began to pound; she felt that old generic guilt, the kind you feel even when you can't think of what in the world you are supposed to have done. She often felt this way walking through the electronic gates at the exit of a store, positive the alarm was going to scream and she was going to be apprehended, even though she had stolen nothing.

The visitors exited quickly, embarrassed, and Erica watched as they headed for the elevators in a bewildered flock. Now it was only Erica, Opal, Sy, and Dottie left in the room. There was an electrical whir as Dottie lifted the head of her bed until she was sitting straight up, the mattress supporting her like a wall.

"What's the matter?" Erica finally asked. "What happened?"

"You know what happened," said Dottie.

"No," Erica went on, "I really don't."

"Well, your sister does," Dottie said.

237

Opal stayed on the window, hugging her knees. "I was just trying to help," she said. "I didn't mean anything bad by it. I just thought he ought to know, that's all." She stood up quickly. "I'm sorry," she said, and she began to cry, her voice splitting. "You were *married* to him; I thought he had a right to know. I thought at least *he* could say something to you."

It was too much to absorb so quickly; it was like walking into a whodunit right in the middle, when you've missed the murder but are left to watch the detached intensity. Meaningless emotion, form without content, like listening to two people make love in the next room. Dottie's rage was obvious and full-blown; her face had darkened, and Erica wouldn't have been surprised if her heartbeats were leapfrogging across the monitor.

"I'm not dead yet," Dottie said, "and you're already replacing me. One foot in the grave, and you girls just *jump* over to your father's side. At least you might have waited, out of courtesy." She paused. "Am I that easy to replace?" she asked. "Do you think of your father and me as interchangeable? After all these years, after the life I've made for us, no thanks to him."

"Dottie," said Sy. "Would you tell me what's going on? Would you just slow down for a minute?"

Dottie turned to him. "All right, I'll tell you what's going on," she said. "Now that I'm dying, these girls here have been contacting their father behind my back. That was him on the phone, supposedly calling just to see how I was feeling. He said that Opal told him where I was." She shook her head. "It kills me, it really does," she said. "Never in my life have I felt so betrayed. I just can't get over it."

"If you'll just listen to me," Opal began, but Dottie waved her to stop.

"Oh, I'm tired of listening to everybody," Dottie said. "I've been doing nothing but listening. Everybody waltzes in here and gives me their opinion, and I'm trapped here listening. Right now I just want quiet. Is that too much to ask?" Then she slowly lowered the head of the bed back down until she was lying flat on her back, staring at the ceiling. No one moved. "*Good night*, girls," she said pointedly. "Good night, Sy."

Before leaving, Erica and Opal stood miserably above the bed one last time, both of them clutching the railing as though afraid they might pitch over the edge and drown.

The next morning, Dottie was silent when they came to visit. She sat upright in her bed, her eyes fixed on the television that hung suspended above her.

"Can we at least *talk* about this?" Opal asked.

"Not now," said Dottie, not looking away from the set.

Erica watched as Opal stood in agony by the bedside. "You don't understand," Opal started, but Dottie stopped her.

"Look," said Dottie, "I've asked very few things of you girls. Obviously, what I asked for was too much."

"Opal," Erica said softly. "Let's go. This isn't the time." She led her sister from the room, putting an arm around her shoulders, smelling the smoke in her hair.

There was nothing to be done. Dottie did not want to talk, and she was cold whenever they visited. "I'll be in touch with you," she said. "In the meantime, please let me be. I need to think."

So they stopped visiting. They stayed at home and cooked extensive meals and watched large amounts of television, and they alluded to their mother in only the vaguest of terms. But both of them were uneasy, and would remain that way until Dottie called. They were still under her influence, Erica realized; even now, Dottie had the power to hold them fast.

On Sunday morning at seven the telephone woke them from their sleep, and Erica knew who it was as she staggered into the kitchen to answer. She picked up the receiver and held it for a moment before saying hello.

"This will be brief," Dottie said, and Erica heard a click as Opal picked up another extension down the hall. "Are you both on?" Dottie asked.

"Yes," they chorused in untried morning voices.

"Good," said their mother. "I'm sorry if I woke you, but I needed to tell you my plans." She paused. "I thought you should know that I'll be leaving the hospital Tuesday," she said. "There's just been too much stress here, too many cooks. It's time for me to get away."

"Are you still angry?" Opal asked.

Erica could hear their mother exhale. "What do you think?" Dottie asked.

"I don't really know," said Opal. "I didn't even do anything. I just called him because I didn't know what else to do. You're *not* being replaced."

"Opal," said Dottie. "Please. I don't want to fight. I think you already know my position, and there isn't anything more to say. I just wanted to tell you my plans."

"So where are you going?" Erica asked. She imagined her mother wandering the globe in a fugue state, still wearing her hospital gown and slippers.

Dottie was silent. "I am going," she finally said, "to that *place*. That fat farm in California, for lack of anything better to do."

Erica was stunned. This should have been a moment of triumph. They had somehow done it, and now Dottie would be flying off to the Lexington Clinic, but it had happened in such a startling and joyless way, that no pleasure could be taken.

"Well," Erica said, "that's great."

"Great," Opal echoed.

"I will be in touch with you," Dottie said. "I just need a while to be alone. If you could pack some clothes for me, and dump everything from my makeup table into a bag, I'd appreciate it. I'll send someone over tomorrow to pick it all up." In the background, Erica could hear the sound effects of the hospital starting its day. "Will you girls be okay?" Dottie asked, and Erica thought back to years before, when Dottie would call them from across the country to make sure they were all right. *Yes,* they had screeched over the wire, *we're fine, we're fine.*

Now neither of them would give her that reassurance. "Will you girls be okay?" Dottie asked again.

Let her panic, Erica thought; let her get a little bit worried.

But Opal broke the moment. "We'll manage," she said.

It was the benediction that Dottie needed, and now she could be released. They said awkward goodbyes, and Dottie hung up. Erica held on for a moment more, and she heard breathing and realized that Opal was still on the line as well.

"Opal?" Erica asked tentatively.

"Hi."

"You're still here," Erica said.

"So it seems," said Opal.

23

The postcards told them nothing. "Doing fine," she would write, or "Getting along." On the back of one there was a photograph of the Lexington Clinic, and Dottie had drawn a stick figure leaning out the window of the main building, shouting "Feed me!!!" That was the extent of what they knew.

In the beginning Opal thought of little else but her mother. She would come into the living room at night and expect to see the glow of Dottie's cigarette punctuating the dark. She would expect to hear the blender whipping up a milkshake, or the distorted thunder of applause from one of Dottie's old concert albums. The stillness repeatedly surprised her.

One afternoon Sy came over to pick up his clothes. "I've left a few things here," he said, "and I think it's time I got them. Who knows when I'll be here again." Opal sat on the bed as Sy shuffled through the rack of the bedroom closet, searching for what was his.

"This evening gown doesn't seem to be mine," he said. "No, red isn't my color; this must be your mother's." Opal watched as he carefully lay three dark suits across his arm. Sy treated clothing tenderly, solicitously. "Your mother's been dropping me a few postcards," he said with his back to Opal. "She says she's doing okay. I'm leaving her alone, as she's asked," he went on. "What else can I do?" He shook his head and turned around. "Well, I think I've got everything," he said, and then he paused. "You and your sister doing okay over here?" he asked. "Rattling around in this big place?"

"We're fine," Opal said. "We're getting along."

"If you need anything," said Sy, "I hope you'll call me. I mean it, Opal." He lifted the suits off his arm and slung them over his shoulder. "Well, I'll be seeing you sometime soon, I hope," he said, and he stepped forward to kiss her awkwardly on the cheek.

That was the way things had always been in this fractured family: People left, and you had no indication of when they would be back. *Soon, soon,* everyone said, and after their departure you had to trust that their sense of *soon* was the same as yours. Everyone took off, but somehow they all came back, in one form or another. You had to trust that this would happen, and that eventually you would get a sign. If you waited long enough, Dottie would wave to you from the stage of "The Tonight Show," and Erica would miraculously appear behind the front door of a tenement building in the East Village. And finally, Norm Engels would get up the nerve to lock himself in his den on Coconut Court, away from his wife Ellen and all the trappings of his current life, and hesitantly pick up the phone.

But there were limits to what people could do, and what you could ask of them. For now, this was enough. Her father had actually made *contact,* had given her a sign, and because of it everything had been set into motion. It was like a Rube Goldberg cartoon: The daughter calls the father, which in turn makes the father call the mother, which finally sends the mother hurtling across the country.

Dottie had been gone three weeks now. For three weeks Opal wondered about her, felt slightly afraid of her, even from such a distance. But then winter began to loosen its hold on the city, and Opal felt herself growing distracted, itchy to be outside. All along Central Park West, fingers of ice were cracking off awnings and the branches of trees. Opal and Erica pushed open the windows of the apartment and let air travel through the rooms. One day Walt called and asked Opal to meet him in the park. "Come on," he said. "I never see you anymore. You can't hide out forever."

So she went for a walk with him along the reservoir, while the first crop of springtime joggers ran by, snow cracking in puzzle-pieces beneath their feet. "When are you coming back to the show?" Walt asked. "Joel has hired—get this—his *daughter* to do busywork. Her name's Holly, spelled with a 'y,' although it should be an 'i,' and she's supposedly studying Literature at a junior college. Her favorite writer is Charles M. Schulz. You better come back soon, Opal."

Opal smiled. "I will," she said. "I'm getting restless."

"Too much family," said Walt. They had stopped on the path for a moment. "You need a break from them," he said. "I used to get all wrapped up in my parents' lives. Once I actually tape-recorded one of their fights—I hid my cassette player under the couch—and later I played it back to them so they could hear how they sounded. They were furious, of course. But then I eventually realized it was *their* business, not mine. They would have fights, and I just wouldn't listen." He paused. "You've been in that apartment too much," he said. "You need to get out of there for a while, I think."

"How do you know what I need?" Opal asked lightly.

Walt tilted his head. "Just a guess," he said. "That's all." He lifted the edge of her scarf and held it between his fingers; Opal didn't breathe. They stood like that for a moment, until a jogger approached, and they automatically separated, letting him pass between them. Opal could hear the tinny scratch of music wafting from his headphones. "Sometime," said Walt, "you'll have to come uptown. See the way the other half lives. Three guys in a Roach Motel."

She couldn't say a word, but just nodded to everything he said. They continued to walk, their gloved hands linked now. So this was the way it began, Opal thought. First comfort, then tension, then comfort again. Like a creature waking up from a deep sleep and arching, then settling back down to sleep some more. You were with someone because you wanted to be—not because it was arranged, or because, like your mother and father, you were desperate. She thought of her parents getting married in a synagogue in Brooklyn. In the middle of the ceremony, they must certainly have looked at each other in disbelief. This is what it comes down to, Dottie must have thought, as the cantor sang and the ring was yoked onto her finger.

244

Opal returned to "Rush Hour" the following week, and fell quickly and gratefully back into her old routine. The only difference was Walt. When he passed her in the hall now, he let his hand bang dully, almost accidentally, against her hip, and they shared a follow-up glance. She and Walt had both been invited to the Friday-night wrap party—Mia's doing, Opal was certain—and until Friday, it seemed that they were going to maintain a certain tense distance. Walt's hand rested lightly on the plane of her hip, and then he moved on, calling to someone farther down the hall.

It was a relief to leave the apartment in the morning, to have a mission every day. Opal once again found herself stationed in front of the Xerox machine; sometimes she didn't even close the flap on top, but instead let the stark green light bathe her hands and face, temporarily blinding her. In the background she could hear props being wheeled onto the sound stage, and doors slamming up and down a corridor, and one of the comedians practicing a Tarzan yell for Friday's show. Her first day back, Joel Macklin and one of the casting agents had asked after Dottie's health, had said they had heard Dottie was out of the hospital, and wondered how she was getting along. Opal had nodded and muttered that Dottie was progressing well; she couldn't tell them that she really didn't know, that the only information she had came from three brief and cryptic postcards.

They had held her place for her on the show, and although she was pleased, Walt told her not to be too thankful. "They don't even *pay* us," he said. "They're lucky to have you." But she couldn't get over the fact that there had been a great upheaval—a hurricane, almost—and everything that had been mercilessly slammed around had somehow settled back down to earth, with little visible damage. Her job was waiting, and Walt was waiting, and in September there would be a room for her up at Yale. All she had to do was write a letter to the Dean, asking to be readmitted, and tell him that she now understood the error of her ways.

But she wouldn't have spent last semester any other way; she still would have sat up late at night, monitoring her mother's commercials. Back then, Dottie needed a guardian, or at least a willing audience: *someone* to observe her as she flew by in that final burst of color. The commercials were still on the air, although much less frequently now. Sometimes Opal and Erica would come across one late at night, and they would watch it silently, neither commenting nor turning away. The commercials were a reminder, telling them that even if Dottie wasn't here, she was still somewhere *out* there in the world.

"Do you think she's still angry?" Opal asked one night. She and Erica were lying across Dottie's bed, watching. Their mother waltzed by in pink chiffon.

Erica shrugged. "Oh, she always jumps to extremes," she said. "That's the way she lives. God," she said. "Look at that."

"The thing is," Opal said, "I don't even think I did anything wrong. I just started writing to him because I was curious." She paused. "Haven't you ever been?" she asked.

"I've been curious," Erica said slowly, "but it was never a pressing need. Families always seem to me like this weird accident."

"What do you mean?" Opal asked.

"I don't know," said Erica. She gestured with both hands, fingers splayed. "It's almost as if a bunch of people who have absolutely *no* reason to be together all drew straws and somehow wound up on the same commune." On the screen, Dottie twirled in slow motion, her dress belling out around her waist. "It was sort of like that with Jordan," Erica said. "Sometimes I would look over at him and he would have a nosebleed from doing coke. There would be a little piece of tissue hanging out of his nose, and I would think: Who *is* this person?"

"So that's why you left, because you couldn't take it anymore?" Opal asked, and Erica nodded. "Like Mom," Opal added.

Erica didn't answer. Opal tried to imagine how her mother had finally gathered the nerve to leave. Maybe Dottie had looked around at the furnishings of the life she had painstakingly set up with Norm Engels, and wondered how she had arrived here, and how she might possibly get out. "Do you remember the last time we saw him?" Opal asked.

"Yes, but I can't believe *you* do," Erica said. "You were so little."

Opal nodded. "We went to that park near Aunt Harriet's, and we were really restless and wouldn't sit still. He told us we would grow up to be fidgety women. Do you remember?"

A slow smile formed on Erica's face. "Oh, Opal," she said, her voice subdued, "was that what you thought?" She clapped her hands together. "You heard it wrong," she said. "He said we would grow up to be *frigid* women, not *fidgety* women."

Opal flushed. He had actually said that? She had remembered it wrong all these years, and now she was stunned. "But that's even worse," Opal finally said. "I mean, what a thing to *say*. Who would say something like that?"

Erica looked at her. "Anyone," she said simply. "People will say anything." As she spoke, her face was calm as a Buddha, as though she herself had never been angry, had never stormed through the apartment with her hair lashing her face, smelling of pot and patchouli and strawberry shampoo, hating the terrible commune she had been born into.

But now Erica was back, and she moved easily among all the things she had once hated; now she actually lay across her mother's bed. She and Opal talked of their father as though he were not a terrible man, but instead someone who had been overwhelmed by everything around him: his huge wife who filled most of the bed at night, and his two girls who carried their Barbie Dreamhouses with them everywhere, like businessmen clutching attachés. It was too much, too much, and Norm Engels was not one for excess. He was Mr. Sprat, he was the Hollow Man, and he belonged somewhere else: down in Florida with his wife Ellen, lost in whatever life he had chosen for himself. She remembered that she had not even spoken to him, had not heard his voice.

"Opal," Erica said. "Are you all right?"

On the television now, Dottie Engels paused for a moment and directed a long wink at her daughters.

The wrap party was held at the Tet Offensive, a new club in Tribeca that in all likelihood would have the life span of a

247

butterfly. The evening's show had not been one of the season's strongest; the guest stars were a duo of aging, skeletal British rock stars who doubled over their guitars as though in severe abdominal pain. The whole cast and some of the staff headed downtown in waiting limousines. Opal and Walt took the subway together, slipping tokens into adjacent turnstiles and walking out onto the brightly lit platform.

"Look," Walt said, "there's almost no one here."

Opal looked around the station. Two women sat motionless all the way down at the other end, and a man lay sleeping across a bench. The only real sign of life came from behind the blue glass of the token booth, where a man nodded his head over a pile of money. She and Walt stood bundled up in the middle of the platform, and there was an awkwardness suddenly; Opal prayed for the train to come. When it did, they stepped into a nearly empty car and sat with their legs lightly touching. Walt, she saw, was smiling and looking away.

"What kind of people," he asked, "would agree to put their names on ads in subway cars as *hemorrhoid sufferers?*" He pointed. "If I were Mrs. Rita Velásquez, I would be embarrassed to show my face in public ever again. I mean, now everyone *knows.*"

"Maybe she's an exhibitionist," Opal said.

"Are you?" Walt asked.

Opal shook her head, embarrassed. They sat in silence for the rest of the ride. Over the loudspeaker, the conductor spoke some garbled words with a certain amount of urgency, and the train came to a resolute stop between stations. Walt slipped his arm through hers and continued to read and deconstruct the ads across the way.

When they finally arrived at the Tet, as everyone seemed to call it, they flashed their invitations at the door and walked past an eager and self-conscious crowd of hopefuls straining behind rope. Walt walked slightly ahead of Opal, still holding her hand, and he led her down an aggressively dark hallway lined with a tangle of jungle foliage.

The club itself was the size of a small stadium, with a lacquered dance floor lit by revolving lights. "Come on," Walt said, and they

248

descended a set of shallow steps until they arrived at the dance floor, where the music began to encircle them, percussive and overwhelming. Across the room she could see Stevie Confino dancing with a young blond woman in a checkerboard dress, and nearby Mia and Lynn were doing precise Egyptian-style steps, heads and arms moving side to side, both of them concentrating on each other without ever touching. In the corner of the floor the two legendary rock stars were standing spindle-tall and motionless. The party was just gearing up; in an hour it would burst open into something else entirely.

Walt and Opal managed to clear out a small circle for themselves on the floor. The circle got smaller and smaller, and soon Walt was flush against her. He was working now, she saw, dancing just for her—his eyes near-closed, points of sweat above his upper lip. He brought his mouth down to her neck and skidded there for a second, then settled. They stayed like that, Walt's face buried deep in her neck, her arms wrapping him. She stared out across the room, thrilled and wild-eyed.

Opal imagined her mother walking in here and looking around in wonder, shaking her head at this new world, everyone young and nervy and stripped-down and gleaming. All about the room, huge-screen televisions broadcast a series of disjointed images: a black woman walking a big white Afghan, a man in leather following another man down a narrow alley, an airplane cutting through a sky the color of blood. Even here, in the middle of all this, you could watch *television* if you wanted. Without a second thought, Opal closed her eyes.

24

Because she now loved the apartment—loved its assortment of rooms, and the soft furniture planted beneath windows in slants of sun, loved its glowing chrome kitchen stocked for eternity with good things—Erica knew she would soon have to leave. It was amazing the way you could be lured back and *held*; sometimes you had to slap yourself awake to remember this was only a stopping place, a watering hole. Erica had once read a magazine article about grown children who move back into their parents' apartments, and the idea of it had been unthinkable. But this wasn't quite the same; she was in her mother's apartment, but her mother *wasn't*, although Dottie's ghost seemed present at times, especially late at night, when Erica went to fix herself something to eat in the dark kitchen. She would feel a hesitating ripple in the air, and would whip around to look. Everything was in order: The pilot lights kept vigil under the burners on the stove, and the refrigerator did its usual ice-making song and dance. Is it me? she wondered, holding her plate and pausing for a moment in the middle of the room.

What had happened was this: Erica had suddenly become seized with loneliness. It struck her in the way that hunger sometimes did—in great, unpredictable gusts. When it did, she would walk around the apartment like someone who has been dealt a blow to the head, and who is trying to gather her wits about her. The apartment was shocking in its silence and its cleanliness—two aspects that Erica had not known, living with Jordan. Opal was around less and less often these days, and lately she had begun staying out all night. She had "met someone," she announced one night over dinner, and before Erica could respond, Opal was stammering and shredding her napkin and looking pleased in a way that Erica had not seen in a very long time.

It reminded her of when she had first met Mitchell, and how they would sit at lunch together in the snack bar, separated by the distance of two red plastic trays that were still warm and wet from the dishwasher. She knew, if she saw him now, that he would be full of good advice about how she should conduct her life. He would lean back in his green swivel chair, the unoiled springs groaning beneath the serious weight of him, and he would link his hands together behind his head and say: *Let's see.*

Her loneliness, she knew, was specific to Mitchell. She had always been able to be alone with herself; that had never been a problem. But knowing that he was *out* there, and that she was still here, was too much for her. It was a simple equation, but each time she thought it through to its conclusion, she was left with an overwhelming despair. Erica was back in the lap of her childhood home; she could stay here forever, she knew, and lie in her big bed all day and night, as she used to, smoking dope and watching the smoke disperse around her. She could start listening to her old records again, slide the orange crate out from under her bed and flip through the collection. She thought about her set of Reva and Jamie albums, and how they had gone untouched for years. These days, she knew, Reva and Jamie had become a lounge act, performing Sixties hits in revolving restaurants at the tops of hotels in lesser cities.

It was all very tempting, in the way that sometimes the thought of touching the third rail in the subway is tempting: You know what the results will be—the way your finger will beckon death into your body—but you are curious anyhow. Staying in this apartment would be a slow but equally certain death. Erica would fulfill all her old fears about herself. She would eat herself silly in the bedroom of her childhood, and she would never be able to leave.

What she needed, she realized, was an addition to this life. Living here for a while wouldn't be damaging if there was somewhere else she could go during the days, if there was another landscape that wouldn't claim her with the same kind of fierceness, but would instead just *shift* to allow entry. Erica thought at once of Mitchell, and the psychology building where he worked. She would go see him, talk to him; maybe, she thought, he could help her get a job there. She wanted to work, wanted to do something other than sell her innermost thoughts about being heavy or sad or lost. It wasn't just Mitchell she wanted, although even now, focusing on the idea of work, she could still picture Mitchell's face and hands, and then finally his whole body came spinning to the surface.

Erica found her keys and left the apartment before she could think this over. It was eleven-thirty in the morning, and Mitchell was supposed to be at his office, unless he had changed his schedule since she had seen him last, unless he had packed up and left town with tiny Karen, abandoning his doctoral thesis and all those fat women who relied on him.

When Erica arrived at the psychology building, the fluorescent lights in Mitchell's office were humming like mad; she could hear them from outside in the hall. A tall woman in a lab coat walked past, and Erica pretended to be studying the bulletin board next to the door, where stapled-up flyers in jazzy colors tried to persuade you to go to graduate school.

Mitchell's door suddenly swung open without warning. He stood yawning in the doorway, the lights humming like a fleet of desperate mosquitoes behind him, and when he saw Erica he stopped with his mouth slack, and took a step backward. "Oh, Erica," was what he said.

"Hi," she said, her voice tentative. She wanted to show him, somehow, that she wasn't *armed*, that she wanted nothing from him, but it occurred to her that this wasn't quite true. She wanted whatever she could get.

"I was just going to get some water," he said. "Want to come?"

They walked upstairs together, and when they reached the fountain on the landing, Mitchell bent over and took a long drink like an animal at a trough. She looked at the curve of his broad back, saw the way his flannel shirt was riding up and escaping the

252

harness of his belt. When he was done he stood up, his beard spattering water, and then Erica took her turn. As she leaned over the low ceramic ledge, she thought that this was nearly a ceremonial rite: the two of them drinking together, as once they had eaten together, and made love together. Everything between them involved the taking *in* of substances, and she hadn't let any of it go.

She wiped her mouth with the back of her hand. "I wanted to talk to you," she said. "I wasn't sure if it was okay."

"You stopped coming by," Mitchell said. "I didn't know where to reach you. I actually called you at your apartment, but I kept getting *him*, so I hung up. You never answered the phone." He paused. "Then I read about your mother," he said. "I felt really bad, but I didn't know where you were."

They walked back downstairs to his office. When he opened the door, the white lights were loud and hard. "I'll turn them off," he said, and he slapped his hand down on a wall switch, and the windowless room went black and quiet. "Here," his voice said, and in a moment he had pulled the chain of a small green desk lamp. The glow in the office made it look like a bedroom. She thought of Mitchell unbuttoning his shirt, his fingers skittering over a row of buttons.

"A lot has happened," she said, sitting in the folding chair by his desk. "My mother, of course. It was terrible; I can't begin to tell you. We had a fight and she just took off." She shook her head. "But it's not just that," she said.

Mitchell sat across from her. He put his hands flat down on the blotter and said, "What else?" She remembered him with a pink index card in his hand, his eyes searching her face. It distracted her now, made her forget what she wanted to say.

"I left Jordan," she finally said, as if in afterthought.

"Oh," said Mitchell. "Well." His face was impassive.

"Not because of you," she added quickly. "No need to worry."

"I wasn't worried," Mitchell said. "I just wish I had known what was going on with you," he said. He looked down at his desk and began to fiddle with his magnet of paper clips, scooping them out of their tight, connecting bundle and letting them rain back down. "I've really missed you," he went on. "I know I probably shouldn't, but I do. I'm still with Karen, of course, but sometimes I get frustrated about it all. Things get fucked up."

"Fucked up how?" she asked.

"Oh, nothing new," Mitchell said. "Same old patterns. Sometimes I just want to shake her. She won't eat anything; she's like a bird. I think she eats in secret, when I leave the room. There's a lot she keeps from me." He paused. "I know this is stupid," he said, "but sometimes I think about what it would be like to get up in the middle of the night with you and have a little feast, like in *Tom Jones*. You know, spread everything out on a banquet table and just eat. I guess that's pretty transparent. But I never said I was complex."

She thought of the two of them sitting at Mitchell's table at one in the morning, tearing apart a leftover roast chicken, their faces and fingers streaky with oil. It was easy to take the image farther, to build it into a series of tableaux that, taken together, equaled a whole life. But it was dangerous to even let herself imagine such a life. Erica forced herself back to this moment, to the fact that they were sitting in his office with a desk between them, that she needed to do something with her life—that she needed, in fact, a *life.*

"Mitchell," she said, "I can't make myself crazy over this. I need something that's good for me." She hesitated. "I was wondering if there might be any jobs here," she said. "Really, I'll take anything. I'll sit in a room interviewing fat women, or bulimics. Whatever."

"Come on," Mitchell said. "That's not why you're here."

"It is," she said. "It's part of it."

Mitchell's voice went flat. "Well, there are only lab jobs," he said. "But you're overqualified. You would just be working with *mice*, Erica."

"I am not overqualified," she said. She had no qualifications at all, in fact. She had somehow been able to send a blur across Mitchell's reasoning so he thought she had some power in the world, some recognizable worth. But just because he saw it didn't mean that it was true.

"Oh, I guess I could find you something, if you really want it," he said. "At least you would be *around* me." She didn't say

254

anything. "Don't you want to be?" he asked. "I don't know what it will *mean*, but still, Erica." His voice drifted off.

The overhead lights may have been silenced, but even so, there was a new hum in her head now—a steady, bristling drone. She stood, and in a moment Mitchell was standing too. He edged around in front of the desk and put his large hands on her hair, just touching the top like a halo. They kissed, and without thinking she leaned into him, against the scratch of his sweater and the softer scratch of his beard.

Out on the street, Erica let herself walk and walk. On the corner of 14th Street and Sixth Avenue, she stopped with all the other walkers and waited for the light. She peered down the broad gray street, at the storefronts and outdoor tables of jangly items that made you feel there was no room left in the world: keychains and mugs with wacky sayings and authentic hookahs and Smurf dolls fresh from Taiwan. Clusters of shoppers were scrabbling like crabs across the surfaces of tables. A small fight erupted. Someone was apparently being accused of stealing a Smurf doll, and voices were rising up over the traffic. Erica started to watch. Her eyes drifted slightly to the left, and that was when she saw him.

She was not positive at first; he was wearing a familiar, ratty overcoat and rummaging among a table of bongs and spoons, lifting them closer to his face for inspection, and he might have been anyone. But when he looked up, Erica saw that he had a woman's eyebrows. *Jordan*. What was he doing here? she wondered. Probably waiting to meet a supplier; Jordan went to other neighborhoods to do that occasionally. His coat seemed so insubstantial; she could imagine him catching cold and not knowing how to take care of himself. He would lie feverish in the loft bed for days, sitting up just long enough to cut himself a line or skim another chapter of *Steal This Book*.

Erica quickly turned away so he would not recognize her. Jordan was a shaving, a clipping, a filament—anything slight and flyaway. But there would always be girls around to tend to him and cradle him and sing to him the songs that were lodged inside his head forever. She felt bad that he hadn't gotten what he

255

wanted, that during the weekend of Woodstock he had probably been home making a diorama or learning the New Math. Nobody got a second chance at these things. He was disappearing up the street now, and soon she would think of him less. Other things would replace these thoughts; there was only so much room inside. She was not a deep well, a bottomless pit, as she used to imagine herself. There were limits, she thought, and it was a relief to feel that there were *edges* around you, a membrane that kept you from spilling out into the world.

25

They traveled three thousand miles to see their mother, and when they arrived, she was nowhere to be found. Opal and Erica stepped into the clamor of the San Francisco airport and looked around for Dottie. She would be huge and glowing in a dotted caftan, Opal imagined, perhaps just a little less huge than usual. Before they embraced, they would have to exclaim over how well she looked, tell her she was really making progress. But Dottie wasn't there. Instead, they saw a young man holding a cardboard sign that read "O. and E. Angels," and Opal realized that this meant them.

"It sounds like a football team," she whispered as the man put their luggage in the trunk of a car. She imagined telling her mother the story later. Even now, after not seeing her for six months, she still pictured Dottie rolling her eyes and opening her mouth to laugh.

It was the heart of summer, and New York had become a difficult city. Both Opal and Erica knew that the apartment would eventually be turned over to their mother; this was their final summer, this was *it*. In the fall Opal would move back to New Haven, and Erica would start looking for a cheap place downtown, near NYU. In these last days the apartment seemed even more mythical than ever. The air conditioner seemed to put a preserving layer of frost over everything. Nothing changed up here on the twelfth floor; it was like Shangri-La.

When Dottie called, asking them to come, telling them she would send them airline tickets, Opal had been reluctant. It was a complicated reluctance, she realized; she didn't want to leave her life, even for a few days, but also, she was afraid. Who knew what Dottie had become? Right now she was just a voice on the telephone, just a stick figure on the back of a postcard.

"Please, girls," Dottie said when she called. "It would mean a lot to me. I'm not allowed to leave while I'm on the program; it's a house rule. But I really want to see you. You can stay at a nice hotel nearby. Come on."

It was as if there had been no rift between them. She didn't mention Norm at all, and apparently wasn't going to. Obviously, Erica said later, Dottie was trying to apologize in her own oblique way. "We should go," Erica said. "Among other things, I'm curious."

So now they were traveling in the back of an airport limousine down the Pacific Coast to Carmel. The day was unrelentingly clear, the sun slashing in across the backseat. Dottie had the ability—the talent, really—to conjure just about any desired response from both her daughters. *Come,* she said, and they jumped on an airplane and flew all the way across the country to see her, because she was their mother, after all, the biggest mother anyone could have, and she took their breath away.

But nothing could have prepared them. The woman who met them on the sun deck of the Lexington Clinic bore little resemblance to Dottie Engels. It was like identifying a body in a morgue, Opal thought, like the moment when the filing cabinet is slid open and you are made to look.

As she stood out in the warm light, observing her mother for the first time, she tried to find something to latch on to; her eyes quickly moved up and down, then side to side. Her head ached from the lack of recognition; everything was familiar, but seemed *off.* Opal felt as though she were a stroke victim reaching for a word, but the word no longer fit. *Chair,* she thought. *Table.* She turned to Erica for guidance, but Erica also looked confused.

Dottie Engels was no longer fat.

Nothing bloomed outward; there was no real girth to her. The weight that remained seemed unevenly distributed, hanging on her like loose clothing. For the first time Opal realized that her

258

mother was not tall; it was as though her height had deserted her along with her width. What remained was a small woman with red hair and round shoulders and a round face, who looked out of shape, as if after a long winter of hibernation. She almost looked delicate, Opal thought.

"God," Erica said, and they both just stood there, still holding their luggage, unsure of how to proceed.

Opal remembered one of her favorite books from childhood, *Are You My Mother?* about a baby bird that falls from a nest, and goes around asking this question of a variety of animals and objects. But *are* you my mother? Opal wanted to ask now, before she would even move closer and let herself be hugged. This woman didn't look like the type who would throw her arms around you and press you close; instead, she would probably hold you a little bit away from her body, and your cheeks would gently brush against each other, the way women sometimes do when they meet for lunch. But Dottie Engels's embrace was surprisingly muscular; she moved forward to hug both daughters, and her eyes were shining. Still Opal hung back a bit. Tell us a joke, Opal wanted to say; anything loud and raucous and out of date, so we can be sure it's really you.

"This has been extremely rough going," Dottie said later, when they were sitting in her room upstairs. The room was small and clean and antiseptic, and both windows provided dramatic views; it was like the living quarters in *The Magic Mountain*. Dottie heated some water for tea on her hot plate. "Which isn't to say that rough is necessarily bad," she went on. "It looks like a country club, right? But you should see how difficult the regimen is; that's the reason I couldn't meet your plane. I had a yoga class I couldn't get out of. I told Linda it was just for the afternoon, but she said no. There are no exceptions around here. I apologize; I hope the ride was okay."

Opal could not stop staring. She wanted to look and look.

"I know," said Dottie. "You can't believe it, right?"

Opal shrugged. "It's a shock," she said. "You didn't tell us."

"Well," said Dottie, "it's not so easy to talk about. I didn't want to jinx it. And part of me doesn't even believe it."

259

"How can you not believe it?" Erica asked. "You can just look in a mirror."

"It's difficult to explain," Dottie said. "I still don't feel thin. I feel fat; I think I always will. I keep expecting to look at myself and see the old me."

Oh, me too, thought Opal.

"Sometimes," Dottie said, "my body aches the way it used to. A doctor here was talking about people who have arms or legs amputated, and how they still feel pain in places that don't exist anymore: 'phantom limb pain,' it's called. That's the way I feel now." She shrugged. "I told a friend here that someone ought to write a book called *Fat Like Me*, about a thin woman who pretends to be fat so she can see what it's like being a member of an oppressed group."

Opal smiled. Dottie looked thin, but she also looked older somehow. She perched on her small metal bed and drank her cup of tea, and Opal stared at her, unabashed, the way Dottie's fans used to stare in restaurants or on the street. "Look all you want," Dottie said. "It's free."

"I'm sorry," Opal said. "I didn't mean to."

But Dottie assured her it was fine. "You know, I'm used to being stared at," she said. "It's been that way my whole life; first for being fat, then for being famous, and now for *not* being fat *or* famous. So it really doesn't faze me. Life's one big freak show." She paused. "I don't know what will happen when I leave here," she said. "I'm not getting my hopes up. Sy wants to go look at fabric in Africa, and he wants me to come with him. Can you picture me on an elephant?" She smiled. "One of these days," she said, "I'm going to walk into Ross's office and say, 'So, can you get me some work? Then he'll be the one to have the heart attack."

"When do you think you'll be able to leave?" Opal asked.

"I can't be sure," Dottie said. "The important thing is to keep the weight off. Some people leave here and they just balloon right up again. I still think about food a lot; sometimes I think I would sell my soul for something really bad, like Twinkies or Devil Dogs. And cigarettes, too. We're all addictive personalities here; we have these therapy groups and talk about our addictions."

260

The voice was the same; the familiar ironic tone, the rasp that could continue a routine even while people were roaring and waitresses were setting down drinks on tables. This was the same voice that could lift above any audience and keep going. Now Dottie told stories of the weight-loss program: the careful diet, which a clinic nutritionist had personally prepared for her, the endless mornings of exercise, the yoga classes, the behavior modification therapy.

"It's all natural," she said. "None of that vacuum cleaner surgery where they suck the fat right out of you. Here they make you lose it yourself." She paused. "At first I hated being in a place with only fat people," she said. "It's like looking in a mirror—a fun-house mirror. Some of these women, when they heard I was here, came up to me and told me how much they always loved my work, and that I was an inspiration to them. A couple of them had even brought along dresses from my line; I couldn't get over it. I'd be sitting there in the dining room, looking at somebody, thinking *That woman's dress looks familiar,* and then I'd remember why." She paused. "There are a couple of other celebrities here, too," she said, "but I'm not allowed to reveal their names. You'd think we were at the Betty Ford Clinic or something." Dottie sipped her cup of tea. So Opal kept staring, and Erica did too. They sat in unnerving silence for a while, looking at Dottie as though she were a museum piece, until finally Dottie stood up and stretched. "Okay, the show's over," she said. "I've got to move around a little; it's part of the program. Come, I'll show you the place."

She gave them a tour of the clinic, taking them to see the gleaming gymnasium with its rows of weights and dangling rings. One lone man lay under a set of barbells, just paused there, like a mechanic slid beneath a car. They moved on, past the small, sunny dining room, where Opal could hear the laying of silver, and out to the saltwater swimming pool and sauna. As they walked past the sauna, Opal peered inside. She was startled to find a large, naked woman asleep on a slab of wood. This was Dottie's whole *life*: living among strangers, lying beside them on burning planks.

When it was time for Dottie to go to dinner, Opal and Erica took a cab out to their hotel. In the room they put down their

261

unopened luggage, and lay flat on their backs on the matching beds, staring up at the stippled ceiling. For a long time no one said anything. From outside in the hallway Opal could hear someone shoveling ice from the ice machine. It was evening at the Ramada Inn in Carmel, California; guests of the hotel were fixing drinks, unwinding, removing clothes, and lying in their own climate-controlled rooms.

Over at the Lexington Clinic, Dottie Engels was sitting in a dining room full of the hopeful and the desperate, her dinner portion meted out on her tray, the sliver of fish as dry as a relic, the carrots tiny and slender, as though they had been uprooted prematurely. Dottie would stay at the clinic for several more weeks, and then she would return to New York and try to cook herself similar dinners, try to take care of herself in this new manner. Out on the streets of the city, few people would recognize her. Dottie could walk down any street and holler in people's faces, but they would just squint at her and wonder if perhaps she was someone they had gone to school with. The face is sympathetic, they would think, but then they could take it no further.

Finally Erica spoke. "It's going to take some getting used to," she said.

"I don't think we will," Opal said.

"Oh, I'm not so sure," said Erica. "Things happen, you get used to them. Then they're just not so important anymore, you know? Other things take over."

But Opal didn't know if this was true. The change both astonished and frightened her; she felt as though her mother had not so much changed as disappeared. Opal turned on her side away from Erica, away from the light. "You okay over there?" Erica asked.

"Fine," said Opal, and she reached for the phone to call downstairs for dinner.

The next morning they met their mother early. She wanted, she announced, to go running. "Every day I have to exercise a little," she said. "I can run or swim or use the weight room. I thought we could all jog together for just a couple of minutes. Nothing too strenuous, I swear."

"I don't have sneakers with me," Erica said, with obvious relief.

But Dottie was unmoved. "Oh, we can just run barefoot along the beach," she said. "We won't go far, and we'll go very, very slowly, Erica. I swear you'll be able to handle it. We can stop anytime you like. I mean, I'm hardly Babe Didrikson myself."

At first Erica resisted, but finally she came around, and they walked outside and went down a steep flight of wooden steps that led to the water. Opal could feel the wind and sun in even measure. They started tentatively, kicking up small whorls of sand. Dottie stayed in the middle, and every once in a while she would shout out something encouraging, like "Keep it up, girls!" or "Just a little longer!"

I have never seen her move, Opal realized, and even though the pace was almost stunningly slow, she was impressed. Dottie's head was tilted up, her mouth open to take in more air. Erica looked winded too, trailing a foot behind, and Opal could hear her breathing come in small gasps. *You get used to it*, Erica had said. Opal saw the three of them years before, fleeing the house in Jericho in the early evening, climbing into the station wagon and driving off, and she remembered how, just a few nights later, lying in what had once been Cousin Kenneth's room, she began to forget the way her own room looked: the flimsy white furniture she had once begged for, the stuffed animals propped on the window in a military row. She also began to forget the way her father looked and sounded; his voice faded out and his body left his suit of clothes, like a soul ascending. The same might be true for one's own body, Opal thought. Dottie had shed a skin, and maybe eventually she would forget what she had been, would forget the way she had once stood onstage, her body filling a sphere of projected light.

Now Opal listened to the way the three of them were breathing in synchrony, and she marveled at how they all gathered in great, exerted breaths and then let them go. They pushed themselves forward, and their breathing rose and fell, almost, she thought, as if they were hyperventilating.

HINSDALE PUBLIC LIBRARY
HINSDALE, ILLINOIS